C000000633

This is the third book in the Rupert Brett Deal series.
The current titles are listed below in chronological order:

By Simon Fairfax

SIMON FAIRFAX
A DEAL WITH THE DEVIL

A CIP catalogue record of this book is available from the British Library.

Copyright Front Cover images:
SAS logo- ninety-seven97.deviantart.com
Terry Seaward photography.- police boat.

Contains public sector information licensed under the Open Government Licencev3.0.

http://www.nationalarchives.gov.uk/doc/ open-government-licence/version/3/

ISBN: 978-1-9996551-0-5

info@simonfairfax.com
www.simonfairfax.com

For my mother
for all her love, help and support.

By Fortune's adverse buffets overborne
To solitude I fled, to wilds forlorn,
And not in utter loneliness to live,
Myself at last did to the Devil give!"

—Johann Wolfgang von Goethe, Faust

CHAPTER 1

May, 1995

The oil dark waters of the Irish Sea were occasionally streaked with a light, pale luminosity, as the clouded sky freed a captive moon. It was a good moon for hunters, bad for the hunted. The clouds were merging, hinting at the promise of rain. A darker shadow was outlined against the seascape. Bulky in shape, evident against the choppy sea.

The steady chug and churn of the diesel engine powered the fishing trawler *Celtic Needle* steadily onwards, riding the crest and fall of the waves. They had passed the Isle of Man sometime back and were now about to enter the territorial waters of the west coast of Britain. It had been a long night and the men on board were tired; straining against the roll of the boat and tense with fatigue, wanting the journey to be over, their dangerous cargo home and safely in port. They were showing no running lights and the crew all scanned forward across the bow, as men at sea do.

The coarse Belfast accent of the skipper cut across the din of their passage: "Keep your fockin' eyes peeled, we want no cock ups here."

The others said nothing already straining their eyes against the night. The outer door to the cabin banged open, a figure appeared bearing mugs of tea. The man rolled naturally with the rise and fall of the boat, second nature after years at sea. He deposited the three mugs on the bridge and was rewarded with a 'ta' from the skipper who continued making tiny adjustments to the trawler's progress, fighting the swell of the waves.

Six miles east other craft were making headway in the opposite direction, moving away from the coast line, outwards towards the 12 mile limit of their operation. The 31 foot Mitchell mono-hull ploughed steadily forward, its twin diesel engines easily coping with the steady swell of the sea. It had passed the 6 mile marker of coastal waters and was authorised to proceed to the 12 mile limit. It was tense on the bridge, a lot was riding on finding the lone vessel in the many square miles of the Irish sea. The skipper, Billy, guided the craft in a broad sweep, constantly scanning the horizon. He was relaxed but alert; as ex-army, he had been on taut missions before and little fazed him. Next to him stood Ben, the youngest of the three Maritime police. He watched through night vision binoculars, trying to spot their prey. Behind the raised seats of the bridge, a third crew member scanned the radar; his face eerily green in the glow from the screen, his full concentration focused on the sweep of the radar arm.

"If only we had the new AIS, it would make our lives a lot easier," Ben muttered.

Billy snorted. "Huh. By the time the fuckwits in Whitehall think about spending the money, it will be obsolete!" he predicted cynically.

They both laughed. The new Auto Identification System was now developed, but not fully operational and certainly not on police boats. They both cast a glance over their shoulders at the stern figure to their rear, bearing the pips of an Inspector on his waterproof jacket. Billy didn't care. Even as a 'lowly PC', once on board, as the skipper, he outranked everybody, even if the head of the Met were present. Normally the boat was crewed by three police officers, but tonight was special. The rear of the boat was crowded. In addition to the Inspector there were six members of the Firearms unit led by a sergeant. In contrast to the three crew members, the firearms team were all in black and wearing bullet proof vests, Kevlar helmets and an array of other equipment. No deck shoes for them, but tough-soled, lace up boots, squeaking as they gripped the floor of the rolling boat.

The Mitchell carried no fixed armament, but each member of the firearms team had a Browning High-Power side arm, together with H & K MP5's, supported by slings. They were eager and ready. This is what they had trained extensively for and they were keen to put it into practice. Protected from the ever worsening elements by the enclosed cabin, the team remained fresh and alert.

Outside in the choppy sea, another craft was running parallel to the Mitchell. A huge twin hulled RHIB, powered by two massive Merlin diesel engines pushing it through the swell, was rising and bouncing into the troughs of the waves. Open to the elements, it was tiring work. Tim, the skipper, was in constant communication with Billy. Mike, his crewman, stood at his side awaiting orders to assume the front position when the firearms team was aboard and contact made with the target vessel.

"Billy," he shouted above the noise and spray into his radio mike, "anything? It's getting worse out here, there's a storm coming or I miss my guess."

Billy responded confirming nothing as yet on the radar and turning his head slightly he shouted over his shoulder at the Inspector: "Are we sure this is reliable sir? Not a sign and we have squared off the route they were to take." They radioed the progress report to the command centre in Manchester, where the HQ of the North West police consortium was based.

Inspector Raglan scowled, making his features even more taciturn, moving closer to communicate more clearly against the noise of weather and din of the engines. He did not feel great, but was never going to show it to the Firearms team or the Maritime police and suffer the loss of face: "The Garda and the RIC have been liaising well for once. The source is reliable and they have lumped up one of the crates holding the load. The battery is by necessity small, but once we are in range, it will definitely show up." Raglan sounded more confident than he felt. For the first time doubt began to creep into his mind and his masters would not be happy if this mission failed. Too much planning, cost and exposure of contacts had gone into this.

"If nothing else, it will help with positive ID of the boat and with the weather coming in," Billy gesticulated to the sky with a nod of his head, "we may well need it. Main comms are already shaky with the weather. Soon we will probably lose them completely."

* * *

Aboard the trawler *Celtic Needle,* the atmosphere was a little more confident.

"Liam, we're inside the 12 mile zone. It all looks good, on course, and should be home within the hour."

Liam MacCabe gripped the wheel tighter. His rugged, red-faced features, lined by a thousand seas, creased into a frown. He was still not reassured. "Good. Now we just a need a bit o' luck to miss the Cutters and we will be home and dry. I didn't like it when Sean missed the trip. I hope I'm wrong about that wee man. Wasn't right him goin' ill at the last minute. Stay by the radio Dohnal, if anything goes wrong, we need to send it in."

Dohnal looked up from the charts, unsettled by the warning. *It was unlike Liam to be worried,* he thought. He was normally so indomitable and assured. His eyes were drawn sideways to the third figure seated at the bridge. The man had the haunted, drawn features of one who had seen too much, and participated in evil for most of his adult life. Tir Brennan was a killer: an enforcer for the IRA. He had more blood on his hands than almost any other in the Loyalist paramilitary organisation. The hollowed face showed no expression as his body moved easily with the roll of the trawler, broad shoulders loose in repose. Dohnal hoped to God everything was alright with Sean, *he wouldn't want to have Tir Brennan after him, that's for sure.*

The squall hit suddenly, bringing with it sheets of rain that so often appear in the Irish sea. Visibility reduced drastically and the trawler suffered under the weather's attack, losing speed down to 8 knots and needing constant adjustment to her direction. At the same time, the police boats changed course running along the 12 mile limit.

Ted, the third crew member of the police boat, strained in his seat against the sudden change of course and looked back at his radar screen. It beeped, the sweep of the radar arm showing a shadowy shape. He waited for a second sweep of the bar. There it was again, more definite now. Elated he called it out: "Skip, I've got a contact. Bearing 25 degrees from our position, heading inland. Estimated speed; 8 knots. At this speed...we'll close in 10 minutes," he calculated.

"Good. Keep on it." He spoke into the microphone to contact Tim on the RHIB. "Tim? Over." he was treated to a crackle of static and no human response. He looked over and Mike made the universal sign for dead communications, miming a handset and sliding his hand across his throat a number of times. They switched to personal radios and he alerted him of the supposed contact before sharply changing course.

The atmosphere on the boat changed immediately. The Firearms team became quietly excited, tense with the prospect of a boarding. Raglan permitted himself a quiet smile, gripping the chrome upright pole harder, as the boat lurched forward to a greater speed of just under 18 knots. The chase was on.

The Firearms team re-checked their equipment for the last time and readied themselves for the transfer to the RHIB. It was a potentially hazardous manoeuvre, but one they had practiced in all weathers and conditions: now it was the real thing. With constant checking of speed and direction the boats tracked a course, bringing them up at the rear of the trawler to remain undetected and confirm its identity. When they were within one mile of the trawler, an electronic beep sounded on the bridge, as the mobile tracking device picked up the signal being clandestinely sent out from its source.

The RHIB skipped and slid close to the Mitchell police boat and with consummate skill borne of long practice, Tim pulled up against the hull of the boat making it look easy in the difficult conditions. Secured in place, the two craft acting as one, the Team now disembarked the boat and hopped onto the RHIB. It took a matter of seconds as the hours of long practice paid off. Nobody wanted to end up in the Irish Sea in the middle of a squall. Hand actions now took over and once all secure, each member of the Firearms team hooked a foot to secure their position. Mike then cast off and Tim powered away from the Mitchell, skilfully avoiding the choppy wake.

In a matter of minutes the RHIB was much closer to the target vessel and it was easy to make out the words *Celtic Needle*, written on her stern. As a final confirmation Tim ratified identification to Billy at the helm of the main police boat. He stared down at the photo of the trawler that was stuck to the bridge as an aide to identification, noting now (as it appeared in the rain strewn darkness) that the stern matched that in the picture. The Celtic Needle was typical of the trawlers built in Skibberdeen, Co. Cork from where she hailed. High prowed, main superstructure settled amidships and a huge cable drum, located in the stern, supported on massive steel struts. The cable was all in-board as no fishing was taking place. The naturally low stern was already sitting low in the water and the flat platform was constantly washed by the chop and lee of the waves.

Tim and the team were going to attempt one of the most dangerous boarding strategies. They had, upon seeing the design of the trawler, already decided upon this course of action back at the harbour: but it was still perilous and unpredictable. Ironically, the atrocious conditions had helped their cause; for as the swell rolled and fell, so did the stern of the trawler causing the rear platform to be almost at the water line. Only yards away now, the RHIB was steadied under Tim's expert guidance; Mike at the prow, arm raised awaiting the exact moment. One misjudgement and it would be chaos. Mike, gripping with one hand turned over his shoulder and shouted: "Yes!" Simultaneously chopping his hand downwards in a precise movement.

Tim had anticipated it, being at one with the boat and sea. The RHIB shot forward closing the remaining distance and, in a perfectly timed manoeuvre drove the RHIB hard up behind the trawler crashing the bow onto the stern platform. Mike locked on and held the RHIB fast. The Firearms team swarmed onto the deck of the trawler, needing no second bidding. They split into two groups, running either side of the trawler's deck, MP5's held ready to fire. Shouting "Armed police!" as they burst along the deck, driving forward to the main bridge in the superstruc-ture; pulling open the sea doors on either side in swift unison. The noise of the storm masked their progress and the crew were unaware of the two team's presence until the doors were flung open. The crew's reactions were predictable as each man span around, tensing, looking for a way out. Each member of the police team picked their man shouting:

"Down, now! On the floor, arms behind your head." Any resistance being met by force from the armed team.

The one man the team had been alerted to watch carefully was Tir Brennan. The man acted instinctively like a caged animal. No way was he going to be held captive. He had instantly rolled off his seat as soon as the sea doors opened. He had been facing the port side door and had a split second's warning as the dark figures entered. Going with the roll he reached down to his waist band trying to tug out the .38 Smith & Wesson from his belt. But the team was well trained. He looked up into the cold, gaping barrel of an MP5 as a knee landed hard into his lower back, smashing him forward, driving his jaw into the unyielding deck. His right hand, now trapped behind his back, could no longer draw the weapon.

"Arms up." He was ordered. Through mashed, bloodied lips, he mouthed curses and swore at the team. His jacket was ripped up, the gun removed by a gloved police hand: "Weapon, suspect armed." Came the shout of warning to the other team members. Brennan's arm was twisted and driven up between his shoulder blades, forcing the last resistance out of him. He relaxed and spat a bloodied gob of phlegm at one of the officers, who ignored it, too alert and high on adrenalin to be concerned over such a futile gesture. The sergeant in charge of the team moved to the bridge controls and throttled-down the trawler to a little above idle, just enough to prevent it from wallowing in the choppy sea.

"There should be four, check below in the engine room." He ordered. Two of the team peeled off to go below ships to the engine room and galley. The rest ordered each man to his knees, careful not to block or stray behind the line of fire of the covering team member. A set of fixed wrist cuffs was produced for each captive. The first in line kept his arms behind in the accepted manner.

"No, in front, we don't want you drowning now, do we?" came the black humour of the team member. The arms were arranged crossed at the wrist, to make any attack or resistance awkward. Each man was then told to lie face down on the deck. The bridge door opened and the final member of the crew entered, similarly bound and assisted by one of the firearms team.

"All secure below boss," he confirmed. The sergeant then contacted the Mitchell from his personal radio.

"All secure here. Request skipper for Celtic Needle and return to port. Over."

The response was given; the RIHB broke away and returned carrying Ben who took over the helm of the trawler accompanied by the Team overseeing the prisoners.

An hour later, as the first speckles of dawn light perforated the dark sky, land formation began to take shape on the horizon. The return journey had been uneventful and the full haul of the night's work had been revealed: two pallets of what looked like, high class cocaine. The beeper concealed in one of the pallets, alerting them to the exact location hidden on board. As they neared the safety of the sea walls, the prisoners were all lined up on deck and Brennan who until this stage had appeared truculent, appeared suddenly to relax, missing his footing in a roll of the swell. The vigilant officer ahead was alert and wary, saw him misbalance and prepared to assist, extending a steadying arm. It was a mistake.

Brennan, flexing his jointed wrists to the right, appearing to balance himself, continued the movement, bringing his right elbow up in an arc. It came crashing down in synchronisation with the stamp of his right foot, catching the officer on the collar bone and driving all the force down diagonally through his body. He crumpled with a "*whoof*" as all the air was driven out him, his internal organs in crisis. Brennan lurched forward for the deck rail, setting himself up for a vault into the sea, a shale beach now lay only thirty yards away and potential freedom. It was a brave or foolhardy move borne of desperation. Freedom was in his sights. It was dashed by a blur in front of his vision, fractionally ahead of the collision between the stock of an MP5 and his nose. The MP5 won. Brennan was forced backwards away from the rail, his nose a pulp gushing blood.

"Stay down you bastard." The sergeant ordered the dazed figure. He turned to his fallen colleague who had a gone an ashen shade of grey: "You all right?" he enquired gently of his junior officer. "I know, they don't teach you that one in the classroom. I've seen it once before, some martial arts guy we took in once nearly killed one of my mates. Always have to be wary when the cuffs are in front. Though how the hell he thought he could get there," he nodded toward the shore, "fuck knows, the undertow here is lethal."

CHAPTER 2

WEST KIRBY HARBOUR

The three boats pulled into the harbour at West Kirby. The small port was ideal for their purposes; the police authorities wanted to unload all the prisoners unseen. The plan had been to take to the sea again and pull into the port of destination in Birkenhead.

As the prisoners had been taken ashore, each was loaded into the waiting unmarked white police vans, one to each vehicle so that that they could neither collude or rehearse their stories. A man alone and alienated from his friends was much more likely to talk. As the vans drove away, Inspector Raglan returned to the group of Marine police who had handled the operation so well.

"A good night's work men. Now I need a skipper and mate to take the Celtic Needle around the coast to Birkenhead. We have been keeping a watch on all traffic and suspicious characters around the port. Some are known to us and some new faces, but nothing concrete. The trawler will have a full complement of the Firearms Team hidden away. We just need you to take her in dressed as fishermen and we might, just might, nab a couple of their contacts on this side of the water. The IRA won't trade in drugs in their own backyard, but are quite happy to bring misery and agony to us on the mainland. So we'll let the Drugs Squad pull everything off," he nodded to the team currently going over the *Celtic Needle* with a fine tooth comb, "and then we'll be off.

LONDON

The telephone rang loudly, reverberating off the walls of Chief Superintendent Webster's office. The room had been made to feel like a comfortable study by its occupant and belied the steely character and determination of its owner. It was from this command centre that Webster ran a Special Task Force formed in 1985 to deal with cross boundary crime that did not fall into any one category. On this occasion he was the lead officer, liaising with the Drug Squad, HM Revenue & Customs and the Anti-Terrorism unit from Special Branch, co-ordinating all the information and reporting to the Home Office and MI6.

Retrieving the receiver he answered: "Webster."

"Inspector Raglan here, sir, from Liverpool. I wanted to update you before sending in my final report." It had been four hours since the Celtic Needle set off on her last voyage around the coast into the heart of Birkenhead and moored innocently as close to the mouth of the harbour as possible. Openly inviting the contacts to approach her.

"Ah, morning. Any joy?" he asked casually, belying the tension he felt regarding the huge mixed operation he had put in place.

"We waited as instructed, sir. A sea going cruiser passed nearby and pulled up as if to make contact, but something must have alerted them, maybe a hidden signal; flag at half-mast or something…" he ventured. "Anyway we got the name and who she is registered to and we'll follow it up. But no hope of getting the people, just a lead to follow."

Unconsciously Webster let out the breath he had been holding against the news.

"Well, it was a long shot at best." He sighed. "What was the haul?"

"Pure cocaine, uncut and street value in the millions. The drugs boys are delighted. The IRA have been stuffed again, no funds for them and no doubt a huge debt owed to whoever supplied them. We will have a full analysis in due course."

Webster let Raglan continue, his mind working overtime and thinking how he would report this to his masters at the Home Office. Well, he considered, the drugs secure; a ring broken and terrorists arrested. The sad thing was their mole in the IRA cell was now almost certainly blown and would have to be relocated for safety. But it was a small price to pay for the success of the mission: a pawn to catch a king he mused.

"Good. I will look forward to reading your report in due course. Please keep me informed of any new developments." He replaced the receiver. The next call was to the Home Secretary. Webster span it as a great success to Michael Howard: no one rose to his position within the police, or indeed any other institution, without being as much a politician as a policeman. The net result: Britain's borders were as safe and secure as they could be now the IRA corridor of smuggling had been broken.

His final comments were to be more prescient than even he could realise: "Yes, thank you Home Secretary, well they do say that 'he who deals in drugs does a deal with the Devil!' " The Home Secretary chuckled drily at this refrain and asked to be kept abreast of new developments.

BOGOTA, COLOMBIA

High in the Eastern Hills which limit the sprawl and urbanisation of Bogota, the climate was cool, the air clear and it defied the stifling smog of the City centre spreading below. Bogota itself is beautiful: a relic of the old Spanish Conquistadores wealth and splendour of a bygone era. From the beautiful museums, universities and the cobbled streets, to the modern high-rise offices and apartment blocks. It was a thriving city, but one that earned an unenviable reputation more: it was considered at this time to be one of the most violent and dangerous cities in the world, with a staggering murder rate of 81 per 100,000 of the population. The problem was the black economy fuelled by a certain commodity: cocaine. The drug lords ruled the city and its environs, their powerful tentacles stretching nationally and internationally with a fearsome reputation for reprisals in the event of disloyalty.

It was here that Juan Ballesteros, high up in the hills, ran his newly formed drug empire. Escobar had been dead some two years ago and, as with many cancers, others took his place. As one of his former trusted and senior lieutenants, Ballesteros had taken to his new role with alacrity after Escobar's assassination.

The newly refurbished and extended house in the old Spanish style was an exquisite example of ostentatious bad taste, from the appalling décor to the ubiquitous use of gold plate everywhere, even the door handles were gold. It shouted from the rooftops: *I've made it and I'm going to shout about it*, like so many ego-centric, successful, nouveau riche before and after. He sat in his study, awash with heavy drapes, pictures of Old Masters and overstuffed leather furniture, behind a large Spanish style Rosewood desk; pictures of his family adorned the top along with brass lamps, throwing a warm glow across the space. A thin trail of cigar smoke dribbled up from his thick lips. His swarthy-skinned, round face glistened with a sheen of sweat in the warm room, highlighting the dead eyes concealed within the pudgy face.

The man seated in front of him, Pablo Rojas, was nervous; letting Juan Ballesteros know that a consignment of drugs had disappeared was not a good experience. He too was sweating, but out of fear, not temperature.

"What do you mean it has gone? We were told that these terrorist bastards were reliable. That they had Ireland sewn up. How could it disappear?" his voice a quiet refrain.

Rojas swallowed, he knew that the quieter his boss spoke the more dangerous and ruthless he became. He had seen many a man tortured and all the while Ballesteros would whisper quietly in their ear, of how much pain he was going to inflict and how the victim would die. It was therefore all the more menacing at this moment of gentle inquisition.

"The boat was travelling across the Irish sea. All was OK, they had passed the half way point and radioed in to say all was going well. Next we went to the UK harbour for the pick-up. But the flag, it was at full mast, they nearly missed the signal. So they shot off and we made enquiries, and the boat was hit by the police mid-channel. They have the drugs and all the crew. We-"

"Including *Señor* Brennan?" he interrupted. Rojas nodded.

"*Si*, including him. We need to find out what happened and I am working on it."

Ballesteros nodded. "Find them. Find what happened and we need to send a message to the IRA. No one crosses me: I want my money or my drugs. Either will do. Now we must wait for the new route to Europe."

"It is moving already, *Jefe*, the first run of this year will be in the UK, June. It will be good, no one will suspect, a great route. The quantity may not be as great, but we can move that up and distribute easily from now on." Rojas made to move and left the office as quickly as he could. At the open doorway he breathed a sigh of relief. It was short lived. Ballesteros called out after him.

"Remember Pablo, a message, my money or my drugs, no excuses."

"*Si, Jefe.*"

CHAPTER 3

June, WEST END, LONDON

The new offices of HBJ International were bespoke, a glistening edifice of steel and glass, having only been finished 3 months ago and most of the snagging list covered, they were now a joy to work in. *One of the benefits of having an American parent with lots of dosh,* thought Rupert Brett, reflecting on when Jarvis had bought out H & B at the start of the recession. Most of all, they had air-conditioning and as the midsummer sun beat out across the capital, it was actually a blessed relief to be indoors. *Far better,* he thought, *than the old Regency offices in Grosvenor Street - they would have been sweltering in there now.*

Brett was enjoying himself. The market was rising, investments were flying out of the door and starting to make record yields the like of which had not been seen since the late 80's. The deep recession of the early 90's seemed a distant memory to many, especially, Rupert thought, *the new clutch of graduates that had started with the firm last October. All 'green and keen' having never known the hardships of a bear market, they were rising on the ever present 'green shoots of recovery' the Chancellor had promised which had now materialised into a full grown jungle. The bull market seemed here to stay, and long may it continue,* Rupert prayed.

Although email was starting to do the rounds internally within the firm, everything external was still sent by post: early nods, sales particulars and, in this case, invitations. He inserted his finger and ripped open the stiff envelope retrieving the embossed invitation.

"Well, well," he mused out loud, "Mrs. Brett will be excited."

"What's that Rups?" called a voice from the outside his new office. The tall Patrician figure of Mike Ringham appeared in the doorway. An old friend of Rupert's from his university days, they had briefly had an estrangement after his run in with the corrupt developer, Simions, who was now jailed, over false murder and corruption charges. But, some ten years later, they were back to their old friendship, or so very nearly that it did not matter. Two years ago, Mike had also moved to HBJ from Cowell Rubens as a safe haven in the recession and a promotion.

"Ah Ringo, look at this, the fruits of my toiling."

He handed the invitation up to his friend, whose face was a picture as he read the words inscribed: "Wow lucky bugger, 'The Directors of Featherstone Securities PLC request the pleasure of the company of Mr. & Mrs. Rupert Brett; to the Final of the Queen's Cup at Guards Polo club. My, my, we are moving in elevated circles. Not the Cartier Cup but the Queen's Cup. Claire will be thrilled," he exclaimed.

"Ha, you're just jealous and it's not the 'Cartier Cup' they're just the sponsors, it's actually the Coronation Cup," he finished pedantically but with a smile on his face that robbed the words of any sting. Rupert was privately pleased that he could now tease his old friend after the gap between them. As head of Capital Markets in the UK, his position was right up in the top echelon, especially as he was one of the highest fee earners, and felt he deserved all the freebees he could get.

"Of course, I do know that, dear boy," he patronised. "I know the Hipwoods rather well and they've invited me to the player's circle before now," he continued in the game of one-upmanship. "But these chaps, Featherstone, are rather interesting. How did you find them?"

Rupert answered modestly: "For once, not my own work, I am afraid; it was our American cousins who teed up the contact. They have huge investments in Europe and have been buying in the UK this last year, with which I have been only too willing to help. They like big lot sizes and bundles or portfolios where they can either break up or securitise the debt. In short, anything with an angle. The problem I have had lately is that as prices have risen and yields hardened, we have had to look further afield to get good value. Even the major provincial cities are now on fire with yields being pushed down all the time. Also very difficult to find deals off the market, everyone is so worried they are going to be tucked in and the property turned on them!" he finished exasperatedly.

Rupert's brief but lucrative foray into Buenos Aries five years earlier had proved invaluable and had given him the taste and experience of dealing with foreign investors and linking up international deals, with investors often being foreign and therefore offshore. His work in the market with opening the new office had been cut short. Largely because spying for the UK government had caused him to be shot at and chased half way across Argentina just before a very unhappy Argentine government had caught up with him. *The consequences* Rupert shuddered at the thought, *still gives me nightmares now.*

"I know the feeling," Mike sympathised, whilst he too enjoyed the rising market, keeping apace and finding stock was proving to be harder all the time. He continued in his upper class drawl: "On another note, are you and Claire free for dinner on

Saturday, we have some clients who have become sort of friends and thought it might be mutually beneficial?"

"What, not frightened Claire will pinch them?" he mocked.

"Not at all, she at least has honour among thieves, well sort of," he teased. He also knew full well that as an in-house agent for CR, Claire had enough clients of her own and would not be trying to take out more externally.

"Ordinarily I, or rather we, would love to, but I have TA training this weekend; won't be back 'til Monday."

"I don't know why you still do that game; you're getting too old," he chided.

"Queen and country, dear chap. Anyway I'm 35 not 55 and it keeps me lean and trim." He stood up to his full six foot height and patted his flat stomach. Apart from a few more grey hairs appearing in his shock of wavy brown hair and wrinkles around his eyes, Mike Ringham had to admit that Rupert still looked in very good shape and his blue eyes were still clear, with no sign of jowls appearing or a paunch at his waist. Rupert looked pointedly down at his friend's stomach where middle age spread and too many corporate lunches were beginning to show. Mike embarrassedly looked down at his middle, instinctively pulling in his stomach muscles. He turned to go with a final retort: "Well, I'll think of you playing at soldiers, whilst I am tucking into a very good red I have in mind."

Rupert stuck two fingers up, grinning at the departing figure of his friend. He picked up the receiver and dialled Claire's direct line at CR.

"Claire Brett?" she answered.

"Hi Darling, you're going to love me."

"What, even more than I do already? Impossible," she retorted. "Mmmh, unless you've bought me an impossibly expensive present."

"That's what I love about you: not a mercenary bone in your body. But not quite an expensive present, more of an exclusive one. We have been invited to attend the final of the Queen's Cup at Guards, guests of Featherstone Securities. So keep the 21st June free."

"Wow, clever you! Shame it's not the semis, they're usually better games and you get to see two matches. Still, not bad."

"Ungrateful wench!" he chided. "I'll take my lover instead."

They flirted with each other for the next few minutes and before the call ended she teased, "And I might have some exciting news for you as well."

"Really, do tell?"

"Ah you'll have to wait 'til this evening. Listen, must go, another call coming in. Love you." And with that she had gone.

Rupert shook his head in frustration and considered his next move in the market. *So, I am going to have to take a tour of the provinces and try to find some product,* he thought. What he really needed was a bundle of kit, comprised of multiple properties, that would generate huge fees; get the interest of Featherstone and re-sales on the split of the portfolio. But he knew he would grasp at anything he could if it had an angle. 'Have to keep the client warm' was the mantra and he knew it was what the graduates had yet to learn.

CHAPTER 4

June, BOGOTA, COLOMBIA

The Colombian winter was always a good time for business to be conducted. The cooler weather promoted action and the drug cartels were no different. A council of war and, therefore, progress had just been held; the distribution routes were now wide open with the new routes proving successful. The conversation turned to past events in the Irish Sea.

"Now, tell me, Pablo, what of this man Brennan? What do the Irish say?"

Pablo Rojas took a deep breath, this was not going to be easy. "The man Brennan, he is on trial and will probably get fifteen years minimum. We will see where he

goes, but he will be well protected, the terrorists stick together and we do not have strong connections in the British jails. The IRA council say it was unfortunate and they will of course help in any way in the future, but…" the words hung in the air for a painful moment, "They will not repay us, they say it was just bad luck and will not pay any money. To mount a war in Ireland as a reprisal will not succeed."

The silence continued, Ballesteros' eyes bored into Rojas, who held his stare. The chess master eyeing his pawn.

"OK we wait. We use to recoup our money and when their job is done we kill Brennan and send the head back to them. That is the message. OK? They have many people friendly to their cause in the US, there they are vulnerable as well. I don't care how long it takes, but we send the message. Now leave," he commanded.

* * *

21st June, GUARDS POLO CLUB

The atmosphere was one of excited expectation. The final of the Queen's Cup was widely regarded in polo circles as one of the most prestigious trophies to be had outside Argentina. The crowd were informed and appreciative of the players' skills and were there, by and large, for the spectacle of the sport, as much as the sense of occasion. Unlike the Coronation Cup, which now attracted coach loads of inebriated spectators more there for the day out than the spectacle of the sporting event.

As Rupert observed, being his first time to the Queen's Cup Final: "The atmosphere is different to the Coronation Cup, isn't it? Rather more refined and a feeling of belonging."

Claire responded with her usual acerbity. "Yes, so much better with the women not all dressed as though to a cheap wedding with fascinators bouncing on their heads and impractical high heels that dig into the pitch. And no ghastly louts in stupid shorts getting pissed and ignoring the game."

Rupert chuckled. "Ouch. You're such a snob!" he chided.

"Well, I mean." She sighed and continued, "But, yes, 'guilty' where polo is concerned. The last thing I want to see is people here just to get pissed or seen to be seen, and not here for the game. It would be like me turning up on the terraces of a football match, all dressed up to the nines and constantly talking to my companions whilst the game was in progress, making stupid comments. You can imagine how that would go down!" she reasoned.

Rupert held up his hands in mock surrender knowing when to capitulate and the subject of polo was one of those times. It had been like a religion to Claire ever since she had played in pony club; or more particularly, like a drug, he corrected himself.

The Featherstone Securities hospitality marquee was located in one of the prime positions about half way down Pitch1, which was one of the two main playing pitches at Guards Polo Club. It was beautifully decorated inside and the atmosphere was one of a rarefied party. The guests were all suitably attired, (not a fascinator or pair of shorts in sight, Rupert smiled inwardly) and the urbane directors were moving smoothly around the various clusters of guests, making appropriate noises and massaging egos as the need required. They were, by turn, very solicitous of their agents and looked after them accordingly. The head of the UK team made a bee line for Rupert, when he saw him over the crowd of heads. As his main contact for Featherstone, Hugh Congreave was a very important client of Rupert's.

He approached all bonhomie: "Rupert, how nice to see you. So glad you could make it," he enthused, shaking his hand firmly. Rupert in turn smiled and turned to Claire.

"May I introduce my wife, Claire? Claire this is Hugh Congreave, our host."

Hugh Congreave turned on his megawatt smile, beaming from a tanned face and swept off his Panama in polite deference and shook hands with Claire.

"Ah, now, I've heard great things about you. Swops deals,

running the market ragged and setting the pace. The directors at CR sing your praises, m'dear."

Claire played the game, smiling in return. She saw through the smooth exterior, but was still impressed. The man before her would, she guessed, be in his fifties; a voice that held a trace of colonial accents (*Kenya or South Africa?* she thought), skin perma tanned and lined from too many tropical suns. He was, she considered, still a handsome man and wore the grey in his hair well. The overriding impression was that of a ladies' man and a shark, she concluded. A handsome shark, but still a shark. She responded in kind, "Ah if only. Instead, I am fighting to keep up with the amazing deals you all seem to be doing at Featherstone, great start to your new second fund launch."

"Well, thank you. Yes, we are trying for larger lot sizes to increase our buying power and need to get the cash away in big chunks. We could even end up buying in debt to do that. So, if you have any clients who might want to off-load, please let us know."

As an aside, in the full flavour of the dramatic, Congreave turned as if to jokingly sideline Rupert. "Of course we don't need to bother about other agents coming to us directly..." he finished sotto voce.

"Hey now, easy tiger, I want an introduction fee on this 'arrangement'," Rupert joked. The banter continued until, spotting someone in the distance, Hugh made his apologies and swept off to charm another contact.

"Mr. Smooth or what?" Claire decried.

"I know, he has a certain charm, though I wouldn't trust him further than I could kick him."

"My thoughts exactly. Still, he pays the bills and he is a good client of yours so, keep it coming."

"Indeed. Drink?" he offered from a table of champagne glasses, then instantly regretted it. Claire had been pregnant back in the beginning of June but had lost it and they had been trying ever since, with Claire unusually abstaining from alcohol. The loss had hit them both hard, Rupert feeling in some way that it was his fault and Claire felt she had let Rupert down for not being able to carry his child. He looked shamefaced.

"Rups no, what will be will be. You carry on, just don't get legless, you're too heavy to carry."

The lunch was next and they were seated with other property people who had never been to a polo event, so inevitably Rupert, and especially Claire, were pressed for knowledge on the rules and details of the game. In the midst of the talk Claire turned to one wag who was decrying the game as one for wusses.

"So what is your game then Henry?" she enquired, knowing full well what he was going to say.

As if by walking cliché he replied: "Rugby. Prop forward for the Hants Tigers," he declared proudly, flexing huge shoulder muscles and a thick neck. Rupert saw it coming and almost felt sorry for the sap, but said nothing, enjoying the entertainment.

"Really?" Claire said feigning hero worship. "Wow, you must take some hard knocks, smashing into other players with your physique, at what, sixteen miles an hour or so in full flight I bet?"

The peacock, rose to the bait with all the aplomb of a red grouse on the glorious 12th.

"Absolutely. I weigh over 18 stone, you imagine colliding with me in full swing," he boasted. "That's 32 stone with a collision speed of around 32 miles an hour. Man's game rugby, tough," he finished emphatically. Henry preened like a typical 'rugger bugger'; Rupert winced seeing the course of the conversation and how it was going to end- badly for him. A couple of the wives at the table were rolling their eyes at all the testosterone and machismo.

"Really? Gosh," Claire answered gently as though terribly

impressed, continuing as though talking to a recalcitrant 10 year old. "Well imagine this. In polo we are also allowed to ride off or in your terms 'have a collision'; but a High Goal polo pony will travel at between 40 to 45 miles an hour and weigh half a ton, plus the weight of the rider. That, in case you haven't worked it out, is 1 ton plus travelling at a collision speed of around 90 miles per hour! Would you care to try it, being a real man and everything?" she finished, slaughtering him. The wives smiled and the men coughed embarrassedly. Henry left to fetch more wine, making his excuses. Rupert winked across at her: his darling courageous wife. She smiled beatifically in response, which set his soul alight.

The game started at 3.pm and with lunch over, one of the agents and his wife, Steve and Lisa Channing, asked if they could go and see the pony lines. Claire was only too happy to oblige. They walked off their lunch down towards the lines of polo ponies, all tied to the steel rails ready for tacking up. An articulated lorry turned up at that moment, stopped with a hissing of airbrakes and the rear ramp was lowered, disgorging 17 polo ponies, one after the other, like Noah's Ark in reverse. The beautiful, gleaming animals all burnished, copper, liquid gold and chestnut, ready to do battle on the hallowed turf. Their bodies a picture of athletic sinew and muscle, fluid under their shiny coats.

"Amazing," exclaimed Lisa, "So many in one lorry and why do they need that many?"

Claire explained that this would be for just one player and they need to change at least once per chukka to keep the horses fresh and that the game comprised six chukkas each of 7.5 minutes. She continued: "Sometimes they will bring them on later and ride them again, but never for more than seven minutes in total. It is not allowed and would be unfair on the ponies.

They are all at peak fitness, but it still takes its toll, especially the stopping and turning."

"Like playing 7 a side rugby, very knackering," Rupert commented.

Steve Channing snorted. "Yea, I am sure dear old Henry would appreciate that. You certainly put him back in his box Claire." He grinned. "Not that he didn't deserve it."

"Well, pompous arse. I'd like to see how he feels falling off a horse at 40 miles an hour," she scoffed. The others laughed and looked on with interest as piles of tack all came out of the side lockers of the trailers. One of the balls escaped it's net bag and rolled towards Steve who picked it up. He examined the white sphere, gently throwing it up in the air and catching it in his palm.

"It's made of plastic, I thought they were made of wood? Larger than I thought, too." He turned interrogatively to Claire.

"They used to be made of wood," she informed him. "In fact that's where the name of the game came from. The balls were made from the root of the willow tree, well after they gave up playing with the heads of their enemies! And the Indian name for willow is 'Pulu'. The British colonials in India bastardized it to polo and so the modern game was born."

"But what's inside the ball? It's quite light." He flicked the ball up in the air again catching it deftly.

"It's like a Crunchy or Aero bar, filled with millions of tiny air holes, so virtually hollow, in a funny sort of way."

"Interesting."

He pitched the ball back to an Argy groom who caught it just as deftly, calling *gracias* to Steve. Returning to their seats at the marquee, they prepared for the afternoons spectacle. The commentator's voice boomed out over the crowd, announcing the entrance of the two teams onto the pitch.

The gladiators had come out and saluted the crowd, accepting the applause as they rode around in a semi-circle, returning to their lines after their name was called out, together with their handicap. Rupert could not help feeling as he always had, that it was just like gladiatorial combat, these superhuman horsemen, armed with mallets, clad in leather armour and helmets. Chris Adams, the seconded SAS sergeant who had saved him in Argentina, had had the same feeling and admiration for them, having witnessed the Argentine Open first hand, and he *was* a hero, as Rupert knew only too well.

The game started and it was a master class of how to play polo. The two teams, playing with their patrons, rich captains of industry (one a famous property magnate) gathered pace and tension. The horses streaked up and down the pitch, stopping and turning within three paces from a full gallop; spinning and setting off again at full speed in a matter of strides. The 'little white ball', Steve Channing had lofted in his hand, being blasted at up to 140 miles an hour around the pitch. The two teams were pretty evenly matched with a drawn score one minute before the end of the game at 18 all. Then just before the final whistle of the final chukka, an Argentine 'hired assassin' sneaked in, taking the ball nearly the whole length of the 300 yard pitch to score a glorious goal, sealing the fate of the match.

After the game there was the usual tumultuous applause, with a prize giving, including one for the 'Best Playing Pony' and the guests started to depart, facing the traffic back to London for the most part. Before their departure, Hugh Congreave smoothed up, asking if Rupert and Claire had enjoyed the match and if they wanted to stay on for the infamous After Party, for which he had complimentary tickets. The parties were the stuff of legends and lasted until the early hours. As Monday was always 'polo day off' it was a night to howl for anyone connected to the game.

"Very kind of you, Hugh, but I think we will give it a miss, have to be up bright and early tomorrow to find you some deals," Rupert joked.

"Very good. We must have lunch as soon as the requirements have been refined for the new fund. I will arrange a date," he promised.

Farewells bade, they made their way to the car park and their tortuous journey home to Richmond.

The next day saw Rupert in the office reading the early morning edition of the Telegraph. Opening the social pages he saw pictures of the Final which he had attended and there in a separate leader column was something that caught his eye. "Wow," he exclaimed. "Lucky escape." He picked up the receiver and dialled Claire, who answered at the second ring.

Without preamble he launched in, "You will never guess what, have you seen the papers today?"

"No. Why, what has happened?"

"There was a massive drugs bust at the After Party last night. Not just any drugs but cocaine and two people have been hospitalised as a result!"

"My God, I am glad we didn't go. It's odd though, drugs, apart from a bit of weed, are unusual around the teams, especially the high goal. It must have been someone up from Town who is connected. Anyone we know or just general comment?" Rupert confirmed no names, just some anonymous party goers rumoured to be from London, "and nothing to do with the polo world per se," he finished.

"The good directors of Guards won't like that. I can see all kinds of fallout. Listen, I've got to go, my other line is going and I am expecting to exchange today. Speak later, love you."

"You too. Bye," he chimed and put the phone down.

CHAPTER 5

August, DEAUVILLE

The delightful Normandy coastal town of Deauville was generally acknowledged to be the holiday destination for the Parisian elite. The town with its cobbled streets; quaint half timbered architecture; and the quay side harbour, which rolled gently up from the sea, flanked by multi-coloured houses which would then open on to elegant piazzas. There was a discreet, but evident, smell of money about it.

The August heat was tamed and diluted by the refreshing sea breezes, drifting up from the English Channel: in short it was the epitome of chic. It was also the final leg of the 'High Goal Circus' before the polo cabal returned to Argentina for the winter. Some would drift across to Australia and New Zealand or even India, but this was the last glamorous location in the polo calendar. The 22 goal competition was attended by all the Argentinean contingent up-rooted and moved on from England. The whole entourage arrived en-masse and enhanced the carnival atmosphere of the town.

The famous casino was the focal point for the town, along with the Hotel Barriere, racecourse and numerous boutiques. Unusually, polo and racing met here, as the two pitch club was situated in the centre of the town surrounded by the racecourse, which could be very distracting. This day was the opening ceremony and the polo teams had, as tradition dictates, paraded through the town on horseback, lauded as gladiators by the knowledgeable crowd. Champagne flowed, without recourse to cost or quantity consumed. Even the players who would one day be censored, were known to go on to the pitch 2 or 3 three glasses of champagne up and play perfectly happily. It was still the province of the gentleman professional player.

A talented amateur, Vicomte Luc de Patenaude, was the product of an old French aristocratic family. The generations had made good on their inherited fortunes in pharmaceuticals and industry. He was therefore able to adopt a playboy lifestyle, from his base in Paris, which included him playing the High Goal as a patron. Alcohol was the poison of choice for the polo crowd, but the Vicomte demanded something more exotic. He had found a supplier for his Parisian habit and he had found it here at Deauville. The supplier was of an unexpected source, but had assured him that the product was very pure and of good quality.

A week later, De Patenaude had just finished his game and had been knocked out of the tournament at the quarter finals. He was not happy; his capricious temper was boiling over and he had stormed off from the team marquee. Long, sun bleached hair flowing, rubbing a day's growth of stubble on his chin, still in his polo whites and boots, he strode to his Alpha Romeo Spider. It was a beautiful car, a rare model *Beaute*, of which only 120 were produced specifically for the French market. It was liveried in two tone white and blue, with white leather seats. Another beautiful model was at this time running after him: his long suffering girlfriend, Elise.

"Luc, *arrette, arrette!*" she cried to no avail. *He does did not deserve such a lovely machine,* she thought. But money and virtue are not easy bed mates. He fired up the engine, which roared into life with a beautiful, guttural roar, as had been intended by the Ferrari engineers. He crunched into gear, revved it hard and shot off, treating Elsie to a pall of white dust and flying gravel. She shook her fist at the retreating car, stamped her foot in frustration and turned back to the club house.

De Patenaude was angry, hung-over and suffering withdrawal symptoms from the drug his body craved. Like most playboys of his type, he had toyed with racing cars and was a competent track driver. In his current state, he drove with stupidity, causing near accidents from other drivers, forcing them either off the road or to give-way to his dangerous driving. He arrived at the Hotel Barriere in the centre of Deauville, screamed up the cobbled drive-way and left the car, vaulting over the door, throwing the keys at the concierge, who caught them deftly in one hand. He was used to the vagaries of the these spoiled Parisians and knew that there was always a big tip to compensate for their arrogance. Luc strode into the foyer, locks flowing behind, ordered a telephone from the desk and dialled a number from a piece of paper produced from his wallet. The recipient at the other end answered.

De Patenaude responded in fast, accented Spanish. "It is Luc. I need to meet with you. Soon. When can we meet?"

The other person responded that they could meet early evening, just outside of the town; there was, he described, an old café and wine bar, *Lafayette's,* that was easy to find and convenient. It had a car park at the rear and they could meet there. They agreed on 5.30 and Luc, ungraciously, slammed down the phone. "Merde!" he cried and strode off into the bar in search of drink and trouble.

Five thirty arrived none too soon for the Vicomte. He had been sniffing all the way to the café and pulled in early, tapping the steering wheel of his car in frustration, awaiting his contact. He was now getting desperate, twitching and sweating, needing the fix badly. At just before 6.00 the contact turned up. Alphonso, "Al" to his many friends, chugged up in an old diesel Peugeot 206, lurching to a halt as the brakes caught. Al creaked open the door and lithely slipped out of the car. He was almost weedy in stature appearing held together by sinew, skin and bone alone with a face creased and nut brown from too many South American suns.

"*Hola,*" he greeted De Patenaude, all grins, as though being late was perfectly normal and time only an indication. "*Como estas?*"

The Vicomte was not in the mood: "Have you got it?"

Al was not perturbed. "*Si,* here, but come to the car," he swept his arm across to the Peugeot. De Patenaude approached the car, opened the passenger seat and slid in, leaving the door open against the humidity. Al produced a plastic bag of white powder, which he proffered forward to the Vicomte, who opened it and dipped his index finger in to sample the powder. Sucking the finger, he immediately felt the hit of the drug and rolled his tongue appreciatively.

"Good," he exclaimed, "but it has an unusual flavour?"

Al shrugged in his Latin way as if a full explanation had been given. "I do'n know, 'ees good, that I do know. If you don' wan' it, jest let me know. *No es una problema,*" he decried.

"No, I'll take it." A mouth-watering price was asked and paid by the Vicomte. The Francs were paid over and the Vicomte left the car, returning to the Alpha. Al left quickly, leaving the Vicomte in the rear car park alone. De Patenaude, produced a small piece of glass; rolled a 50 Franc note and hoovered up a line of the cocaine in each nostril. He breathed deeply, relaxing as the drug hit his bloodstream. He started the Alpha and headed out, back towards the town.

Later that evening, the French police were alerted to a traffic accident on the main road into Deauville. A blue and white sports car was wrapped around a tree, mangled beyond recognition, and the sole occupant, unrecognisable. Miraculously the car had not burst into flames, but lay smouldering by the road side, hissing in obscene objection to its fate. Police, ambulance and fire fighter teams fought to free the driver, who was pronounced dead at the scene of the collision. No other vehicle appeared to have been involved. Maurice Durand, the *Brigadier-chef* in charge of the scene was about to write off his report as accidental and in the way of the French authorities, fit the incident to the accident, rather than the other way around. It was then that one of his men found the bag of white powder that had been flung into the passenger foot well. Upon seeing the bag, he realised that his job had just become so much more complicated.

"*Oh merde!*" he cried. "*Maintenant la putain d'equipe de drogue serait im pliquee.*" He walked over to his Peugeot 406, sat and picked up the police radio hand set, annoyed at what he was duty bound to do; report it to the drug squad OCTRIS.

CHAPTER 6

The Old Bailey, LONDON

The number Two Court had been a sensation of security and outrage as the criminal charges had been brought against Tir Brennan. Brennan called it a 'British quisling court' and that they had no right to try him, as he did not recognise their Power of State. The motion failed and the trial proceeded.

The jury, who were under strict security protection, took precisely one hour to reach a unanimous decision and found him guilty on four counts of terrorism, murder and extortion. He was sentenced to life imprisonment, but no less than 25 years. In an unusual move, the judge saw fit to grant a plea that he be imprisoned on the Irish mainland; and as some of his crimes were committed in Southern Ireland, he was to be sent to Mountjoy prison in the centre of Dublin, so that he could receive visitations from family during his long incarceration.

The press and the relatives of those killed by this evil monster were furious at the clemency of the court. However the ruling stood, with Brennan transported to Mountjoy prison in Ireland under the cover of a huge security escort.

* * *

Bogota, COLOMBIA

The late August Spring heat was starting to build in the capital and the waves of heat haze danced on the winding road as Pablo Rojas drove up towards the hacienda above the city. He was, however, smiling; he finally had some good news concerning Brennan; and the latest shipment of cocaine had reach mainland Europe safely, already being distributed through their network of contacts, with the money rolling in. The next supplies had reached top production levels and were almost ready to be shipped north to the US for future transportation.

The reinforced steel gates of the estancia opened inwards, upon him being identified by the cameras and then, 20 yards in, two armed guards left a secure post, hidden in the shrubs, checked it was really Rojas and pressed a button that caused a sharp-toothed hydraulic ramp to slide down, permitting his Mercedes to pass. Twice now, rival gangs and angry victim's families had tried to gain access with a view to murdering Ballesteros - as had happened to his predecessor. There was, as Rojas well knew, a group called *Los Pepes,* also known as *Los Perseguidos por Pablo Escobar*, a militant vigilante group, who had killed many of his men, family and lawyers in revenge for the deaths of their family and friends. This was quietly condoned by the Colombian government, who it was said, turned a 'blind eye'.

Upon finally reaching the casa, he strode up the steps, passed the two further armed guards and into the hallway, leading to Ballesteros' study. He knocked and entered, finding Ballestros by a small log fire, lit against the cool of the day at this altitude. The rainy season was about to start again in September and already the humidity had dropped away, even in the city. After the salutations Ballesteros asked: "So Pablo, what news?"

"We have good news, *Jefe*, the drugs are through to France and *Señor* Brennan, he is jailed in Ireland at Mountjoy prison." He waited for his boss to nod in agreement. "Now, we have people there who owe us; drugs people, white, not obvious, they can be controlled, guards bribed. Or maybe, just maybe, we get him another way." He smiled nastily. "We will see who visits him; family, friends, maybe we work it from there. He will understand that there is a price to pay for crossing us."

The trail of smoke rose from Ballesteros' mouth as he squinted against the strong pall of cigar fumes. "Good, let us hope that we see some retribution soon. If he gets out, that too is good. Once he is out, he will make a mistake. Then we will have him."

* * *

October, LONDON

After an astonishingly good summer, London had turned damp and cold very quickly, with a promise of a desultory winter to follow. Hugh Congreave and Rupert had finally managed to put a date in the diary, where holidays, functions and the launch of a new fund had not caused cancellation.

They were sat at a corner table of The Wolseley, as Rupert's treat for the client. Located in the heart of St. James, the Art Deco restaurant was a calm haven compared to the hullabaloo of the frenetic world outside. They were celebrating a portfolio deal Rupert had put together and delivered for them to the tune of £87m. It was a block of six industrial estates that they had bought off-market, from a distressed developer who had sold the holding company that owned the properties. In that sense, it had not been a strict property deal per se, but a corporate acquisition: exactly the sort of thing that Featherstone liked. Congreave raised his glass in salute.

"Here's to you Rupert, great deal." They chinked glasses of Moet and sipped the bubbly liquid appreciatively. He continued: "Do you know why I really liked the deal?"

Rupert nodded. "Because you had the opportunity to buy in the debt and get a free loan off balance sheet, which the City or anyone else can't touch, so it is ring-fenced and you can do with it as you like," he offered.

"Exactly, we're happy; shareholders are happy and big bonuses all round. This is just the sort of thing we need more of, but I know I don't need to tell you that. The other point is, and as you have worked client side in the past you will understand," he referred to Rupert's year with corrupt developer Paul Simions, "is that the fees are compressed and therefore smaller, just one set. You see?"

Rupert again nodded in understanding, his fee alone had been 0.75% of the £87m. "Yes, of course, and I wish I could find you more of them. But, unfortunately, they don't grow on trees."

"I know, I know. In fact it may be better that we look overseas. Possibly the US." Rupert was surprised but as the first course arrived he had to bide his curiosity until the waiter disappeared. "Why the States?" he questioned.

He smiled his shark smile with a superior grin on his face. "A very good question. You see, last year they passed the Riegle-Neal Interstate Banking and Efficiency Act which has had a significant effect upon the way banks can lend and, more importantly for us, what they can then do with the loans." Rupert raised an inquisitive eyebrow.

"Go on," he encouraged.

"Well, here's the thing. The banks over there have a deregulation of how the money is lent; at what ratio and the basis of the valuation. Now everybody wants to own their own property and release equity from it to move up, buy a second home or just have a great holiday. So now they can with the de-regulisation. They have just started what has become known as a 'credit default swap'.

Rupert frowned. "What the hell is that? Damn, these Yanks love their big, clever names. Spell it out for me in English so a poor, ignorant surveyor like me can understand," he finished exasperatedly. Congreave laughed.

"OK, in simple terms; they go out, gets lots of individual loans from home owners, new and existing and get great big bundles of debt. Now here's the clever part. They put these bundles together in packages - just like we did with this last deal - and can now trade, sell them as commodities. Simple. We get loans and property all in one big fell swoop." He grinned, rubbing his hands together. Rupert was more than a little sceptical.

"All well and good, but with all these small lot sizes, the due diligence must be horrific in terms of hours and therefore costly. Who does all that and checks on the security of the borrowers? Who ensures that they can repay the debt satisfactorily? Bloody nightmare!"

He waved his hands dismissively. "Oh we don't worry about that, its' all above board and valued locally by the individual brokers-"

"Yea, who all want a big fat fee and would sell their own grandmother for one, I bet," Rupert interrupted cynically. "Sounds like a recipe for disaster to me," he prophesied.

"Ah you're too cautious," he chided. "Just remember you heard it here first: it is being called the new 'Sub-Prime market' and 'credit default swap'. Pioneered by JP Morgan, no less. And I hear Lehman Bros are taking a huge stake in this new market, so it can't be bad."

Rupert couldn't help himself: "Yes and you remember here, that I said it will all end in tears!" he joked, robbing his words of any sting with a smile. "So, with all this activity in the US, are you still buying in the UK or have I no longer got an active client?" he joked but half worried that one of his main clients had suddenly shut up shop.

"No, not at all. We are still looking, but if we can get huge tranches of debt and property, we can leverage that and be more proactive in the UK."

"I am delighted to hear it. So who is looking in the US and where?" Rupert was intrigued to know, as the waiter removed the starter and brought the main course.

"Mmm, yours looks good, what is it?"

Rupert looked down at the plate. "Something I enjoyed in Italy; small medallions of loin of pork, pan-fried with herbs and goats cheese in a liquor sauce. When done properly - as here - it is amazing. Now, tell me who is searching?" he asked, helping himself to vegetables.

"Ah yes. Well, we have a number of agents combing throughout the good areas and have effectively mapped the US, picking the top provincial spots first, to buy up before the rest of the crowd get there. As to who, well a network of agents, in fact some of your chaps from the New York office actually. They're doing a bit of a road trip. Sounds quite fun really."

"Wow some road trip," he commented between the mouthfuls of pork. "Still, I suppose just like in the UK, it is possible to find the hot spots."

"Indeed and frankly it is not my problem, I just sign off the syndications and get the goods."

All seems a bit hit and miss Rupert thought, *where are the regulators? It could all go so massively wrong with huge exposure to a weak, overinflated market!* But he kept his thoughts to himself and smiled encouragingly. He returned the conversation to the UK market as the meal progressed. Safer ground, he considered. After coffees, brandy and cigars, the two men, suitably relaxed and partly inebriated by the considerable consumption of celebratory alcohol, parted on the steps outside.

As a final refrain, Hugh Congreave ordered him: "Rupert, don't for god's sake be put off, we still need great deals in the UK: keep 'em coming, eh? But if you hear of anything in the US from any source happy to pay a fee, y'know. No reports, just bang it in, alright?"

Rupert smiled in reply and promised to look for deals and report anything he heard in the US. They parted on excellent terms, promising to do it again soon.

Upon returning home that evening, he relayed to Claire what they had discussed over lunch.

"But that is madness," she exclaimed. "If all the reformer regulation has been set aside with this new Act, surely it leaves it open to abuse? And I heard something about this JP Morgan deal. It was with Exxon and some of my clients reckon it will come back to bite them in the arse in due course. But you know, it's not just limited to the US. I heard one of the other's today saying his secretary is buying her first flat; has obtained a 100% mortgage and the lender agreed to finance this off 4.5 times her salary. 4.5!" she decried. "How the hell is she going to repay that back? Live off hope and promises? You know people have such short memories. This is how it started last time. And look what happened there."

Rupert agreed. "Yes, the trouble is, if the wheels come off this time, with the momentum in the US and the way the markets are linked internationally, it will screw up big time. Hey ho, let's just keep making money whilst we can," he finished philosophically.

"You are as bad as the rest of them - deal junkie!" she chided him.

CHAPTER 7

It had now been six weeks since Rupert had lunched with Hugh Congreave and he had not found him any more deals. Two transactions were in lawyers hands for other clients, but nothing for Featherstone. One other deal closer to his heart had come to fruition: Claire had found that she was definitely pregnant. He smiled to himself at the thought that he was going to be a father. The thought was short lived as the next telephone call was one of those that he dreaded.

"Rupert Brett," he answered.

"Mr. Brett." Rupert recognised the voice instantly and was dreading the next words. "Chief Superintendent Webster here, how are you?"

Rupert had first come across Webster back in the 80's and had been asked by him to help break a money laundering ring. It had, as with all things concerning Webster, become dangerous, and in Italy he had been kidnapped and nearly murdered. They had been on speaking terms ever since and through this escapade he had come to the notice of the Foreign Office, especially with Rupert's military background through the TA. He had helped them in Argentina, averting a second Falklands invasion. Every time they crossed paths something bad happened and he knew instinctively this was not a courtesy call. Rupert had from time to time passed information to Webster; if he came across double dealings of a criminal nature in the market. His name was kept out of everything and it had resulted in certain individuals having their collars felt for crimes that would have gone unnoticed in the usual course of events.

"Good morning," he replied warily, "What can I do for you?"

"I wonder if we could meet up for a chat. I need to discuss something with you and ask a few questions on something that you may be able to help me with. Not over the phone." Although presented as an invitation, Rupert knew it was more of a gentle order. Webster was a consummate politician and had not risen so high in the ranks of the police without being very able at manipulating people.

"If it is just a chat, certainly," he confirmed as wary as ever of Webster's Machiavellian tendencies. "When and where?"

"How about my office, say late afternoon, after work? Six o'clock?"

"Fine, I'll be there. See you at 6.00." Rupert put the telephone down and remembered the small office down in Piccadilly, which had been the starting point for his first foray into Webster's world. He shuddered involuntarily and picked up the receiver to call Claire.

She answered almost straight away. "Hi Darling, how's it going?"

"Oh you know, doing deals, living the dream. I've got a shit of a client, who I could cheerfully strangle because he is being so thick and can't see the angle and I feel sick all the time," she added sotto voce. "Apart from that, brilliant. How are you?"

Rupert laughed at her. "Fine. Fine. Just to say I will be late home tonight, going for an early doors sharpener with Freddy from valuation. I want to square something away with him."

"OK," she responded, "What time will you be back?"

"Oh about 7ish, you know how it is."

"Indeed, no probs, see you later." The call finished abruptly. Despite his best efforts, and Rupert knew that for all his ability in the market, the one person he could not successfully disseminate to was his wife. He knew she was not fooled and there would be a third degree later. He thought back to the time he had to tell her about the trip to Argentina and how that had gone down. *Not good,* he thought, *not good.*

* * *

Rupert tried to put the later meeting out of his mind and the hours seemed to drag by. Finally 5.30 came and he left the office, arriving at the address he remembered from years ago, pressed the buzzer and was let into the reception area. As he recalled, it looked as little like a police headquarters of one of the most dangerous and active forces as it was possible to be. But then again, it was a very unusual department and this was the nub where the big cheese sat. The walls were the same plain colour, divided by a dado rail. The receptionist was of a younger vintage and gave him an encouraging smile as he entered. He was asked to go up the carpeted staircase to Webster's office on the first floor. Ascending to the first floor landing, he was met at the door by the man himself.

"Mr Brett, good of you to come and see me. Come on through." He gestured with his hand, leaving the doorway open as he moved sideways.

Hasn't changed, Rupert thought, *still as smooth and direct as ever.* He looked more closely at Webster: still the same erect bearing, sharp, indifferent coloured eyes, he had grown a little more jowly with age, but the same polish to the skin. He was smoothly dressed in a well cut suit, more appropriate to a merchant banker than a policeman, Rupert noted.

The office had changed little: it still had the feel of a study, the large repro antique desk, with two telephones and a green shaded 'bankers' table lamp; Georgian fireplace and shelves of books. All pretty much as he remembered it, even the same smell of pipe smoke, although he had never seen him smoke.

"Have a seat, do. Coffee, tea or dram?"

"Well, it's been a long day," he declared, sitting down, "I will have a single malt, if you have it?"

Webster moved to a corner cabinet. "Certainly, and I'll join you." He poured two shots of whiskey into heavy tumblers with Rupert thinking that all this conviviality was not a good sign: this was more than a question and answer session. He steeled himself for what was to come. He sipped his whiskey appreciatively, the quiet before the storm.

"Now," Webster began, "a number of seemingly unconnected events have been occurring around the world which, until recently, had little or no bearing on anything that I have been dealing with. However, a month ago I received, through various channels, a telephone call from my opposite number in OCTRIS. He tel-"

"OCTRIS?" Rupert queried.

"Ah, the French anti-drug squad. Stands for Office Central for the Repression of Illicit Drugs, or something like that. However, what is important is that the agency OCTRIS, is very well informed with ties into all the French agencies including, police, customs and gendarmes. It has links all over Europe and into Africa. They're based in Nanterre and are extremely well organised. Pierre Cardon, is their deputy chief; he and I get on very well. Now, Pierre has been following a line of drugs, more specifically cocaine, that is very pure. They have not been able to track down the main suppliers, but from the small amounts confiscated, they know type and origins to a certain extent."

Rupert was interested: "What, you mean they can tell which side of the hill it was grown on, like wine?" he offered slightly sarcastically, not really seeing what all this had to do with him. Webster snorted impatiently, wanting to explain his whole story, not appreciating Rupert's sense of humour.

"Yes, in manner of speaking. It has its own DNA, which can be traced back and logged with other drugs found. A picture is then built up, showing, with known traces of origin, where each sample is produced. This provides links to couriers, how they travelled, where a product is distributed from etc., etc.,"

"Really? Interesting, I didn't realise it was so sophisticated."

"Indeed, it helps all agencies, across all borders, track drugs from source and build an accurate picture of where they came from and, to a certain extent, when, where and by whom they are distributed. This includes what we do here in the UK, when a new source of drug or distribution is found, we analyse and trace it. Anyway, they have traced a new batch of drug doing the rounds in Paris, to be of Columbian origin and very pure at that. Most recently, there was a death of a son of an influential family, Vicomte Luc de Patenaude. Have you heard of him?"

"Vaguely, it rings a bell," Rupert responded.

"Well, the reason I ask is because, apart from being an international playboy, he was also a famous polo patron and had, until just before his death, been playing in the Deauville Cup."

"Ah, I see. Yes, now I remember; his team was the *Les Tigres,* I think."

"Just so. Well, he met with an unfortunate accident on the way home from a trip to a bar out of town. He was spotted there with another man in the car park and a substantial amount of cocaine was found both in his car and in his system. What was more interesting is that the post mortem analysis found a toxic substance in the drug and apart from affecting his driving - he wrapped his car around a tree - it would probably have killed him in due course anyway. This batch was the same as turned up in Paris and we know it originated from Colombia."

Rupert opened his mouth to speak but Webster silenced him, continuing, "Now, you will remember this, back in June there was a drugs bust at the Queen's Cup final at Guards, no doubt you were there?" Rupert nodded seeing the direction the conversation was heading. "And you will probably remember two of the people arrested were hospitalised and one subsequently died."

"From an overdose, yes, and don't tell me this was the same batch that killed the Vicomte in Deauville?"

"Yes, the same batch, but not an overdose. We believe it was the same sort of poisoning suffered by the ill-fated Vicomte. Now, not all the drugs from this source (we have found other relatively healthy consumers) appear to be contaminated. But it all matches the DNA of the Colombian source." Rupert waited knowing there was more to come. Webster watched him as he surmised all that had happened: "Both of these sources are directly connected with the polo world and, more specifically, all big, high level tournaments."

"Yes, the High Goal circuit," Rupert commented.

"High Goal?"

"Each player gets a handicap, like in golf, only in reverse, nought being crap, 10 excellent. Each tournament is graded, anything above 18 goals is High Goal so that the aggregate of the four players must add up to, in this case 22 goals, which is the highest rated game outside Argentina. A big deal in polo terms. Like watching the FA Cup Final or Twickenham, only over a period of weeks not just in one day," Rupert explained.

Webster had a pertinent question: "And the same group of players moving from place to place?"

"For the most part, yes. Certainly the Argies, they are part of the circuit and will return home after it all ends in Deauville for their summer and the High Goal in Argentina. Then it starts all over again in January at Palm Beach in Florida," Rupert explained.

Webster cast his penetrating eyes on Rupert: "Interesting that you mention Florida. We have also been liaising with the DEA in the States. You may not know, but they divide the country into Divisions and one of the unsurprisingly busiest is the Miami Division, which of course happens to include Florida. They also have a co-ordinating SOD, Special Operations Division. This deals with data, analysis etc., and surprise, surprise, the drugs that ended up here and in France, were an identical batch to those being found in the States and Florida."

"And the drugs entered the States how? They have, if I understand correctly, really tough standards on drug smuggling and very tough DEA agents?"

"Oh don't be naïve, Rupert," Webster chided. "Nowhere is air tight, the southern border with Mexico is so porous. Until they build a wall or an impregnable fence, it will always be that way. Miami itself is a haven for smugglers, due to its huge exposure to the sea and close proximity to South America. No, that bit is relatively easy. Getting drugs in is the easy bit, however getting them distributed worldwide after that is the hard bit, especially into the UK."

"So, let me see if I understand this correctly," Rupert stated. "You have a production facility in Colombia that is distributing into the States, then worldwide. All of this distribution, shown by analysis, coincides with the High Goal polo circuit and you think, somehow, the two are connected. That is ridiculous," he finished scathingly. "What do you think they do, use their horses as drug mules?" he finished, laughing at his own joke. Webster was not amused.

"Well, you may find it funny. But we have evidence that this has been happening for two years and this year's quantities have risen considerably. This coincides with a significant bust we made in the Irish Sea earlier this year." He went on to explain to Rupert what had happened.

"Wait, this was this IRA guy, what's his name... Brennan, just sent down at the Old Bailey?" Webster nodded. "OK, call me stupid here and I'll bite, but why you? You are a cross-over task force for special cases. Why not the drugs squad?"

"But that is exactly what it is: terrorism and drug smuggling, a cross over jurisdiction which I am co-ordinating. We think that once we shut down the Irish route across the sea, there was a big falling out and they - the Colombians - have concentrated on their apparently lucrative route through the States to here."

"I thought that the IRA didn't deal in drugs, as it killed their own people?"

"They don't, but having forsaken politics for profit, they are quite happy to make a buck or two off their home turf."

"OK, I get it, drugs are being pushed out of Colombia and supposedly moved to coincide with the polo world, all emanating from the US. I am dreading asking this, but why tell me all this? How on earth can I help? As far as I can see, all I have to offer is a little bit of knowledge of polo. Big deal, thousands like me." Rupert spread his arms and shrugged.

"Yes, well, I was getting to that," Webster responded insidiously. "You see, you have a number of qualities that would be perfect for what we have in mind." He began to list them, counting on his fingers: "You have signed the Official Secrets Act; you have undertaken espionage before; worked with me and other agencies; have a knowledge of polo, as you say; and last but not least, understand property so can be there perfectly legitimately, looking for deals for clients." The silence lasted for a minute, Rupert shaking his head in amazement.

"No! Definitely not. NO!"

"But you don't even know what we would like you to do for us," Webster wheedled.

"Don't tell me, be a professional polo player and go undercover to be an IRA member at the same time." This time Webster did smile at his sarcasm.

"Dear me, no, nothing that dangerous."

CHAPTER 8

Tijuana, MEXICO

Not long after Rupert Brett had left the offices of CSI Webster, an activity that Webster had described to Rupert was taking place with military precision on the other side of the world. The cartels of Colombia, having formed their own routes to the States, had either agreed deals with the Mexican suppliers and cartels or eliminated them.

At this moment, a train of drugs was being transported by open farm lorries stacked with watermelons and was making its way on the last leg of the journey to an estancia just outside Tijuana, on the north side of the city and close to the border with the US. The massive Colorado Hills swept up majestically from the bowl encapsulating the city. The city had grown as one of the main manufacturing bases for markets north of the border in the States. The manufacture and supply of medical instruments was much cheaper this side of the border, and so easy to export north to the US companies. They vicariously employed and owned them through holding companies and corporate structures.

But there was a secondary, more sinister base to the Tijuana economy: drug smuggling. Its close proximity to the border inevitably led to use of the city and its environs, to aid the smugglers entry to the US with their lethal cargo. *Casa de Luz*, was a sick name for the luxurious house set in its own compound. It did not provide light, but dealt death and darkness from the tunnels beneath the house. Miguel Sanchez, nominally the 'Owner' of the property, was at this moment overseeing the unloading of the latest shipment of cocaine delivered up from Ballesteros' factories in Colombia.

"Come on, we want this on the rails by sundown," he ordered. The thin, wiry, brown skinned men laboured like ants. Almost running with boxes of drugs from the four lorries parked near to the cellar entrance of the house. They looked just like typical farm labourers, grubby from the fields, but the cargo was cocaine, not water melons.

One of the foremen from the lorries came up to Sanchez, enquiring of the tunnel. "The tunnel is in there?

"*Si.*" Came the monosyllabic reply, seemingly shutting down any further discussion. But the driver was inquisitive and had been paid to be so. He was pushing his luck.

"Where does it go?"

Sanchez gave him a hard stare. "Over there." He pointed across the border, scowling at the other man. He shrugged, grimacing, "OK, just curious. None of my business."

"No it's not. Get back to work," he ordered. The driver, an undercover agent for the Colombian Nat Police drug squad, knew how quickly a knife or a gun could appear. He sloped off, hair rising on the back of his neck; he had done well to get this far in. He now knew how and when the drugs would be moved, and he would report in due course.

What he would have loved to do is follow Sanchez down to the doors of the tunnel, see the railway tracks, and follow them to the other side. There was even a telephone line, running the full length of the 4 foot high tunnel, with electric lights and a drainage system. Sanchez picked up the receiver linking to the factory over the border in San Diego. It answered after a few rings.

"*Hola, Sanchez*," he fired off in fast Spanish. "Yes it is on its way now, the first shipment is leaving us. Ok." He knew that the small cars or carriages, would now roll their way under the border and be in the US destination in just under half an hour."

CHAPTER 9

LONDON

After Rupert Brett had left Webster's office, he scowled and shook his head. *No fucking way*, he thought, *not after last time. And Claire would kill me. She would be proud of me this time though, I said no.* He grinned to himself. He would have been less than happy if he had overheard a conversation emanating from Webster's office at that time. He was speaking with Simon Johnston, head of MI6, who Rupert also knew from his last adventures.

"Yes, predictably he said an emphatic 'No'. So it looks as though we shall have to go with plan B. How will you get it done?"

"Well, same as last time, only rather more clandestinely. Robinson has some old school tie connection with one of the senior chaps at HBJ. We will pull strings from there. Perfectly legitimate. Brett, as you say, is head of capital markets, always travelling, and the Americans are looking to counter invest and vice versa. Perfect time for him to go and look at a bit of Real Estate in the States."

"He will, of course, smell a rat."

"Oh undoubtedly, but when it is put to him as a fait accompli, I am sure he will come around and he can take that lovely wife of his along, too. She will love being in amongst the polo set she seems to enjoy so much. Anyway, he can smooth over there, meet up with the contact from New York office, do a bit of hand pressing and look around. He has a nose for it, I am sure he will pick up something. Agents like him really are spies in disguise. Their very job needs them to be like it. Only with them its property information, not state secrets." He smirked, the grin evident in his voice.

"Yes, well, I wonder which one of us he will contact first when the penny drops? Or maybe we will have to make the penny drop in due course. But this is serious or we wouldn't be asking him to do it. And of course his rather special skill sets and experience make him ideal for the job. Still, he does not quite see it like that." Johnston agreed and promised to keep him informed.

Rupert had no idea what was being planned for him as he entered the house they had moved to in Richmond. They had sold their flat at the top of the market, just before the last recession. Having judiciously sold and rented for two years; foreseeing the recession, much to the horror of their friends who had thought them mad, to cries of: 'dead money', 'going backwards', 'foot off the housing ladder' etc. But by doing so they had kept the high value for their flat sale in the bank, watched the market collapse and bought back in at just the right time, managing to swap a flat in central London for a period semi-detached house in Richmond overlooking a small green, which would have cost them twice as much at the top of the market.

As the front door slammed, Rupert hung up his overcoat on the rack and walked down the hallway; he was treated to wonderful smells emanating from the kitchen filled with herbs and spices.

"Wow, that smells good. Lamb curry?" Claire turned around. She was wearing jeans and a baggy sweater and came over, kissing him hard on the lips. He pushed her back, taking a closer look at his wife. He saw sparkling green eyes, heavily styled, full, strawberry blond hair, a bloom in her cheeks and her skin looked as though she had been on holiday.

"How do you do it? Most woman get pregnant and look terrible. You look like a goddess," he flattered. His eyes took on a lascivious look. "How about a quickie before supper?"

She scolded him with a quick look, but her eyes smiled. "No Rupert Brett, I've got a curry to finish, it is all I seem to want to eat at the moment and I'm starving," and she turned quickly towards the new electric Aga. Rupert was not to be dissuaded. He came up behind her, cupping her breasts which had started to swell with the pregnancy, although nowhere else had yet started to show. "Oh come on, just look at these 'babies'," he exclaimed squeezing them gently, "they're fantastic and getting bigger!"

"No Rupert, you bloody octopus," she chided, slapping the wooden spoon she was holding down on his hand. "Maybe later, if you're good. Now set the table." Rupert put on the time honoured, shamefaced look of a man who was about to shrivel up and die without conjugal rights, but to no avail, Claire stood firm, although she was feeling as horny as him, the pregnancy seemed, she was pleased to realise, to have exacerbated her sex drive, in addition to her hunger, which won out.

It was throughout supper that Rupert explained what had really happened after work, citing that he had not wanted to worry her.

"Hah," she cried. "I knew it; I knew you were lying. You can't fool me, I was going to interrogate you later under sexual torture."

"Wish I hadn't told you the truth now." He winked at her.

"You really said 'No' straight out to Webster?" He nodded "Well done you. Although I would love to go to Palm Beach and see the polo. Now that would be cool. It is supposed to be a great tournament, publicised as '*the best winter polo in the world*'. A number of friends have been and said half the fun is the razzmatazz the Americans bring to the scene, it is really smooth apparently."

"Well, sorry to disappoint you. I could always offer to spy for them if you wished...?"

"Don't you dare. Now I have another mission for you, come upstairs..." she arched her back as she rose from the table and sashayed wantonly, her hips swaying from side to side like a hooker on the street tempting clients. Rupert followed her quickly, entering the bedroom just after her. She was not there, he turned around and as he did so she appeared from behind the door, pushing him back onto the bed. "Now the torture begins!" she whispered at him huskily.

Rupert had awoken the next day with a smile on his face, not least of which because he had assured Claire, yet again, that he had said no to Webster.

Two days later the smile was no longer there. He had been summoned to a board meeting of Regional Heads of Departments. It was a 'strategy meeting': something he hated along with all the politics that went with a big company, especially a big company owned by Americans. The meeting was coming to an end and then the agenda reached: *Future Placements.* Rupert had no idea what this meant but was soon to find out.

Andrew Hastings, the head of the UK board held forth: "Now, as you are all aware, we are investing more time abroad and bringing in clients who are multi investors, crossing borders and investment strategies. This falls in line with the American strategy for a bigger global market." He droned on and Rupert wondered where all this was leading. He received the answer after another five minutes. "So, Rupert, we want to make you

Head of Capital Markets with responsibility for the US and Northern Europe."

Rupert was amazed and barely heard the other two names for Southern Europe and the South East Asia markets. The other two candidates seemed equally surprised by the announcements. In reality, Hastings and the board were going to announce this in the New Year, but Robinson's intervention had just speeded things up. The details were explained and the positions were to commence forthwith. Rupert was approached by Hastings afterwards.

"Pleased Rupert?"

"Delighted, just didn't see it coming."

"Well, you have, amongst other clients, been working hard on Featherstone and the chairman there stated he was going to the states into this new *Sub-Prime market*, wants us to see first-hand what it is all about. Sounds exciting." Rupert sensibly held back his thoughts and reservations on the Sub-Prime market.

"Indeed, Andrew, yes I shall look forward to it. When do we meet up with our counterparts?"

"Well, I understand a trip has been teed up for the New Year in early January. So you, not we, will be off for the US then. They have mapped out the States, and you will meet and greet, press the flesh, that sort of thing and see if we can drum up some cross-Atlantic business." It was then that Hastings slipped in the deadly information, very deftly with all the political aplomb of his powerful position in the company. "Yes, apparently they are working down to the richer areas, one of them is the northern Florida range, vast swathes of land and property there and the owners equivalent to American royalty, I'm told. Should be rich pickings for investors as well." He eyed Rupert keenly, all bonhomie and goodwill. And for someone so astute and sharp in the outside world, with a keen sense of self preservation, Rupert could at times be remarkably naive when it came to looking after himself. Explaining the position to Claire over supper he was thrilled with the new promotion.

"So where will you start your road trip?" she queried a little wistfully.

"Oh it will only be for two weeks and hopefully *we* - you will be able to fly by then and you can come with me - can go travelling. I can't leave you behind, you'll easily be able to get time off then: everyone skiing, the market is always dead for the first two weeks of January anyway."

"Oh wow, winter sunshine in grim January. Now tell me where are we going?" she interrogated him and before he could answer, interjected, "You will have to cancel TA manoeuvres then as well."

"Oh that will be fine and to answer in reverse order: Florida, the land of winter sun."

It was the words 'winter sun' that struck Claire first, ever the more Machiavellian, with a woman's fine-tuned sense of intuition, they floated in front of her eyes, bringing back the discussion of a few days ago about the Palm Beach polo. She shook her head closing her eyes.

"Rupert, they've done it to you again."

"Done what?" What are you talking about?"

"Doesn't it strike you as odd that you are suddenly put in the position that Webster et al wanted you in at exactly the right time and place? Wasn't it last time that Robinson, Johnston or whoever, pulled strings to get you to Buenos Aries? Think about it."

"No, no way. Look it is all legitimate, with Featherstone etc., it is just a coincidence. And if it is a ploy, why promote the other two with the Far East and Southern European markets, mmm? No, too big a stretch. No way," he kept convincing himself. "You're too suspicious, playing your spy games in the market, Lady Borgia," he finished, smiling. Claire smiled too but was unconvinced and was just waiting for the hammer to fall. *But,* she thought, *if he goes, I go too.*

The next day, Rupert began making plans for the trip in the New Year and, amongst others, put in place his request for leave from the TA in the days he had previously agreed to serve.

His CO, Major Dove, agreed to the request with an alacrity that surprised him.

"Off to anywhere exciting?" he asked once he realised it was work orientated and part of a promotion.

"Well, in manner of speaking, I suppose I am. Florida and then a trip further around the wealthy states in the US. Press the flesh and get the goodies from the Yanks to invest over here. Should be fun," he concluded.

"Sounds like it. I hope you have a great time and think of us slogging in the mud back here in blighty," he ordered.

Rupert thanked him, left the offices in the barracks in Clapham and got into his Audi Avant RS 2. He was particularly proud of the car and glad of the chance to drive it as he normally caught the tube. His mind had put all thoughts of Dove's attitude out of his mind as he drove through the thinning traffic, which offered a few small opportunities to try the car's stunning acceleration from various sets of traffic lights as he headed towards Richmond.

After Rupert had left Dove's office, the Major picked up the receiver and dialled a number in Whitehall.

"Johnston?" the direct dial number answered.

"Good evening, Major Dove here. How are you?"

"Very well and hopefully better if you have some good news for me," he responded directly.

"Indeed I do. Brett asked for leave this evening, so I should give it a day or so before putting the wheels in motion. What will you do, ask to see him, or will that be Webster's domain? "

"I think it will be a joint interview, get him here, chat it through and explain how easy it will be for him to help us now that he has agreed to go and will be there anyway," he predicted.

"Good luck, I don't think he will go easily and try to keep my name out of it, please."

"Will do and, er, thank you for your help."

"Not at all. Goodbye." The call was terminated. *Mmm*, Dove thought, *I think they have underestimated just how stubborn he can be. We'll see.*

The weekend went by with Rupert and Claire planning not only Christmas but the trip for the New Year. Rupert was delighted everything was falling into place. Nothing came on the horizon and Claire, who had enquired about his conversation with Major Dove, was starting to feel it might be alright and that she had worried unnecessarily.

Monday at the office, Rupert received a call from Johnston. He was annoyed, worried and aggressive all at the same time: he realised exactly why he had called, no naiveté this time.

"Mr Johnston. I told you 5 years ago the answer is no and it is still no. Why are you calling me?"

"Two things have come to my attention. One you have had a discussion with Detective Super Intendent Webster and as I understand it, you will now be in a position to help us, with very little effort on your behalf; it will save misery to millions of lives caught up in both areas that you have discussed with Webster," he finished ambiguously. "Look, you don't have to do anything but be yourself and keep alert."

Rupert appeared to ignore his plea. "How did you know I was going 'there'?" he asked.

"Requests from military get processed, certain areas have stars attached to them, get flagged if actioned. That sort of thing," he said vaguely, avoiding the point. Rupert knew that he had little choice short of resigning his position within the firm, but he had a key card he wanted to play.

"When and where?"

"What do you mean?"

"To meet with you. That's what you want isn't it and I'll bet Webster or some other sneak will be there."

"Ah, yes, I see. My office, you've been here before and I will arrange for clearance and a pass at the reception desk. When, well to suit you in the next 48 hours. We need to brief you and put all this in motion. So as soon as possible."

"You may need longer because you haven't heard my terms yet. If I don't get it, I'll resign. Yes, to cut across your arguments now, it will be difficult, but I'm at the top of my game, I can walk in anywhere and probably get a better package. I'm happy at HBJ but if I don't get what I want, I'll walk and you'll be left with no one until next year."

"Alright, I'm curious, what do you want so insistently, money?"

Rupert snorted at him in disgust. "No, don't be so crude, just one word, bearing in mind this is an open line: Adams."

There was a pause as the implication of the one word percolated through to Johnston.

"Can't be done, and it won't be dangerous, just a recce, no spies or terrorists or hostile governments. We have good people here who-"

"No. And that's what you said last time. Him or no one and I'll see you and him in your office. Let me know when you've arranged it. Goodbye." Rupert slammed the phone down. *What am I going to tell Claire?* he thought.

CHAPTER 10

Rupert had tried to contact Chris Adams, the SAS sergeant who had worked with him in Argentina, directly at the home number he had for him, but to no avail. He tried telephoning Stirling Lines, that proved a dead end too. Chris Adams had been an usher at his wedding and since their joint operation and subsequent friendship in 1991, they had stayed in touch and met up whenever they could, given Adam's peripatetic lifestyle.

When Rupert arrived at Thames House, the MI6 headquarters, two days later, he was escorted from reception to a secure room on the first floor having handed his briefcase in at reception. The door was opened for him and he entered the bland room; thick, frosted glass that faced the Thames, solid walls and thick sound proof carpet. No pictures, just a thick, glass-topped table and chairs. No telephone or cupboards, a purely functional, secure room. There were three other men awaiting him. Sergeant Chris Adams came forward first, ignoring all protocol, offering his hand and clasping Rupert on the back with his left arm in a powerful half bear hug.

"Chris, you bugger, how're you doing? You are looking tanned and well."

Adams was just over 6ft, and whilst not bulky, had a natural power to him, all oiled sinew and whipcord strength, born of hard work and exercise, rather than in a muscle bound gym environment. His dark hair had receded slightly to Rupert's keen sight, skin tight over his prominent cheek bones and there were a few more lines around the eyes joining up the crows feet, from squinting into too many suns. His grip on Rupert's right hand was that of a Grizzly and Rupert could sense the feeling of power and energy exuding from him in a wave. He was, Rupert considered, obviously in top shape and it was great to see his friend again.

"Hah, I was sunbathing on the coast until you disturbed my holiday," he joked, dissembling as always. Rupert knew he would not get the truth until they were alone and then only part of it. "You look fat and soft as ever, enjoying the good life. Easy this surveying business as I seem to remember." Rupert laughed it off, pulling his stomach in still further. The other two men permitted them a moment or two of indulgence. One was Webster with whom he shook hands and the other Simon Johnston, who as with Adams had changed little: still the solid countenance of an athlete going slightly to fat, and fighting the onset of middle age. The hard, shrewd, cynical eyes still carried a piercing stare which bore into him, or so Rupert felt.

"Mr Brett, good to see you again and despite Sergeant Adams's opinion, you look fit and well," he joked, breaking any sense of formality. "Now, please sit. Coffee, tea?" They both refused. "Don't worry, you won't need notes." He assured him as Rupert automatically reached for his non-existent briefcase, "I will give you a file. As before, all the information will be in it. But to re-cap for the benefit of Sergeant Adams."

Johnston went over everything that had happened since the interception in the Irish Sea. The plan was simple: go to America with Chris as a junior surveyor as before. Do exactly what was expected of him as a surveyor. Mix with the polo crowd and see if anything comes to light that is suspicious.

"You will have a DEA contact over there, Seth Meacham,

who is part of their Special Operations Division. He has your mobile number and the hotel landline where you will be working. Please make sure your mobile works in the States and is set up for their banding."

"Already done, I have one of the new Motorolas, works both side of the Pond. The office has checked."

"Good. As before, an encrypted sat phone will be sent across and to the Consulate in Miami if we feel that there is a need or urgency. However, I suspect that this will just be a surveillance mission and nothing more. It's in a briefcase as before and all secure. All the numbers are in the files." He pushed two buff-coloured folders across the table. "Sergeant Adams, your background cover as before will hold good. Spend a bit of time in the London office and make up whatever story you want. Back on the firm payroll. The reception has been told that you're back, all covered. Although, I still don't see why Brett needs protecting, it is all very low key. All you have to do is observe. How are you going to play it with the polo side?" he asked, turning to Rupert.

"Well, as you know, polo is a very closed group and there are groups within the groups. No more so than the High Goal scene. Now, that is divided again into two contingents. Patrons and Players. Clearly, I am not a player but I am going to hold out that a property source I represent is looking to sponsor a High Goal team for the Queen's and Gold Cup in the UK for this, or possibly next season."

"And can you pull this off? What if someone bites?"

"Oh I can use Featherstone's name and credentials if pushed. It only has to hold up for a short period of time anyway. If it gets back to Hugh Congreave, I will just say it was a misunderstanding and blag it. Easy, I do it all day long," he boasted. "But, in any event, the polo world is a gossipy place once you're on the 'inside'. Polo and property have always been easy bedfellows and it all feels right to anyone in the game."

"Alright. Anything else you need?"

"Luck!" they both chorused in unison.

They both left the building and wandered around the corner to a for a cup of coffee. Once settled in a corner, away from anyone within earshot, the overriding music masking their conversation, the two men caught up with recent events.

"Chris, it's good to see you and I'm glad that you could make it. I told them I wouldn't go without you."

Chris smiled in reply, his face looking younger and less tough: "Ah, delighted to be of service," he mocked. "Well, here we go again, but I think it will be a lot less tense than last time."

"Blimey, I hope so. Where did they drag you from or can't you say?"

Chris smiled again, pleased at the effect the words he was about to say would have upon Rupert. "Colombia, anti-drugs sortie. Can't say any more in detail, but it was rather ironic when I heard where and what I was being asked to do."

Rupert laughed. "Is this all to do with the new agreement President Mitterand signed back in 1989: war against drugs; helping the Colombians fight poverty, that sort of thing? Coffee not cocaine. Etc., etc?"

"Yes, that sort of thing," he answered diffidently, "joint effort from Europe. Can't say anymore, I'm afraid, even with your clearance." Rupert held up a placatory hand.

"No, understood and I don't want to know: it will only get me into trouble. So the plan is to get you back in and seen around HBJ for a few days. I don't know...back from the Birmingham office or something. I am sure that snake in the grass Hastings had something to do with this behind the scenes, so he can arrange it. I should have listened to Claire. She had the right of it all along. She should be the spy, not me," he exhorted.

"Talking of Claire, how is your lovely wife? I still can't

understand why she would up and marry you when I am around."
He laughed.

"Ah, very well and I am sure she misses you. But some news:
she is pregnant," he enjoined.

"Rupert, mate, that is great news. When is she due?"

"Oh not for months yet and she will be just over 3 months
gone when, you'll be pleased to know, she will be joining us in
the States."

Chris Adams' face clouded slightly into a frown. "Is that wise?
I mean I know they say that there is no danger, but wherever
drugs are involved there is always danger, however small."

Rupert looked around furtively: "Well do you dare to tell her
not to come when polo is involved and the chance of winter sun?
Not to mention keeping an eye on me." Chris shook his head
grinning. He knew only too well Claire could, when pushed,
have the flexibility of a mountain.

"Ah, thought so. And, talking of strong women, how is
Sophie?" Sophie Carswell an MI6 agent, had been in Argentina
with them and played a major part in preventing disaster. She
and Chris were, the last time Rupert had heard, an item, although
that was 6 months ago.

Chris grimaced, moving his head to a one sided tilt. "It's
difficult, we are still sort of together, but both our work gets in
the way, massively. We are both being posted all over the place
and, well you know how it goes, one of us may not come back
one day. Don't get me wrong, when we are together there is no
one on this earth I would rather be with and I think she feels the
same. But..." he shrugged. "Well, when I leave The Regiment,
I've only got another 6 years or so tops, then we'll see if she hasn't
found some rich diplomat by then," he finished smiling.

"Not with you around matey, but don't leave it too late."

"Now, we need somewhere secure to discuss things," he continued. "Can we meet tomorrow at HBJ's offices? I will get a

meeting room booked and you a desk to make it look Kosher."
Everything arranged, they parted company and Rupert went
back to the office. That evening at home went pretty much as
Rupert expected. Claire was not happy with an 'I told you so'
attitude. She then proceeded to tell him she was going at any
cost and not leaving him at the mercy of drug dealers and other
nefarious persons. She was, however, considerably mollified by
the presence of Chris and told him that it was the most sensible
thing he had done over the last week. His wife, he considered,
was a force to be reckoned with.

CHAPTER 11

Mountjoy Prison, DUBLIN

The prison was located in the centre of Dublin, in the Phibsborough area. It was a daunting place with a castellated style entrance supported by two towers in dull, grey granite. It was difficult to access and anybody who had attempted an escape had failed by virtue of its close proximity to the Gardia and the difficult streets that made a fast getaway almost impossible. However, the IRA's GHQ staff had decided to get Tir Brennan out and back in service. He was too valuable to them as an enforcer and assassin. They knew it would be only a matter of time before someone shanked him with a homemade knife or toothbrush blade; or hurt one of his family in retaliation for the missing drugs. It would, of course, be an almost certain death sentence for the assassin, but that would not matter. Some prisoners were desperate or their loyalty sold to their families elsewhere, for whom they would rather die to keep them safe. It was a cruel world and only the most desperate survived.

A plan had been hatched and explosives were smuggled into the prison, in food and heels of shoes, pens, anything that would accommodate small amounts of plastique to be assembled. All it needed, they reasoned, was enough explosive to blow the doors leading to the exercise yard. From there, a rope ladder would be flung over the walls, with Brennan and two others making good their escape. The plan was well thought out, as a series of escape cars were set up to act as a diversion, rather like a shell game, no one knowing who was in each car.

But the plan was doomed to failure. They could not get direct access to the exercise yard door and whilst they struggled internally, timing being everything, the ladder had been thrown over the wall and was spotted by a warden who raised the alarm. Major searches were undertaken and the explosives discovered hidden in a cell. A new plan had to be hatched, and so a far more daring plan was orchestrated.

In the office behind *The Brigade* pub off the Falls Road, one of the joint chiefs of staff looked at the proposals, shaking his head in disbelief.

"Do you think it will work? It's like something from fockin' James fockin' Bond," O'Donnall exclaimed.

"I know, I know but we've planned it to the limit. It's all in place, everyone is up for it. We go in two days. We get word to Brennan and he, Muir and Sean will be ready. Do we agree then?"

The three council members gave their agreement. The most daring plan ever attempted in the Republic or the British Isles was about to be put into action.

An American sympathetic to the *Cause* was flown in and visited the Eire helicopter company in Dublin. John Roberts called into the airfield as arranged. Calling in to the office of Eire helicopters, he introduced himself to the owner, Michael Carr.

"John Roberts." Carr and Roberts shook hands.

"Mornin' to you."

"I'm over here for a recce for some film work and need to be taken up towards County Laois. Aerial work and maybe fly back down shooting all the way.

"How many crew will you have with you?"

"Oh there'll be three plus me, for the 'sound team'," he answered in a Boston accent.

"Well best will be the five-seater Allouette. Here, let me show you."

The two men walked over to the hanger where the fleet of helicopters was stored. The Allouette II was parked near the front of the hanger, an opaque, Perspex fuselage, offering full 360 degree vision surrounded the cockpit and the aircraft was mounted on skids, with retracted wheels. Roberts opened the large door and peered inside, seating himself in the front seat adjacent to the pilot. He smiled across at Carr in affirmation.

"She will be perfect. Love the visibility and my men can hang out and get great shots of what we want. Listen, we are on a tight time frame, can we do this the day after tomorrow?"

"Sure. We'll need payment upfront, of course, but if that can be cleared-"

"No problem, it'll be cash and I can pay now."

This was music to Carr's ears. "Come down to the office and we can get the paperwork sorted and a flight plan agreed." The pair walked out of the hanger and across to the office. On the way, Roberts stopped at his car and retrieved a brief case carrying it into the office. He was shown through; papers signed and the cash paid over to Carr, who was more than happy with the day's first transaction.

"What time will you want the flight booked for Thursday? The pilot I have in mind can be available all day."

The American considered briefly, looking at the light through the open window. "I would think, given the light and this brief patch of good crisp weather we are having, which I understand will hold good for the rest of the week, say 9.00 am here for take-off? Then up to Stradbally. There is a field up there where we can land easily, pick up a colleague who is bringing all the photographic equipment and off we go. Is that OK?"

"Sure, sure, we'll be a wee while getting the flight plan booked and then all good to go." Carr stood, offering his hand and shaking Roberts firmly.

"Thank you, Mr Carr. I will see you on Thursday, now you have a nice day," he chimed, American twang at the fore. He left the office, got into his car, a Ford Mondeo that had been stolen that morning with the plates changed, and drove out through the airport gates. Roberts stopped at the first public telephone box to make a call back to *The Brigade* pub off the Falls road. It was answered by a rough, guttural Northern Irish voice. "Brigade?"

"Morning, John Roberts here. Can you pass on a message for me? Tell Steve I've booked 18 holes for Thursday and we tee off at 9.30. Tell him to take the day off work and I'll call around tonight. OK?" The barman gave a consent to pass the message on.

"Thank you. Have a nice day." The call ended and 'John Roberts' headed deeper into the city centre and the prestigious North Star hotel on Amiens Street. The lovely Georgian hotel attracted many Americans staying in Dublin, visiting the 'Old Country' and where better, he mused, to hide a tree than in a wood. Although a true American citizen, he had booked in under his real name of O'Calley and went to meet his wife for lunch. He now had two days of sight-seeing before taking the helicopter flight, followed by a ferry crossing to the UK and a long haul flight from Manchester airport back to the US. He was then to be met at the hotel by another man, who would take the car off him and finally arrange a 'taxi' for the return trip to the airport on Thursday morning.

Thursday morning, as promised by the Met Office, was cold, with a thin wintery sun piercing through the clear, freezing air:

"Perfect for filming," Roberts declared as he was introduced to his pilot, Captain David Bryan, a tall, sparse, ex-RAF pilot, now working the civilian passage, as so many did after leaving the Service.

"Morning to you. Captain David Bryan," he offered, shaking hands, "Yes, good day for flying and filming, we'll have you ready for take-off in 10 minutes. I'll just go through pre-flight checks and we'll be up and away." Bryan smiled and marched off to the aircraft, which was sitting on the concrete outside the hanger. Five minutes later, he signalled Roberts to join him in the Allouette. Rotors turned, turbo's whined and in a short space of time the helicopter rose steadily up from the concrete apron, gliding into the air with a chatter of rotor blades. The aircraft dipped, turned and Captain Bryan set course for Stradbally.

Located to the south west of Dublin, Stradbally was a small agricultural town; isolated and perfect for the plan the IRA had in mind. They arrived in just under half an hour, dropping down into a field indicated by Roberts, where a car waited. As soon as the aircraft touched down, a man ran forward, from behind Captain Bryan's line of sight, ducking under the rotor wash as the blades whirred overhead. The masked man pulled open the cockpit door on the pilot's side and thrust forward a Colt M1911 .45 semi-automatic from his Barbour pocket straight into Bryan's face. The sun glinted off the barrel of the slim pistol, its wide bore seemed to be pointed straight at Captain Bryan's forehead.

"Keep the rotors running," the masked man ordered, through the slit hole for his mouth, accentuating the harsh Belfast accent. "If you do as your told, you won't get hurt. It's not you we want, it's your chopper and for you to do a job for us."

Bryan nodded in agreement, knowing that the mask meant he was probably safe if he did what they said, as he could obviously not identify the man. Roberts stepped out of the cockpit, turning to greet another masked man who appeared out of the bushes, carrying an Armalite AR-18 rifle, the chosen weapon of the IRA, smuggled in from the States. The second man entered the cockpit carrying another Colt M1911 and stashed the Armalite by his legs.

"Now," he instructed, "I want you to fly back to Dublin, following the canal. No heroics, I know what you're thinkin', that you're the pilot and in control. Well, let me tell you, I can fly well enough to get this thing down safely. So try to fock around and I'll shoot you in the head, kick you out 'und carry on. It won't be ideal, but I'll do it. Just don't be a hero, OK? Do we understand each other?"

"Loud and clear," Captain Bryan answered; he knew that he would have a better than fair chance of surviving this if he did what he was told, remembering all the details he could of the men involved and passed them on to the security forces afterwards.

"Good. Do not set or register a new flight with Air Traffic Control, just do exactly as I say."

They moved forward in silence, following the Royal Canal, and as they approached Dublin airspace the final horrifying part of the plan was told to Bryan.

"Right, we are going to land in Mountjoy prison and pull out two members of our organisation. We are going to land in the prison exercise yard and you will be guided down by one of the men we're to pick up, he'll have a red handkerchief. Do you understand?" he shouted into the microphone of the headset he was wearing.

"Understood," Bryan shouted back in confirmation. He altered course slightly, heading for the final destination.

Ten minutes later, the Allouette hovered over the exercise yard where down below a football match was being played between the prisoners. It had all been carefully orchestrated. There were eight guards in evidence and all watching the prisoners, alert for any trouble. One glanced up at the hovering helicopter, unaware that O'Hearn, another prisoner, was signalling with a red rag, giving semaphore instructions for the pilot to land. The guard watching the approaching helicopter assumed that it was the Minister for Defence who was due a visit. Just as the aircraft was touching down on its skids, three fights broke out amongst the watching prisoners. The eight guards launched in to break up the fights and were at once set upon by the prisoners with cries of "stick the boot in".

Immediately Tir Brennan and O'Hearn ran for the helicopter. The masked gunman had stepped out of the cockpit, encouraging them, waving the Armalite, ready in case any of the jailers tried to put up any resistance. As the general alarm sounded over the klaxons, the waiting gunman standing on the concrete of the exercise yard, began spraying the air with bullets, and quickly jumped back into the Alouette helicopter as soon as the other two men were securely inside.

"Go, go!" he ordered the pilot, who opened the throttles and the engine strained in response, pulling the aircraft up out of the exercise yard to a chatter of rotors.

O'Hearn, ecstatic to be free, thumped the masked man's shoulder: "We did it, we did it!" he cried. "Well done, mate, fockin' well done!" The masked man turned, grinning at his erstwhile IRA member. Brennan was as dour as ever.

"We're not out of the fockin' woods yet, we have to get away."

O'Hearn rolled his eyes and shook his head. "Come on, just to be out of there for a while, it does you good. You haven't been in there for five years."

Brennan answered with a scowl: "Where to now?"

* * *

LONDON. 3 hours later

The Home Secretary's office was a buzz. The news of the escape had filtered through from Dublin. An Under Secretary marched into the Minister's office.

"Have you heard the news? Damned Brennan has been snatched from Mountjoy prison, in a helicopter of all things. In broad daylight, can you believe it?"

The Home Office Minister looked up from his desk, peaking over the top of gold-framed half-moon spectacles. "Yes, I heard something to that effect. You really will have to learn to calm down, Jeremy, this won't do at all. Firstly, it is not our problem, it will all fall on Eire. Rather clever really, onus on them not us. Secondly, it may not turn out to be such a bad thing. Why do you think we conceded on protocol and allowed that scum to be kept there, now how did the Judge put it? Ah yes, 'to permit compassion on the members of the family, with consideration for the longevity of the sentence', did you really think we were doing this out of benevolence?"

Across London another conversation was taking place on the same subject via a telephone call from Whitehall.

"So," Webster confirmed, "they tried a second time and succeeded." The Irish security officer agreed. "I hope that the pilot was alright?"

"Yes, they flew to a disused racecourse in Baldoyle outside Dublin. Tied him up and left him there. He is slightly shaken but generally in good shape. And from there, well, we assume that taxis or stolen cars took the men away. Probably members of the IRA's Dublin Brigade. So we will track them down if we can and try to get them back."

"Understood. Would you keep me informed as well as MI5? It is a sort of cross over point here and we all need to understand everything as soon as it happens."

"Of course. I'll let you know as soon as I hear anything. My guess is that they'll be across the border now and away to a 'safe house'. Although Brennan will be a hot potato, he'll be difficult to hide." Webster agreed and the call ended. The next call was to Simon Johnston at MI6.

"Webster here. You've heard?" he asked cryptically.

"Mmm, interesting turn of events and pretty much what we expected. The helicopter was a ballsey shout though. I bet some poor sod is getting his ear chewed off in Mountjoy about this at the moment."

"Yes," Webster agreed. "The Gardia think he will be over across the border. I think it is more likely he will be over across the pond before long."

"Which," Johnston said "is exactly where we want him. They will all come crawling out of woodwork now. It will be very interesting to see what we find and hopefully that will include a high-up drugs connection, not just low level suppliers. The Gardia have no clue we helped set all this up, I hope?"

"No, not a sniff of suspicion. So now we just sit back and wait to see what Mr Brett turns up in the States. Are we going to tell him Brennan is loose and possibly free in the US?"

"No, let's not alarm him unnecessarily and in any event, it may not happen. I want him over there first and he has Adams with him as he requested. All will be fine," he prophesised.

At that precise moment, Brennan was being stowed onto a fishing trawler for his second trip across the Irish Sea in a few months. This time, there was no informant and the trawler was off to fish in earnest. A friendly boat from the UK mainland would be meeting with it just outside the 12 mile limit, Brennan would be transferred and then off to Liverpool docks.

CHAPTER 12

Christmas Day had been and gone, the last time Rupert and Claire would have a child-free Christmas, they hoped. They had spent the day at Claire's parent's home in the Gloucestershire village of Edgeworth. It had been freezing and a true feeling of Christmas prevailed with a harsh Hoare frost, gilding all the trees in silver. They both reflected how it would contrast with the temperatures they would soon encounter in Florida. Claire's parents had been less than happy with her proposed trip. But, she assured them that she was passed the tricky three month period and all was well.

They now found themselves at Heathrow airport, on a flight bound for Miami International airport in Florida. The early morning flight was nine and a half hours, but they were travelling business class which in Claire's eyes made it bearable. They were waiting in the departure lounge; Rupert had gone for coffee and had left Claire alone to mind the bags. Looking up from a magazine she spotted a familiar figure walking towards her, smiling as he approached. She saw the same upright bearing and lithe ease of movement, with rangy muscles rolling beneath the leather jacket and button down shirt.

"Chris!" she cried, jumping up into his arms as he got near. He enveloped her in a bear hug and picked her up, the aftershave he wore suddenly familiar to her, reviving memories of Argentina.

"Darling Claire, you look more beautiful than ever, pregnancy suits you," he charmed in his Welsh lilt. "So you've decided to run away with me and leave that dreadful Rupert bloke?"

She broke free, giggling at him like a gauche school girl on her first date. "You don't change, so smooth," she chided. At this point Rupert returned with two coffees.

"When you've quite finished chatting up my wife, I suppose you want coffee too?"

"Black, two sugars," he retorted and Rupert padded off again, sighing, shaking his head, muttering: "I thought the boss had coffee brought for him..."

They both sat down. Claire gave Chris an intense scrutiny, noticing the deep tan lines around his eyes, which crinkled as he smiled. "How have you been? As you probably know, Sophie and I manage to catch up from time to time when she returns to the UK says she hasn't seen you in a while: abroad?" she asked quietly, knowing that she would receive an edited version.

"Oh, you know how it is Claire, here and there. But yes, very well, very fit and as good as I have ever been. But Sophie makes me think from time to time about what it is all about. But I love what I do, and so does she. It doesn't make it easy. But we meet up whenever we can. Either me to London or her to Hereford. We don't ask too many questions of the other, but it is the best we can do and it will continue until something breaks, or changes..." he let the words hang in the air. "I think about it all the time and I know that in a few years I will be forced out of the Regiment by virtue of age. Then what do I do, go back to the regular army? No thank you. Maybe I'll re-train as a surveyor?" he joked.

Claire scoffed at the thought. "Yea right! You'd be bored

within a few months." It was at this moment that Rupert returned with the coffee and the conversation ended.

The call for their flight was announced shortly thereafter and all three boarded the plane. Nine and a half hours later they arrived in a warm Miami International airport but they had yet to face the stern interrogation of the US customs officials. It was a universally acknowledged truth that getting into the country was strictly policed and monitored at the airports, whereas getting out was, by comparison, merely a nod and a tick; they didn't care what you took out, just what you brought in. The lines formed, they were scanned, questioned and baggage scrutinised. Once finally through, they left the air-conditioned airport terminal to a blast of warm air rushing through the automatic doors and headed for the Hertz rental office.

"Oh feel that," Claire exclaimed. "Warmth, it's only early morning and it must be at least 20 odd degrees. After wintry London, this is bliss."

"Yea, probably a bit less, but feels so warm after the chills of winter back home," Rupert agreed. They reached the car hire office and were shown to a massive Ford F-250 7.3 litre monster pickup truck, which Rupert had reserved via the admin department at HBJ in London.

"Wow, what a beast. Rupert, did you order this?" Chris asked, clearly impressed.

"I certainly did, when in Rome...! I was reading about them, they are amazing and will go anywhere. And as some wise soul once said: *get something heavy*. Also, we might be going off-roading, who knows where these properties or ranches will be. This is perfect."

Chris nodded, smiling, thinking of the sage advice which had saved their lives in Argentina.

The enclosed rear flat-bed was secure, with a hard top canopy, so they dumped all the luggage in there and returned to the four-door cab, which was encased in sparkly chrome and shiny paintwork.

"It's like getting up into a lorry," Claire declared, opening one of the front doors and stepping up into the raised cab. "You're right though, Rups, all leather everywhere and it smells of 'new car'. Look at all these knobs and gadgets?" Chris got into the back and made himself comfortable in the large rear seats.

"Starship Enterprise. Beam me up, Scotty," Rupert joked as he started the engine, which fired into life with a mighty roar of the turbo charger. "Oh listen to that?" he enthused, revving the engine gleefully.

"Boys and their toys." Claire rolled her eyes in dismay.

* * *

NEW YORK

The leviathan TransFijord cruise ship was being pulled into the New York harbour, having entered the mouth of the River Hudson, and was being 'tugged' to the Manhattan terminal. It had completed the cross-Atlantic journey from Manchester in perfect time, despite rough seas and bad weather. Most passengers had stayed well and happy due to the massive stabilisers counteracting the rolling waves. But below decks, deep in the bowls of the ship, it was much more uncomfortable, and unable to come up for air, Tir Brennan had suffered.

"I shall be glad to get off this fockin' boat," he snarled, hating being cooped up in the tiny area behind the engine room, where he had spent most of the journey.

The crew, many of whom were Irish and therefore sympathetic to 'the cause', had helped smuggle him aboard and had fed and looked after him during the voyage. But they were all getting fed up with the moaning. The Chief Engineer, was not a man to be trifled with and had risked a lot keeping Brennan's presence secret.

"Oh stop you're moanin', you could be stuck in a prison cell for the rest of your days. But you're here, free, or will be once we get you on land," he quipped, not at all afraid of Brennan's terrible reputation. On board, down here, he was king, not some killer for hire, which is how he viewed the enforcer. Brennan turned quickly, grabbing the front of the engineer's overalls, bunching his fist, gripping the cloth, raising a fist to smash him. The chief was unperturbed, a winner of many a waterfront brawl.

"Yea, go on then, try and see what happens," he snapped. "I'll rip your fockin' head off. No guns here, mate, just try it, and see how far you get without my help and the boys on board, eh? I've got no family back home or here. Nothing to frighten me with Brennan, so go on, take your best shot," he goaded, raising his hands, tensing the muscles in his bull neck, arms apart ready for the blow to arrive.

The light in Brennan's eyes dimmed, realising that the stocky chief was right, but he hated backing down. He sneered in response, letting him go. "We'll meet at another time, then we'll see," he spat.

"Yea? Well let me know and I'll be there. No pop guns, just you and me, tooth and nail," the chief responded, standing square and looking indomitable. Brennan snorted and turned away.

Two hours later the massive ocean liner was docked and the passengers were all leaving the ship. The dockside a flurry of activity, stevedores milling, passengers saying goodbyes, promising to keep in touch with new found friends, whom both knew they never would; it was organised chaos. The strict routine for loading up new supplies and work parties came and went.

One of the other crew members motioned Brennan up to the

next deck, and gave him a wooden case to carry. The pair moved up the decks, on to the service area and down a gang plank. He recalled the words of the chief two days earlier, briefing him on what to expect.

'*Do not appear to rush, return on to the ship many times*' and this was secretly reinforced by his 'shipmate'. '*Too many stowaways try to get away straight off,* he *had been told. They always stand out and get caught. Better to go back and forth, look casual and get noticed by port officials, become part of the scenery.*' This he did, carrying crates, chatting amiably in loud voices with others, who were part of the shore crew and after three trips to and from the ship, he slipped into the warehouse where the stores were being kept. The customs officials and other longshoremen noticed nothing untoward and later, as a van backed up, dropping off more supplies, he slipped in the back as planned. The doors were closed by the driver and he moved off, proceeding slowly so as not to attract attention. Tir Brennan was safely in the United States.

* * *

FLORIDA

Rupert drove the Ford out of Miami airport onto the main freeway Route I95, heading north in the warm sunshine, with the air-conditioning on. The freeway traffic was moving steadily and the large, comfortable truck seemed very at ease, smoothing along at 70 mph in the express lane. The scenery changed as they left the Miami area: from ugly industrial areas, to open freeway and semi tropical landscapes. They passed suburbia flanked by palm trees and then hit the open grasslands. The ubiquitous Atlantic Ocean lapped the shore just below, only yards from the highway, down a gentle slope of grass and shingle. When they stopped for a break, the tang of the sea floated perceptibly on the air. They passed the mass of Fort Lauderdale, the next stop was Wellington.

The journey lasted for an hour and a half and they finally saw signs for Palm Beach and Wellington. They then followed the signs and arrived at West Palm Beach.

"Amazing," Claire exclaimed. "Like Venice with attitude. It's huge; I imagined a discreet area, more like Midhurst than a major town." Arrayed before her were waterways, lagoons and low rise towers of apartments and, of course, the ocean, framing golden sands. There was, they all felt, an overwhelming feeling of wealth.

"It's like a scene from *Hotel California*," Rupert declared.

"Now you're showing your age," Claire retorted.

They moved on to Wellington and a different feel pervaded, one of class and opulence- old money. Less razzmatazz and more discreet buildings; elegant driveways and quiet roads. They were booked into the Hampton Inn, a Hilton hotel in keeping with their status as top flight surveyors. It was an elegant, but modern affair, located in the centre, just off Forest Hill Boulevard and close to the polo grounds. The grounds of the hotel were all beautifully manicured, with small gazebos dotted around, accessed by block paths and fringed by palm trees. A gentle breeze blowing in from the ocean moving the fringed leaves. Lush, green lawns opened onto terraces and the central swimming pool: an oasis in the heat.

"No, no," Claire declared, getting out of the Ford and stretching like a sinuous panther. "Take me home to freezing England, rain and fog. This is all no good at all." The other two men laughed in response.

"It is all a bit smooth, isn't it? Ah well, I dare say we will get used to it," Rupert sighed dramatically.

The hotel reception was a mirror of the punctilious grounds outside and having signed in, they were treated to a chorus of 'have a nice day'. Up in their rooms the views were spectacular as Claire opened the bay windows onto a balcony.

"Yep, I could definitely get used to this," she sighed. They showered, changed and then Chris arrived to go over the plans before they slept, although all three were determined to fight the jet lag by staying awake as long as possible.

"Right, so who do we meet first?" Chris asked when he had settled down with a cold coke in hand.

"The local contact for HBJ is a chap called Philip Rosti from Ocean Realty; and the man down from the New York office is Matthew Wood. I have spoken briefly to Wood and he seems like a good guy, very New York, if you know what I mean. All hale and hearty and about as sincere as an albino sunbather." Rupert smirked. "That is tomorrow. Then I have a number to call, so we can get in contact with the DEA agent assigned to lead this case from here." He looked at his list of notes; "a chap called…Seth Meacham. We will set up a meeting for the day after tomorrow. We should all be reasonably acclimatised by then."

Chris took a deeper interest. "With the DEA involved, we will certainly have a good team on side if anything goes wrong. I did some cross training with those guys before, when we did a joint operation. They are some of the best trained Feds in the US. The hand gun course they have to pass is bloody hard, they use nearly as much ammo as we do in training. I'll be interested to meet this agent."

Rupert acknowledged this with a nod. "Right, I'll get on the phone give him a call, then a quick dip in the pool sounds in order."

Chris, who was dressed in shorts and trainers, nodded. "Good. I'll join you later, I'm off for a run first, get the kinks out of my body from the flight."

Claire raised her eyebrows: "Really? In this humidity?"

"Ah, it's nothing to where I have just come from," he commented cryptically "I'll be fine, a few miles, then a dip in the pool. Perfect end to a perfect day."

Rupert shook his head, feeling guilty that he too should be running as they had in done in Argentina. "I'll join you tomorrow. I'll stick with a few lengths of the pool today."

Chris nodded in agreement and left the apartment.

"The man's a machine," Claire commented after he'd left.

"I know, it makes me feel tired just watching him. But, that's his job and, as he has said on many occasions, no point trying to vault a six foot wall with a five foot pole!"

* * *

NEW YORK

New York had long been acknowledged as the home land for IRA sympathies in the US. Its network of safe houses and underground links provided safe passage around the city for anyone visiting or on the run, it was stronger than anywhere else in the USA. Sean's bar in Lower Manhattan was one of those places. It was the start of the conduit that would secure Tir Brennan a base, from which he could operate in the States undercover. Having parked the van, the driver Mike, led him into the bar and ordered a couple of beers, awaiting the arrival of their contact. It was a relaxed atmosphere. The green, white and orange colours of the Irish flag prevalent all over the bar, with images of Shamrocks and draught Guinness on tap. If Brennan had shut his eyes, he could have imagined that he was back home, just listening to the voices and humour pervading the bar.

Just then the door to the bar opened, letting in a gust of cold air and a thick set man, wearing a coarse worsted jacket, plaid shirt, jeans and boots. As he crossed the bar he nodded 'hellos and smiles' to many of the customers, sharing banter on the way. Approaching the bar, he ordered a pint of Guinness and turned to face Mike and Brennan.

"Mike." He nodded at Brennan's driver. "So how do you like our fair country?" he asked his accent an impure mix of New York and Irish. He held out his hand to Brennan. "Con," he introduced himself, "it's good to meet you."

Brennan shook his hand, but did not offer his name in return, however his sour features creased into a smile. "Good, I like the smell of freedom. Better than a stuffy boat," he finished quietly.

"Aye, that it is. Let's go over there where we can talk quietly." Connor motioned to one of the wooden booths surrounding the outside of the bar. The three men sat down, supped their pints and the rules were explained carefully to Tir Brennan who listened with interest. Connor continued, "It's easier now with the Clinton administration in power, much more sympathy than with poor old Joe Doherty back in '88," he commented, alluding to the infamous case of the IRA killer who broke out of a maximum security prison in Northern Ireland, fled to the US and was then arrested and sought asylum.

"Now, we get a lot more authorities turnin' a blind eye, if you know what I mean." He winked at Brennan. "So, here's what we'll do. In a few minutes, we'll finish our drinks and head out through the side door behind me. A car will be waiting. That will take us to the first safe house. You'll be moved around for a number of days, just to be safe. Now don't take this the wrong way, but each time you will be blindfolded, so you won't know where we are." Brennan made to object, his hard features setting in a sneer. But Connor held up his hand, the nice easy going

'Irish charm' disappearing behind a mask of granite. His eyes bored into Brennan.

"I know what you're going to say and stow it. We take a big risk with our operation. We keep it sealed. No one person knows everything and that way, if anyone gets caught we all stay safe and locked down. But if you don't want in, you're free to walk out of here now, I'll give you a few hundred dollars and you can be on your way. Your choice." The pint glass in his hand held mid-way between mouth and table. Brennan had seen the move before and knew it was a weapon waiting to be utilised if necessary: beer thrown first to blind and a glass to the face. Once again Brennan was forced to capitulate and he wasn't happy.

"OK, I agree," he shrugged, "just hate being blindfolded."

Connor, visibly relaxed and the glass returned to the table. "I know and I sympathise, but it is how we do things. Safe for you, safe for us."

The three men finished their beers and made to leave. The driver Mike stood up first, shaking hands.

"Good to see you, Con, no doubt we'll be in touch. Tir, good to meet you and luck to you." He turned with a wave of his hand and disappeared out of the bar into the cold night air.

CHAPTER 13

FLORIDA

The next morning, the three of them awoke early their bio-clocks still attuned to English time. This time, Rupert joined Chris for an early morning run, and he left Claire dozing in bed. After a steady run along the beach, Rupert returned to find Claire up and dressed for the pool in a tiny, black bikini, striking against her pale skin.

"Wow," he exclaimed. "That doesn't leave much to the imagination," he commented, admiring the tiny triangles struggling to contain her breasts and the thong bottoms, which were high cut against her curved hips. Her tall, willowy figure, honed by riding and aerobics classes, showing them off to perfection. She was still showing little signs of her pregnancy, only her already ample breasts had started to swell a little. Claire cut a pose, hands on her hips, jutting her left hip outwards towards Rupert in a sensuous manner.

"It is one of those that Franky sends me from Argentina. Anyway, give me a break, I won't have a figure to show off with for much longer," she decried, smoothing her hand across her slightly convex stomach.

"Always for me," Rupert reassured. And went over to kiss her, hoping to take it further. She started to return the kiss and then his sweat soaked torso pressed against her.

"Yuk, get a shower and then maybe," she chided placing a hand on his chest. He laughed pulling away slightly and grasping her hand, drawing her gently with him. She giggled pretending reluctance at first and then followed him into the bathroom. Like so many American showers, it was huge and easily big enough for two people. With the water running hot, Claire discarded the bikini and joined Rupert. As he stood facing the water she gently soaped his back, rubbing away the sweat of his run and massaged his hair with a fragrant shampoo, whilst he sighed with pleasure.

"My turn," he stated, turning Claire around, running a lather of cream all over her body, gently soaping her breasts and rubbing her extended nipples. She moaned with pleasure, letting her head fall back onto his shoulder. His hands moved downwards, tracing small circles with his fingertips, finding the soft creases of skin just below her hips. He slid a hand down to the creases below. She mewed with pleasure as he explored further, rubbing gently, building her climax.

Claire could finally stand it no longer; she turned, kissing him hard on the lips, their tongues twining. He reached behind her and lifted her up, at which she locked her legs around his waist as he entered her, leaning back against the shower wall, water cascading over them. They rocked gently together, seeking a mutual rhythm in the unusual position. They found it, riding a wave of pleasure, they tensed, hitting a perfect climax, in silent screams, gasping for breath amidst the droplets of water.

"Oh my God, I can't move," Rupert declared a minute later. "That was amazing, I am going to get a massive shower installed at home." They both laughed and Claire gently slid first one, then the other leg to the floor. They towelled each other off and Claire shooed him out, saying he would be late for his meeting.

A half hour later, Rupert appeared downstairs with Chris, ready to meet the two American realtors. They were easy to spot, both formal amidst a sea of shorts and polo shirts. Rupert decided that Philip Rosti was the young blond, who looked very Californian; button down shirt, conservative tie, blazer and chinos. Matthew Wood was pure New York: thousand dollar silk blue suit, polka dot tie and shiny Oxfords. Pure preppy America at its best. Chris and Rupert strode up to them as they rose from their early morning cappuccino's. The assumptions were correct. Rosti came forward, all gung ho.

"Philip Rosti, Ocean Realty, pleased to meet you." A firm hand shake and all American smile. Then Wood introduced himself.

"Matt Wood. Morning, good to meet you. Welcome to America." The nasal twang of New York over-laid on Ivy League vowels. The obviously gym-honed figure moving well in the expensive suit and not a gelled hair out of place. Another firm handshake and a perfect smile. They followed the two men and Rupert noticed with an inward smile, that like all Americans, Wood's suit trousers were not quite long enough to English eyes, showing socks and not breaking on the shoe. Even in films they were never cut correctly and it gave Rupert an immediate and rather ridiculous feeling of superiority. Moving into the dining room, coffee and croissant ordered, the four men got to know each other over breakfast. Wood continued, explaining in terms very reminiscent of the words Hugh Congreave had used back in the UK, of the current position in the market cycle.

"We basically have a Bull market, building up steam and no end in sight," he puffed. "The deregulation is due to the new Inter State Banking and Efficiency Act and it is now wide open, so we intend to clear up ahead of our competitors. Now, I hear that you have some investors that might want a piece of the action, Rupert?"

Rupert nodded and expanded on Featherstone's requirements, dropping a few more names into the conversation as he went.

"Sounds great," Rosti exclaimed. "Well, we can certainly help you here. Show you around, see some property, great real estate and top market product. Your clients in Britain will love it, guaranteed," he finished enthusiastically. The conversation drifted in this direction with Chris, as Rupert's 'wing man', giving the Top Gun reference that everyone seemed to like, and offering input as necessary.

With the conversation nearly at an end, Rupert asked: "Tell me, Philip, do you ever get to the polo tournaments here? I only ask because my wife is with me and she adores it. Also, I have an ulterior motive in that a client is thinking of sponsoring a team in next year's High Goal in England. I thought I would put out some feelers now to see if there is some interest from the Argy's playing here."

"Sure thing. You've come to the right place. I know a lot of the Patrons, they sponsor the games and have teams playing; big clients of mine. One in particular is looking to become really involved in this Sub-Prime market. A guy called William Lester the Third. I'll introduce you, great guy, you'll love him. I'll be pleased to introduce you around, it's a very friendly crowd. I'm sure that the Argy's would jump at the chance; they don't, as a rule, get paid that much and the chance of a firm tournament commitment in the UK would get them running after you, I'm sure. Let me know when you'd like to go over – it's only ten minutes away - and we will hook up," he offered enthusiastically.

"Perfect. How about the day after tomorrow? I want to get chatting before the tournament actually starts and they start concentrating on the game."

Arrangements were made, Rosti agreed to come across and they would follow him to the grounds. Matt Wood agreed to pick them up the following day and introduce them to some major investors based in the area before he flew back to New York, his corporate duty done.

* * *

Bogota, COLOMBIA

Rojas sat in front of his boss and was feeling pleased with himself. All was going to plan and he had two lots of good news for Ballesteros.

"*Jefe*, we had confirmation a few minutes ago that all shipments are now in America. All the tunnel led transportation went well; and the shipments to Miami from the power boats got through with 90 percent success. We lost two loads to DEA but we always lose some." Ballesteros agreed with a shrug, it was, he knew, an acceptable percentage. Any higher and he would be suspicious that they had an informer in their midst.

"Good. And what else?" he asked, sensing that more was to come.

"We hear that Brennan is in New York. He made it out of Ireland, came across on a liner."

Ballesteros lost all feigned complacency. "Where is he now?" he demanded.

"We don't know exactly, they keep moving him around, from safe house to safe house. We know a few places, but not all. He will show up somewhere, then we will have him. Rest assured."

"Good. Now when are the drugs due to be moved across to the plant?"

"From Miami in the next few days. From San Diego next week. All will arrive at the plant in time for packaging and transportation by the beginning of February. UK, then Europe afterwards. Such a great system," Rojas added, pleased with himself.

* * *

LONDON

"Johnston?" he answered to the ring of the telephone on his desk. He listened to the voice at the other end. "Good, thank you for keeping me informed. Good bye." He dialled another number and DCI Webster answered.

"Johnston here, I've just had an agent call me from the States. It appears that matey boy has managed to get to New York safely."

"Really. Any clues as to where he is, or more importantly, where he may be heading?"

"No, all we know is New York. But we have an inside track, if he moves we'll find him. I take it you've heard that the three of them all landed safely in Florida and are to meet with the DEA tomorrow?"

"Indeed. Do we mention anything to Adams or indeed Brett, if at all?"

"No, I can't see how it will concern them. Even if Brennan does head down there. He is more likely to lock horns with the Colombians or whoever they are using. No, can't see that being a problem, let sleeping dogs lie."

"What about your other man there? Any news from him?"

"Nothing, all quiet, he is in place but no news. I'll keep you informed if I hear anything." The two men rang off.

* * *

FLORIDA

Following the meeting with Matt Woods and Philip Rosti, arrangements were made for visits to various properties and senior principles.

"The feeling I am getting," Chris commented, "cutting through all the bullshit and smiles is: have we got anything they want and can we deliver? If not, company loyalty or not, that shark from New York wouldn't give a rat's arse."

"My sentiments exactly. The local guy is OK and I am sure he will be helpful, showing us around and introducing us; as long as he feels there is something in it for him. So we have a few days of meetings, getting to know all the bigwigs and see what we can find out. Would be good if we could arrange to meet those with a mutual interest at the polo club and cement the two causes together."

"Good idea," Chris agreed "It would also give us a little more credibility: money, money and contacts," he repined cynically. Rupert laughed.

"See, you're back into the cynical, nasty, surveying mode before you know it," he said, clapping Chris on the shoulder as the two made for the pool to meet up with Claire.

A morning of relaxing by the pool ensued and after lunch, the three headed for the polo grounds. Like so many of these large private club affairs in America, it was very smooth and the grass, would not, they all felt, have dared to be out of place for a moment. Yet for all that, it had a rather 'folksey feel' due to the chalk tracks that dissected the grounds, offering access to the pitches, club house and other sporting facilities. They found the entrance to the club with a prominent brick wall, rendered in white stucco bearing the legend 'Palm Beach Polo & Country Club'. They drove along the chalk road into the grounds, following the signs for the polo club.

"Wow, amazing clubhouse," Rupert commented as they approached the centre of the grounds. Before them lay three main stands with white pillars and what looked like three ancient Roman villas on the top, protecting the 'Patrician' viewers from the sun as they watched the gladiators performing in the area below them.

"It is quite a special place," Claire agreed. "Everything is manicured to within an inch of its life. Different to the UK; I mean we have smart clubs like Guards and Cowdray," she continued, naming the two most prestigious clubs in the UK, "but nothing like this. Just look at that Club house, compare that to the 'mud hut' at Cowdray."

"Apparently it was built by one of the wealthy Patrons, Bill Ylvisaker, so Phillip Rosti was telling us. Still around apparently and a big fish in the local scene. The main bar and restaurant are supposed to be something special. Then there is the Player's bar as well as the nightclub upstairs, where all kinds of bad behaviour takes place. I think Mr Rosti is a bit of a bad lad!" Rupert finished wryly. The other two nodded their heads, smiling.

They pulled up in the car park near the stands, got out and took in the surroundings, looking out over the expanse of the two 13 acre grounds; immaculately, laser-levelled seas of emerald green. The goal post flags at each end of the pitches gently flapped listlessly in the faint breeze to a back drop of palm trees, lakes and small lagoons. It was a beautiful setting.

"Mmm, I could get used to this," Claire sighed.

"The thing I like about assignments with you, Rupert, is that I know I am never going to be slumming it!" Chris opined.

"Yes, it's a hard life but someone's got to do it." The three headed off towards the direction of the main bar called the *7th Chukker*. Upon entering, they were hit by the refreshingly cool temperature. The bar was an oasis of gleaming wood, tiled floors, old leather armchairs, bar stools, a marble topped bar and taupe walls. The 'Library' to the rear had soft down lights, illuminating the many shelves of books. It was a homage to wealth and class, and the feeling of a preppy gentleman's club prevailed. Antique ceiling fans were suspended from above and twirled gently. Moving towards the bar, Rupert ordered drinks.

"What is that?" Chris asked, eyeing the cocktail suspiciously when Rupert returned to the table, carefully carrying three glasses containing an amber liquid and green vegetation.

"A mint julep. Apparently this is the place to have them. When in Rome... Cheers," he said raising the chunky glass upwards in the eternal salute.

"Oh that is good," Claire said, smacking her lips appreciatively. "But only one."

Even Chris was impressed. "I could get used to those," he commented, nodding at his glass; then he looked around, eyeing up the other occupiers of the bar, assessing, looking for clues as to manners or attitude in accordance with his training. He could tell instinctively if someone was going to be trouble and was expert at spotting concealed weapons. Nothing stood out and all of the occupants appeared to be American, not Argentinian. "You know, it all looks very normal and civilised here," he continued sotto voce. "Do you really think we are on a wild goose chase? It could be any number of reasons and coincidences that tie up with the polo world and proposed smuggling. I mean, look around you, I could see the odd user being here and some wild parties, but smuggling?" he finished, grimacing.

Rupert continued in the same hushed tones, below the general hubbub of conversation.

"I know what you mean. But the powers that be seem to think so, and if we find nothing, we all have a good jaunt on HM Gov and go home." He shrugged. "We'll see who and what we meet when Rosti introduces us around and then I can start to talk to the players and maybe the grooms; inveigle my way in, see if there is anything suspicious and report it. Anyway, we are meeting the DEA agent tomorrow, let's see what he has to say first."

CHAPTER 13

The following morning, Rupert and Chris were due to meet with Seth Meacham of the DEA. The trip was a return journey down the I95 to the DEA's field office in Fort Lauderdale. The office building was located in an innocuous office park, close to the airport in the main town. The brick buildings were shaded by the ubiquitous palms and they parked outside, under the shadow of the mature trees. The plaque outside one of the buildings showed Drug Enforcement Agency in bold letters. They pressed a buzzer; smiled for the video camera, declared their identity and were allowed in.

The reception was on the first floor with no seeming way of getting into the ground floor offices from the tiny entrance. At the top of the stairs they were again buzzed through glass doors that were obviously armoured, by a vigilant looking receptionist. Her face was almost devoid of makeup, hair pulled back in a severe style and she was conservatively dressed in a dark two piece suit with a 'no nonsense' manner about her.

"Good morning. Rupert Brett and Chris Adams. We are here to see special agent Meacham," Rupert offered smiling at her.

"Good morning," came the stern reply, impassive features and no response to the smile. "Can I see some identification please?"

Rupert and Chris handed over their driving licences. The receptionist took the documents, scrutinised them carefully, handed the licences back and asked them to take a seat, her manner slightly more relaxed than earlier. She picked up the internal telephone, held a brief conversation, replaced the receiver and called over: "Special Agent Meacham will be right with you."

Rupert nodded a 'thank you' whilst he and Chris exchanged a knowing glance that spoke volumes.

Five minutes later an electronic click of an internal door heralded the entrance of Seth Meacham. The two men saw a beefy individual, of around forty years old, 6'2", square shoulders, deep chest and a lined face, framed by swept back hair, longer than the buzz cut they had been expecting. He would probably have played Quarterback for his university, Rupert reflected. There was still an athleticism to his movements, but he noticed a slight almost imperceptible limp, to his right hip: *maybe an old football injury or gunshot wound* Rupert thought.

He walked over and introduced himself: "Special Agent Seth Meacham. Good to meet you both." Rupert and Chris shook hands and found an acute strength in the large ham-like fist offered to them. *Definitely Quarterback*, Rupert thought, as he winced inwardly from having his hand crushed. Chris, whose own strength was exceptional, if not as obvious as Meacham's, held on a little longer than was necessary, not to be intimidated. The two men gauged each other with a brief mental and physical assessment and let go of the grip with evident mutual respect.

"Come through to my office." He gestured towards the door and proceeded to operate an electronic key pad with an appropriate code to which the lock clicked open, whilst he pulled the door, motioning the other two men through. Stepping through, Rupert was immediately reminded of the film *Point Break,* where a young Keanu Reeves steps into the frenetic FBI field offices. Glass cubicles fed off glass walled corridors and open plan spaces abounded, alive with computer screens and hushed telephone conversations. Serious individuals in suits looked around at their entrance and returned diligently to their tasks after a quick assessment.

"Welcome to the Miami Division field office," he said sweeping the offices with a wave of his arm. "From here we co-ordinate the operations for this area. The States is divided into 21 domestic field divisions, covering the whole of the country. From here we go down to the Florida keys and up to the border with the Atlanta Division and across to New Orleans."

He led them through to his office; another glass cubicle at the end of the corridor overlooking the car park. It was spacious, functional and fairly sterile, bearing hardly any personal effects or pictures. On the wall they noticed a badge of commendation and a few plaques.

After offering them a drink, and with coffee ordered, he continued. "What we do, by and large, is prevent the influx of drugs into this area of the States. Now because of our close proximity to the Caribbean and Mexico, we're pretty busy. We stop a lot of the drugs, but it's a long coastline and pretty porous. They bring it in on light planes, power boats speeding under the radar. We're well funded but we can't get 'em all," he finished.

"Real Miami Vice stuff," Rupert enthused.

Meacham snorted nodding and rolling his eyes. "Yea, but we don't get the same clothes budget, Ferraris or the beautiful women," he joked giving a nod to the main tenets of the TV series. "I run the Special Operations Division which supplies information to the sharp end for drug busts etc. What we do here is work the intelligence, crunch the data, watch the players and use this to make the arrests. We have teams of agents who actually go out and arrest the smugglers and main dealers, this in conjunction with local law enforcement officers and others. The focus has been on marijuana, but over the last two years, particularly down here, we have found more and more cocaine and therefore the emphasis has changed in this direction. Now, I have been briefed by my Administrator that you and the FBI have a theory about how the drugs are then being sent on to the UK and Europe?"

Here he left a question mark hanging in the air and both Rupert and Chris sensed that they may not be as welcome here as they had first thought. Rupert took up with a conciliatory tone, as he had no wish to antagonise the DEA agent who may be required for considerable assistance: "Well, to be fair, we are just as sceptical as you. Basically, we work together and as we are in Capital Markets and have a rudimentary knowledge of polo, they asked us to help if we could."

Rupert deliberately made no mention of Chris's skills or real profession. He didn't know why; it may, he felt, have helped or hindered the situation. Chris, as always, played along, taking the role of junior surveyor in the proceedings, a route that had worked so well for them in Argentina.

"What puzzles me more than anything," Meacham continued, frowning, "is why would they pick a couple of Limey realtors to come out here and do a spooks job? I mean why pick on you two? Did they just drop a pin into the realtors handbook and say: *'they'll do'* or what?" He finished raising his eyebrows to emphasise his puzzlement and he was clearly not happy.

Rupert glanced across at Chris who's face remained impassive and gave a tight smile. More than ever he was now determined not to give the full facts away, so proceeded to tell half the truth, more than a little irritated with Meacham's attitude, yet determined not to spoil everything. Keeping his tone even, he answered the obvious challenge to their credentials.

"Mmm, well first of all we are not just 'Limey Realtors', we are Chartered Surveyors, which takes a degree and five years to qualify. Not like over here, where, I understand you Yanks," he stressed the insulting slang, "take a couple of weeks and an exam a monkey could pass. Secondly, the reason we were chosen is that we are both members of the TA."

At which point Meacham was clearly puzzled and as Rupert had hoped, he bit: "TA?"

"Oh sorry, forgot," he continued, deliberately adopting a pompous tone, quoting George Bernard Shaw " *'two countries separated by a common language'* eh? Members of the, in your terms, Reserve Army, which means we have signed the Official Secrets Act and come under the auspice of the government. As to why us specifically, because in the past we have helped out, albeit inadvertently, the police, with a matter of money laundering and murder back in the UK, which took us to Italy and organised crime.

"Subsequently we have helped on one or two matters relating to criminal activity in the UK where we were able to assist the authorities with our inside knowledge. We are therefore known to the law enforcement teams, and given the nature of the suspicious activity here in the polo circuit, they felt we would be able to fit in rather nicely, as I and my wife have a knowledge of the game. It is, you may be aware, a notoriously difficult circle to enter and be part of. You cannot just waltz in and be accepted, it takes time and knowledge. We can, of course, combine this with a genuine interest in the Real Estate market, which I believe has no relevance to the potential drugs smuggling, but it gives us an excellent cover.

"Now, for the record, I happen to agree with you, I think we are on a hiding to nothing and will return in two weeks saying it is all a waste of time. But, like you, we have an obligation to the Crown and Government and do what we are bid. You never know, we might actually make some money out it."

Chris found Rupert hugely amusing, as he gave Meacham a metaphorical bloody nose and could not help but indulge himself in a wry grin. He was especially amused to be described as a member of the TA with Rupert's artistic licence, but inwardly agreed that his real persona should be kept secret.

Seth Meacham smiled at him, but the smile didn't quite reach the eyes.

"OK, I probably asked for that, but I just wanted to see what I was dealing with. Glad to have you on board. Now let me level with you. Yes, drugs get in, no doubt about it, we can't stop it all, as I say, and this is a big distribution area for the rest of the States, although a lot comes in under the Mexican border. But with the slack controls and lack of direct backing from central government, my colleagues down there are up against it at times. But that's politics.

"Yes, we also believe that a certain quantity is getting out of here to Europe, UK, wherever. The chemical analysis proves that, which has probably been explained to you?"

Rupert and Chris nodded in response.

"Right, now it goes out of the country but we can't find where or more importantly how it is being smuggled. Yes, we have kept an eye on the polo crowd. We don't usually have sniffer dogs on this side of the airport; it is usually Arrivals. But we have been extra vigilant to try and catch anyone out. *Nada.* If they are doing it, I don't know how. It would also take massive organisation to co-ordinate. The quantities being bandied around by our respective intelligence communities are huge, we are not just talking about a small stash of coke stuffed in a luggage compartment of a suitcase. We are talking hundreds of kilos. I mean, where do you think you will start that we haven't already looked into?" he finished rather defensively.

It was Chris's turn to question now, wanting to get a better picture in his head, and Rupert gave him the lead.

"The answer is; we don't know. Can I ask you a question?" Meacham nodded. "Well, speaking to some of the guys who have been in training in Belize and a few who went across to help in Colombia with your guys, they seemed to think," and at this point he held up a placatory hand, "and I'm only getting this second hand; that the distribution areas are known. As with any organised crime, the main players can be identified, but due to lack of evidence, not locked up. So where, in your opinion, is it being distributed from for domestic distribution, here for example? It's just occurred to me that it might be a good place to link up."

"It's a thought we have already followed," Meacham answered. "As I said, we specialize in wire taps, traces and other undercover stuff. But nothing has shown up or given an indication that this is going on here. So, however they are doing it, it is not mainstream but something special."

"I see, interesting. So really, that leaves us no further forward," Chris continued probing. "But if we find anything, you have the authority to investigate for us, is that how it works?"

"Sure," Meacham asserted, "if you get anything you want checked out, I am here to help. Now I know we are pulling together, that is great and if we can stop the trade, all well and good. Here's my card; if you need anything just shout." He passed across his card with a direct dial and mobile number on it. Rupert and Chris reciprocated with their own business cards and mobile numbers.

"You've got the hotel number, just in case the mobiles don't work here at any time?" Rupert asked.

"Sure, no problem and I will let you know if anything comes up. Now if you'll excuse me, I need to get on." He motioned to the door. Rupert and Chris said goodbye and left the building. They waited until they were outside before speaking.

Rupert's intelligent brain whirred away, uncomfortable at the result of the meeting with Seth Meacham. He wasn't happy that he'd been provoked by the belligerent agent. He wasn't happy that he'd responded in kind, pushing back hard; and he wasn't happy at the conclusion: whilst he hadn't made an enemy, neither he felt had they found a firm ally, despite what Meacham had said.

It had struck a discordant note and Rupert, in all his dealings in the brutal world of commercial property, had learned to trust his instincts. The real question was: did Meacham dislike them poaching on his turf or had he been put up to it? Out loud he said: "Welcome to America! Blimey, I thought he was going to throw us out at one point and send us home with a slapped wrist. Either someone didn't brief him properly or he's got his knickers in a twist about something."

Chris snorted in agreement. "The guy did seem a bit of a prick, not like the other DEA agents I've met. But then he didn't, and indeed doesn't, know our background, which is good. Thank you, by the way, for not exposing my real ID. I don't know why, but I'm just glad you didn't."

"Yea, I don't know why I did that. Could have been easy, 'oh by the way my colleague is really an SAS man so piss off and don't get so snotty.' Instant respect and all that, but something held me back. I always like the opposition to underestimate me in all negotiations. Although, he is not really opposition, but easier to get one over on them if needs be, I suppose. It was the way I was taught; go in soft and then get harder if you wish, but difficult to reverse it, if you need to."

"Well you certainly slapped him down, in the nicest possible way. Loved the bit about a monkey getting a licence!"

"Yea that was funny, but it is a bit Mickey Mouse; any idiot can do it. They think we are just estate agents. Lucky for him, Claire wasn't here, he would really have gone off with a flea in his ear."

"Amen to that," Chris concluded. "So as always, we are, in reality, on our own."

"Nothing new there then. So we follow our previous plan, shake the tree and see what falls out."

"Worked in Argentina," Chris agreed with a nod.

CHAPTER 14

The drive back to Palm Beach was full of speculative conversation between Rupert and Chris. The plans for the rest of the day were a trip out with Matt Wood to meet with the local investors who were getting into the Sub-Prime market everyone was talking about.

Entering the hotel, they were met by Matt Wood looking as immaculate as ever in another blue silk suit, shot cuffs and, Rupert noticed, too short trousers. He repressed a snigger as he came forward.

"Matt, good to see you. Thanks for coming in and arranging this."

"No problem, that's what I'm here for, to oil the wheels and hopefully we'll see some business out of this. Chris, good to see you again. You're keeping your tan, I see. Where did you get that?"

"Oh a bit of winter sun in the Canaries, always go at this time of year," he responded suavely. Matt Wood nodded, not sure exactly where the Canaries was, but his curiosity was satisfied. They moved off to Matt's rental car, a large Chrysler LHS sedan, that he had parked in the shade. As the powerful V8 engine started up, they were treated to a blast of cool air from the climate control system fitted in all American cars.

"Nice car," Rupert commented, to make conversation as much as anything else.

"Oh, it's only a rental, but its comfy. I certainly wouldn't want to drive down from New York to the boony's" he derided, displaying the usual New Yorker's scathing attitude to the provincial areas of the States.

"Yea, I know what you mean, it's a big country." The conversation continued as they discussed markets, Fed rates and the Fannie Mae - the Federal National Mortgage Association - which amongst other factors was having such an influential affect upon this new Sub-Prime phenomenon. Chris, as always, had done his homework well and was able to contribute creditably to the conversation, giving credence to his cover. He had learned a lot from Rupert during their time together in Argentina and his natural intelligence had soaked up information like a sponge.

They had five individuals to see that day, all representing, in one form or another, major participants and clients of investors involved with property and loans. Each visit was pretty much a repetition of the last: strong characters, money men all out for what they could get for the corporate entity they represented. The last call was to someone who Matt Wood described as a major player.

"William Lester the Third has interests in all areas, but especially Real Estate. Plays in the big league; has a number of offices, including one in New York. We've done some deals for him up there and he has expressed interest in buying bundles of debt for the new Sub-Prime. I get the impression that he wants some off balance sheet, to put together a separate finance deal for another project."

Rupert decided he was going to have to bite his tongue and take someone seriously who called himself 'the third' as a suffix. Curious, he asked: "Where does he get his money from?"

"Old family money, so I understand, you'll see what I mean

when we get there as we are meeting at his family home. Although, he has expanded on the portfolio and assets some since he took over from the Old Man. I would have thought that he is stretched pretty thin at the moment," he commentated ruminatively. "What you would call asset rich, cash poor. Still, if he wants in to play the game, I am not complaining. It's all fees, right?"

Rupert nodded, understanding the situation only too well as so many of his clients had been the same in the early 90's recession. The Chrysler pulled up outside an impressive entrance, guarded by two huge wrought iron gates, set into brick pillars. Matt Wood pressed the buzzer through the open window of his car, confirmed his identity looking into the camera and in due course, the large electronic gates swept majestically open. The gateway opened out onto a wide, paved driveway fringed by palm trees and leading to the main house, some 300 yards in the distance. They drove slowly up the driveway which ended in a circular rotunda, surrounding a central, ornate fountain.

The house itself was magnificent. It looked rather like an ancient Roman villa, with a two storey central portico, flanked by wings, the gables pointing forwards in an H-shape, all under pitched, roman-tiled roofs. The whole house was extensive and further buildings lay behind the main residence, in what looked like a pool-house and stables, together with staff quarters, all in the same vernacular architecture. Chris made a silent whistle, well aware that this was one of the prime areas for Wellington real estate. "This must cost a pretty penny, not only to buy, but keep up."

Matt nodded in agreement: "As I said, asset rich. This would be into the tens of millions, he's got around 50 acres attached to the house and fantastic views to the rear across to the ocean." Leaving the car, they were assailed by scents of jasmine, horses and the sweet, salty tang of the sea arriving on a gentle breeze.

The front doors opened and a large figure appeared, dressed in white cotton trousers, linen shirt and Argentinian Capybara moccasins. Rupert estimated him to be about six foot three with a solid build and a reasonably trim waist. His hair was very dark, unnaturally so to Rupert's eyes and he reassessed his initial impression of age to well-preserved sixty, rather than late forties. A vain man and a powerful one, hanging on to youth, Rupert decided, the perma-tan and dyed hair helping to cement the illusion to the casual observer.

Power and authority clung to the man as he strolled forward, completely at ease and assured that the world would do his bidding. Rupert had seen the like many times in his career and he knew it was something that you were born to. It could not be successfully transplanted or learned, it had to be there from birth. A small cigar, almost like a cheroot, hung negligently from his left his hand as William Lester approached the three visitors. The voice, when he spoke, was a deep, cultured, rich baritone.

"Matt, good to see you, thank you for coming over; sorry we couldn't meet at the office but I had to be here this evening, family affair later." Although he apologised for the inconvenience, waving his hand back towards the house, the tone implied that he would not have expected the outcome to be any different.

"Not at all, really good to see you," Woods replied smoothly as the two men shook hands. "Now let me introduce you to Rupert Brett and Chris Adams. They're from England, out of our London office, as I mentioned on the phone. They have come to look around and see if we can't do some business across the pond. The Brits seem to want a little bit of the action we have going here."

"Mr Lester, how do you do? Rupert Brett."

"Chris Adams. How do you do?"

William Lester stepped forward shaking hands with both men assessing them on his terms, seeming to like what he saw.

"Good to see you both, please call me Bill. Now come on in and have a drink, the sun must be over the yard arm somewhere," he joked, ushering the men forward up to the main entrance.

The three men entered through the front doors into a large entrance area, full of light and space, galleried above at the first floor level with a balustrade surround, running the whole way around the huge room. Before them was a beautiful, sunken, open plan sitting area leading to a stone flagged terrace, with a fabulous vista beyond to the ocean, violet in the evening light. The walls were painted in a pale taupe, cleverly lit by concealed up-lighters and table lamps to create a feeling of warmth and space. Set around the room were sofas and comfortable armchairs; occasional tables and a baby grand piano, burdened with many photographs of family and special occasions. It was a beautiful room, Rupert observed, combining classical lines and decor, yet not losing a homely feel. William Lester strode around to a large fitted dresser upon which were set out an array of drinks in sparkling decanters.

"Now, what'll you have?"

Matt Wood went for a bourbon.

"Do you have a beer?"

"Sure. Chris?"

"And for me please, Bill," Chris confirmed. With that, Bill Lester opened a panelled door in the dresser to reveal a deep, concealed fridge, stocked with different beers.

"Now, I can offer you, Bud, Red Stripe or Quilmes?"

Both Chris and Rupert chorused "Quilmes" having developed a taste for it during their time in Buenos Aries and were glad to finally have the opportunity to try the beer again. Drinks served, the four men moved out to the terrace, watching the sun move down across the sky.

"It certainly is a beautiful house and setting you have here, Bill," Chris offered.

"Why thank you. It has been in my family for three generations and hopefully more to come. I like it, close to the ocean, somewhere for the horses and ...its home," he finished, smiling. "Now," he continued, getting straight to the point, "how can we do some business together?" The fast change of tack may have thrown lesser men, but Rupert was somehow expecting it and took it in his stride.

"Well, we rather like what we see happening over here and as I am sure Matt has mentioned, we have various interests from UK clients who are looking to expand and diversify. Particularly as the UK market is getting pretty overheated and we need some value and balance to our portfolios. So, Matt indicated that with your and other investors' portfolio of assets, under this new Sub-Prime market, there might be some areas of mutual benefit where we could co-invest and possibly look to take some securitised stock off your hands."

"Interesting and perhaps more so in that I didn't realise that the Brits would be so far sighted as to get in now whilst the elevator is still on the ground floor," he finished metaphorically, arching an inquisitive eyebrow.

Rupert acknowledged the jibe with a smile and continued: "Well, you know we have been doing this for rather a long time and we are certainly not averse to risk and return; providing of course, that the return indemnifies the risk. Now, it seems to me that the circumstances that you have here with a relaxing of the rules, offers a perfect opportunity to get involved and we have some investors who are potentially keen."

The initial parry of swords and thrusts over, the conversation moved on to more meaningful discussions and it was sometime later that the meeting broke up with a promise of more talks and the possibility of co-investment occurring. When Matt Wood dropped them off at the hotel later that evening, they could finally talk openly.

Chris, who had joined in the conversation with the potential 'money men', was slightly sceptical about the property side of the visit. "I'm not sure whether that was a waste of time or not. Do you really think any of them are going to let us play in their back yard? I mean, I can see the reasons, potentially, but of them all, Bill Lester seemed the least sceptical. He seemed a bit off though, not sure what to make of him, it all seemed a little too smooth, if you know what I mean?"

Rupert leant his head to one side in a gesture of uncertainty, shrugging his shoulders. "I don't know. I mean, I understand where you are coming from, but I've seen chaps like that in the UK. Wealthy IDB's who-"

"Wait, I thought I knew all your acronyms. Everyone says the forces are bad, but what the fuck are IDB's ?"

Rupert savoured the moment: "In Daddy's Business! Oh do keep up 007, please." He received a cuff around the head for his humour and then continued, "Seriously though, they have a certain attitude and aura; expect everything to happen for them and everyone to run around after them. But I grant you, it was strange not to meet at his office, maybe he didn't want any staff knowing he was meeting with foreign investors, after all, the other money men didn't seem to mind."

"Yea but he said, he was having a bash there tonight."

"Indeed. So where were the flowers, the band, people running around getting it all prepared, the food, tables? Come on, he'd have more flunkies than a box of j-cloths if he was having a party there and where was his wife?"

"Good points and well made. I tell you though, talking of family, did you see the picture of his daughter on the piano? 'I would', I'll tell you," Chris exclaimed. Rupert shook his head grinning.

"Oh really and what would Sophie say? Cut these off." He gestured crudely.

"Yea, it would all be for Queen and Country, just like her when she is abroad, I bet," he said, putting a brave face on it. "All that aside though, I still feel something isn't right; from the DEA guy up to this evening. My antennae are starting to twitch and probably for no reason that has anything to do with drug smuggling and polo. Maybe I've been around you too long and your double dealings." They carried on into reception, pausing their conversation until they were safely alone in the lift.

"Well, we'll see, but maybe this won't be a waste of time. It will be interesting to see how it all pans out when we meet some people at the polo club. Property and polo are always easy bedfellows, as you know. Wouldn't surprise me to see William Lester the Third there as a fully paid up member. It was one of the things we never got into with all the business chat."

"Yea, good o'll Billy boy," Chris chided, continuing, "Tomorrow Philip Rosti is going to introduce us to people at the polo club, correct?"

"Yes, we are meeting him here at 12.00, then off to the club for lunch and to watch one of the opening games of the C.V. Whitney Cup tournament, 26 goal, seriously good," Rupert enthused.

CHAPTER 15

NEW YORK

The Brown Stone house on Francis Avenue was typical of the surrounding buildings; wide pavements, with steep steps up to a recessed door and as with many of the town houses, it had been converted to apartments set out on each floor. Tir Brennan's final 'home' in New York was to be one of these apartments. Dave, his 'minder' for the first few days of his time there, had been curt and succinct upon his drop off: "No surnames, no details, you keep yourself to yourself, then everyone will be happy. I don't want to know anything about you. If you want anything, let me know and if you go anywhere, let me know. The rules are simple and it keeps us all safe. OK?" Brennan had nodded, impressed again with the tight security of the operation. All tight cells, no compromises, no one knew what anyone else was doing, unless they needed to. A perfect, secure system.

Connor had been as good as his word and after three separate stops and different safe houses Brennan had now been in this final residence for a day and was beginning to like it. It was, to his mind, comfortable, well set out and, as always with an eye on trouble, he had noticed that he could slip out on to a flat roof and be away; out of the back window into the garden and skip into next door's property over the fence. It was also a thousand times better than a prison cell in Mountjoy jail, he reflected.

Brennan was now ensconced in this apartment for the fore-seeable future, and he was expecting a visit from Connor that morning. As agreed, just before 10.00, the doorbell rang and he saw through the video camera it was Connor, wrapped against the cold New York winter. Brennan buzzed him in and opened the inner door to his apartment at the top of the first flight of stairs. Connor was stamping his feet.

"Damn, but it's a cold one, must be minus 5 out there," he exclaimed.

"That it is, but at least it's not raining like back home. It's the rain that's so miserable."

Connor nodded in agreement, as every time he had been over to Northern Ireland it had been raining. "Now, how are you settling in?"

"Fine, its grand and the neighbourhood seems good. Just need to start doing something to earn my keep. No one has yet explained to me how I can help or what you want me to do. Everything comes with a price, so I know that whilst I'm here it's not going to be one big holiday."

Connor nodded in agreement with a knowing smile on his face.

"Yea and it might be sooner than you think. Let me explain how it works over here. There are a number of factions, and de-spite the mid-Europeans moving in, we, along with the Italians, still cover a lot of ground. Now, whilst we don't trust them all the time nor they us, we sometimes do each other favours. Sometimes someone not connected needs to pull a job, so we lend them someone and vice versa. Do you see what I mean?"

Brennan nodded so Connor continued, "OK, well we're both

Catholic, after all, and sometimes our aims are the same. We make money over here and need to keep funds moving to supply the Old Country. Sometimes we also share information and this is where it gets interesting.

Brennan interrupted: "Is this what I've heard about the Mafia helping us out? Tit for tat, use us where one of theirs will be suspect?

"Exactly and whilst they have no monopoly, they do like to know what is going on. The main suppliers come from South America, as you know, and more particularly, Colombia. And you know all about the guerrilla group FARC and the drug lords in Colombia. Hell you've helped train them for God's sake."

"Sure, but I still don't see how this involves me. Do you want me to go down there and train someone?" Brennan queried, not seeing where this was going.

Connor humoured him: "Let me bring you up to date. With Escobar gone, largely due, I might add, to FARC and the home grown vigilante group Los Pepes, the new cartels have opened up. One in particular-"

"Ballesteros," Brennan interrupted. At which Connor nodded.

"Exactly, Ballesteros. Whose men have been making enquiries about you, they know you're here." Brennan shrugged, he had been hunted before by experts.

"Now, here's the interesting bit. Given your history with Ballesteros, we thought that you might like to get back at him and maybe settle the debt and get some cash back as well."

"Tell me," Brennan encouraged Connor.

"We hear from the Italians that large shipments of Cocaine have been coming across to the States over the last few days. Not just through the boats into Miami, but across in San Diego for distribution. They are not moving it all internally; not nation-wide, but specifically to Florida of all places. This is according to the Teamsters union with whom the Italians have big contacts.

Now the US is the biggest consumer of cocaine in the world, but not Florida. I mean it's strange, ain't it?"

Brennan frowned, like most successful killers, he was intelligent, well organised and methodical. He considered all that he had just heard, assimilating and digesting the information. His first question was a good one:

"Where in Florida, Miami? Because if so, that is surely for organised Crime, no part for us there, we'd just be stepping on the Mafia's toes?"

Connor shook his head. "Not as far as we are aware, the schedule for all transportation is a series of warehouses, then to be picked up by vans, couriers, you name it, no final destination."

"Clever. So what are we looking at; snoop around and see if we can pick up some trace, nick it off them, flog it and give the Colombians what cash they want for the load we lost?"

"Why not? It's simply fuckin' audacious, they'd never believe we'd try and who would suspect us? I'll get people on it now and we can keep talkin' to the Italians."

Brennan nodded in agreement. "If this goes on, I'll go down there and look around. If it looks good, I'll need some people to pull it off, can you arrange that?"

"Sure, this is what we want you for. You're under the radar and experienced. Maybe go down soon; we'll get you on a truck, a long drive, but safer and no one'll notice. I'll make some arrangements."

Brennan went off to the kitchen to make some coffee and returned a few minutes later with two steaming mugs, to find Connor already on the phone talking in cryptic words to some unknown source. He came off the line, gratefully accepting the hot mug of coffee. Sipping it noisily so as not to burn his tongue, he winced at the heat and continued.

"Right, initial plans are in place. I'll be back in the next two days. You sit tight and we'll get you ready to go. Anything else you'll need?"

"Yes. I'll need a gun, a good one. Pistol, preferably a Sig Sauer 9mm with the SAS finish."

"You don't want much do you? I'll see what I can do." Coffee finished, Connor made to leave.

* * *

FLORIDA

As planned, Philip Rosti arrived to take them to the polo club and introduce them to the members that he thought may be useful. He was dressed in chinos and blazer, every inch the wealthy realtor, but as Rupert knew only too well, every faction had its uniform and this helped them bond.

"Philip, good to see you again, thanks for coming along," Rupert greeted him. Claire and Chris came up forward and shook hands. "This is my wife, Claire, who is joining us on the trip and is the most knowledgeable about polo."

"Claire Brett, how do you do?" she responded.

"Well, thank you, ma'am," he responded with old fashioned American manners, giving Claire a once over and clearly liking what he saw, giving her an American, thousand kilowatt smile. "Glad you could join us, I'd be delighted to show you around."

The emphasis was definitely targeted in Claire's direction and Rupert smiled, used to this reaction; men naturally liked his wife, she had an allure which drew them in. It was, he had realised early on in their acquaintance, an uncultivated charm which naturally appealed to members of the opposite sex. She could also play upon this quality when she wished, which Claire did to good effect in business, using her sexuality to her advantage.

"That is very kind of you. I have waited to see this particular tournament for a long time, so great to now be part of it all, in a manner of speaking," Claire responded in kind, smiling winningly at Rosti, who seemed to melt slightly. Chris too had seen the effect of Claire's allure and smiled to himself.

"Shall we?" he gestured to the foyer doors, before Philip Rosti became overheated. They went to their respective cars, which offered more flexibility for when they left the club, and prepared to follow Rosti, but not before Rupert had teased his wife: "You are such a tart, he'll be your slave for life."

"I don't know what you mean," Claire responded coyly, unabashed. "I'm just an old married mother-to-be!" Rupert snorted in response, following Philip Rosti out of the car park.

Upon arriving at Palm Beach polo club, they found that they were no less impressed than on the previous occasion they had visited the club. The same immaculate lawns and building presented themselves, only palls of white chalk dust hanging in the air signified a greater degree of traffic than before. Upon reaching the car park in front of the stands and clubhouse, they saw a fine array of parked cars: limousines, Mercedes, Porsches and other sports cars including, Rupert noticed, a very rare Ferrari Dino in bright Ferrari red. Rupert getting out of the Ford, could not resist, as he walked over to the beautiful car.

"Wow a Dino, these are so rare, it's the 246 GTS, just like the one driven by Tony Curtis in *The Persuaders*," he exclaimed. The others came over to admire the beautiful, bright red Ferrari. "Oh, I would love to have a ride in this," he purred, enviously stroking the curved raised wheel arch. Claire sauntered over and very deliberately draped herself provocatively over it, leaning forward, accentuating her cleavage, pouting at him, her strawberry blond hair showing strikingly against the vibrant red of the Ferrari.

"I think I need a cold shower," he sighed, linking his arm with

Claire's, pulling her gently off the car; she smiled innocently at him, Rupert caught sight of Philip Rosti, who looked very hot and bothered.

The club house and bar when they entered was alive with members and spectators; a cacophonous hubbub of voices all competing with one another. A glitter of smiles; a flick of hair; a waft of cigar smoke mingled with the scents of expensive perfume and the tinkle of laughter. Beautiful, elegant women, dressed in an array from designer jeans to elegant 'Pretty Woman' dresses; good looking, preppy youths; swarthy Argentinians and powerful captains of industry holding sway. Money and power were evident. It was simply perfection.

"If ever America claims to be classless, this would dispel the view," Chris commented looking around the room, clearly impressed with the quality of clientele but his own words came back to him, *'a little too perfect.'*

"Amen to that," Rosti intoned. With drinks in hand, he then proceeded to work the room, clearly a well-known entity amongst the polo fraternity, of whom most it seemed, were either clients past, present or future. One or two present were people that Rupert and Chris had met on their tour of 'money men' the previous day. The crowd then seemed to part and there was William Lester the Third.

"Well, Rupert, you didn't tell me you were here for the polo as well?" he boomed out, his deep voice resonating around. "Good to see you. Hi Chris, glad you're here," he said, shaking hands with Chris, all smiles and bonhomie.

"Bill, I wondered if we might meet you here. Good to see you. May I introduce my wife, Claire? Darling this is William Lester. We met him yesterday at his rather lovely house."

"Ah yes, Rupert mentioned it. How do you do?" Claire smiled winningly at him, turning on the charm.

"I am very well," he responded, oozing charm towards Claire, whose hand he held just a little too long. "Do you know anything about polo at all?" he addressed the question at all three guests, but it was clearly aimed at Claire, whose attention he held with eye contact.

"I've played a bit in England and Argentina," Claire answered, "and we saw the Open together in Argentina when we all there a few years ago. Amazing skill, and I am hoping this will be as good." She gestured towards the polo fields beyond the open clubhouse.

"To match the Open? I doubt it, but it should be a great tournament. But all three of you were in Buenos Aries?" he queried raising an inquisitive eyebrow, looking at Chris Adams.

"Yes, Rupert and I opened an office out there for HBJ some years ago, breaking new markets. We did some deals too, forward funded the harbour project. They were exciting times, weren't they, Rupert?"

"They certainly were and, of course, Claire timed her visit to coincide with the Open at Palermo. Amazing, as Claire says, have you been?"

Bill Lester reappraised Rupert and Chris, realising for the first time the true value of their seniority and experience.

"Well, yes, I have been once or twice," he murmured deprecatingly, "and I happen to agree with you. Not only that, we have a few of the same Argies here. So, whilst it may not be 40 goal, it should be an excellent tournament."

He turned around, looking over the heads of the immediate crowd. "Now, let me introduce you to my wife." The crowd seemed to magically move at his words and a woman appeared at his side. "This is my wife, Samantha. Samantha, this is Claire, Rupert and Chris, they are over here from England on a business trip, although I should think Claire is more interested in the polo," he finished charmingly.

Chris saw it was the beauty from the photograph on the piano in Lester's home that he had admired so much and who, he had assumed, was Lester's daughter. To Chris's eyes she was in her early thirties and appeared taller than her photo. Her auburn hair curling over her shoulders, framing the high cheek bones of her face, whilst confident eyes of a startling aqua marine hue appraised them. She shook hands with Claire and Rupert, then moved forward to engage with Chris. The sensuality of the woman was an allure that she wore as definitively as the perfume which clung around her like an aura. She had broken the golden rule of never wearing white jeans at polo but as they clung to her curvy figure, somehow, she seemed to get away with it. She shook hands with Chris in a surprisingly firm grip.

"I am very pleased to meet you." She had the slight twang of a southern belle, which seemed easy on Chris's ears, as she emphasised the intonation. Rupert and Chris saw a beautiful woman: Claire saw trouble.

"The pleasure is mine," he answered, accentuating the lilt in his usually mild Welsh accent. The flirting, while discreet and within the bounds of polite society, nonetheless caused a frown to fleetingly appear across Bill Lester's face.

"Right," he interjected, "how are you all doing for drinks? Now, you must be my guests at our table for lunch, great place to see the play." Rosti seeing that his work was done, deftly moved off to work the room in search of clients. The remaining three Brits, gracefully accepted Bill Lester's invitation and walked across to a beautifully set table, where a discreet waiter hastily laid three more place settings for lunch.

Over lunch, Claire sought to engage with Samantha Lester and see if she could find out more about her. The reasoning being that a wife or husband could often tell you more about the partner than anyone else.

"So Samantha, do you play or just a keen aficionado of the game?"

"Oh, please, call me Sam. All my friends do."

As an olive branch between two strong, attractive women, it was a good sign and Claire accepted it gracefully. The lunch proceeded in this vein, with the conversation bounding around the table on all sorts of subjects, including property. It transpired that Bill had a team playing in the tournament which he was sponsoring, as a non-playing patron.

"That's very interesting," Rupert commented upon hearing the news, seeing it as an opportune time to introduce his cover of seeking sponsorship amongst the Argentinian players and gaining a connection.

Bill Lester took the bait: "How so? Surely it is not unusual?"

"Well, maybe not in the US, but in England the patron usually plays and is 99% of the time outclassed and really should not be playing at all at the higher levels. So one of my clients -who incidentally is also interested in entering the markets we discussed yesterday - is also potentially interested in entering a team for the next UK High Goal season as a non-playing patron. It is a hundred percent tax efficient over there."

"Interesting, well you'll get no shortage of takers, I'm sure. They don't get paid very much and the cost of living in Argentina or Chile is much less than here or the UK; the players view any form of payment over and above the basic level and accommodation etc., as a serious bonus. I will introduce you around after lunch and the game or maybe later in the week as the players tend to be a little tense after a game and wish to be alone."

"Careful Bill," Samantha cautioned jokingly, "they'll be stealing your team and opening up over here as well." The others all laughed but Rupert felt that there was a slight sting to the comment that he couldn't put his finger on. The rest of the luncheon proceeded smoothly and they all decanted to join the rest of the crowd at the magnificent viewing stands overlooking the playing fields.

The crowd represented a mixture of the knowledgeable and those who were there purely for the social event, to see and be seen. But the game was closely fought and as with all such tournaments, the early rounds were highly competitive; no one wanted to be knocked out this early in the competition. Bill's team was playing, and comprised of two strong Argentine players, Manuel Cordon and Pepe Lopez, who were 10 goals each respectively. They commanded the game as one would have expected, bringing home a 12-10 win with panache and smooth moves, lauded by the home crowd. After the game, they parted with Bill Lester promising to arrange a meeting with his two Argentinian players in due course. The conversation in the Ford on the way home was an interesting one.

"Wow some *'daughter'* he has there then, Chris?" Rupert crowed

"Did I miss something here?" Claire asked

"Hah, piss off!" Chris laughed at him. "OK, the joke is on me. I saw the photo of Sam, amongst others in his house last night, and thought it was his daughter. Hell, you can see why, no wonder the guy dyes his hair, she must be about half his age," he exclaimed.

"Yea, there is something not quite right there, you listen to 'Auntie Claire', that trophy wife is trouble," Claire warned.

"Oh nothing wrong with a bit of harmless flirting," he remarked, innocently smiling back at her.

"Yea right, if that is all that is on her mind, I'd be very surprised. She may be Bill's trophy wife, but she is still a man trap," Claire stated vehemently.

CHAPTER 16

LONDON

Johnston had called Chief Superintendent Webster to keep him updated as to the current position in Florida.

"Yes, we had a call from Brett yesterday, really just confirming all that they had achieved. I must say, that despite a large contingent of drugs having entered the States and being moved around, nothing seems to have happened untoward. If it wasn't for the fact that a conclusive analysis of the drugs all pointed to an American and vicariously Colombian connection, I would be beginning to seriously doubt the existence of anything unusual happening over there. Or more importantly, our chances of finding anything.

"However, two important facts have come to light: our man Josh Harding thinks he may have found something of relevance and is reporting back; and secondly, we have lost track of Tir Brennan."

Webster was not altogether surprised. "Do you think that he's just laid low within a safe house in New York?"

"No, it is more than that. There were occasional sightings or hopeful sightings, nothing is ever completely quiet, but these have just stopped. If he is hiding, then it is in deep cover for a move and if not, then he has gone somewhere to be useful to his American colleagues. I would desperately like to know where that is, but we can only rely upon our American cousins, we have no right to operate out there in full display, so we will just have to see where he turns up." Due to the nature of his role, Johnston did not reveal everything, even to Webster. Just as the intelligence services had moles deep within the IRA, so the same applied to the States. They lived a difficult and dangerous life; constantly under strain, running and hiding from both the society they were spying on and the one they were spying for, unable to get formal help as they did not officially exist.

Webster was not happy with the news. "So what have you managed to glean from Mr Harding? Anything concrete?"

"No, we have him in place because he can fit in. He is innocuous, so he should be safe. We just need to see what he can bring in. He is due to report back in again tomorrow. However, just to be on the safe side, I am going to send an encrypted phone out to Brett and Adams and give him somewhere to turn to. Although, there is little chance of him being overheard or suspected."

"Well, that is your province, not mine. Probably good to keep Brett informed; he is remarkably resourceful and with Adams as the muscle, they form a pretty formidable team."

"I agree, a shame we couldn't have recruited him permanently, but I suppose that would negate his legitimate cover in these circumstances."

"That is axiomatic. If you are going to lie, tell as much of the truth as possible: the golden rule of undercover work and, in this case, the perfect fit." The two men agreed to speak the following day and ended the call.

* * *

BOGOTA

The drug wars in Colombia had been hard fought between factions in the early 90's. FARC had, by joining with Los Pepes, the backing of the populace and, to a certain degree, the government. But it had also caused the cartels to try and infiltrate the terrorist group and bring it down from within. This had been partially successful and although they had no high ranking people within FARC, Ballesteros' cartel still had informers that fed general information to them. The information that had been fed back to Rojas was troubling him enough to take it back to Ballesteros.

"We hear that they are sending one of their men up into America to meet with someone in the States. We don't know who yet, but we know that this, this person, or agent is one of their best and manages to go undercover unnoticed."

"Why are you bringing this to me?" was the stinging retort. "Find out who it is, eliminate them or turn them; then come and see me, that is what I pay you for," he ordered. Rojas was unnerved; the conversation was clearly at an end. The final chilling words spurred him on: "I want Brennan dead or here, alive and this agent neutralised. See it done, no excuses."

Rojas nodded and muttered to himself on the way out of the casa, slamming the door as he left the building. On the spur of the moment, he had decided against reporting the other piece of intelligence he had received from north of the border. There were, he had been told, uncomfortable questions being asked, which as yet had revealed nothing and hopefully, nothing would come of it. But there were starting to become too many issues and moving parts: Brennan, the FARC agent; movements of drugs and co-ordinating the shipments; now this problem of unwelcome questions. Rojas shook his head in exasperation, he had to get a grip and resolve these issues once and for all. People must be made to realise that crossing the cartel was not to be tolerated.

* * *

FLORIDA

Josh Harding considered himself lucky and if you had asked a year ago, if he would be doing this and getting paid for it, he would have laughed at you. He was a tow-headed young man, looking younger than his 23 years with a wiry frame, and an easy smile. Josh had read Classics at Cambridge, obtaining a creditable 2:1, and from there had been recruited to join the Civil Service and more particularly MI6. The life he had envisaged was one of dry Martini's, fast sports cars and femme fatales. The reality had been nothing like that, it was, he reflected, more double 0 zero than 007.

The training he had been given to this stage, starting out with his initiation at Fort Monkton near Portsmouth, had been more cerebral than physical. It been an interesting time, where amongst other skills, they had been trained to integrate and learn from people, all the essential skills of a field agent. They had to get on with everybody, not like some elitist James Bond type spy. The instructor had quoted Kipling at them "...to walk with Kings and princes and not to lose the common touch...". But it had sunk in and when Josh had returned from a pub with 6 names and addresses of strangers, as part of his tests, he knew he was in the right field.

He had been a grammar school boy who had risen like cream to the top. Josh, who had played polo at Cambridge university, had easily been accepted initially into the polo world, you cannot fake the background or the skills necessary to be in polo, because everybody knows everybody: one or two calls would be all that it took to check up. Josh's good credentials were readily accepted without suspicion, which is why he had been chosen for this, his first role by MI6. He was now finding out all he could about the Argentinians attached to the Meredith team in accordance with his brief. There were some grooms from Mexico as well, which had seemed to appeal to MI6 in view of the border controls and connections.

They were a rough bunch, straight from the pampas in Argentina; seeking a new and better paid life outside the mother country, ultimately returning home at the end of the 'Circus' round of world tournaments.

Although superficially kind and open, there was, he found, a level through which he could not travel. Whether it was a language barrier or simply a distrust of white Europeans, he could not fathom. Initially, working as a groom for the English patron, Brad Stevens, whom he had met in the UK, he had just inveigled his way in to their confidence. But as time had moved on, certain patterns and movements had started to trigger alarms within his trained mind.

He had started carefully looking through personal effects at certain times, seeing what he could find. This particular evening Josh had been on 'late stables' looking after a horse with a swollen leg. Once he was sure that the open topped lorry filled with all the grooms from his bunk house had left, he stopped hosing the leg of the horse and returned it to its stall. Josh then quietly made his way back to the accommodation over the stables, where all the rooms were set out from a central corridor, like a classic dormitory. The external wooden staircase was the only way up, apart from the fire escape to the rear; he knew that he was reasonably safe from detection and would get plenty of warning if anyone was coming back earlier than expected. He looked carefully through the window and saw a couple of players sitting on the verandah outside their accommodation, drinking *Mate* through metal straws, sucking up the herbal tea of their staple diet. In an effort to fit in, Josh had adopted the habit, but he was not as keen as he professed to be and would rather have a cup of coffee given the choice. Still, he reflected, there were worse sacrifices to be made. He would make the search and then go and find Vikki, Meredith's attractive daughter, with whom he had started a flirtatious romance.

His heart was beating faster as he passed the door to his own room near the stairs. Every strain and creak of the wooden building set his nerves on edge. He had found that he was ridiculously tiptoeing, when he knew that he had every right to be here, it was just his clandestine activities that set his nerves on edge. Josh came to the next two doors on either side of the corridor, hesitating and, although he knew no one was in, he knocked tentatively, his knuckles sounding like a thunder clap to his ears. There was no reply and realising that he had been holding his breath, he slowly released the air from his lungs with a sibilant sound. Josh tried the door and to his relief it opened quietly, the cheap handle on the lock fitting turning in his hand. None of the doors had expensive locks, just Yale type latches that could be dropped shut for basic privacy.

The room looked like all the others: a bedside cabinet, small wardrobe, basin and a few pictures on the wall, including one of the Argentine flag. Josh methodically worked the room, checking all the usual hiding places. Nothing: the room was bare and boringly normal apart from some money taped to the bottom of each draw of the bedside cupboard. He didn't stop to count it, but estimated that it would amount to only a few hundred dollars. Basic spending money no more. Josh looked at his watch; he had been in the room about 10 minutes, so far so good. Checking carefully that he had left everything as he had found it, he quietly closed the door. He repeated the same procedure for the next 5 rooms, halting outside the sixth door, this he knew belonged to the head groom, Rizzo, who groomed for the 9 goaler Marcus Ortiz. This time the handle did not turn; the door was locked.

Producing a set of picks from his pocket, Josh spent the next 5 minutes picking the basic lock. It was, he thought, not as easy as in the films where the hero flicked it open in a matter of seconds. They had all been taught these basic skills, but each lock was different and as with every specialist trade, it required constant practice once the essential skills had been learned. Once in, everything looked in order. He checked all the cupboards, under the wardrobe and drawers. Nothing but the usual clothing and nick-knacks.

As he was about to leave, he saw the two large bags of *Mate*. One he noticed had been opened, its top rolled closed and the facing end outwards, then re-sealed just folding the paper. Normally stored like tea, in an airtight container or taped shut, to maintain its potency, this struck Josh as odd. Curious, he again checked his watch; he had been inside for 45 minutes, he needed to return to his room, shower and see Vikki.

He opened the *Mate* bag and inside there were two more clear bags, each containing what looked like sweets. Each 'sweet' was shaped like a conical frustum and looked like a white dowel. Josh squeezed one within the bag, between his finger and thumb; they were rock hard. He dared not open the packet, so he took a photograph with a small pocket camera, from two different angles.

Satisfied, he replaced the bags, folded the *Mate* bag closed and replaced it on the cupboard, in a parallel position to the unopened bag. He really didn't know what the contents of the plastic bag were, or rather he did, but he had no idea what useful purpose they could serve and certainly no possible connection with the smuggling of drugs from one continent to the other. They might be drugs in some form and without opening the packet, he had no way of knowing for sure.

He pulled the door to, hearing the Yale latch click shut and walked quickly along the corridor. Returning to his room, Josh hastily shed his clothes and running back out to the bathroom, he almost collided with Vikki having been shown in by Marcus Ortiz who still lingered in the doorway, smiling benignly as he warned, "Miss Vikki, you know that your father doesn't like you being up here."

Vikki swirled her blond hair around and pouting, looked coquettishly at him, "Well, what he doesn't see, won't hurt him, will it Marcus?" As she arched an eyebrow and Marcus shook his head, retreating through the doorway to the staircase. Turning, Vikki took in Josh's appearance for the first time. "Mmmh, I love the outfit," she cooed, looking pointedly at the towel wrapped around his waist, as the sole item of clothing he was wearing.

She closed the distance between them, embracing him, reaching behind his head, pulling them together and kissing him hungrily. She wrinkled her nose in disgust. "You need a shower! Marcus said you'd been up here for ages."

"Well, where do you think I was going dressed like this? To the mall?" he laughed, ignoring her comment on the time he had taken.

She turned him around and smacked his arse through the towel. "Hurry, I'll be waiting," she cooed, striking a lascivious pose, with one hand on her thrust forward hip. Josh hurried to the bathroom, eagerly anticipating the return to Vikki.

* * *

The following morning there was a lovely blue sky over Palm Beach, as Josh Harding walked out of his bunkhouse accommodation and strode towards the large, open barn and stables on the team Meredith complex. His mind was elsewhere, thinking about the previous evening and his return to Vikki, who had been waiting in his room upon his return. He had found her clad only in the very briefest of underwear, posing provocatively upon his bed, leaving nothing to the imagination. Their coupling had been hot and the sex spontaneous. He would have gone on into the night, but the sound of the ranch truck returning down the drive had alerted them just in time and Vikki had run to the fire escape at the rear of the corridor, grabbing her clothing, which she hastily put on as soon as the fire door was closed. Josh was still smiling at the experience and expectantly looking forward to their date that evening.

He carried on into the stable block slightly later than usual and jumped as a voice startled him.

"*Hola*, Josh, you're late," the voice said in Spanish, as Rizzo appeared out of the shadows, his solid frame approaching Josh from behind, dark eyes shaded by the ubiquitous Argy beret. "You're jumpy," he chided, "a little night activity, eh?"

Rizzo grinned, but turning to face him, Josh wasn't sure whether there was some ambiguity to the comment or the crooked smile of the head groom. He regained his composure, quickly laughing off any embarrassment and playing the game.

"What do you mean?" he asked innocently grinning in a worldly wise manner, "Oh I get it, Marcus told you about my 'visitor'. Well, you know how it is?" he smiled, spreading his arms, shrugging in a 'boys will be boys' way.

"*Si*, but you want to be careful," he continued "it could get you into a lot of trouble, you know, playing around where you shouldn't." At this he put a meaty, brown hand on Josh's shoulder and began to grip hard, looking directly into Josh's eyes. "We don't like people messing up and interfering in our ways, *comprende?* I hope that you stuck to your own room as well, I was told that you spent quite a while up there. Let's hope it was worth the risk, eh?"

The grip increased and Josh decided he had had enough, his face became a grimace of an unfriendly mask. Rizzo was challenging him in more ways than one and was clearly expecting him to either remove the hand; over arm him; or strike to release the pressure.

He did none of these things. Instead, he turned away 180 degrees, and continued the rotation so that he was now on the outside of where Rizzo's arm had been; the grip was broken very effectively and Josh was where every fighter wanted to be, on the 'outside gate' and in close. He faced him, not backing down, ready for more if it came, the moment for friendly banter had clearly passed.

"I don't know what the fuck is wrong with you, Rizzo," he snarled. "You may be *Segundo*, but what I do in my own time is up to me, now back off."

"You watch out, *guiri*, and be careful," he answered, using the Spanish slang for an Anglo Saxon foreigner. The two men parted company with Josh going to check on the horse he had been treating the previous evening.

What the hell was that all about, Josh wondered, *had he made a mistake? Left a tell-tale clue or sign? Or was Rizzo genuinely worried about annoying the boss?* He decided then and there to get into town, have the photos developed and faxed to the UK as soon as possible. He would do so whilst taking Vikki out tonight, to avoid suspicion.

CHAPTER 17

Rupert was a having a good start to the day. He had taken up Wing Chun practice again with Chris who had introduced him to the martial art during their time in Argentina. He had continued to take lessons each week back in London and whilst still not in Chris's league, he had moved through the grades to the first level of brown sash biu jee form.

As he now found it was the time when training changed and you realised what it all meant, with previous levels coming together. After an hour's practice and with bruised and lumpy forearms, but a happy grin on his face, Rupert left with Chris for meetings with two more investors which proved potentially fruitful. A tacit agreement was reached on how they could co-invest and set off the debt being ultimately bought by Featherstone Securities. Hugh Congreave was delighted when Rupert telephoned to tell him.

"Hah, I thought it was quiet here. You're secretary said you were on holiday. So, you took me up on my offer, eh? I knew you couldn't resist a lucrative deal!" Congreave crowed, feeling he had got his man hooked.

"Well, I didn't want to say anything until I had seen the lay of the land. But yes, you were right," he continued disingenuously, "great opportunities and little risk. Now I'm packaging up some deals and we can, by all accounts syndicate them as you previously indicated. Who are your lawyers over here?"

Spendell & Rushton, based in New York, I'll fax over the details to your hotel." Congreave noted the number Rupert gave him and promised to send them over and warn the contact at S & R that Rupert would be acting for him.

"Now, one other thing," Rupert continued, "it seems that, particularly here, polo and property are closely linked: patrons sponsor teams, do business at the club etc., so in order to get in closer, I have dropped hints that I was representing a client in the UK who *may* be interested in sponsoring a High Goal team next year. Looking at players, hinting at large sponsorship deals, that sort of thing, nothing concrete of course, just bread on the water. It adds to my credibility as a high roller, do you see?"

Congreave cut across: "And you want to know if you could use our name if pushed?"

"Well, yes, it may just help in all directions." Rupert held his breath, this would, he knew, be the icing on the cake. He was surprised by the reaction.

"It is quite a coincidence that you should mention this. We have a board meeting set for later this month and one of the things on the agenda is the Entertainment budget for this year. Now, as you well know, we took a marquee at Guards last year and we may just be tempted to go one stage further and do a team: either for the Queen's or the Gold Cup, but not both. So in answer to your question, yes, do put some feelers out as to who would be available, drop some hints, you know the form. However, do not make any definite commitments. But if you feel that it will help to make our case and seem as though we are in earnest, crack on. Does that help?"

Rupert's expectations had just soared: "That is perfect and quite enough for me to find out some ground rules: who, where and how much? I will put some costs together and come back with some ideas, you never know, it could be great publicity for you. The only team in the High Goal without an over the-hill-patron and a great chance of winning!"

Congreave chuckled, knowing exactly what Rupert was alluding to and that he was the first to recognise it as the reason he never entered. Although a keen amateur player, he did not want to be laughed at as fat old man trying to keep up with talented professionals.

"Keep me informed, Rupert, and get me some good deals!" With that he put the phone down.

Rupert punched the air with glee, thinking: *a holiday for free; a chance of some great fees and some freebie polo to watch, what more could an agent want? And all this nonsense about drug smuggling seemed a waste of time: perfect.* Rupert would have been dismayed to realise that his bubble was about to be burst.

* * *

Later that day, Josh met Vikki as arranged, with her driving the 3 Series BMW which she loved.

"Nice wheels," he commented, slipping into the passenger seat and grinning knowingly at the watching grooms, including Rizzo, to whom he gave a knowing nod.

"I know, Daddy gave it to me for my 18th birthday. Isn't it cool?" As if proof were needed, she sped off, foot to the floor, rear wheels spinning on the dirt drive from the stables.

As they sped off, Rizzo watched from the first floor bunkhouse; he pulled out his mobile phone and dialled a number.

"Does that make you feel better about Rizzo?" she asked as Josh had mentioned the contretemps with him earlier that morning.

"It sure does, he can be such an arse sometimes."

"I know, Daddy wouldn't put up with him, but Marcus insists he comes as part of the deal. I don't even think he is that good a groom."

"No, I agree with you. I'm just glad to be away from him for a while." He changed tack, "Listen, just before we go to the bar, I need to pop into the photo shop, get a few prints and send something off to the UK. It's sort of a project for university," he added, keeping up the ruse that he was still a student as part of his cover.

"You 'pop' all you want, then we are going to have some fun at the 'Horseshoe'," she cried, gently mocking his English turn of phrase.

The short drive to town was quickly covered and they pulled up in one of the side streets, next to a photo shop. Josh jumped out, handed over a film to be developed with the hour service and returned to Vikki in the car.

"I need to be back in 1 hour, send them off and then we can enjoy the night."

Vikki rolled her eyes: "Why the hurry?"

"Oh, I am behind on a deadline for a project, you know how crap I am about school work," he commented, falling into the American vernacular.

An hour later, Josh returned, picked up the photos; sent two by fax directly to London and posted the originals using registered post. He then returned to the bar with Vikki, happy that he had put in motion the findings, although he was still not sure what relevance or use the plastic objects could have. The night turned out to be wild, meeting with friends of Vikki's who were clearly out to party.

The next morning, Josh woke with a massive hangover; they had caught a cab back as Vikki was way over the limit. The evening had been fun but he was now paying the price. He wandered out into the warm sunlight, having risen early with a thumping head. He pulled the long-peaked baseball cap lower over his face to shield his eyes from the bright sunshine.

One of the benefits of being a groom, Josh knew, was mucking out the horses after a heavy night; the high level of ammonia in the horses urine would clear the head and has some chemical affect, which banishes the hangover. He went to work in the stalls, mucking out his charges and, for good measure, barrowed the soiled bedding onto the enormous muck heap, where standing atop, he forked the heap. The newly stacked bedding was piled in steps and he broke the crust on the older manure, releasing a steaming, acrid, ammonia filled vapour.

"Ah, that's better," he muttered as the eye-watering concoction reached his sinuses, clearing head and lungs. He shook his head, smiling, with the refrain of *'never again'*.

Returning to the horses, he saddled one specific horse, who needed to be ridden alone. Normally grooms would ride one and lead up to four around the exercise track, doing the mandatory 5 minutes' walk, ten minutes trot and 15-20 minutes canter, followed by a warm down. But today this horse needed to be ridden singly to check it out properly

The track was sand covered and roughly oval in shape like the old Circus Maximus of ancient Rome. It was located a few minutes' walk from the stables and Josh rode gently out onto the track, squinting under the peaked cap. There were already a number of grooms on exercise, including Rizzo with a string of three, cantering around. There were calls from the others and everything seemed fine to Josh as he entered the ring, inserting himself amongst the other strings, without causing them to lose pace.

Even Rizzo saluted him with a nod and a reptilian smile. *Oh well*, he thought, *at least everything seems to have straightened itself out here.* He noticed Rizzo was riding with both leading horses in his left hand, rather than one either side. *Odd,* he thought. After the requisite time and warm up, he started cantering the horse, checking for any lameness in the action.

He was in the middle of the track, circling at a canter. Hearing the rumble of hooves, Josh was surprised to be caught up; normally a single horse would be going faster than those being led in a set. Then he realised that two strings were approaching at a slow gallop. Josh looked over his right shoulder to see Chico, one of the other grooms, approaching fast and then Rizzo appeared on his left: he was boxed in. They closed on him, Rizzo flicking his foot, kicking Josh's stirrup up, unbalancing him and then the same happened on his right. Both feet were pushed forward, tipping him backwards. He instinctively grabbed at the reins to help his balance, and the horse leapt upwards at the pain, causing Josh to topple over backwards into the path of the oncoming string of five horses being ridden at speed.

Josh somersaulted over backwards, losing his baseball cap and cried out in horror as he crashed onto the sand track into the path of the oncoming string of five ponies. He raised his hands in a futile gesture of defence as the steel shod hooves crashed into him, rolling and crushing him like a rag doll, his head smashed first one way then the next, blood streaming from a fatal wound to his temple. He finally came to rest, ten yards further on, his smashed head at an unnatural angle. Pillars of dust devils whirled around him as though in salute to his death.

Rizzo had halted his string quickly, along with the other riders, including Chico. He turned to see the result of his planned assassination, and to leap forward if he were needed to finish the job. Realising it was not necessary, he signalled to the others and looked around to see if anyone else had witnessed the collusion, resulting in Josh's death. He scanned the tree line screening the track from the rest of the yard and saw movement. Rizzo hurriedly altered his attitude, suddenly all concern and horror at the 'accident'. He had seen Vikki approaching on her pet Appaloosa, still unaware of what had just occurred.

It was the halting of exercise and the focal point that first drew her eye. She cantered over, dropping from her horse screaming: "Josh! Josh! Nooo."

She tried to run to him, but was restrained by Rizzo, now dismounted and pretending to help the stricken figure of Josh, lying in a bloody heap on the sand track.

"No, don't look," he urged, dissembling care and concern. "There is nothing you can do, he is dead."

"Let go of me, you bastard, let go," she screamed at him, wildly thumping his chest. He grabbed her in an even tighter bear hug, pulling her away and she was powerless to resist his forceful embrace. She started to cry hysterically, sobs shaking her frame, covering her face with her hands. Then, breaking away from Rizzo, she began running towards the house to call for an ambulance.

* * *

LONDON

The following morning, news reached Johnston at MI6 that his operative Josh Harding was dead. It had arrived just as he was examining the faxed documents sent by Josh to MI6 headquarters, showing the photos he had taken of the plastic pieces. Johnston was examining them under a magnifying glass and in front of him, seated at the desk, was one of the lab analysts that the security forces employed.

"Well, what do you make of it? Are they drugs?" he queried irritably.

"Hard to tell really, but I would say no; more like plastic, but as to their use, I have no idea. The photos are hazy and the fax copy doesn't help. We may be able to tell you more when the original photographs arrive." Johnston made a guttural noise in his throat that could have signified any number of things. At that point, the door opened and an 'Eyes Only' document arrived marked urgent.

"Very well, let me know when you have more." After the door closed, he fingered the document warily, suspecting the worst and that Brett had been hurt in some way. He was not expecting the death of Josh Harding. He swore harshly at the information given; he would now have to inform the parents, who had only a 'vague idea' what their son did for the Civil Service. He picked up the receiver and dialled a number, it was, he reflected, early morning in Florida.

"Good morning, I would like to be put through to Rupert Brett, please." The hotel receptionist confirmed the name and said she was putting him through. Three rings later it was answered.

"Hello?"

"Mr Brett?"

"Speaking. Who is this?"

"It is Johnston, here in the UK. How are you?" Pleasantries abounded for the next two lines of conversation and then Johnston cut to the chase, cryptically phrasing his next sentence in ambiguity.

"Following up on some leads which we discussed in the UK, can you go and pick up a package I've sent through to you?" Rupert confirmed that he could. "Good, I had it sent straight through to the Consulate in Miami, easier that way, no fuss, if you take my meaning." He finished in a breezy manner. "Let me know when you return and we can chat. Cheerio." The line went dead.

Rupert looked at the telephone, slightly nonplussed. His warning antennae started to come alive. Something had clearly happened and whatever it was, it would not be good news. He finished dressing and went through to Chris Adams' room.

He entered Chris's room, to find him showered and dressed after an early morning run and explained to him the details of his brief discussion with Johnston. Chris raised an enquiring eyebrow.

"It'll be the encrypted sat phone. Which means that something either has or is about to happen that cannot be discussed over an open line. Not good," he surmised.

* * *

NEW YORK

The man who Tir Brennan had known as 'Dave', left the apartment which, until recently, had housed Brennan and slouched onwards down the street, heading for the local coffee bar. Smoking as he went, it appeared to all that he hadn't a care in the world. He dropped the butt end of the cigarette he had been smoking, grinding it with his foot into the pavement. As he passed the call box on the corner, he snapped his fingers as though recalling a call that he had to make. Turning, he fished into his pocket almost as an afterthought to any curious observer, retrieved a few coins, dialled a number and made a call. The call to his 'handler' was curt: "It's me. He is on the move, headed south towards Florida from what I can make out. I'll call again if I hear anything."

Dave gently pushed the receiver buttons down, but for forms sake kept talking in a jocular manner, continuing a one sided conversation. After a couple of minutes, he left the phone booth and continued on his way to the coffee shop.

At that moment, the subject of Dave's discussions was on course for his destination. Tir Brennan was acting as driver's mate in a Scania T Longline lorry heading south towards Florida. They had already made two drop offs in Virginia and this final load was going all the way, filled with white goods, destined for Miami. The huge cab was comfortable and on impressive air suspension. The driver, a quiet individual not given to long conversations and who Brennan thought mercifully, was not into Country & Western music. They had just crossed the state line into North Carolina and were heading straight down the East Coast on the I95 which led into Florida and Miami. The total journey was about 1,300 miles, but they had to abide by tachograph rules in case they got stopped by Sheriff and Highway patrols, no suspicion must be attached to the journey: steady and safe were the orders.

CHAPTER 18

FLORIDA

Rupert elected to go in the car with Claire to pick up the package from the consulate. She was less than happy at the turn of events and wanted to know first-hand what the package was and if, as they suspected it was a sat phone, what implications it had upon them all. Despite this, the drive back down to Miami was a lovely diversion, taking in some stunning coastal scenery and listening to her favourite track of the moment.

"*All I wanna do is have some fun,...*" she sang along, joining in the chorus of Sheryl Crow's ballad. "Have I told you I love this song?" she laughed.

"Yes, just once or twice," he responded, laughing. It was to become the anthem for the trip in her mind, summing up the relaxed southern way of life in America.

The journey passed without incident and they arrived at the consulate in Miami, with Claire looking after the pickup truck, whilst Rupert walked into the Consulate to see what had arrived for him. Producing his passport and signing a receipt, he was presented with a familiar shape. It was a briefcase of a typical style and size, he did not need to open it to know exactly what it contained.

However, the occupant of the car that had followed them down from Wellington, was rather more curious, dialling a number on his mobile phone.

"Yea, they just pulled up at the Consulate and the Brett fella' returned holding a brief case. What do you think it is, cash for deals or bribes?"

"No," came the response. "I have a pretty good idea what it contains and it won't be money. Things have just got more complicated." *Things were racheting up,* he thought, *I'll need to report this, it means we have less control.*

Rupert returned to the Ford, opened the door and Claire asked: "Well?"

He proffered the briefcase up into the car as an answer. "Just as we suspected; an encrypted sat phone."

Claire rolled her eyes. "This is turning into a nightmare like before. I wonder what is happening now? I hope to God that you don't have to do anything dangerous, Rups, please " she pleaded.

"Oh, it will be fine," he murmured. "It will just be some more info for us to pass on, probably to Meacham or whoever. I really can't see what else we can do. I am mixing with the polo crowd and the property chaps, all to no avail. Yea, there are the usual dodgy types who you would expect, but nobody who I think has *drug smuggler* tattooed on his forehead," he joked.

In response, Claire raised an eyebrow, knowing how trouble seemed to follow her husband. They left the car park and re-traced their steps on the return journey back to Palm Beach and the hotel. The car that had followed them down also left at a discreet distance behind, knowing that there would be very little to report now.

They returned safely to the hotel to find Chris waiting for them expectantly.

"Well?" he queried.

"As we expected, the usual." The three went up to Chris's room and sure enough, the briefcase contained an upgraded and modified version of the encrypted satellite phone that had become so familiar to Rupert during their time in Argentina. The encryption programme was fool proof, not even the CIA could get through and decode what was being said or transmitted. Setting the codes that had been picked up by Rupert and Chris's phones separately and covertly, they then dialled into Johnston. He brought them up to speed with what had happened to Josh Harding, confirming in his opinion that it was murder, or at least attempted murder and not an accident. Rupert's response was a mixture of anger and incredulity.

"What?" he demanded. "You had someone in place all this time and didn't think to tell us? Why the hell not?" he questioned hotly.

Johnston ignored Rupert's outburst and his response was annoyingly measured and calm to Rupert's ears.

"Well," he began, "firstly you were the belt and braces; and secondly we wanted this to be approached from two different directions. Harding on the inside, so to speak, and you and Adams on the outside. That way we could compare the intel and, if necessary, bring you two together."

Rupert was unimpressed and Chris was fairly sanguine. He encountered this form of duplicity all the time in his line of work and the powers that be were never to be fully trusted. Physically forcing himself to calm down, Rupert asked, "So what next? What do you want us to do now exactly?"

"I will send you the details of the address and I would like you to go over there and pick up his personal effects. Say that you are acting on behalf of the family and that the English patron

Brad Stevens has asked you to pick up his effects etc. Stevens is away, back in the UK for a few days and will be back next week, so it will all ring true. Finally, I will also send you through some images of photos sent by Josh Harding the day before he died."

"Photographs?" Rupert questioned. "Of what?"

"As far as we can ascertain, they are made of plastic and resemble small, plastic, cone shaped objects but with the top cut off. Almost like dowels used in woodwork if you know what I mean."

Chris who had been listening in interjected, "And you think that these photos, or more particularly the objects themselves, are the reason he was silenced?"

"We do. On a hastily scribbled note he wrote that they were the property of someone called 'Rizzo'. I don't know who this person is or who he works for, but it should become apparent when you visit the ranch. Let me know how you get on."

"Will do," they both chorused and the link was terminated.

The two men looked at each other, initially without saying a word and Rupert broke the silence, "You know the other day when you said that your antennae were twitching and something didn't feel right? Well, tell them to get back in their box next time," he commented.

"Huh, well we didn't shake the tree this time, but something has certainly fallen out," Chris surmised. "But," he said studying the recently arrived images, "I don't see how this connects to drug smuggling, do you? I mean unless these are coated drugs and not plastic."

"No I don't, maybe it was just a coincidence and this poor chap Harding came across something else unrelated and he was killed for it?"

"Well, let's go on over there." Chris continued to study the address Rupert had written down following the conversation with Johnston. "Meredith Ranch... wait, I think I know this place, or rather of it, it is the Meredith team's home base. We met the patron, Martin Meredith, remember? He is one of the big property guys and investing heavily in the Sub-Prime?"

Rupert snapped his fingers. "Of course, tall, lean, good looking sort of chap, rather sharp faced."

"Had a pretty daughter with him at the polo club too, as I remember," Chris grinned, lightening the mood.

"Hah, sure it was his daughter?" Claire interjected. "And if you two think you are going anywhere without me, you are mistaken." Rupert eyed his wife, recognising that firm expression and knowing that she would not take 'no' for an answer.

"OK, before we go I am going to call Seth Meacham, the DEA agent," he nodded at Claire who looked momentarily puzzled. "To see if he has heard anything."

"Just one thing, Rupert, don't tell him anything about the photos just yet," Chris cautioned. "I know that we agreed on a frank exchange and all that shit, but information is power and I want to keep that nugget of information close to our chests."

"Yes, I couldn't agree more. He'd want copies; ask who, how, where, why. I'll just say we're going over as we know the family through polo, all a big coincidence etc. Keep it light." Chris nodded in acquiescence.

Five minutes later he finished the call with Meacham, clicking the red button on his Nokia as he ended the conversation. "You know, I still think he believes we are a couple of amateur sleuths running around like headless chickens on a fool's errand. He didn't seem really interested at all and to all intents and purposes he felt, or implied, it had nothing to do with drugs whatsoever."

"Have you ever thought that he might be right?" Claire asked, raising an inquisitive eyebrow. "I mean, you two do tend to go off Famous Fiving at the first sign of trouble!"

Chris squeezed her shoulder gently, smiling at her. "Now, now, Auntie Claire, boys will be boys."

They set off for the Meredith home, which was some twenty minutes' drive away, passing small estates set back from the roads along sweeping driveways. Small lagoons and majestic palms vied for dominance in what was, from the outside, a sybaritic paradise, enclaved for the rich and entitled. One felt that nothing would dare to go wrong in this perfect environment. They had driven out on route 98, heading west, following the directions they had been given, through Twenty Mile Bend and after another five minutes found a discreet sign set back from the road heralding *Meredith Ranch*. There were electronically operated wooden gates and a cattle grid within the drive.

"They clearly don't want anything to get out by accident, do they?" Rupert commented. He pressed the buzzer and after giving his name, they were admitted and the gates purred open. They had now become used to the sweeping elegance of the Florida estates and were presented with a long drive, bordered by sentinel palm trees and indigenous acacias. There were perfectly formed post- and rail- fencing enclosed paddocks in all directions, occupied by tail swishing horses, gleaming in the sunshine, who briefly deigned to raise their heads in curiosity, as a respite from munching lush grass.

The drive gave way to an open area, similar to Lester's home, with stables and corrals to the right and the main house to the left. The main house was modelled on an old ranch house, with a sloping veranda running along the whole of the main frontage and separate wings stretching back, all dressed in a dove grey, clapperboard cladding. Large gables appeared at each stage, looking out over the courtyard. It was an elegant country house that had a distinct feel of home to Rupert.

"Well, I could live here, hard but I'd make the effort," Claire commented sarcastically.

"Yep, tricky choice, but if I had to."

The drive was cluttered with a number of cars, some of which seemed out of place; one was a black Chrysler.

They made their way to the front, stepping up on to the cool shady veranda. Upon ringing the bell, the door was opened by a pretty young woman who Chris recognised from the polo club as Meredith's daughter.

"Good afternoon," Rupert began. "Sorry to disturb, my name is Rupert Brett, my wife, Claire, and colleague, Chris Adams. We are here to pick up Josh's things, to return to his parents. They-"

He was cut short as the pretty face before them crumpled into a mask of tears. She raised the back of her hand to her mouth.

"I am sorry," she blurted out. "It is just that when I hear his name..." she stumbled to a finish as another figure appeared behind her. It was Martin Meredith.

"What's going on? Oh, it's you. Rupert Brett, isn't it? What are you doing here?" he demanded brusquely.

"Hello Martin. I was just saying to your daughter, that we have been asked by Josh Harding's family to come over, pick up his things and give them some background to this, um, awful tragedy. They can't get flights at the moment, you see, and any word directly from us would help." By way of explanation he covered the awkward silence. "We know both them and Brad Stevens. Connections through polo etc.," he finished.

"Ah yes, of course, er, come in," Meredith offered putting a protective arm around his daughter's shoulders.

"Thank you," Rupert muttered as the three entered the house. There was another awkward silence as they waited to be shown through, then Meredith's daughter regained her equilibrium.

"I'm sorry, my name is Vikki, please, come this way, I'll show you through to the stables and his bunk."

"Vikki, are you sure-"

"I'm fine, Daddy, I've got to go down there sometime. Follow me." She bravely led the way through the side of the house and out of a back door. A gravelled drive led to the stable block and barns, opening out onto the track where Josh had died.

"This way," she offered. Claire separated slightly from the two men and gently latched on to Vikki, opening a conversation with her, gently comforting and probing at the same time. Rupert and Chris taking the hint, carefully moved discreetly away, so that by the time they had walked to the stable block they were about 25 yards apart.

There was a Sheriff's patrol car parked at the foot of the stairs, which led up to the bunk house. It was empty and the two way radio was emitting tinny voices, with various coded calls, through the open window.

"The county sheriff came earlier and some more people, forensics or something, I guess," Vikki offered rather hopelessly nodding towards the patrol car. "His stuff is in his room; first door on the right at the top of the stairs." They thanked her, then Rupert and Chris proceeded to climb the wooden staircase to the first floor. Entering the building, they walked to the door of Josh's room and found a deputy sheriff there looking through the room and its effects.

He turned around on hearing their footsteps and moving towards the door to block them from entering. "Afternoon, can I help y'all?"

"Yes," Rupert responded. "We are friends of Josh's family over here. They're unable to make it due to flights, so asked us to come over and pick up his things and, if possible, try to understand what happened and report back to his family."

"I see, well, you can't come in yet, the sheriff and others need to check this more thoroughly and make a report. Procedure, you understand. Did you know the boy?" he asked.

"No, not really, just a nodding acquaintance through polo and things in the UK, small community, as you probably know."

"Uh huh," the deputy responded. "If you wait here, the Sheriff will be up in a minute. I am sure he would be pleased to talk with you. In fact, come along with me now and I'll introduce you." He moved around, locked the door whilst Rupert and Chris made eye contact, neither liking the way this was going. They followed the deputy out, down the stairs and across to the stables that the Sheriff was clearly using as an office. The first loose box off the central line had been commandeered and the sheriff emerged just behind a swarthy Argentinian groom, berry askance, almost running away down the central isle.

The sheriff was a middle aged man with a barrel chest and a paunch jutting above his gun belt and straining against his shirt buttons. He was about six foot in height and appeared almost as broad as he was tall. In a field of irony they found that his name was 'Slim' Reed.

He spoke with slow measured tones, "Good afternoon. How may I help?"

The deputy filled him in on what Rupert had said and Reed returned his attention to the two men.

"So, what are you doing here and by that I mean here, in this part of world?" He pointed down to the floor by way of emphasis. So Rupert gave a full explanation: work, polo connection, part vacation, Sub-Prime attractions, and mendaciously adding that they had been notified by the family connections to help if they could. In all this the sheriff said nothing and just listened.

"Quite a coincidence, you being on the spot when this happened? I mean, were you planning to meet up or just in the vicinity?"

"No, we were not even aware that he was here. Brad Stevens knew, of course, and the contact came through him." Rupert braved it out on a wing and a prayer. "But, um, this all seems a lot of activity for what I understood to be a tragic accident. Is anything untoward?"

"Now why would you think that, Mr Brett?"

"Well, I suppose compared to England it just seems very thorough, if you see what I mean?"

Sheriff Reed eyed him again and Chris, who had remained silent throughout. "And you Mr Adams, you a realtor, too?"

"I am indeed," he answered, "we work for the same firm in London."

"I see," he said, clearly dissatisfied with their explanations. "Why don't you step into my 'office' for a minute and I can take some details." He gestured towards the open loose box. At that moment there was a loud concussion from within the adjacent, larger stable door, with bars on the opening. The sheriff jumped and as Rupert started to turn, Chris had already spun round, ready to face the threat; knees bent, arms extended in a full fighting stance. Chris looked round slightly abashed. *Not cool,* he thought to himself, *not cool at all.* Sheriff Reed raised an inquisitive eyebrow.

"That'll be the Meredith's stallion," he commented sardonically, "mean devil, doesn't like people much, nearly killed a groom last year by all accounts. They'll probably be bringing a mare into the other side of his stall.

"Rob, make sure we aren't disturbed, 'und tell the last two Argy's I'll see them in a minute." He turned back to the two Englishmen. "Now, names, hotel where you're staying. Rob gave me the gist of it but just explain to me again who you are and what you are doing in my bailiwick."

He motioned them into his makeshift office and asked them further detailed questions. Rupert explained to the Sheriff at length their reason for being there, how the international 'realtor' market differed from just selling houses, which is how most Americans viewed a realtor's role.

"I see, well to tell you the truth, this seems a little too pat to me. You turning up here so soon afterwards, I mean. Anything else you'd like to tell me? For example, have either of you served?

Especially you, Mr Adams," he asked, raising both his eyebrows and tilting his head slightly to one side, jowls moving and clear eyes focusing on Chris particularly.

Rupert answered. "Well, yes, I am a member of the TA in London, which is rather like your reserve or National Guard."

"Uh huh." He turned again towards Chris, who made a decision to come clean.

"The same, but before that in the regulars, Royal Green Jackets."

"I thought so, I can always tell; you 'have the look'. I was in the 101st Airborne. In fact, you Mr Adams, look a lot like some of the special forces guys I knew."

"Yes, the military certainly stamps its mark, that's for sure," he answered noncommittally.

Following Chris's lead, Rupert also decided to open up a little more. He liked Sheriff Reed and felt they could work together, maybe even more so than the taciturn DEA agent Meacham.

"You see, Sheriff, we have helped the government in the UK before on one or two matters, completely unofficially, of course," he began and then proceeded to explain with most of the truth about the other reason they were there. Keeping the subterfuge about Chris's real identity and true status, but explaining their cover story. "We would of course appreciate you treating this in confidence, as we don't want to tread on anyone's toes, so to speak," he finished entreatingly.

The shrewd sheriff smiled to himself. "Yes, now that feels a little more like it. I knew there was more to you two than met the eye. But drugs, here, for more than a little recreational use?" he scoffed at the idea. "I mean, I can see the Argy's smuggling a bit in, but in the quantities you're talking about? Miami yes, drug capital of America. But someone would have heard or a cartel operation would have moved in. And the DEA would be sure to hear about it. I know Seth Meacham, he's a good man, if a little touchy, but sure, he would have heard."

"I realise it may seem a little farfetched, but we are only doing a little snooping around, as asked." He had not told sheriff Reed about Josh Harding's true status and continued mendaciously, "but tell me, was Josh's death an accident? I mean, you don't think he stumbled accidentally onto some drugs and was going to report it, do you?"

"Well, you tell me. He was out exercising the horses on the track you saw out there," he nodded outside the barn, "fell off, and was trampled by the horses following behind. Unfortunate, but there it is."

"And that killed him outright?" Chris asked sceptically. "Who was there, did he say anything before he died? I am just curious, you understand. I mean, jockeys fall in races in the UK and don't get killed, even with a race full of horses jumping and running after them. Just seems a little odd and final to me."

"Yes, he appears to have been killed outright, but there will be an autopsy. There were three grooms on sets including the Argy who ran him over; and young Vikki came up just after he fell off his horse. Unfortunately, she saw the body and everyone was milling around, from what I understand. It's not really strange, you see, they don't wear hard hats, like in England, it is all baseball caps or those fancy berets the Argy's wear and no body protectors."

"How many was he leading when he came off?" Rupert asked.

"Well now, I grant you that is the odd thing, just the one he was riding."

"Yet he fell off? An experienced groom, on a well-trained polo pony?"

"What, you think he was pushed? Maybe, we'll look into it, call it professional courtesy, one soldier to another.

"Just one other thing," Chris asked. "Who were the others on the track when he had his fall?"

"As far as I am aware, Andreas, Ramon and Rizzo. But do not start asking any questions yourself. I will help where I can but leave the investigating to me. Do we understand each other?"

"We do, just curious, that's all," Chris confirmed. They got up to leave.

"And if you hear anything from your side, please keep me informed. Let's work together, if we can. I will release the things once we have the results of the autopsy. I'll call you when we're done."

"Fine. We'll leave you to it, I need to get back to my wife." Chris and Rupert shook hands with the sheriff and left. Outside, back in the sunshine, they checked they were not being overheard and quietly confirmed their thoughts.

"This is starting to get intriguing. It will be interesting to get Claire's view on the 'accident', particularly, as she will no doubt have Vikki's take on it." At that point Claire appeared around the corner of the barns from the direction of the house.

"Interesting day?" he asked, irony infecting his voice. In answer, she nodded, indicating to Rupert that they get in the car before chatting.

The journey back in the Ford was an interesting and enlightening one. Rupert explained all that had been said between them and the sheriff. At the point where he described the elements of the fall and that Josh Harding had not been wearing a hat, she snorted in response: "Yea right, fell off his horse when he was singling it? An experienced groom who Vikki said was a really good rider and had played extensively? I don't think so. OK, no hat, fine, but they all do that. It is stupid, I know, and very macho, but there is more to this than meets the eye. I know I chided you two for seeking adventure earlier, but now I am beginning to believe something is wrong."

"Sorry," Chris asked, "but what is 'singling' and why the relevance?"

"Singling is where a groom takes just one horse out rather than a string; it might need extra exercise or checking, so they ride just one horse; really easy for a groom and never likely to fall off. Also, any string following would, in my opinion, be easy to stop and really unlikely to do the damage that killed him."

"OK, so it casts more suspicion on his death. Go on, what did Vikki say?" Chris encouraged.

"Well, in amongst the sobs, she clearly thinks it's not right and that in her words; 'Rizzo is a bastard and had something to do with it'. Even given her emotional state, I think that she could be right."

"Rizzo again," Chris commented. "I really would like to have a chat with this guy and see what he has to say." The menacing tone in his voice belied the lightness of his words. Rupert turned to look at him, knowing that he was angry at Josh Harding's death.

"OK, we take this steadily. Let's just assume that his death was suspicious; we still don't know what was the cause or rather the magnitude of the offence. I mean was it just to stop him telling the authorities about whatever drugs he found? Or was it something more sinister and the photos he sent back to MI6 have a much greater impact?"

"Vikki said that Josh seemed excited and concerned to get the fax off urgently, but he claimed it was just a dissertation for a university project. One thing though, it was pretty apparent that this Rizzo character did not like him and they had a run in the day before apparently, when he threatened him to mind his own business."

"But that means he must have the negatives somewhere," Rupert commented, quite excited at the prospect. "I wonder if Sheriff Reed picked them up. I would love to see the originals; could we call him, do you think?"

"Don't see why not, we have already declared our hand, to a certain degree." Chris punched in the numbers on his mobile and called the sheriff.

"Sheriff Reed, Chris Adams, we just met. Yea, thank you for your time too. Listen, just mulling things over on the way back and Vikki mentioned to Claire that Josh was keen to get some photos printed, did you happen to see any negatives in his affects?" Chris listened with interest to Sheriff Reed and said goodbye.

"No photos, no negatives, nothing. If Vikki hasn't got them and we must assume she hasn't, someone's been a naughty boy. The more I think about it, the more I want to chat with *Señor* Rizzo."

"So, if we assume guilt by implication," Rupert continued the thought process, "that means the photos are important and we need to look at them more closely."

* * *

Back at the Meredith ranch, another call was being placed on a mobile. "Yes, they were just here," he reported in Spanish. "Gone, but they spent a long time with the Sheriff and the woman spent the whole time speaking with *Señorita* Vikki. Just thought you ought to know. Yes, of course, I have destroyed the photos, but clearly something brought them here. OK, OK, but the sooner we get the shipment up and away, the better. I thought you ought to know so you can tell the boss. *Si*, ok."

The call ended and the man at the other end put the mobile down, rubbing his temples in an effort to relieve the pressure and stress building within his head. It was getting complicated and he now had to report to the boss. He dialled a number in the States.

"Yes," came the response from 'the boss', and again the Sheriff's visit and that of Rupert and his company was relayed. "I see. No, don't do anything, leave it with me, I will pass instructions in due course. I will call you again from a different phone. But another matter; we know from the south that their agent is on their way. All we know is that the name is *Shivren*. I know, weird, but that is all we have and apparently the agent is an American or European, so it makes it that much more difficult him or her."

"OK, I will tell everyone."

"Do: we are close, don't cock it up now." The line went dead.

CHAPTER 19

Shivren, as the agent was known, went through passport control and was picked up by agents friendly to FARC in America. The car took the agent from Miami airport and up to Palm Beach and on to a hotel. All instructions and equipment, including an untraceable mobile phone, were passed on during the journey. It was clean, simple and *Shivren* was just another tourist arriving by private taxi to the hotel.

Tir Brennan was on the last leg of his journey and had just been dropped at a safe house on the outskirts of Wellington. It was not as smart as the town house in New York, just a bland, suburban semi, with a yard, decking and well maintained paintwork. It was just one in a street of many. The car that had brought him from the truck stop, pulled into the drive and waited for the garage door to open automatically. The car pulled in and Brennan stretched, pulling his case from the back seat of the Chrysler. He entered the house through an internal door from the garage and was met inside by his local contact, Tom Doyle. Doyle was an average sized man, with a moon face and innocuous looking. Which was exactly why the IRA liked him; he could pass anywhere unnoticed, nobody remembered him.

"Hi, welcome to Florida," Doyle smiled in greeting, shaking

Brennan's hand. "Good to meet you after I've heard so much about you."

"Thank you, but don't believe everything you hear," Brennan responded in a rare attempt at humour. The two men exchanged pleasantries as Brennan acclimatised himself, inevitably looking for escape routes and weak points. Once settled in, Doyle continued to brief Brennan.

"The agent from FARC has now arrived in the States and is booked into a hotel in Wellington, we'll arrange for a meet up in due course. You'll be right at home though, she is from your homeland-"

"She?" he exclaimed.

"Yea, didn't you know?" he replied, grinning. "Here's the funny part; they think she is a man and they can't pronounce her name properly, they call her 'Shivren', but her real name is Siobhan Clifford."

"Siobhan Clifford! My god, that's a name from the past. I knew the wee girl in Ireland." Brennan was genuinely stunned as his thoughts drifted back to a red-haired girl with pig tails and freckles. He remembered crowded streets filled with kids playing and another boy, her brother, Michael, now dead, lost to the cause. He'd had a teenage crush on her; she was a pretty thing with a great figure, but it had not been fulfilled. The rumour was that she preferred girls and had worked for 14Int, the British military intelligence regiment that often worked closely with the SAS. In reality, she had been one of the best undercover double agents the IRA had in the active force until Argentina in 1991. "But I thought she had been lost to us?"

"I don't know the history and I don't want to. But I do know that she is a great asset and helps us in America when we need someone undercover. No one ever suspects her so she will be perfect to discover where the drugs are being hidden. Someone will talk they always do, trying to impress a pretty girl. She is also great for here," he pointed over his shoulder in the direction of Palm Beach "as apparently she is good with horses."

"Aye, she would be. Her uncle had a farm on the outskirts of town. My God, Siobhan," he muttered again as his mind drifted.

"We're going to try to get her a job as a groom or, if not, at least somewhere near the Argy community. She has lived in Colombia for the last 4 years so she speaks Spanish like a native, but she won't let on, of course. Now, you and she need to link up, and try to find where the drugs are being stored. We know from our sources that they are being held at different places around here; we followed two trucks that came from San Diego and the tunnel."

Brennan raised an inquisitive eyebrow.

"Yea, I know," Doyle answered, "they have this amazing tunnel from the Mexico side to somewhere in San Diego. We only get to know where it leaves Mexico and that it arrives somewhere in San Diego, everyone who has got close has been welched on and never seen again. We only pick it up from trucks and delivery stops made by the unions where we have an agreement with organised crime when it suits us both to help each other.

"Right, so we know that all the deliveries including those arrived by boat have been stashed in warehouses around this area. But we don't know how they are to be moved or when. Until we know that, we can't hit them. If we just get one, the others will move and they will double security. Most of all, we need to find out what the fuck they are doing with the cocaine and how they get it out of the country. At some point, a lot of the stuff will have to be in one place, before they ship it."

"So, whilst Siobhan is listening and trying to find out more, what the hell do I do? Sit on my arse all day?"

Doyle snorted in disgust. "No, take it easy. I want you to meet some boys we have down here, and if appropriate, meet with Siobhan somewhere once she is established. I'll be bringing some people around later. Also, I have a gun for you, no serial numbers and its clean anyway. I'm afraid I couldn't get a Sig." He opened a drawer and produced a Glock 17 with a 19 round magazine. Taking the gun, Brennan ejected the magazine, pleased at the crisp action and proceeded to eject all the shells, feeling the tension in the spring as he reloaded them, one by one. Satisfied, he checked the slide action, pulling the mechanism back. There was now a bullet in the breach, but due to the Glock's lack of proper safety catch it could now be carried with the hammer down. It was one of the reasons the intelligence agencies preferred the weapon, that and it's light weight and ease of concealment. You just pointed and pulled the trigger which released the three stage safety features.

* * *

PALM BEACH

The following day, Chris and Rupert started with a run, followed by a Chi sao or 'sticky hands' session of Wing Chun and then met Claire for breakfast. She was starting a really good tan and had that pale skin that if taken steadily, goes a golden brown without burning. To Rupert's eyes, she was becoming even more attractive as her pregnancy and tan progressed. They moved out onto the sun terrace and took up residence on three empty sun loungers at the deserted end of the swimming pool.

"I don't know, we work out and you look better than either of us," Rupert complained, admiring his wife who, in one of her Argentine bikinis, was stretching with feline languor on one of the loungers.

"That's because I'm a woman," she replied tartly. "So, what is the plan for today?"

"A polo match this afternoon, cocktail party and dinner at the polo club. But before that we have to meet with Bill Lester as he doesn't want to discuss business this evening in front of others. He also said that he would introduce me to his two star players today about the possibility of playing in the High Goal in England."

At that moment his mobile rang. Looking down at the screen, he recognised the number and mouthed 'Seth Meacham' to the other two.

"Hi Seth, how are you?"

"Good, thank you. How are you enjoying Palm Beach?" he enjoined sarcastically. Rupert sensed that there was more to this than a social call. Then he remembered that Meacham and Sheriff Reed knew each other.

"Yes, an interesting place, great fun," he commented neutrally.

"Yes, I hear that you've been making your own fun or rather trying to. Sheriff Reed and I had a little chat earlier today and do you know what? The more I think about it, the more and I hate to say this," he continued in his deep baritone, "but you and Chris may just have something."

"Really, why do you say that?"

"Well, information has been trickling through, from inside the organisation, intercepted phone calls and other areas," he continued ambiguously, "about foreign nationals arriving and a shipment of drugs, or rather various shipments being stashed, along the lines we discussed before. Now don't get excited, I'm still no nearer to finding out when, where or who, but something is moving and there is a lot of coded chat going on. I guess what I am saying is; you may not be that far off the mark. But one thing is for sure, it is being co-ordinated locally under one umbrella and that means a single boss."

"Wow, so our government was right."

"Maybe, but going back to Reed, I still don't see how this fits in with this guy Josh Harding, unless there is something that you aren't telling me?"

"No, not all," and Rupert continued with the story he had told Sheriff Reed.

"So you think that he stumbled onto something and was killed for it?"

"Yea, well Claire, my wife, and Vikki Meredith, Josh's girl-friend, both know quite a lot about polo ponies, exercising habits etc. They are both suspicious about the nature and finality of the accident. Also, there are some missing photos, with no negatives, or packaging. Just disappeared and these were apparently taken the day before he died. It all seems to revolve around this groom Rizzo; his name keeps coming up."

"Rizzo? Never heard of him, but I'll notify everyone and keep an eye out. Have you told Reed this?"

"Yea, he hasn't seen any photos either."

"But listen, whoever is behind this have started to get rid of people, just be careful, I don't want you getting hurt. I don't care if you are a part time soldier or not, these people play rough and have no feeling for the sanctity of human life. And keep your wife safe too, nothing is out of bounds for drug dealers," he warned. Rupert looked slightly alarmed, gazing across at Claire who gave him an inquisitive glance. He agreed that they would take precautions.

As an afterthought, Rupert asked, "Oh, one other thing, you mentioned *foreign nationals*. From where or is it just vague intel?"

"Ah, you're going to love this. There was a prison break in the UK a few weeks ago, did you hear or read about it?" Rupert muttered that he hadn't. "Well, this guy Brennan, who escaped, apparently we have reason to believe that after his escape he made it to the States and is on his way down here. Could be to get in on the drugs deal, who knows?"

"Brennan is here?" Rupert exploded.

"Yea, we also hear that a FARC agent is on his way, by the name of Shivren, one of their best apparently, could be a fun party," he laughed humourlessly. "Which is why I urge you to take care."

Rupert agreed and promised to keep Meacham informed. He clicked the call end button and sat lost in thought. The other two cried out in frustration: "Well?"

"What, oh sorry, yes," and Rupert proceeded to relay the side of the conversation that they could not hear, missing out the part about fearing for Claire's safety

At the end of Rupert's monologue, Chris aired one very important question that had not occurred to Rupert.

"Do you think that 6 and Webster know about the possibility of Brennan being in the US? Because," he continued, "I wouldn't put it past them to use us as a stalking horse to see what comes out of the woodwork. I mean, at least Meacham is on side now and yet curiously, he had no wind of this before we arrived on the scene, it all seems a little too neat to me."

"Yes, from past experience, I wouldn't put it past the bastards. OK, what do we know for certain, because I think we need to report this in now that Meacham has told us Brennan may be on his way, 6 need to know. But before we do that, I think we should move inside, you never know who may be listening. Claire you can stay here if-"

"Oh no," she interjected. "I want to hear this and give my view." She slithered off the sun-lounger and stood up, pulling a sarong around her, slipping her feet into beach sandals.

They used Chris's room as it had the sat phone in it and sat around the low coffee table with a pad making notes.

"OK," Rupert began, holding his thumb up as he began to summarise the points upon which they had confirmation "Going back to the beginning, we know that the drugs trade going into the States and Europe originates from Colombia. Two. We also know that it was these same drugs that were intercepted by Webster's man in the Irish Sea and resulted in the capture of Brennan.

"Three," he continued extending his middle finger, "we have been told that the drugs follow the pattern of the international polo set calendar and that they can be traced back to distribution in the States.

"Four, the DEA is aware of drugs through wire taps etc.; knows they're here and that a FARC agent (incidentally that is another Colombian connection) has been sent up for reasons as yet unknown.

"Five, an MI6 agent has died, possibly murdered, just after he sent information back to 6 about a suspicious find from within the polo world.

"Finally," he extended another finger. "Brennan turns up here after losing drugs to the cartels and we know that there is a friendly direct link between FARC and the IRA. Did I miss anything?" Claire looked up from the notes she had written on the pad and Chris took up the summary.

"Yes, it is what we don't know that matters. For instance, we don't know where the drugs are being held; how they are moved for distribution and more importantly; how they are exported without being detected."

"And," Claire continued. "What the direct link is between the polo world and the cocaine, if indeed there is one. Dare I say it, one step forward two steps back?"

"Yes and no. We came out here on a theory of possible involvement and Rupert asked for my protection. We all thought it was pretty thin and it would be just a case of '*well we heard a rumour, get the government agents to follow up and send in the cavalry*' but this is starting to get nasty. It means we or someone, maybe Josh Harding, is getting close to exposing whatever is going on. But it also means I need to really protect you two,"

Chris nodded at Rupert and Claire, "because despite poncing around pretending to be a surveyor, this is the real reason I am here and don't forget it," he finished seriously.

"Good points Chris and well made. But, how do we find out what's going on? Bear in mind that the tournament finishes here in what, 2 or 3 weeks at most? Then everyone in the 'polo circus' will be packed up and on a plane to England. So we have to find the connection and fast, before they leave. Always supposing, of course, that there is a connection with polo and they are not being transported coincidentally at the same time. So let's look at this another way. Keeping within the confines of polo, how would you transport them, Claire? I mean your knowledge is greater than mine or Chris's."

She thought out loud, bouncing ideas around to the other two, "OK, we have humans, horses and kit. The lorries don't go, so no hollow compartments etc. You can't stuff a horse's bottom full of drugs or get them to swallow it, unlike a human, they are too fragile: they would die of colic."

Rupert wrinkled his nose in disgust as Claire continued, "I know, but you have to consider all this, you asked me to," she said, defending her crude comments. "Same with the men, the quantities that are being bandied about, is more than a few Argy grooms and players could carry in condoms in their bodies etc., so that leaves kit. Hats, boots, no.

Sticks, well I suppose being inventive, you could hollow out the heads of the polo mallets, but that would still be a comparatively tiny quantity. Balls, well in quantity, yes but they are all made out of precast plastic at a factory, mostly from Dallas Polo or similar. Rupert, you saw that when I explained to that agent at Guards, Steve...Steve Channing. They are made of filled plastic, as sealed units. And that's it." She raised her hands, shrugging. "That is all that differentiates a polo player or groom from another traveller."

Chris Shrugged in a gesture of hopelessness. "So, we are no further forward. But my guess is, something will break and we have to keep looking. Whatever happens from now on, no lone meetings and, Claire, you stay safe in plain sight all the time. It is my job to protect you. This is getting serious." They nodded in assent and then using the encrypted sat phone sent the notes made by Claire on to Johnston at MI6 headquarters, reporting both their known facts and theories.

"OK, we have a meeting to attend with Bill Lester. Claire, you stay here and we'll be back to pick you up for lunch at the polo club," said Rupert.

"Yes, sir!" she said, giving him a mock salute.

Rupert shook his head, closing his eyes in mock disgust. "See what I have to put up with? Insubordination in the ranks. I bet it's not like this in the SAS."

"No, worse," Chris joked. "We're an unruly lot. But Claire, I meant it, with people; stay in crowds and beware of anyone approaching you out of the blue, however seemingly innocent they are, especially women, remember Valentina and Siobhan? Because if we are onto something and they think we're involved, they will get at us through you."

Claire frowned, looking worried, remembering the two women from their trip to Argentina. Both in their own way were ruthless killers. She agreed to be wary.

* * *

As Rupert and Chris left the hotel, a call was being made to the boss in Florida.

"Yes?"

"The two surveyors have been informed about the drugs in the area, the FARC agent arriving and Brennan."

"Good, we'll lead them in the wrong direction and, if necessary, there may have to be another 'accident'."

"But," the caller continued, "and this is worrying, they know about the photos, probably from Vikki Meredith and have alerted the Sheriff." There was a silence on the phone. Plans would now need to be altered.

"Right but leave that side of it to me. We need to find *Shivren* and sort out Brennan; he is dangerous and will have local help. I do not want this turning into a bloody gunfight just before shipment, it will bring unwanted attention."

"OK, I will report back as soon as I hear anything."

CHAPTER 20

Throughout the short journey over to Bill Lester's house, Rupert and Chris again went over what they knew, trying to find a key element that they had missed. Nothing new came to light and they seemed to arrive at Lester's home in record time. As they drove through the gates, a large brown UPS delivery van headed towards them, flying past, aiming for the still open electric gates.

"Do you think he was in a hurry?" Rupert queried sarcastically.

"I guess 'white van man' mentality thrives the world over, whatever the colour of the van."

Arriving at the end of the drive, they pulled up to see piles of oblong cardboard boxes stacked up on the drive bearing the legend 'Dallas Polo'. Next to them was an irate Bill Lester, gesticulating to the two Argy grooms who were busy loading them onto a trolley to be moved around elsewhere on the estate. As they left the Ford, he exploded.

"What the hell is it with couriers? Don't they realise goods go around the back? This shitty stuff is not even for me," he roared, appearing to cover embarrassment with bluster.

"We were just saying that drivers were the same the world over, not a care, just want to get home for their lunch."

"Amen to that! Now, sorry boys, bad manners, come on in." Bill Lester waved them towards the house, magnanimously looking over his shoulder at the two grooms with a look that could kill.

However, Chris was curious about the piles of boxes, "I hope you don't mind me asking, but if they're not for you, what are they for? Surely an Argy can't drink that much *mate*!" he joked.

"Damn polo balls. The Argys buy them here, much cheaper than the UK, ship 'em over and make a few bucks. They do quite well out of it apparently, all the Argy grooms and pros do it, anything for a buck, these guys. Probably keep a family back home for a week on the profit. Anyway, you didn't come here to talk about polo. Go on through to the den; we can talk in private there."

They went through a hall to a cosy room of decent proportions that had the intimate feel of a London Club; with recessed window seats, leather Chesterfields, dark salmon walls, low lighting from table lamps and thick carpet. Lester ordered coffee from a telephone on a large desk and they settled down as Bill Lester launched in with his usual enthusiasm.

"Now, let's get down to it. I know that before, you outlined a strategy for conversion of stock and you said that your client, Featherstone Securities, was in the game for a big ticket deal. My question for you is, how much? I need to move on other deals that are being offered and to look at those; some are up-state in New York, requiring either re-gearing or liquidity."

"Well, I have authority to move across a 100 million dollars' worth of collateral to secure a portion of the syndicated debt. This will of course be subject to contract, surveys and–"

Lester waved his hand across his face in a rude dismissal. "Yea, yea, I know all about the caveats, it was the amount that interested me."

Rupert unabashed by his rudeness continued to fill in the

details of how the deal would be organised. They left an hour later with a potential deal in the bag.

"Lester is an arrogant prick, but he does make the wheels go around, doesn't he?" Chris commented.

"He does, although probably like me, you wanted to punch him in the nose a couple of times back there. But as we say, think of the money."

"Huh only a couple? Yea but I won't be getting any of it this time, not like Argentina."

"Oh yes you will," Rupert responded confidently, "you will be getting half of my commission."

"Rupert, you-"

"Shut up already, not another word. I got you into this, you saved my life on more than one occasion and you know what? You deserve it."

Chris nodded, acknowledging the compliment and to cover his embarrassment responded curtly, "Come on then, we have a lunch to go to."

* * *

LONDON

It was evening in London when the transmission came through to Johnston's offices. He had been both impressed with the concise analysis and disturbed by the content of the report. To him, it had been too much of a coincidence that Josh Harding's death had been an accident and Johnston concurred with the view presented by Brett and Adams. He picked up the receiver and dialled on a secure line to DCI Webster, bringing him up to date.

"So, they confirm that Brennan's on his way or indeed there already, eh? I am glad that Sergeant Adams is there with them, this could get quite nasty."

"Oh I don't think so, it will probably end up being a scrap between the IRA, the FARC and the drug cartels, and frankly they can beat seven bells out of each other for all I care. We pick up the pieces. Two for the price of one.

"But one other thing occurs. You remember the death of the Vicomte outside Deauville? Well, I know that the autopsy said that he died of a drug overdose and, if I remember correctly, there was another toxic substance present. Did they ever identify it in the report?"

"The answer is, that we never actually saw a copy of the report, just a summary. You know what the frogs are like. I will speak to my contact at OCTRIS and see what I can do. Why are you raising this again after so long?" asked Webster.

"Eh? Oh just an idea from something that they mentioned in their report," he responded vaguely. "I won't say anymore in case I have it all wrong, just a hunch. Please, let me know once you have the full report."

Webster agreed and as soon as he finished the call placed another to his opposite number in OCTRIS.

* * *

BOGATA

Ballesteros had learned the lessons from his predecessor Escobar and although not directly at war with the other cartels, he still moved around regularly for security reasons. He had a *Fincas* further out in the country, 12 miles south west of Bogota, alongside the beautiful lake of *Embalse del Muna* where he met with his family and rode one of the Andalucians that he kept stabled there. The lake was surrounded by rich, lush vegetation, amid gentle slopes leading to a range of hills surrounding the waterside. It was perfect riding country and here, in some ways, he felt safer than ever, although perimeter guards both on and off horseback were always near, screening for any potential threats.

He had just returned from his morning ride and was now in conference with Rojas who was reporting upon the movement of the next shipment north of the border.

"It is going well, *Jefe*. The drugs are being packaged at separate warehouses and will even now be in course of distribution amongst the couriers. Everything is *tranquilo.*"

Ballesteros turned, using the shade of his wide brimmed Stetson to better see clearer into Rojas eyes. "And what of this FARC agent and Brennan?"

"We have killed the suspected spy who was at the rancho; Rizzo got rid of him carefully, a terrible accident, nothing suspicious. He was nosing around so we were cautious. Brennan we hear is now in Florida and we will find him as we have someone on the inside of their operation," Rojas continued, happy in the knowledge that their army of spies and informers, all lured by money, power or blackmail, would deliver. "He must meet with *Shivren*, it will mark them both out, but also we now know that *Shivren* is a woman."

For once Ballesteros was surprised and his emotion was written across his face.

"Are you sure? The FARC agent is a woman?"

Rojas nodded in affirmation. "*Si*, we have information from inside FARC, but only that she is *anglos* nothing more."

Ballesteros patted Rojas on the shoulder. "Good work Pablo, *muy bien*. I want this Brennan alive, if possible. I want him here and I want to kill him; no one steals from me."

* * *

PALM BEACH

Siobhan Clifford had settled in well to her new surroundings as quickly as she could. She was also delighted to be told that she wouldn't have to work as a groom, but that they had found her an easy job waitressing at the Palm Beach Country Club. The idea of having to groom, ride all day, muck out and put up with Argy's hitting on her had not appealed. *Not after all these years. To get back in the saddle for an occasional ride, yes, but all day? No thank you,* she thought. The club had quarters for staff and it was the perfect cover. She could easily meet Tir Brennan there without compromising her position, lots of cover from crowds: perfect.

Her American contact had picked her up and dropped her at the club with a light suitcase and she was enrolled into the system for contract staff. The club particularly liked British staff and were always busy whilst the major tournaments were on, so it had been easy to arrange for her placement. Uniform in place, she too let her mind drift back to Northern Ireland and the lean figure of Tir Brennan. She had remembered him as a teenager; wiry with an easy grin, but a certain shyness that had set him apart from the other more boisterous boys. Good times she remembered, with her brother and Tir going around in their gang.

But then 'The Troubles' had cast their shadow and everyone had changed forever, something Siobhan of all people knew. Her brother was now dead and she hadn't seen Tir for years but had, of course, heard about his exploits. Her life as a deep cover agent embedded in 14Int had not be conducive to meeting up with IRA enforcers, and her cover blown in Argentina five years ago had meant that she now lived between Colombia and Buenos Aries, working for FARC, often working undercover in the US.

Her call to the States had been to assist Brennan in stealing the cocaine. She knew that as a trained agent and an attractive woman, she could get information where men could not and she was more often than not above suspicion. Men, Siobhan found, were very stupid where a pretty woman was concerned and inclined to boast, telling more than they should. She was confident that by asking discreet questions and inveigling her way in, she could, in a short period of time, put a fairly complete picture together.

Others were also making their way to the Palm Beach Club. Rupert, Chris and Claire were slightly late for their lunchtime appointment with Bill Lester and his friends. Again, they had perfect seats out on the terrace from the restaurant and the table was set for twelve, as someone was evidently playing cupid for Chris's benefit. Bill Lester, ever the gracious host, came and offered introductions.

"Rupert, Claire, Chris, I believe you know everyone from last time, but this is Anita, daughter of an old friend of mine." Anita was a stunning brunette, classically dressed with large 'bumble bee' sun glasses which she brushed back onto her forehead, locking her mane of hair in place. She treated Chris to a thousand kilowatt smile with tantalising, knowing eyes.

"Hi, nice to meet you," she enthused with a gentle southern drawl. Chris responded in kind and shook hands. She was, it transpired, to be sat adjacent to him at lunch. But on his left he found Samantha Lester, looking as beautiful as ever in tailored trousers, an elegant cream blouse and around her neck was an unusual necklace of two intertwined polo sticks of rose and dark gold. She purred at him, placing a kiss on each cheek and he was left with the everlasting presence of her delicious perfume throughout the meal.

Claire found this by-play hugely amusing; she saw Chris caught between two predatory women and catching his eye, mouthed 'Good Luck', raising her glass in a silent salute.

The meal that followed was a delight of delicious food and cold wines. However, the game was a disappointment and appeared to all concerned a rather lacklustre affair. Neither side appeared to be trying hard and it was a confusion of whistle blowing and fouls that can often bring down a free flowing game into a desultory spectacle.

Although, the real action was taking place off field at the lunch table, with honours going to Samantha, despite Anita trying her best. The repartee and flirting continued apace, but to their frustration neither woman could gain ground and each time it appeared that a true side of Chris's character or depth of personality appeared he blandly and obliquely changed the subject. When he felt a leg rubbing sensuously against his own, Chris knew it was time to do something and excused himself, asking where the men's room was located.

He stalled on the way, meeting some of the property people with whom he had become acquainted since their arrival and engaged them in conversation. *Anything,* he thought, *to be away from the predatory lion's den of the lunch table!* At this point, Rupert appeared, grinning from ear to ear at his predicament and accompanying him to the lavatories. Laughing away before the basin, Rupert mocked his friend and guardian, "You know, for the big, tough, ninja SAS man, you do get yourself into some real scrapes where women are concerned," he chuckled and for his pains received a clip up the back of his head from Chris who despite himself was also grinning.

They were still quietly laughing as they left the Men's Room and looking straight ahead Rupert stopped so suddenly Chris banged into him from behind.

"What the hell-" he muttered.

"Quick back inside." Rupert about-faced and Chris to his credit reacted instantly, retreating behind the door. "Look carefully, straight ahead at the bar, the waitress about to take the tray into the restaurant." Chris peered around the door which was now slightly ajar and froze.

"Shit!" was all he could say.

There in front of him, carrying a tray, was Siobhan Clifford. The same mass of red hair, now pulled back in a ponytail; the sprinkling of freckles across the nose and pretty hazel eyes that looked as hard as ever. To Chris's judgemental view she had put on a few pounds since they last met five years ago, but still looked fit and in good shape.

From behind him, Rupert questioned, "I'm right, aren't I? It is her?"

"You are. Siobhan fucking Clifford! What the hell is she doing here?" Then suddenly the dots started to join up and they both said in unison: "Shivren!"

"They never could pronounce her name properly, you remember the trouble Rafe had? Bitch, so she is up here for FARC and to meet with Brennan. This is turning into one hell of a party, Rupert."

"Yes and I don't think that it is any coincidence that she ends up working in the polo club. You know how good she is at gathering intel, pound gets a penny she'll be working on it here. We have to get out of here before she sees us; I want the element of surprise here, don't you agree?"

"I do. Look, you discreetly get back to Claire, probably go outside and up the external staircase, make my excuses; say I was taken unwell and I'll meet you both at the car," Chris ordered, retrieving the car keys from Rupert.

"Will do." With that, Rupert looked carefully around the door and made his way hurriedly across the crowded room and returned out on to the terrace via the external steps. Claire looked around upon his return approach from the unusual direction, and as with all close couples, sensed something was wrong just by the look on his face. Rupert came up behind her as she was now standing watching the second game which had just started.

"Is everything alright?" she asked "You were a long time."

"Well yes and no. Chris has taken unwell and asked to be excused, he has gone back to the car." And he continued in a quieter voice so as not to be overheard. "And I took rather longer because I just bumped into an old colleague of ours up here on vacation, you know her in fact, Siobhan Clifford." Then continued in a normal voice. "So we need to get Chris back really, poor chap's not feeling at all well."

Claire's face changed dramatically and she blanched under her tan at the mention of the woman's name. She recomposed herself quickly and continued, "Yes, of course, poor Chris, I will just say good bye to our hosts."

Their host was upset at the hurried departure but not as much as Samantha and Anita, who both silently blamed the other for ruining a good party. Bill Lester gave his wife a stern, forbidding look and she returned it with a serene, diffident smile. He looked searchingly at both Rupert and Claire, realising that this was a farce.

"I'm really sorry you all have to leave, I hope it wasn't something Chris ate that upset him?" he apologised, but with an edge to his voice. He evidently didn't like his plans going awry and people under his sway as guests, business associates or otherwise being affected. A multitude of emotions were playing across his face, of which neither Claire nor Rupert could put an exact label on.

Excuses made, they left by the external staircase which led down to the car park and made no conversation until back at the Ford, where they found Chris waiting for them in the passenger seat of the car. He was grim faced as they got in and slammed the doors on the outside world.

"Of all the people I expected to see here, she is not one of them. Fuck it, this has just taken a whole new turn. Claire, for the record, I want you out of here. Apart from anything, Siobhan knows you. Before now it was just supposition, no one really knew our true purpose or my real identity, this has now all changed. If we were seen or are seen, or our names are mentioned in conversation around the club, she will hear. You know how good she is at gathering intel, she was 14Int, for fuck's sake."

"Look, I appreciate your concern, but I'm not going. I'm staying with you two; I'll be safe either at the hotel or in your company and notwithstanding this, I am having a great time and I might be able to help." Chris shook his head in disgust.

"Okay, I wasn't going to tell you, but when you called for my help on this, I was actually in Colombia on anti-drug missions. Now, I am not going to go into the details, but this I will say, what I saw down there; what they do to people; it's inhuman. You know why the bad guys are feared? Because as tough and hard as we can be, we cannot sink to the level they do. All through history, Romans, Mongols, Nazis, Stalinists, you name it, they were all ruthless when crossed. They suppressed by fear and retaliation.

In Northern Ireland, the Regiment wanted to take out the 'Players'; we all knew who they were and it would have decimated the IRA overnight. But then we would have stooped to their level and it would have meant war. A war we would have won very quickly, but at a huge cost to propaganda. So we use the courts, due rule of law and prevention, depriving them of funding whilst protecting the innocent. But these cartels, they have no moral compass at all; if they knew of Rupert's connection to you and his involvement and they thought by harming you they could achieve their aims, they would in an instant," at this Chris clicked his fingers.

Claire had never heard Chris talk so much or so emotionally before, but she felt safe here, and felt she was far from the 'front line' Chris described.

"Chris, I really appreciate you caring, but we have one more week or so, then we return home. I am staying with Rupert and you. But thank you, I do appreciate your concern."

In response, Chris just looked at her in despair. He knew what it meant to kill, but he never considered himself a killer. Not, he thought, like the terrorists or drug cartels; they would just kill for the sake of it if they felt threatened, without compunction or remorse. He knew he would be called upon to kill again, but only on orders, and in the line of duty. Not for pleasure or because someone was disloyal or slighted the government. It was a fine moral line and not one he ever wanted to cross, although he had seen members of the Regiment go down that dark road to perdition. But how to get a civilian to understand that line and fear as a result? He could not seem to get Claire to understand, to appreciate the lack of value human life has to these people.

"OK, let's get out of here," Rupert said, breaking the spell of silence, turning the key in the ignition and firing up the Ford. "Shit, this puts a whole new complexion on everything. But let's just look at this logically for a second, now that we have got over the shock of seeing her again." They drove quietly out of the carpark but did not realise that they were being watched by more than one interested pair of eyes.

Rupert continued, "Right, we can assume that Brennan is here to link up with Siobhan. So for that reason alone, it means they are definitely planning something with the drugs that are already here.

"Doesn't take a rocket scientist to guess that they are planning to raid a location, gain some goodies and lo and behold pay back the Cartel what they owe them. Or maybe not, just keep the cash and say 'fuck you, come to Ireland to get it'. Not an attractive prospect, I grant you. It is, after all, one thing to be big and tough on your home turf, but another thing entirely when you would stick out like a sore thumb in Northern Ireland.

So, we have the IRA and FARC trying to steal the drugs; the cartels and someone up here trying to distribute the drugs; and us along with MI6, DEA and the Sheriff's department trying to stop them. Have I missed anything?" he finished sarcastically.

Chris followed up, "Yes and no. We know that the various caches of cocaine are being stored in and around Miami and presumably here, if we assume that the polo community is the distributor. Two things: someone up here has to be bossing this operation and at some point the cocaine must be packaged and distributed for shipment."

Claire interjected, "Again it either comes down to polo or property, one is regulated and the other very tight on ideas. But the two are closely linked at this point, as everyone involved at the top is involved in both sides. Talking of which, did you see Bill Lester's face as we were leaving? I didn't know if he was frightened, angry or upset."

"I know, something is not quite right there; he is clearly under pressure from one direction or another."

"Yea, that's the impression I got yesterday from our meeting. The way he went off because those boxes of polo balls were delivered to the front door not the back. "You'd think he was Hudson in Upstairs Downstairs!" Rupert quipped.

"Boxes of polo balls?" Claire queried.

"Yea, apparently they were for the Argy's; they buy 'em here cheaply, take them over with their gear and sell them in the UK for a profit. Well, when we arrived yesterday a van driver had just left and dumped tons of boxes of polo balls on the front porch. He was not a happy bunny."

Claire sat in silence, lost in thought as they drove back to the hotel.

CHAPTER 21

U pon reaching the hotel, they returned to Chris's room, pulled out the sat phone, reported in to London that Siobhan Clifford was in Florida and awaited the response which they knew would be cataclysmic. Rupert did a handwritten note reporting on the terms of Bill Lester's deal and faxed it across to Featherstone Securities for the attention of Hugh Congreave, who would pick it up in the morning, UK time. Then Rupert placed a call to Seth Meacham at the DEA.

"Meacham."

"Seth, Rupert Brett here, how are you?"

"Good thanks. What can I do for you?"

"Other way round actually. We have just had a very interesting day at the polo club."

"Congratulations, I'm very happy for you. And?"

"OK, joking aside, we have just seen and recognised the FARC agent who you know as Shivren."

"What, where?" he exclaimed.

Rupert proceeded to tell him all about her, their mission in Argentina together and how she had betrayed them, nearly causing their deaths. He did not elaborate on the nature of the mission just that it was valuable to the government.

"So, you're telling me that a rogue agent, trained by British Intelligence no less, is now loose on US soil gathering information and working in conjunction with FARC and the IRA Brigade to bring off a potential drugs heist? Outstanding!" Once he calmed down, he continued, "You and your ex-army buddy go nowhere near her, OK? We will follow this up now. I'd like a description and any other information you have on her."

Rupert complied and finished up with one final detail, "Oh and her name tag was marked as 'Linda' when she was waitressing."

"Right, you two leave it to me; we will keep eyes on and you informed, clear?"

Rupert agreed and cut the call and then dialled the New York office of HBJ, asking to speak with Matt Wood. It was uninteresting to Chris and Claire who were listening, a frustrating conversation built around short questions and long answers from Matt Wood. Rupert finally cut the call on his mobile.

"Well?" Claire asked, having gathered that something was not quite right.

"Very, very interesting. It seems that dear old Bill Lester's world is not quite as rosy as he would have us believe. He has made some shrewd deals, certainly, but like so many in a Bull market, he has expanded quicker than he should to take advantage of lucrative opportunities.

"In the course of this, he has bought, immediately re-valued and re-geared, leaving masses of debt at various junctures. But in doing so, he has made enemies. Well, you know how abrasive he can be? But most importantly the way the debt and the companies have been structured means that he needs to keep moving forward. Or it will all collapse like a house of cards, with creditors selling off loans to his enemies. More importantly, if they store up enough debt under one umbrella, they could force him to sell various or all of his companies and make a hostile take-over."

"They do that over here? Sell off the debt so easily, I mean?" Claire questioned, knowing how reluctant lenders were to pass debt on in the UK. It was very hard to buy debt, which is why the Sub-Prime market was of such interest to companies like Featherstone Securities.

"Apparently it can be a vicious game on Wall Street, think Gordon Ghekko on speed and you about have it. So the upshot is; he needs cash and liquidity, most importantly, off the record. This is why he needs our money from syndicating the debt; it can disappear or rather appear very quickly for him, he receives a 'get out jail free card' and is away again."

"If Lester needs cash that badly, could he be the one who is bossing the whole operation up here? I mean cash, liquidity, strong connections with the polo world, it all adds up." Chris voiced what they had all been thinking, as the indicators pointed stronger in that direction.

"You know, after we were briefed in London and came here first of all, we were told that we should be looking for drug smugglers. Maybe someone to coordinate everything and by the very nature of the brief probably Colombian or at least South American. I did not have it in my mind, for whatever reason, that he would be American. We seem to have missed a trick," Rupert declared.

"I know, but you were only given half the facts and as with all things you become involved with, tectonic plates constantly move. We didn't even know there was an MI6 agent in place, for God's sake," Claire declared.

They decided to go back to their own rooms, with Chris stating that he needed to run and think, Rupert agreed to join him. Exercise was starting to become addictive again now he was living with Chris. Claire stayed behind to rest and sat on the balcony with the windows open and a balmy breeze blowing into the room. Her mind started to go over everything that had been said in that precise way that made her such a good analytical agent. The telephone rang in the room.

"Yes, hello?"

"Claire it's Vikki Meredith." It took a few seconds for her to catch on and she was slightly surprised at the call.

"Oh, hello, how are you? Is everything alright?"

"Yes, well no, not really. I feel stupid, but I just need to talk. I just wondered if we could meet up and chat. I feel silly but I can't talk to my girlfriends because I have to explain everything and Daddy's out and well, oh I don't know," She trailed off.

"Don't be silly. Do you want to meet up, have a cup of coffee or something." Vikki was grateful and they agreed to meet the following day for coffee. Vikki arranged that she would come to the hotel and meet her there.

Claire replaced the receiver, more thoughtful than ever. *Poor kid,* she thought, *no one to turn to and such a horrible experience.* Then her mind returned to the events of the last twenty four hours and the connections they had discussed earlier. She knew she had missed something that was staring her in the face, something vital.

Rupert and Chris returned from their 6 mile run, relaxed and happier, although Rupert was blown trying to keep up with Chris's pace. They had a light supper in the hotel restaurant and retired early to their rooms. Happy that Rupert and Claire were ensconced for the night, Chris changed into a lightweight black polo neck sweater, black jeans and trainers, left his room and ordered a taxi to pick him up outside. Getting into the cab, he changed the destination from the one ordered at the hotel reception.

Knowing that this was to be a surveillance operation from the start, he had brought with him certain essential items which he thought may be needed: one of these assets was a pair of Yukon night vision binoculars. He liked them because they were compact, non-reflective, waterproof and, most importantly, had a true 160 yard range with high definition. They had been an innocent enough item to take through customs, along with his rather less legal lock pick set.

The taxi arrived at the polo club in 10 minutes with little traffic around and it was just getting dark. Chris paid the driver, let him pull off out of sight and moved around the back, heading for the staff quarters. Large, dense bushes lined the rear drive, highlighted against the chalk of the track. He checked around him, then moved smoothly in between them and settled himself down with a good view of the entrance to the staff accommodation. Various staff came and went, but Chris was patient; he had been in far worse observation posts.

Just after midnight his patience was rewarded. Looking through the binoculars he saw a car pull up and the dark figure of Tir Brennan get out, walking cautiously around the staff accommodation, carefully knocking discreetly on one of the bungalow doors. Brennan immediately retreated so as not to be illuminated by the light thrown from inside the building. But when Siobhan Clifford opened the door no light showed. Brennan slipped quickly inside and the door closed. Chris set the binoculars down and smiled to himself, it was not a pleasant expression.

Checking out the surrounding accommodation, he realised that there was nowhere safe to try to eaves drop, so he made his way to the car Brennan arrived in, made a note of the number and returned to his hide. Inside the cabin, an old friendship was being renewed; Brennan and Clifford hugged each other like the old friends they were.

"Tir," she said in his embrace, "it's so good to see you after so long, you look good, man."

He held her at arm's length. "And so do you, wee lady. God it's been awhile; when they told me your name I was thinkin' back to the past, all so long ago. But seein' you now, here, it brings it all back. Listen, I was sorry to hear about Michael."

Her face clouded for a moment. "Fuckin' Brits, they killed him. Threw him through a window, it was murder and they called it an accident. Bastards!" She spat the word out.

"I know, but he was a good man and a great man to the Cause."

She nodded, closing the subject and they caught up on friends and events since they last met. Finally, she broke the reverie, "Now, we haven't tons of time. I need to fill you in on everything I've learned. You know the drugs are here, right?" He nodded. "Well I overheard some of the Argys talking around the bar. It's amazing what they'll say when they don't think you can understand Spanish. The drugs are being shipped out at the end of the tournament. But I don't know how yet, I might need to sleep with one of them to find out. No, don't look at me like that, it means nothing, you know how I feel, I still prefer my own kind. An' I'll geld him if gets rough, believe me." Brennan knew that she was the girl to do it.

"But what I suspect is that they store the cocaine in various caches around the area, all separate and then they are shipped to the couriers. So we need the locations of the storage depots, hit them and away. We could net a big haul maybe two or three tons. Far more than you lost to the Brits."

"Good work, Siobhan.

"Well some of it is supposition, but it amazing what the Argy's let slip in front of a bit of skirt, with a few clever questions."

"I will get the local guys on to it; they have ears all over the place, especially on haulage. You keep looking from your side and we'll keep in contact via mobile."

"But if I'm right and it is Argy connected, it may be held on a number of polo ranches here. Tons of space to hide stuff and all above board, it's perfect cover. I'll see if I can get in with one of the players or grooms."

"You be careful, these are bad people and we are playing on their ground. I don't want to lose you and your brother."

"Tir, I've been doin' this a long time, I know the craic by now. Trust me, OK?"

They hugged one more time, turned off the lights and Siobhan opened the door, stepped out on to the porch. She pulled out a cigarette, lit up and stood quietly smoking and listening. When all was quiet she flicked the lighter once by her side and Brennan slipped quietly away into the shadows. Stopping by his car, he used the key instead of the alarm fob so no lights showed as the locks popped open. Then he hesitated, there was that old feeling again: the hunter and the hunted developed it, that almost imperceptible sixth sense that warns you of danger. He looked around, carefully scanning each block of surrounding scenery as his hand rested behind his back on the butt of the Glock tucked into his waistband.

His eyes detected nothing untoward under the dim car park lights. He shook his head reflexively, *must be getting old*, he thought. But the feeling was still there. He started the engine and pulled quietly away.

Seeing Brennan depart, Chris ordered a taxi using his mobile and met it at the entrance to the club away from prying eyes.

CHAPTER 22

The following day, Chris woke and made a call to London. Getting through to Johnston, he updated him on all that had occurred since the message of the previous evening.

"This is escalating out of control. Are you armed? Do you need more back up?" he asked.

"No, I haven't been able to pick anything up, but you can bet your life Brennan and Siobhan are. Can you make arrangements at the Consul? I'd like a legal permit as well."

"Will do, now something else, have you received the original photos taken by Josh Harding?" Chris said that they had not arrived and Johnston continued. "Well when they do arrive, take a close look, because we have just had the detailed autopsy report back from the French security services and it shows two compounds in the body of the late Vicomte: one is talcum powder and the other is plastic." he let the bombshell sink in while waiting for Chris's comment.

"Well dealers often cut the product with talc, makes it go further, but it doesn't do a whole lot of good for the users, I grant you. But plastic? What the hell is that all about?"

"You will remember that the objects in the photo looked like plastic? Well I believe that somehow that plastic is getting into the cocaine and that will be the clue as to how they are transporting it. Have you kept the DEA agent informed of everything you are doing? Because you're going to need his help if this blows up. That is what he is there for, so use him." Johnston ordered. Chris confirmed that they had and whilst not being best mates, they had a reasonable working relationship.

"Good because he comes highly recommended, you don't get into the Special Operations Section of the DEA without being a top player," he said.

"No, understood, I can confirm he is in the loop."

"Right, let me know when you get the photos and I will make arrangements at the Consul."

Chris cut the call and locked the sat phone back in the briefcase. Hearing a knock on the door, he opened it to find Rupert and Claire there, ready for breakfast.

"Come in a minute," he said and explained to them everything that had occurred yesterday evening and the information contained within the autopsy report.

"So you went out and saw Brennan and Siobhan meet up?" Rupert asked aghast. "Why didn't you tell me? I could have given back up."

"No, this is my job and it is what I am trained for. With the greatest respect, Rupert, you are not a covert operative. I'm better by myself and if anything blew up, I'd be the one to have to tell Claire, frightening thought," he joked, making light of it.

Claire, in turn, raised an eyebrow, then the internal phone rang before she could comment. Chris answered, thanked the receptionist and replaced the receiver. "There is a package for me downstairs, probably the photos. Let's go and have a look."

Over breakfast, in a quiet corner of the dining room, they looked at the original photographs which had much better definition than the faxed copies. Again, they saw the seemingly plastic cones.

"But they're the same, white plastic cones with the tops cut off." Claire commented quietly, unheard above the din of fellow diners.

"Yea, they look like the wooden dowels I use in woodworking when you put a screw in, countersink it and plug with a dowel to hide the screw."

"Really, Chris, you never cease to amaze me, you work with wood?" Claire asked.

"Yea, I know, but it helps me relax after a mission. Some guys go out and get pissed all the time. Me, I like the calm of it, just me working with my hands and the wood. A huge contrast I know but there we are."

Claire suddenly had an idea: "You know if the balls were hollow, you could fill them with cocaine and plug the hole with these." She pointed to the photograph. "There is no way you could break them and put them back together; it would show and you would be vulnerable at customs. But these are the only things that polo players have that are made of plastic.

"Don't shout me down for this, but I think that I should go down to Dallas Polo, see the guy and ask him if there is any way that it could be done. I mean we don't even know how the balls are made do we?" Claire said.

"That's a really good idea. But I will go, not you, I want you out of harm's way, he might be in on it for all you know," Rupert decided.

"No way," she scoffed at the idea. "I'll pretend I am a journalist working for *Polo Express Magazine*. I know a girl on the staff and she will back me up if I get challenged and neither of you two know enough to get away with it. Also, think about it, what is going to happen in Dallas? The action is all up here."

"Yea, that's what Kennedy thought," Chris quipped sarcastically. But after much arguing, Claire finally got her way and spoke with Gus Rowley head of Dallas Polo and arranged to go down there and meet with him. He was delighted to show her around, but warned there were things he was not prepared to discuss about the manufacturing process.

Rupert and Chris were due to leave after breakfast for a legal meeting on the Bill Lester & Featherstone Securities deal. Claire awaited the arrival of Vikki Meredith, swam endless relaxed lengths of the pool in an effortless manner obtainable only by natural swimmers. She paused and came to the side of the pool, the aquamarine of the water highlighting her beautiful green eyes. Rupert bent down and kissed her, then the green eyed mermaid slid away and he watched in admiration as she resumed swimming, it was an enviable skill, one that he could never emulate, no matter how he tried.

"Damn, wish I could swim like that," he commented. Chris just smiled; as part of his SAS training, he'd had to do sea swims in far from perfect conditions, yet for Rupert, swimming had always been a trial and he would never be able to glide through the water like his wife. They left to head for the meeting.

An hour later Vikki arrived looking wan, with bags under her eyes, making her appear older than her 21 years. Upon seeing Claire, she rushed up and hugged her intensely, seeking solace in the contact with another human being. They walked arm in arm to the shade of a pool side umbrella and ordered coffee.

"Thank you for letting me come over and see you. It is just so difficult having to explain to friends; my father isn't there much and try as he might, he is just not my Mother."

"Where is she?" Claire asked.

"She died when I was young, I don't even remember her it was so long ago. So Daddy has brought me up all by himself and has done a great job, but some things he can't do. Sorry, I sound rather neurotic, I guess."

"No not all," Claire intoned sympathetically, "Sometimes it's just good to talk it all out."

Vikki smiled for the first time since Claire had seen her and continued to talk through everything, admitting that whilst she and Josh hadn't known each other long, she had feelings for him and it had been such a shock seeing him smashed into a ragged, bloody heap on the track.

"And you still think that Rizzo had something to do with it?" Claire asked, steering her in the direction she wanted the conversation to go.

"Yes, he is such a creep. He didn't seem really upset and as I told you before, Josh had had a couple of run ins with him, he tried to get aggressive with him at one point. Oh, I don't know, it all seems so odd," she finished lamely.

Claire decided to fish deeper. "Is there anything else? I mean the sheriff seemed keen to get to the bottom of it. Has anything unusual happened at the ranch? Just something that Josh may have seen that might have got him into trouble?"

Vikki frowned suspiciously. "Do you know something you're not telling me?" she asked.

Claire thought on her feet quickly and decided to weave truth with fiction. "Well sort of, you see, when Rupert spoke to Josh's parents, they said he had written a letter saying that drugs were pretty rampant amongst the Argys. So I just put two and two together and wondered if they were dealing and Josh had found where they hid them. I'm just clutching at straws for a motive, I suppose, if indeed Rizzo was to blame."

"I see, well I can't think where they would hide them, if that were the case."

"Well if it helps find the answer to Josh's death, why don't we go and have a look, search around a bit? All the Argys will be at the club getting ready for a game now." She looked at her watch. "It starts in an hour." Claire held her breath awaiting the response. Vikki thought for a moment.

"Sure, why not? It will give me something positive to do and you can have lunch with me at home."

"Perfect, I've always wanted to play detective. Let me just leave a note for Rupert and I'll be back down in a minute."

Claire returned five minutes later having changed into a pair of jeans and a polo shirt. They left in Vikki's BMW and arrived at the Meredith ranch to find it, as suspected, virtually deserted bar one groom who was out on exercise. Parking the car in the car port, they walked down to the yard and stables.

"Good, he's just started the set so that will give us at least half an hour to look around," Vikki commented. They approached the two lines of stables which in total housed around forty horses. They were in typical linear formation, pitched rooves overlapped the rows and there were large doors at each end creating shelter from the weather. At the end of each row was a tack and feed room. Everything looked tidy, even the stray hay and straw were all swept up.

"Wow, it is immaculate. Whatever faults Rizzo may have, he is certainly a good head lad, if this is anything to go by," Claire commented. "You feel you could eat your food off the floor, everything is so clean."

"Yea, if only he was as nice to humans as he is to the horses," Vikki said. They began a methodical search looking in all the stables and half way down Claire was about to enter the middle box.

"No don't go in there!" Vikki called urgently, seeing her move towards the door. "That is the stallion's 'tease box'. We bring the mare in this side and then slide the partition away and they meet up. But he is dangerous, a groom was badly kicked and bitten last year. Terrible, he will never be the same again." She shuddered at the thought.

"How awful, thanks for the warning." She peered through the open top door and could see nothing untoward; no boxes or anything that shouldn't be there. "Why do you keep him if he is such a brute?" she asked.

"Oh because he is a great stallion with fantastic lines and throws great foals. They all seem to inherit his athleticism and as long as we geld them early, they are much easier to handle than him."

"I see. Well rather you than me," Claire retorted. They continued searching, but nothing was in evidence anywhere. Then Claire spotted two horse boxes, one of which had clearly seen better days.

"What about those?" She asked pointing at the two lorries.

"Oh sure although the old one is just used to transport everything to and from the airport when we take the grooms back. It easily carries all their stuff so we only need to use one driver. Daddy sometimes takes them. They all pile in with their gear and off they go."

"Well, let's have a look." They walked up to the rear of the shabby lorry, undid the locking catches and pulled at the canter-levered rear ramp. Used to the heavy, unbalanced ramps on some English lorries, Claire was wary but it swung down easily, stopping just short of the floor. There at the back, covered with an old tarp, were the boxes of polo balls just as Chris and Rupert had described arriving at Bill Lester's house.

"Polo balls!" she cried, jumped onto the ramp and marching to the back, pulling down one of the boxes. "Let's see if they really are balls or there is something else hidden in the boxes. Here, you try another one, maybe from the bottom, let's see if there is anything suspicious."

Vikki, with some difficulty, pulled a box from the base of the pile and with a long nail, slit the tape holding the flaps closed. Both women carefully pulled open the flaps and inside were dozens of pure, perfect white spheres, each stamped with the legend *Dallas Polo* in bright red ink. Claire pulled one out. It was perfect, unused and certainly appeared not to have been tampered with. The usual minute seam ran around the circumference and at one point there was the tiny almost imperceptible mark where the plastic had been formed as part of the manufacturing process.

She tossed it lightly in the air a couple of times, feeling the almost powdery surface of a new polo ball. She decided that it might be a little heavier than she remembered, but not enough to cause suspicion. She rummaged around to see if anything was hidden beneath, but to no avail.

"Bugger, nothing. I was sure we would find something."

"Same here. Oh well, it was worth a try. Come on," she urged looking at her watch, "he could be back off his set at any moment."

They repacked the boxes, ensuring they were at the back so that the broken seals were not obvious, re-set the tarp, closed the ramp and were walking innocently back down the drive as the groom rode back from the track in charge of five sweaty horses.

"*Hola*," he called, smiling as he passed, slouched in the saddle. The two women responded in kind, smiling and waving at him in salutation, offering no reason for Claire's presence.

"Well, that's that. Lunch?" Vikki offered as they returned to the main house. Vikki threw a salad together and they settled down to lunch with a crisp glass of white wine. Claire sipped it appreciatively.

"Mmh, what's this?" she asked.

"Ah, it's one of daddy's favourites, a Chardonnay from Santa Barbara." With that she got up from the table and fetched the bottle from the fridge, placing it in front of Claire.

Au Bon Climat she read. "I'll have to remember that and see if I can find it in England." She was offered some more by Vikki. "No, thank you, I have the baby to think of, although it is very tempting."

"Sorry, I forgot." Vikki said. "So where do we go from here? I mean we are no further forward, are we? Only our suspicions; but I still think Rizzo is a bad guy and somehow caused Josh's death."

"Maybe it was just drugs in his room or a genuine accident. Whatever, I am sure we will get to the bottom of it before we leave." She was about to tell Vikki she was off to Dallas tomorrow but something held her back, Chris's warning came back to her. It wasn't that she didn't trust Vikki, but she may just say something out of turn which may be heard by the wrong ears, she considered.

Her mobile rang insistently, breaking into the conversation. It was Rupert checking that she was alright and that nothing untoward had happened. He had clearly found her note and did not appear very happy. She assured him everything was fine and that she would be back soon.

With lunch over, Vikki and Claire started the return journey back to the hotel. As they were leaving, they passed the polo lorries returning from the game and Rizzo, who was driving, seemed to pay particular attention to Claire, noting her presence in Vikki's car. Claire felt her skin crawl and she was glad to be leaving.

"That guy gives me the creeps, I know why you don't like him," she confided. Upon reaching the hotel, they parted like old friends, with Claire offering a few final words of advice: "Keep your chin up and if you need to chat or bawl your eyes out, just call me, we're around for the next week."

"Thanks, Claire, it's been great to chat and everything. Thank you." With one last hug she was gone. *Oh dear,* Claire thought, *I feel so old, like an aged aunt.*

CHAPTER 23

Claire had plenty of time to reflect upon the previous day whilst taking the 3 hour flight to Dallas airport. Upon returning to the hotel she had been interrogated by both Rupert and Chris, neither of whom were at all pleased that she had gone off by herself. Her pleas of safety whilst in Vikki's company had fallen on deaf ears. Chris had reminded her that he had said no meetings with anyone, no matter how innocent and that this was not a game. She had been chagrined by their response, but hadn't felt at all in danger, she thought to herself. What was worse, to her mind, was that it all appeared to have been a waste of time as, apart from seeing the cache of polo balls, nothing else positive had come out of the search.

She felt petulant at the time and had departed on not the best of terms with Rupert, who was cross with concern at what he regarded as a careless attitude. *Still*, she thought, *she was in Dallas now.*

Claire had arranged to meet with the owner of Dallas Polo, Gus Rowley, at his main store on the outskirts of Dallas. Passing through the city in the taxi, she faced an array of Lego-like towers, interspersed with old Brownstone buildings gilded with turrets and spires. The vast city, ribboned with wide streets and squares of green, was set against the backdrop of the impressive East Fork Trinity River, which meandered lazily through the urban landscape, dividing it in two.

The taxi stopped outside a huge retail warehouse on an out-of-town shopping complex. She estimated that it must be about ten thousand square feet and all dedicated to polo. Stepping through into the air-conditioned store, Claire felt like Holly Golightly going into Tiffany's. Entering, she breathed in the wonderful aromas of new leather, fresh cloth, saddle soap and a million other familiar smells that she adored. It was a clever array, beautifully and enticingly lit.

Walking through the main isle, she reached the cash desk and asked to speak with Gus Rowley. About two minutes later a broad individual walked down the steps from an upstairs office. Claire saw a craggy man in his late fifties, greying, with a paunch and wearing a check shirt under a cream coloured hunting waistcoat. He extended a large, ham-like hand and introduced himself.

"Mrs Brett, I'm very pleased to meet you, Gus Rowley." His voice was a rich treacle of southern hospitality.

"How do you do?" she responded. "Claire Brett."

"Very well, thank you. D'you find us OK?"

"Oh yes, no problem and what a wonderful shop," she gushed "I could spend hours here, but my husband probably wouldn't like the damage to our bank balance!" she joked.

"Yep, we're pretty proud of it, but please come on up and we can talk." They went up the stairs to his office and Rowley ushered Claire inside. "Please ma'am, take a seat. Now, can I get you a drink, coffee, tea?"

Claire accepted a tea, which he ordered from his secretary. Then he turned his shrewd, business-like eyes on to her.

"Now what can I do for you?" he asked. Claire rolled out the story she had rehearsed, saying she was working freelance for *Polo*

Express Magazine which, of course, Rowley had heard of. He had in fact checked with her 'Sub Editor' Charlotte Green whom luckily she had warned about what she was planning. Charlotte had actually been delighted and wanted a story of whatever she wrote, so all was well. Claire retrieved a notebook and asked various questions, then led on to the equipment and specifically polo balls. Rowley was delighted to explain the process.

"Now I believe you mentioned on the phone that you'd like to see the factory and manufacturing process?"

"Yes, if that is possible? It would be perfect; I've always been puzzled on how you get all the little bubbles inside," she commented disingenuously, smiling in a flirty manner and using all her feminine charm. He responded in kind and offered to drive her to the factory. Leaving the store, they drove in his huge Chevy pickup truck. Despite his courteous manner, Claire found him slightly defensive, as though he were a little suspicious or evasive, she couldn't make up her mind which.

They made small talk in the car, where Claire prattled with enthusiasm about polo and how much she had enjoyed the games at Palm Beach. After around ten minutes, they pulled into one of the more industrial areas. They arrived at an innocuous, white painted factory, with high fencing, razor wire and security cameras.

"A lot of security, do have trouble here or just cautious?" Claire asked pointing at the cameras.

"Well, there is a lot of value here and it is not so much the product, more the method of production. We have spent a lot of time and money refining what we do. There are competitors who would love to know exactly how we make the balls and with what composites."

"Really? Composites, I thought it was just plastic," she commented, noticing that there was no sign defining the name of the company, just a unit number. The surveyor in Claire took in all the details: *large site, comparatively small building, good distri-bution space with large warehouses to the rear and efficient through traffic circulation,* she thought. At the Inward gate, a security guard acknowledged Gus Rowley with a small ironic salute. The premises were busy: a large truck with the words *Resin Plastics* was leaving through the Goods Outwards gate and various delivery vans were being loaded with boxes of polo balls from side loading doors.

Rowley continued: "Now we share the factory with other plastics manufacturers so I will just show you our section of the premises. Although I would still ask that you take no photos, the process is secret and therefore well protected." He passed her through the reception area and a harsh, artificial smell assailed her nostrils. It was an unpleasant carcinogenic aroma that to Claire's olfactory senses, reminded her of burning acrid rubber or extinguished candles. She wrinkled her nose in disgust. Rowley noticed.

"Yep, takes a bit of getting used to," he smiled. The factory floor was fitted with a number of moulding machines. They stood about eye height and comprised of a hopper at one end filled with small, pea-shaped white pellets of plastic. There was a long arm wrapped around with cables and tubes leading to the main bulk of the machine, which could be viewed internally through a large Perspex safety square. The internals of the machine were a series of blocks of moulds, bolted together, that received the molten plastic.

"These poly-propylene pellets," he said, pointing at the small beads of pea-shaped plastic in the hopper feeder, "get pushed through the heated tubes and mixed with talcum powder, then forced through into the moulds," he explained, pointing to the Perspex viewing panel. The machine slid along, small injectors entered the moulds, injecting, then retreating for the next stage as the mould moved, ejecting the spheres ready for the next batch. The moulds were broken by the operator, balls appeared in a chute and were collected at the back of the machine. Claire instinctively went to pick one up from the net, but Gus Corey stayed her hand.

"I wouldn't do that; they are still very hot, reaches many thousands of degrees," he warned.

"Ah, thank you. Did I hear correctly that you said 'talcum powder'?" she shouted above the noise of the machinery.

"Yes, we use it to help the blowing process. But how much and how it is introduced, is a secret. That is what makes our balls so perfect."

"Ah, yes I see," Claire smiled conspiratorially. "It is funny because I always imagined that tiny dimple to a be a plug, but I see now it is just the area where the injector retracts after blowing in the liquid plastic."

"Just so, the actual method of plastic moulding is not that complicated," he answered modestly.

"And the moulds, how are they put together?" she asked having seen the large blocks of metal within the machine which the liquid plastic was injected into. As an answer, he motioned her to follow him away from the noise and into another part of the factory. Through the next door, they saw technicians working on mould assembly and maintenance.

"Hi Steve, can we just show this lady the moulds for a second?" asked Rowley.

The man nodded and explained, "Sure. The moulds are split into these sections and bolted together to form the circular mould for the balls to form in." He exposed the half assembled mould the right way up. "And this tiny hole here," he indicated, "is where the injector inserts and blows in the liquid plastic. It then retracts and you have a polo ball."

Claire realised it was a simplified explanation, but she understood the general principle. She decided to push her luck, and explore a private theory, one she had not even discussed with Rupert and Chris: "So, just for the sake of argument, if one wanted to be sneaky, and hide say, a surprise inside. Do you think it would be possible to hollow out a ball and put something in and then seal it back up?" The two men smiled at each other, thinking that they were being wound up by some ditzy English woman.

"No ma'am. Well you would need to find a way to get in and out without breaking the ball open. A drill sure, would get you inside but to hollow it out? What were you thinking of, a liquid, like a surprise at a party, filling balloons with water?" he laughed. Claire went along and joined in.

"Oh something like that. I would love to play a trick on my husband and have it explode with a purple dye when he hits it." she laughed. Steve smiled indulgently in response.

"Well, you could drill in and yes, if you got a plastic plug, shaped like a cone, pushed it in and cut it off at the outside, that might do the trick." *And there it was*, Claire thought, *the answer to part of the puzzle, which had been staring them in the face all along. All I need to do now is find out how they hollow out the balls before putting in the plastic plugs, like those that poor Josh Harding found.* She cheered inwardly.

The rest of the tour around was perfunctory and Claire couldn't wait to get away and report back to Rupert and Chris what she had found out. Back at the main store, she was just awaiting a taxi to arrive and going over final notes with Gus for her 'article', when a thought occurred to her.

"And you distribute all over the world, I take it?"

"Yes ma'am," Rowley replied, the old easy charm back now he realised she wasn't going to steal his secrets. "We distribute from here to pretty much any country in the world where polo is played."

Trying to sound bland, she phrased her next question carefully. "Ah yes, I saw boxes of balls arriving at Bill Lester's and

Meredith's ranch. Apparently the Argys sell them in the UK." The shutters came down again, he clearly did not like the way the conversation was going.

"As I said, we sell all over the place. We have a distribution centre up in Palm Beach and if some Argy's want to buy a large quantity to take with them to the UK, that is their business. A sale is a sale for us, of course, it is easier and less trouble to sell in the States than abroad," he finished defensively.

"Oh, of course, why not? I mean, business is business. It would be great to get the angle of an international distributor and get a few shots of the distribution warehouse back in Florida. Then we could just use it as the basis of the US operation and our readers wouldn't be any the wiser," she asked.

"Yea sure, why not, I have no problem with photos of the distribution space. I'll give you the address and I'll tell the manager up there to expect you," he replied, back on stable ground again.

"And finally, could you get your secretary to take a couple of you and me, maybe shaking hands, you know the sort of thing."

"Certainly ma'am." The equilibrium returned to his manner. They finished with contact numbers, an address in Florida close to Miami and some photos. Pleasantries finished, Claire thanked Gus Rowley for all his time and left in the taxi. Her head was whirring with thoughts and Claire started to make a phone call on her mobile, then remembering Chris's words of caution, waited until she was booked into her flight at the airport.

"Rupert? Darling, it's me. I've got lots to tell; I know how they are moving the drugs." As she said this, she looked around furtively in case anyone overheard.

"Not on the mobile," Rupert cautioned "Wait until you get back here."

Slightly chagrined, Claire cut the call, her enthusiasm dampened. *Damn*, she thought, *I just want to get back and tell them*. All through the flight home her mind toiled with the problem of how to hollow out a polo ball leaving no mark other than a small entry hole. Eager to catch up with Rupert, she sprang into his arms at the arrivals section of the airport.

"God, it's good to have you back, I am sorry we quarrelled before you left," he breathed, holding her tightly. She looked up at him, an excited look in her eyes. "Me too. Now come on, I've got so much to tell you." They walked arm in arm to the waiting car. The watcher picked up his mobile phone.

"*Si*, I tailed the Englishman, *Señor* Brett, they just left the airport. His wife just came in on the flight from Dallas." He waited for instructions and responded, "*Muy bien.*"

The call ended and the man at the other end immediately dialled another number and reported the movements to the boss of the drug operation north of the border. He was tense, aware of how close they were and how much depended on the outcome of the next few days.

"What is happening about the woman, *Shivren*, Siobhan or whatever her name is?"

"Don't worry about her, she is being watched, we have her under control. I am more concerned about the two Englishmen at the moment. We'll push things and see how they jump."

On leaving the airport, Rupert joined the I95 route back up to Palm Beach, setting the cruise control and driving on auto pilot as he listened carefully to all that Claire had learned during her time in Dallas. He was engrossed in her story, amazed at how much she had learned in such a short space of time.

"I know," she enthused, "it is like that Mosaic thing that Chris mentioned to us."

"The what?"

"You know when he described how they are trained against people asking questions from different angles and by asking the same thing differently or putting pieces of the puzzle together, with seemingly innocuous questions, one is able to build a complete picture without the person realising what they have given away. It is called *mosaic*. Interestingly, I think we do it all the time as agents, without even realising it, just gathering-"

Her speech was cut off as the car was smashed forward with a thud and Claire screamed as the seat belt bit into her chest. Rupert jolted with a start, also thrown against the seatbelt, crushing the wind out of him as his arms braced against the steering wheel. He had not been concentrating, rolling along at a steady 60 mph, letting the cruise control do its job with cars overtaking them. But now in his rear view mirror, the looming mass of a huge Tans Am pick-up truck with a silver, snarling front grill showed in his rear view mirror. He made the mistake of every amateur driver in this scenario: he put the brakes on, trying to stop.

"What the hell?" he cried as his foot hit the brake pedal and the automatic transmission tried to assist his efforts.

This was exactly what the driver of the Trans Am wanted; he flicked the wheel and accelerated. Rupert assumed for a minute that it had been a genuine accident, and that the driver had pulled away as he decelerated to thirty. But that was only for a moment: the huge red monster smashed sideways into the Ford, causing it to weave, closing the distance to the curb and the short slope down to the ocean on the right hand side. Rupert fought the steering wheel, over correcting and finally getting control just before the curb caught the road wheels.

He stole a quick look sideways, just in time to see the large red wing aiming for him again. Adrenalin surging through his body, he had a brief second to anticipate the collision and turn the steering wheel into the oncoming assault. The smash of the second impact was harder, with a grind and banshee-like screech of metal, as the two cars briefly locked and broke apart. Claire screamed again and then fell silent as her head hit the side window with a sickening thud.

Rupert screamed at her, "Bend forward, lock your hands behind your neck and pull your feet back, now!" In a semi daze, she obeyed his instructions and at the same time Rupert yanked back the transmission leaver into second and floored the accelerator. The mighty 7.3 litre engine roared, spinning the rear wheels with torque as the car lurched forward. He nearly made it. The third run by the Trans Am was off target, barely catching the rear wing of the pickup, which was much lighter at the back. It had the desired effect as the Ford fishtailed, whipping right, left and with a final lurch, bumping up the curb and crashing down the slope to the waiting ocean.

Rupert fought vainly to gain control, trying to right the sideways slide as the massive beast splashed into the water almost head on, ploughing up to the bonnet as the sand and water finally braked the car to a halt. The seals were broken on the driver's side and water was pouring in.

Rupert turned to Claire, fearing the worst. He reached over, gently bringing her back upright, her fingers till locked behind her neck.

"Claire, Claire!" he cried, his eyes wide with fear. "Please don't do this to me, please God let her be alright." He saw her chest gently rise and fall as tears of relief ran down his face. Then, he fought with the seat belt release, pushed his door open to a rush of water and sloshed around to her door, fighting the pressure of the ocean. Suddenly, he felt a presence beside him; other drivers had stopped to help and a strong, beefy arm pulled back on the door, aiding his efforts.

"Don't worry, buddy, we'll get her out, just take it easy, she may have injuries," the man said. Rupert, still in shock, muttered a thank you as others appeared. Claire was gently manhandled out of the car between Rupert and the rescuer and laid carefully on the waterside. She then moaned and Rupert cried with relief. The anonymous rescuer returned to the car, then reappeared with Claire's hand bag and Rupert's mobile phone, which had remained dry on the dashboard.

"Do you want to call 911 just in case? I'm sure someone else has done it already, but better to be on the safe side. Would you like me to call? This is one of my regular routes and I know exactly where we are."

"Uh, yes, yes please if you would," Rupert responded.

CHAPTER 24

An hour after the accident, Rupert was sat in the waiting area of the local hospital when he suddenly thought about Chris Adams.

"Shit, I am so stupid," he murmured out loud, pulling his mobile phone open and walking to where he could get reception away from prying ears.

It answered on the second ring. "Hi Rups, where are you? Is the traffic bad or what?" Chris asked.

"In a manner of speaking," Rupert replied darkly. He then proceeded to explain everything that had happened to which Chris listened without interruption, his anger mounting as the conversation went on. Finishing, Rupert finally thanked Chris for saving his life yet again.

"You're life! Has that bump on the head addled your brain? What the fuck are you talking about? I should have been there to protect you!"

"Hah, no, because I followed your advice, remember? You always said get something 'big and heavy' to drive as you never know when you are going to need it! Well, if I had been in a normal saloon we would both be dead now. So thank you again."

Chris laughed drily despite himself. "Well it's good that you listen to me sometimes. Now are you sure that it was a red Trans Am? I don't suppose you got the registration number?"

"No chance, give me a break. Anyway, it's a one plate state, so the number plate is only on the back, by which time we were heading for a swim so I didn't get chance to look."

"OK but what about Claire, is she OK? And more importantly, who is guarding her? She could be targeted again because now they know where she has been and it was probably her they were trying to stop. She was obviously on the right track with her polo balls idea," Chris added, concerned.

"They are doing tests at the moment, I will know in a while. But she is alive and that is the main thing, God I was worried," Rupert admitted. "But as to a guard, I'm here and one of Sheriff Reed's deputies is here as well. It just fell within his area of jurisdiction and he is making enquiries about the Trans Am now. He's a good guy and so were the people who stopped to help after the crash. Especially the trucker, he just pulled open the door like it was a Wendy house. I owe him a beer. Chris, I am going to go and see how Claire is doing, see if there is any news."

"Yes, of course, just one thing, did you get a look at the driver at all?"

Rupert cast his mind back and replayed the film in his head, seeing just before the impact the image of an Hispanic face. "Yes," he cried. "Latino definitely; so it is to do with drugs, not some chance road rage attack."

"I see," was the only comment that Chris made. "Now you take care of Claire, OK?"

Rupert assured him that he would and rang off. Chris thought long and hard about what had occurred and was angry. Claire was very dear to him and this is what he had been afraid of. His next call was to Seth Meacham.

The DEA agent's personal line rang twice and Meacham answered. Chris explained all that had happened, including the reason for the trip to Dallas Polo and Claire's theory about the balls. Meacham swore crudely at the information and vowed to get whoever had tried to kill Rupert and Claire.

"You still think that, somehow, the polo crew is in on this? As I said, we have had sniffer dogs at the airport when they have been through and nothing. Zip. If they have a way of sealing the stuff without trace into a perfectly new ball, in sufficient quantities, they must be magicians," he exclaimed. "I still don't see it, but there must be a connection somewhere. But listen, from now on, you leave this to us, that goes for Brennan and this Siobhan Clifford woman too."

"What have you found out there, have they been in contact?" he asked disingenuously, knowing full well that they had.

"We believe so; we've had eyes on her and are trying to track her mobile calls, but she changes the number regularly. As I say, leave it to us," he ordered. They cut the call and Chris was lost in thought. He felt he had failed Claire; he should have foreseen the play. *He should have been in the car, better still, picked her up from the airport,* he thought and suddenly felt he was behind the game. He didn't like the feeling and vowed to do better. At the moment he was angry and murderous, neither emotion he recognised would do him any favours. He changed and went for a run, pounding away the miles and turning everything over in his mind.

CHAPTER 25

LONDON

Simon Johnston had not been happy when he received the report from Florida. He was cross with Sergeant Adams for not being more proactive and he was furious for the danger and the close possibility of having another two deaths on his hands. Signals had placed the report at 2.10am GMT and it was now 8.20am. Looking at his wristwatch, Johnston calculated it would be about two o'clock in the morning there, but impatient as he was, there was no point in waking Adams up to give him a bollocking. He called Webster instead and fed him all the information.

"So it seems Mrs Brett's hunch about the polo balls was correct. But how the devil are they doing it? That's what I want to know."

"Don't we all. But if I know Brett and Adams, they will now move heaven and earth to find out and woe betide anybody who gets in their way. What also concerns me is how Brennan and Clifford fit into all this. Despite the DEA promising to keep tabs, I want to know first-hand."

* * *

BOGOTA

The news that Pablo Rojas had to impart was good. He was pleased as he approached the estancia on the shores of the *Emblase del Muna* with no trepidation this time. Everything was working out and soon the shipments would be on their way to the UK and beyond. He headed towards the gates of the *ranchera* which were blocked and closed, guarded by two men carrying automatic rifles and a third standing back with an automatic machine pistol and a two way radio. This man called it in as Rojas approached in the Land Cruiser, which rumbled to a halt blocked by the gates.

Seeing it was Rojas, they waved him through, the third guard reporting his approach. The long dusty drive led to the house, set amongst lush fields and a courtyard. Off to the left were adobe stables and a large corral where Ballesteros was watching his eldest daughter have a riding lesson on a pony. He saw Rojas drive up and turned back to his daughter, cheering as she jumped over a small cavaletti led by her instructor.

"Bravo, Sylvi, bravo!" His face all smiles and encouragement. No one seeing the scene would believe that the same doting father was a killer, drug smuggler and about to order another murder in his quest for a fortune.

"Pablo, it is good to see you. A dusty journey no? Come, let's get in the shade." He walked over to the large veranda bordering the estancia. Rojas considered what a different man the drug patron was down here with his family.

"*Si patron.* I have news, the *cringo* woman was put in hospital and they are frightened, we think they will now go home. She is pregnant and not well. She went to see Dallas Polo asking questions. She got nothing from there, just notes for a magazine article. But we do not want her sniffing around north of the border."

"The surveyors, the other one, you said there were two. What of him?"

"He seems to make no trouble and he is not the boss. We are leading him away."

"Why not just kill him?"

"Because *patron*, he is British and connected to the government. If we do, it will make things difficult and could jeopardise the shipment. No unnecessary attention until the shipments leave."

"OK, I leave it to you. And the FARC agent, *Shivren*?"

"We will kill her as planned, we have it all in place and Brennan will follow. Then we will send a message to the IRA."

"*Bueno.*"

* * *

PALM BEACH

At that moment, Siobhan Clifford was calling Brennan on one of the disposable pay as you go mobiles.

"Tir? It's me, listen. I have been working on the guy I told you about, the Argy groom. Yea, on Sunday I'm off there for an *asado*, Monday is polo day off so they always have one. Yea it's at the Meredith ranch. I'll shag him and then look around, I know what I'm doin', don't worry."

Brennan responded with unusual concern. "I don't want to lose you as well as your brother. You know when I left your apartment the other night I had that feelin'; it's never been wrong. I couldn't see anybody, I listened and watched but I know someone was watching."

"Ah, quit you're worry'in. I'll be fine. I gotta go. I'll be in touch." She cut the call and thought carefully through her plans. What niggled at the back of her mind was she too had the same feeling when he had visited her that night, but no one was evident. Too many tense moments on the streets of Belfast had ingrained the instinct into her, she knew better than to ignore it. She pulled the Beretta out of her large leather handbag and slid the BGT ceramic fighting knife out, flicked out the folding 9 cm blade and slid it into the concealed sheath of her half cowboy boots.

Miguel Flores was a very handsome Argentinian groom with whom she had flirted with and led on. He was keen and so handsome that he was almost pretty; with flowing blue, black hair and soft brown eyes. She had managed to get information from him about the drugs without him suspecting, she was sure, confident in her ability to find where the cocaine was being stashed.

* * *

Rupert had spoken at length to the doctor who had examined Claire and was immensely relieved. She had concussion from her collision with the side window of the car but there were no other signs of trauma. The doctor confirmed that they had carried out extensive auscultator tests as they were reluctant to X-ray anywhere near the stomach area because of her pregnancy; her blood pressure was fine and apart from seriously bruised ribs and chest, no bones appeared to have been broken. An ultrasound scan had shown, much to their relief, that the baby was well and healthy.

The doctor had advised that Claire stay in overnight, but Claire declared that she had received worse knocks to the head falling off horses and was returning to the hotel. Rupert knew better than to argue with the life force that was his wife and had summoned a cab for the 20 minute journey back from the hospital. He had been given strict instructions on care and what to look for, not allowing Claire to go unchecked more than every hour, even if she was asleep.

Safely cocooned in her bed, she looked ashen, with a large purple egg-shaped lump on the side of her head. It had just missed the temple: she had been very lucky. Chris came into see them and, although tired, Claire insisted on telling them what she had found out, repeating some for Chris's benefit.

"You did well Claire, really well," Chris praised her, "and I'm sorry for not protecting you better, I should have gone with you or at least met you at the airport."

"Phush, rubbish!" she chided, foreshortening his apology. "It was my decision and even if you had been in the car, I don't know what you could have done. No, the best thing you can do is find this warehouse and see where the polo balls go from there because I still believe that they are the clue to this whole thing. The plastic, the talcum powder, all point to this, once we know how, we can tell MI6 or Webster and then we will be clear. Now, I'm tired and need to sleep," she ordered wearily, her eye lids drooping.

"That's fine, you take it easy, I'll be out on the balcony," Rupert said. Chris took Claire's hand and squeezed it gently. She smiled wanly. "Go. I'll be fine, go and run or something, catch some bad guys..."

"Rups, I think I will take Claire's advice." He looked at his watch. It was early evening, nearly 9.30. "I'm too wound up to sleep. Look after her OK, don't leave the room?" He nodded at them both and left. He did not mention that he had already been for a run and that he had in that time sorted his own plan of action. His mental state was calmer and the cold fury had abated. But it made him even more dangerous. He had planned his every move, considered all the possibilities. He felt that up until now, they had been reacting and following the lead of whoever was behind the drug smuggling: now he was going hunting.

Rupert watched him leave the room and double locked the door. Claire had already settled into a light sleep, with a steady, rhythmic breathing pattern indicating all was well. He turned off the lights, got a bottle of beer from the mini bar and flipped off the lid. Walking out onto the balcony, he slipped into a comfortable rattan chair and propped his feet up on the low table.

Gazing out across the lights of Palm Beach, Rupert's eyes rested on the smoky violet ocean, twinkling with ribbons of light surf and reflected light from the shore. It had an hypnotic effect, calming him. As Claire had said on many occasions, his most lethal weapon was his mind. He had a natural aptitude for spotting angles and deceits, honed by years of deals; analysing the weaknesses of others and their strategies: it was what made him such a brilliant agent. The world he inhabited on a day to day basis would make a Cold War spy's head whirl. Now, with the day's events behind him and a cold anger burning for the harm that had been done to Claire, he began to methodically plan, to think, moving the pieces of information around in his head like a chess master.

Chris had gone down to the bar and exited out onto the terrace, from there he left the grounds and strode to the next hotel, The Meridian. Entering the reception, he went to the bank of public telephones and ordered a taxi for an address ten minutes from the Meredith ranch. He was wearing deck shoes, a light linen jacket, polo shirt and dark chinos. He also had a light carry bag.

Leaving the taxi, he made to walk down the drive of the house and as soon as the cab was out of sight he stopped and walked into the cover of the bushes. Here he changed. Pulling off the polo shirt and replacing it with the black polo neck he had worn previously. He exchanged deck shoes for black trainers, and a light knitted silk beanie with slits cut for sight and breathing. He then stowed the bag hidden under the bushes in the shadows and loped off to the Meredith ranch next door.

When last they were there, after Harding was killed, he had noticed a large red Trans Am parked with the other stable cars. It had been conspicuous, especially to British eyes, by virtue of its bulk and width, much larger than any British equivalent. He wanted to see that car and it's condition.

Reaching the borders of the Meredith's estate, he vaulted the fence and landed silently, making for the buildings to the centre of the ranch. He skirted carefully, marking the position of the main house bathed in external lighting; the stables and barns in shadow and a bonfire near the lake, throwing a vermillion glow across the large group of figures surrounding the fire pit of the *asado*. The sound of voices, speaking mostly Spanish, and the wonderful smells of roasting meat and Rosemary carried across the air, making Chris's stomach growl. He had only eaten a bar of chocolate before he left, not wanting a full, undigested meal to slow him down. Circling in the shadows, he made his way to the stables, painfully aware that Vikki had a pet terrier, who wandered at will.

He made it to the stable block and, as expected, most of the stalls were empty. He remembered Claire saying that polo was the only equine discipline where all the horses were put out at night, with the exception of the lame and the stallion. He entered the shadows of the first long block of stables, easing open one of the large wooden doors at the end of the run, praying that it did not creak. Just a foot was enough; the door swung silently open and he slipped inside. The cavernous barn was lit by one gentle night light of meagre wattage. Chris pulled a small

Maglite torch from his pocket and carefully illuminated the dark corners, proceeding to check each stall. Halfway down, he found the large stallion's double box, thought for a foolish moment of entering and then wisely decided against it. *One,* he thought, *it will play merry hell and two,* he grinned to himself, *I'm a coward!*

As if to verify the thought, he heard the sinister snort of the beast blowing hard through the grill. Chris pulled back quickly before he enraged it, causing a noise. It kicked once against the door, sounding like a loud drum in the night. Chris sprinted on the balls of his feet to the hay bales at the end, hiding behind them, awaiting the arrival of a curious groom. After five minutes he inhaled deeply, breathed properly, and eased out of his hiding place to check the other stalls before moving back out through the same silent door. Other double stalls ran along the outside of the barn but these, he realised, may show him in outline against the ambient light and decided not to risk it.

He moved quietly to the next large barn housing the second line of stables and followed the same procedure, pulling one of the large doors open. He slipped in and started to pull it shut and at the change of direction caused it to squeaked on its hinges in protest. Chris froze, listening for any footsteps or voices. His heart pounded; he did not want to be caught and trapped inside the building if he was discovered. He waited, the chink of light from the dull bulb seemed, in his imagination, to be a spotlight in its intensity. Nothing. He exhaled, breathing normally again. He proceed down the stalls as before and saw a dark shape outlined at the rear end. He walked quickly toward the shape under the tarpaulin. Pulling back the material, he saw the badly dented wing of the red Trans Am and the black scrape marks of another car's paint. He swore under his breath and replaced the tarp. *I will have you, you bastard!* he thought to himself. Chris now needed to know who had been driving.

Moving away from the car, Chris continued his search of the

stables on either side of the main corridor. Then he jumped; the door had creaked on its wooden hinges. Three Argentinians stood there and in the middle stood Rizzo. At least one of the others was from Bill Lester's place. *A joint asado,* he thought, *great, just what I need.* Then behind he heard a bang as the opposite end of the barn had been opened and closed, with the dropping of a locking bar sealing the two doors. A mean looking bulky groom stood there, with a mucking out fork in his hands, guarding the way.

The three to the front had moved quickly, closing the distance and spreading out across the 10 foot wide central corridor between the stalls. They were now about twenty feet away and two were brandishing pitchforks, while Rizzo drew the long knife the Argentinian gauchos carried.

"*Hola cringo!*" Rizzo sneered. Chris backed up towards the single man at the opposite end, but he knew he would never take him, raise the bar and get out before the other three were upon him. "Now," Rizzo continued, "which one are you? The husband; the one who runs a lot; or the *ir`landes?*" he laughed unpleasantly.

Oh shit, Chris thought, *I need a weapon.* In the Regiment they were taught to make use of a weapon, never mind fair play if you can shorten the odds and anything can be used, a stool, a chair leg, rolled up magazine anything that can be offensive in the right hands. He looked around and found what he was looking for but the distance was too great to run for it, they were now within ten feet. He began to back up.

The words of his Wing Chun instructor came back to him: *In a street fight, the adrenalin levels rise instantly making both parties strong and more difficult to stop. So use the circumstances, beg, pretend to cry, it doesn't matter, say you have a wife and child, who the fuck cares, just say anything to throw them. They will relax, their adrenalin levels will fall and THEN you strike.* Chris remembered the instructions, thinking in his job would always be too fast paced to use such tactics. Smiling inwardly and with the benefit of his silk makeshift balaclava in place, he began retreating, pleading, holding his hands out in supplication.

"No, please!" he cried whining, "No, I have a wife and am soon to be father, no please, don't hurt me, just left me go. I'm really sorry, please." He backed away from them. The three grooms looked at each other, laughing. Rizzo laughed again.

"Oh Dio, I think we send him back to his mummy," he said in crude Spanish.

Chris, fluent in Spanish, was delighted with his Oscar winning performance. He was nearly backed into the stall walls and a lot closer to what he was aiming for.

All grooms hang polo sticks up by their heads, using the top rail as a rack. Two were now within reach: a 'footstick' for practice on foot and a full length 53 inch stick. When Chris felt his heel strike the stall wall, he span around and grabbed both sticks: short in the left, long in the right. To his mind he now had a sword and stabbing dagger like knights of old.

There are three levels of Black Sash in Wing Chun: the fighting with bare hands, the Dummy Form and finally the Weapons Form, using butterfly knives and wooden poles. Chris, after 10 years of training, was very proficient in this final and deadly form. He now put it to good use. The groom to Chris's left recovered first and thrust with the deadly sharp tines of the pitchfork.

Chris shouted, stamped his left foot down, parried the lunge with the short stick trapping the end of the fork and moved it laterally across his body, naturally blocking any attack from his right. At the same time, he swung the long 53 inch stick in a vicious arc, the cigar like end of the wooded head down.

The groom, seeing his plight, tried to move back and caught the full force on the top of his head, smashing through the flimsy protection of his beret driving into his skull. He dropped as though pole-axed.

Not stopping, Chris continued through the same line, pivoting on his left leg and blocking the incoming second fork with the short stick, using the Butterfly form in a *jut sao* action. His arms were now crossed, but instead of using the long stick, he let it go, stepped forward, closing the distance and with a bent arm dropped an elbow strike on the collar bone, driving all the energy down through the groom's internal organs as the bone shattered. He cried with rasping breath and dropped to the floor unable to breath, his mouth moving like a goldfish out of water.

To his credit, Rizzo was no coward; he moved forward, knife extended downwards from his right hand in the manner of an experienced knife fighter. He arced with the knife hand and distracted with the left. Chris knew that he had little time as the fourth groom left his guard at the doors and was running to enter the fray. But Chris had an unwitting advantage with his 'weapon' being in his left hand which meant Rizzo had to deal with a left-handed fighter. Chris had no such problem as butterfly knives are used in pairs. The fourth groom was now charging down and, to Chris's mind, clearly not very bright.

Rizzo feinted with his left, jabbing for Chris's eyes, who let it come, blocking with the straight arm and fingers of *biu gee* lapping him as the arms connected. To the uninitiated the *'lap sau'* movement looked like a slap, but it was a powerful pulling movement which was executed with a snap. It pulled Rizzo forward, around and off balance, outside the range of the knife so he could not bring it to bear on Chris, who followed through with the rotation of his hips and shoulders, swinging the short stick into Rizzo's face. It connected just below the eye, smashing the socket and cheek bone. It had happened in a second and by rotating the hapless Rizzo around, Chris had brought him into the oncoming path of the fourth Argentinian groom and his levelled fork.

The tines, powered by the weight of the lumbering groom

pierced Rizzo's skin, just below the shoulder blades. Chris still had control of Rizzo's arm and now pulled downwards, causing the weight of Rizzo's body, impaled on the fork, to drop. The large groom now had a choice: hang on and try to free the fork or let go and be unarmed. Stupidly he chose the former.

His continued holding the fork, which pulled his shoulders and neck down, tilting his head forward. Chris didn't hesitate, instead of raising the polo mallet up, he merely rotated his wrist as fast as he could and the small stick whirred, driving through the air in a short arc. The groom looked up just in time to see the sharp end of the head smashing down on the bridge of his nose. It was the last thing he saw before he lost consciousness.

Chris looked down at Rizzo, whose breath was coming in rasping shudders. There was no pity in his eyes as he looked down. "That was for Claire, you bastard. Come after my people again and you're dead."

He knelt down and started to go through everyone's pockets. Experience had taught him that there was always something interesting to find: identities for reprisals, links, evidence, all sorts of useful information. He also knew that enemies were reluctant to come after you if you knew all about them. Rizzo tried feebly to stop him, so he slapped his hands away, emptying his pockets.

CHAPTER 26

Leaving the Clubhouse early, Siobhan showered, changed and artfully applied makeup, making the most of enhancing her striking hazel eyes. She admired herself in the mirror looking at the end result. *Mmm, not bad,* she thought, *not bad at all.*

She withdrew the Beretta Nano and checked the magazine. She liked the size of the tiny pistol, yet it still packed a punch at .40 calibre with a seven shot magazine. But best of all, to her mind, it only weighed 17 ounces, perfect for her handbag. She eased the fit of the ceramic knife in her boot sheath and, satisfied, sprayed Calvin Klein's Obsession over herself, stepping into the mist. Finally ready, she left the apartment and headed to her small Toyota.

The drive to Meredith's ranch was a simple one and, following Miguel's directions, she arrived in under 20 minutes. She pulled into the drive, pressed the buzzer and the gates swung open. She spotted Miguel at the end of the drive waving at her to stop. Slipping into the car, he kissed her.

"*Ciao, bella,*" he said, using the Italian form of address that so many Argentinians adopted. "You look lovely," he added, oozing charm, to which she responded with a dazzling smile.

"Where to?" she asked.

"Over here, to the left." He indicated the large stables and barns and in the darkening evening she saw the metallic reflection of the lake and the flames of a bonfire and *asado*. There were, she noticed, many Argentinian grooms there from other ranches and some other American girls and grooms. The Argentinians loved the American women and found them easier to seduce than their own women back home. There were also no female Argentinian grooms, it was, Siobhan had learned, just not acceptable to their machismo mentality. *Well,* she thought, *he might think I'm an easy lay, but after tonight he'll get nothing and I'll have gained more than him.*

The party proceeded in good form, with some couples drifting off to assignations in the dark and towards midnight as the coals were dying down, they heard a wrenching noise from the stable block, the water from the lake amplifying the sound. Rizzo cocked an ear and signalled to one of the others that they should check out the stables. A groom strode off and returned a few minutes later, speaking quietly to Rizzo, who quietly slipped away with three other grooms. Siobhan noticed the exit and commented to Miguel.

"Where are they off to?"

"Oh, I don't know, some go early, stable duties, maybe a big day tomorrow, who knows." He shrugged. "But it is not important. Let's go and find a quiet spot ourselves." He winked. She smiled in agreement and they walked arm in arm towards the stables with the bunk house over, but at the last minute he said, "Wait here, I will get a blanket, more romantic in the stables and we won't be disturbed. The others, they think it funny to bang on the door." He shrugged at the childish mentality of the other grooms. Returning with a large, folded blanket they headed for the first set of stables, seeing lights on in the far set and voices carrying in the night from within. Moving along, Miguel looked around almost furtively.

"What making sure no one sees us?" Siobhan flirted.

"What? Oh yes, I must look after your honour," he joked. At the middle of the block he gestured to a large stable, opening the bolted door, "After you, *señorita.*" He bowed exaggeratedly.

"Thank you," Siobhan offered and entered the stable which smelled, she noticed, of clean shavings and another musky smell but was immediately distracted as the door was shut behind her and bolted. Her first thought was that Miguel was playing a trick, then more sinister thoughts occurred; maybe he was getting friends to come and rape her. But he made no sound.

"Miguel, stop pissing about, let me out now!" she cried and then a thought occurred to her: *Had she been blown? How? No one knew her real identity.* She heard the scrapping sound of a partition being pulled back and in the gloom and ambient light she sensed, rather than saw, a wide opening forming between her stable and the next one in the block.

She heard a rustle of straw and heavy breathing; saw a dark shape appear; an accompanying stamp of a hoof; a raw smell of horse assailed her nostrils and she heard the deep whistle of expelled air from bellowed lungs. Her thoughts collided: she had been set up and shut in a box with a vicious horse.

She grabbed her bag, dragging the Beretta from its hiding place, hearing and sensing the presence of the enraged stallion finding a human and, a female at that, in its' domain. Pulling the pistol up she fired quickly at the charging mass, which had reared onto its hind legs. Her shot hit the animal on the shoulder, grazing him, burning his muscle and enraging him further. Before she had chance to fire a second time, a slashing hoof flew down, breaking her arm. It was the last thing she felt or saw.

* * *

Hearing the enraged stallion Chris had an idea looking at the dead Argentinian groom. Murder or manslaughter was much more likely to be reported and followed up than a fight between grooms. He bet that none of the others would report his presence, too many questions, too much to explain. But a death? They would have to report it and although they didn't know his identity, they had a pretty good idea. But if a groom got careless, entered the stallion's box and was killed, smashed by flying hooves? Who was to know?

He smiled a nasty smile to himself. He picked up the pitch-fork in a dirty cloth and hoisted the dead groom into an empty wheelbarrow, carting both around to the stallion's box, *who, if the noises were anything to go by,* Chris thought, *was already having quite a party.* Chris did not see the hidden figure of Miguel, who was appalled and frightened at the sight of the avenging angel that was Chris Adams. He just had time to hide as Chris came into view and had no intention of tackling a man who had taken out four of his friends.

He saw the massive animal pawing the ground in his 'tease box' and quickly unbolted the door, flopped the dead groom inside onto the floor and looked across as the stallion turned his head. In the poor light, Chris looked with horror at the bloody bundle of rags on the floor, which he supposed had once been a human being, the metallic tang of blood hung in the air, with other equally nauseous aromas. He had seen action all over the world; bodies of friends destroyed in action, limbs blown off, eviscerated and blinded. But there was something so macabre about the primeval killing of what looked like a woman, by the long red hair. He stopped dead. Then came to as the stallion rolled back and charged him. He ducked out and slammed the stable door just in time, jabbing it back with the pitchfork which he threw in to complete the picture of a groom defending himself. The stallion enraged by his wound and the smell of blood, treated the new body as a threat and kicked out in defence.

Chris, aware that time was running short, ran to the next box and looked over the partition. He had to be as sure as he could. Using the light from his small torch, he found what he was almost certain was Siobhan's body, only one person in the area had long, red hair like that. He thought back quickly, yes she had betrayed them and once nearly caused them to be killed or captured, but once he had called her a friend and nobody deserved that sort of death, not even a traitor. He shook himself, he had to get out of there fast. Moving quietly out of the barn, he strode away as quickly and smoothly as possible, retracing his steps back out of the ranch grounds.

As he went, he saw a figure gesturing to others to come to the barns. Someone had set Siobhan up, Chris knew, *but who? Were they on to Brennan, is that how they traced her?* He checked his watch in the darkness, nearly twelve o'clock. He had ordered a taxi to pick him up from the next ranch and would be late at this rate. He broke into a fast run, now clear of the sight line and ran through the woods before the fence line.

He barely made it to the pickup point, picking up his bag, changing back to his polo shirt and shoes. He was still sweating when he got into the taxi.

The cab driver seeing that he was sweating commented, "Warm night, isn't it?"

Chris wiped the sweat from his brow. "Yea, I ran to meet you, didn't realise the time," he excused himself. The taxi returned him to The Meridian, he walked next door to his hotel and slipped in unnoticed talking with a couple whom he latched onto, striking up a random conversation as he went and shielding himself from the sight of the receptionist who was luckily on the telephone as he walked in.

CHAPTER 27

Chris had slipped quietly back to his room just after midnight; showered and changed into a pair of shorts and a polo shirt. He called down for room service, saying he couldn't sleep, ordering a sandwich and a cup of tea. Then seeing Rupert's light on, he padded quietly out on to his balcony and whispered across to him.

"I saw your light was still on, I couldn't sleep, is Claire OK?" he asked.

Rupert looked across at his friend and colleague in arms, silently saluting him with a half empty bottle of beer, the third for that evening. Rupert had spent the whole evening looking in on Claire from time to time and carefully, methodically, going over everything in his mind, recalling all facts and events of the last 10 days in Florida. He looked carefully over his shoulder at the sleeping form of Claire, got out of the chair and moved quietly over to the balcony edge, so that he might speak without waking her.

"Yes, fine thank you, sleeping soundly. I've woken her twice just to make sure she is not in a coma but she seems fine. She gave me some grief the second time so I know she is on the mend. You OK? Would you like a beer?"

"No, thanks. I woke up hungry and I realised I hadn't eaten much in all the excitement so I have just ordered a sandwich and a cup of tea. Do you want one?"

"No, I'm exhausted." He was stretching and arching his back. "I think I'll sleep now I know Claire is alright. Good night, let's speak in the morning, I've got a lot to tell you."

"Will do." *Yea I've got a lot to tell you too, matey, but not until we get a visit from Sheriff Reed,* Chris thought, not wanting Rupert exposed. When and if Reed came around asking questions, Rupert should give a genuine response of surprise; there was no need to bring him into the evening's brutality and murder. Therefore, the less he knew at the moment, the safer he was, Chris reasoned.

* * *

The following morning Claire was the first to wake, with a massive headache but nothing more serious. Rupert who had spent a fitful night was deeply asleep as she slipped out for a glass of water and paracetamol. Whilst going back to bed, she heard a loud knocking on what sounded like Chris's door. It was more than the gentle polite knock of a waiter. She was slightly alarmed by the insistence of the sound and quickly shook Rupert awake.

"Whaaa, what?" he mumbled, finally coming round from a deep sleep.

"Rups, wake up, someone is knocking loudly on Chris's door."

"It's probably a waiter, is that why you woke me?" he asked grumpily.

"No, I think it's more than that, please look," she asked.

He gave her a look which could have been taken any number of ways, combed back his hair with his fingers and shifted out of bed. Pulling on a towelling robe, he walked to the doorway, pulled it open and peered out into the corridor. There he saw Sheriff Reed and a deputy knocking on Chris's door.

"Oh, morning Sheriff Reed," he called jauntily, "anything I can help you with?"

"Ah, Mr Brett, morning to you. Yes as a matter of-" at that moment Chris opened the door, appearing with wet hair he was rubbing dry and clad in a towelling robe.

"Oh, Sheriff Reed, good morning. Sorry, I was in the shower, what can I do for you?"

Reed eyed Chris with a searching look and seeing the open towelling robe noticed some of the criss-crossed battle scars on his exposed chest and forearms.

"I need to ask you some questions, if I may? And possibly you too, Mr Brett." He nodded in Rupert's direction.

"Certainly," Rupert replied. "I will be in once I've put some clothes on."

Chris stepped back slightly. "Sheriff, I too need to dress, give me a minute." Two minutes later, dressed and hair combed, he reappeared, opening the door, admitting the two officers and Rupert.

"Now, I am intrigued, what is this all about? Have you found out any more about Josh Harding's death?" he asked diffidently. Rupert too had a puzzled look on his face.

"Well it's interesting you bring that up because, in way, I believe that it may be connected with why I am here. But first, where were you yesterday evening?"

"Yesterday evening, well here. Rupert brought Claire back about, oh I don't know, 9ish and then we stayed on looking after her for a bit. After that, I went to my room and went to sleep early, I was mentally exhausted and worried about poor Claire, terrible thing to happen. Why do you ask?" Chris finished, ever the nice, genuine, shocked surveyor, feigning puzzlement, he had schooled himself for this moment.

"Anyone else see you?" Reed asked.

"Well, yes, actually," Rupert responded, "I stayed up most of the night with Claire, checking on her. I spent some time out on the balcony so as not to disturb her and Chris came out, couldn't sleep or something, and we chatted. Why, what is all this about Sheriff?" he asked, genuinely puzzled by the questioning and turn of events.

"In a moment," he cautioned. "Anyone else see you?"

"Er, yes, actually, when I got up, I was thirsty," Chris explained, "and found I was hungry, not having had any supper yesterday; the accident rather threw us. Well, I ordered some sandwiches and a cup of tea from room service."

The sheriff arched an eyebrow "And what time would this have been?"

"Oh, I don't know, around 12 or 12.30, I suppose. Sheriff why are you asking these questions, has someone robbed a bank or something?"

Reed looked at his deputy who had made notes of everything they'd said and smiled a thin smile, "Well, no banks, no. However," he continued, studying the faces of the two men intently, "yesterday evening sometime after around 11.00 or 11.30 there was a disturbance at the Meredith place."

"Meredith's ranch again," Rupert said, looking at Chris. Knowing how his friend worked, he was beginning to suspect the worst. "That place does seem to be rather unlucky, what now?"

The sheriff launched straight in, wanting to gauge reactions: "Well, two people dead, three in hospital and a groom missing."

"What?" they both cried.

"But how and why?" I mean, who was it, not Vikki?" Rupert asked.

"Now, why would you ask about Vikki?"

"Because she came over to see Claire, she was upset and worried and Claire went back with her for lunch, help her get over Harding's death," Rupert answered.

"I see. Well no, not Vikki Meredith. The two dead people are a woman believed to be this FARC agent you mentioned to me, Siobhan Clifford, and an Argentinian groom who was there for a BBQ, from the Lester's place, apparently. As to how, they were killed by that maniac stallion of theirs, got caught in the stall and were trampled to death, not pretty, not pretty at all."

"Sheriff, that's awful, what a way to go. But I still don't see why you want to know where we were at the time. I don't understand," Rupert said.

Sheriff Reed looked at both men searchingly, keen to see any deviation from their composed yet shocked and sympathetic dispositions; he saw nothing to alert him.

"Well the woman you knew as Siobhan Clifford, she was apparently dating one of the grooms, a man named Miguel. He had taken her to the stables for a bit of seduction. Claims he forgot a blanket and when he returned, she was inside the stall, being kicked to death by the stallion. He tried to get to her but it was too late and the brute wouldn't let him near her."

"How terrible," Chris said, "but did the other man die in the stables, you said two?"

"Indeed. Well we will never know for certain, but he had a polo stick with him and we can only assume that hearing the ruckus, he tried to save her by beating off the stallion."

"Poor chap and very brave of him," Rupert intoned, "but I still don't see how that should involve us."

"Well it seems that when this groom, Miguel, returned, he saw someone lurking about, leaving the stable area acting suspiciously and running through trees. Apparently he was dressed all in black."

"And you think for some strange reason that it was either Rupert or me?" Chris asked. "That's bloody stupid. Why? Also, if it was one of us, just for the sake of argument, how the hell did we get there? We haven't got a car remember, it was written off by some lunatic yesterday," he finished heatedly.

"Number of things. One, we found a red Trans Am in the stables with damage to the front wing consistent with the attack on your vehicle. Two, you knew the woman Clifford and the groom Miguel swears it was a Caucasian, not a Latino and from the description he gave it could be either of you. Three," he continued raising a third finger "the three grooms that are in hospital claim they were set upon by an intruder and ambushed when they heard the stable door creak. Reckoned he, just one man, beat them all up and left them lying there. But they didn't get a good look at him because he was wearing a hood. Finally, I checked with Meredith and they have a groom missing, and the last they saw, he was driving the red Trans Am, now he has just disappeared. A lot of coincidences there, I am sure you agree," the sheriff finished his line of theories, looking at both men questioningly.

Rupert and Chris looked at each other in amazement, shaking their heads. It was Rupert who broke the silence, "And you think that all this points to either Chris or me going over there to Meredith's on a magic carpet, beating up three tough grooms because somehow we happened to know that the car that drove me off the road was there and I suppose you think we kidnapped the missing groom as well, carried on our magic carpet and did away with him?" Rupert shook his head.

"Sheriff, who do you think we are, Superman? And just because a Caucasian who might, just might, loosely match our description was thought to be responsible, you look at us? There are a lot of people that roughly match our description around here and, guess what, they have a car! Do you know who you should be looking for? Siobhan's partner in crime, Tir Brennan. He is about the same height and build as me and Chris, and if anyone would be where she is, it would be him. He is also an IRA killer and they wear balaclavas when doing dirty deeds in Northern Ireland. Find him, I say, and you will find your culprit," he finished heatedly. "Now if you've no more questions, I need to go and see how my wife is."

But before he could leave, the sheriff held up a hand to stop him. "Now just a second. I realise what you are saying, but look at it this way. You two by your own admission knew the woman and had a run in with her before. She was an enemy of your government. You had a run in with the driver of the car that, just by coincidence, happens to be at the Meredith place. You were already suspicious of the groom Rizzo and his possible involve-ment in drugs and I understand that Seth Meacham has already told you two to back off from investigating any further. Also, you could have caught a cab from here and back. Rest assured we'll check, if only to corroborate your story.

One final thing, this dead woman, she had a gun on her, fired two shots; one appears to have grazed the stallion. Now ask yourself this, if she went into the box by mistake, as the groom says, why didn't she just walk back out when she realised her mistake and how did the stallion get from one side of the box to the other? The partition door was slid open, you see."

"A gun? " Chris asked in mock amazement. "She brought a gun to a romantic assignation? Doesn't that say anything to you sheriff? Something doesn't quite ring true here. I mean, maybe he found out she was the FARC contact and set her up. Maybe he is the one who locked her in the stable while the stallion kicked her to death and made up some cock and bull story about an intruder.

"Seems to me you've got your work cut out. But on the subject of taxies, please check my hotel room phone records and, for that matter, my mobile phone; I certainly didn't order a cab last night and I am sure Rupert didn't either," he said, offering his phone for inspection to the deputy who had continued taking notes. Rupert left and returned with both his and Claire's mobiles and the call memories were checked by the deputy, who shook his head.

"Satisfied?" Rupert responded aggressively. "Also Sheriff, we both have alibis for us being here at the times you said."

"And if, as you say, we got into fisticuffs with these three Argy grooms, don't you think we'd have a few black eyes, and please look at my hands, no bruised knuckles," Chris added, holding them up for inspection. "No one in a scrap is that good to get away with no marks."

"Very good, Mr Adams, but the damage was done with a weapon. I've got one who has a puncture wound to his back, a smashed eye socket, he'll probably lose it, and severe concussion amongst other things. Whoever attacked them was extremely aggressive and skilled, apparently he did this with just a polo stick."

"Are you sure it wasn't a falling out amongst thieves?"

"Maybe you're right, believe me, I think that they probably had it coming, but I'm not the judge and jury. Well, we'll see in due course and, to be honest, you have levelled with me as to why you're here and kept me informed. So, what I am saying is, I want to be on your side. But in the meantime, please stay where I can call you. I appreciate your help and give my best to your wife, Mr Brett, I hope that she is feeling better today?"

Rupert assured him that she was and the two sheriffs left the room. Once he was certain they were alone, Rupert went to the door, opened it quickly and was presented with a deserted corridor. Feeling rather foolish at the touch of melodrama, he beckoned Chris to follow him next door to his room. Once safely inside and with Claire looking on expectantly, he breathed out. "Chris, you certainly start a shit storm when you get going. What exactly happened last night?"

He looked innocent and turned to Rupert. "I don't know what you mean? OK, well maybe I know a little of what happened, but I didn't tell you to save you. You could not have pulled such an indignant response and know what had happened." He then proceeded to tell them the whole story.

"So you took out four men armed with pitchforks and knives with nothing but a polo stick?" Claire asked aghast. Although she had seen Chris in combat mode, she still had trouble reconciling the friendly man whom she regarded almost as brother, with the deadly soldier that she knew he could be.

"I did what needed to be done and they won't be sending anyone after you again, my dear, that's for sure," he responded with a hard edge to his voice. "Oh, two things. One, I was wearing a balaclava so all this bollocks about recognising me is crap, but of course I couldn't say that; and secondly, just before they were going to kill me, Rizzo asked was I '…the husband; the one who runs; or the Irishman…' They seem to know an awful lot about what is going on. I've been trying to put all this together in my mind and I don't like where it's taking me."

"I, too, was doing a lot of thinking last night and there are some things I want to run past both of you. What happened last night sort of pulls it altogether even more," Rupert stated as the other two began listening in to what he had to say. "Let's just look at what we do know before I go speculating. We know from Brennan and Siobhan's presence here that there are drugs around. We know that Josh Harding was killed because of something that he found and that link is to the Meredith ranch. We now also know that the attempt on our lives was from the Meredith ranch and that it was to be hushed up. I bet that Argy driver is now safely back in Argentina, tucked up with a few bob from a grateful drug cartel.

"Rizzo is, or rather was, clearly involved very heavily and to begin speculating here, almost certainly responsible for Harding's murder. Claire's trip to Dallas was clearly known about and she was obviously on the right track because they tried to stop her after she had visited the store and more importantly, we must have been followed. But this begs a question: what is making them suspicious of us in the first place? As far as I am aware, we have given no outwards signs of being anything other than we appear to be. That is my first point of concern.

"So back to what we know. Claire's theory about the balls being the conduit seems to be correct, especially as we now know that talcum powder is involved in the manufacturing process and it was found in the drugs in France. So we need to know how it is done and how it is being distributed. But here is the second thing, how did Siobhan know to go to Meredith's place and how did she get found out? Here is a woman who is a very good operator; very well trained; great instincts and years of experience."

"Brennan was known, hence the comment about the Irishman, they could have traced her through him. Maybe they saw her meet with him as I did?" Chris offered.

"Possibly. So she seduces a groom who knows who she is, sets her up and bumps her off. If so, this is big and very well organised, with spies everywhere. Think about it; if they know you as 'the one who runs a lot' they must be spying on us here, which is how they followed me to and from the airport. Or, and this is even more disturbing, Gus Rowley is in on it and he tipped them off. He could of told them a woman was down asking questions about polo balls, that she was on holiday with her husband and could have told Rizzo or higher up to be careful and bang, they think we need to be put off or shut up permanently.

"But in that way, I feel they have achieved their objective; they have slowed us down and put us off the scent. I don't necessarily think it was their intention to kill."

"I did warn you both the cartels are very well organised and with so much money around, they can buy virtually anyone," Chris said. "For my money, Siobhan was on a scouting mission similar to Claire's trip with Vikki the other day. I bet she'd have belted the groom, and then gone searching, but she didn't get the chance. Which means we are still one step ahead."

"Yes, and I know how we can stay there. Claire, you said that we need to go to the warehouse and from there try to find out where the individual deliveries of balls are made, but I think we have missed a step. You see, if the balls are being sent up here for distribution, that is fine, but somewhere between the warehouse and their final destination, in this case grooms, players etc., they are being doctored and that is what we need to know because that is where the drugs will be stored."

"I agree," Claire said, "so all we don't know now is 'how and who' is behind it all. But from what you've said, and given the polo connection, the depth of deceit and the organisation, I am putting money on Bill Lester. He needs the cash and what better way to introduce it and launder it than through property. But if we find the factory or whatever, we may find the answer to both questions. I will go and get changed and we can make an appointment to meet this chap at the warehouse." She made a move to get up. Rupert stopped her.

"No, not you and before you protest, there is method in my madness. First, if Gus Rowley is in on it, he will know you are better and not hurt. Secondly, if I go, I can act the fool with little knowledge and try the Mosaic approach that you mentioned and see if I get any more answers. They'll just think I am getting photos and nothing more, Chris might even be able to snoop whilst I go inside. Finally, I don't want you getting hurt again and that's final. Go to the polo, take it easy and rest, that is what the doctor said. We only have three more days until we fly back."

To Rupert's surprise Claire acquiesced. The crash, he thought, must have taken more out of her than he realised.

Returning to his room, Chris used the time to file a report back to Johnston on all that had happened, and looking at his watch, realised that he should still be in the office, so called him on his direct dial number.

"Johnston," he answered curtly.

"Sergeant Adams here, boss. I have a lot of news, and little time, we need to move out soonest and check something out."

"Fine, tell me." And Chris Adams reported the events of the last twenty four hours, including his involvement and Rupert and Claire's lucky escape. Johnston listened carefully, asking the occasional question for clarification on certain points. Blowing a soundless whistle when he learned the identity of the FARC agent.

Then as Chris finished, he asked, "And you're certain that you weren't identified?"

"No. They can only speculate, no one saw my face and if Siobhan Clifford hadn't been caught up in it, we wouldn't have even been questioned. I doubt the Argy's would have reported it at all. Just bad luck, but as we don't have a car, it was even more unlikely that we were involved. I sowed the seed that it was Brennan as he had a greater motive and would have been there trying to protect Siobhan."

"Good. One other thing, report this to Seth Meacham at the DEA, but do not tell him of your involvement, just say that you heard the FARC agent was killed and that Brennan was the likely suspect for the fracas with the grooms. He will, I suspect, not take kindly to us playing rough house and killing people on his turf."

"Will do, boss. Also has anything arrived for me? This is getting quiet serious and I need a weapon."

"All taken care of and should be with you today. Remember,

your main priority is to look after the Bretts, make sure you keep them safe, no cock ups, OK?"

"Boss," he replied, cut the call and repacked the sat phone, locking it away in his case. As if in answer to his prayers, he then received an internal call from the hotel reception informing him that there was a courier awaiting his signature for a package and he was under instructions to only accept Chris's signature. He duly went down and signed for the package, which turned out to be an oblong box made of stiff cardboard and securely taped together.

The courier was not a typical van driver or motorcyclist, but was wearing a suit and tie and had arrived in a conservative saloon car. He eyed Chris more as an equal than a customer and asked for identification before Chris signed for the parcel. Suspecting what it would contain, he produced his military ID which produced a quiet smile from the 'courier', who handed over the package and departed without another word. In his room, he ripped open the box and there, as he suspected, was a weapon.

It was a Sig Sauer P226, TacOps model, with spare ammunition for the 19 round capacity magazine, a cleaning kit and a special Alien gear 'conceal' belt holster. Chris smiled, his favourite make and model. He loved the trigger pull, the large magazine and had never had a jam with the weapon. He knew from experience you could drop it, kick it, get sand in it and it would still fire as well as the day it left the Swiss factory where it was made.

He stripped the weapon, cleaned it, checked the action, fitted the outside belt holster and practised drawing the Sig from different angles and stances. He spent half an hour doing this and then checked for concealment. He was not happy with just a polo shirt, so put on his linen jacket. This in itself presented a problem, he found that the extremely light nature of the material caused it to stay in place and move with him, refusing easy access to the pistol. He 'loaded' the right hand outside pocket with his wallet and tried again. *Better,* he thought, *but still not happy.*

He then filled the coin section of his wallet with some dollars, adding weight and returned it to his pocket. This time as he swayed, the jacket stayed virtually still before it caught up with his movement, offering an opening for his hand to grip the Sig. The action was much better, with the pistol appearing almost like magic with the same speed that he had perfected without the jacket. He made a few more passes, then satisfied, loaded the weapon and stored it behind the bath panel.

Next, using his mobile, he called Seth Meacham and brought him up to date on all that had happened. He found Meacham to be his usual cynical self, but also rather concerned for Claire and Rupert. He did, however, surprisingly favour Chris's proposed theory of Tir Brennan's involvement.

"Yea well, I've been in touch with Sheriff Reed and because of the drugs connection you alerted us to, we are sort of working together on this. We looked at this woman's mobile phone records and although she only had it for a couple of days, it's a pay as you go, she called another mobile which is now untraceable. I'm betting that it was Brennan's phone and we know for certain that they met up. I bet it was him that put those guys in the hospital. But I do say this, Mr Adams, trouble sure does follow you and your partner around! I just hope that you weren't involved; as government helper or not, there will be hell to pay. You hear me?"

"Oh don't start on me, Seth. I was tucked up in bed here worried about poor Claire. And even if I was there, do you think I could take out three tough Argy grooms? That Rizzo alone looked one tough son of a bitch. I was just a foot soldier not Superman, now I'm just a realtor trying to help," he decried.

"Fair enough, just stay out of trouble," he said and put the phone down. *Now why don't I believe you, Mr Adams; there is something about you I don't like or trust,* he thought.

CHAPTER 28

The call was made for Rupert to attend a meeting at the Dallas Polo warehouse off the I95 south of Wellington. First, he ordered a cab to take them to the local car hire office to sort a car for the next few days. They picked up an innocuous, black Taurus 4-door saloon.

"Hah, bit of a come down from the mighty Ford, insurance hire car companies are going to refuse to deal with you. First Argentina, now here, you'll be getting a bad reputation," Chris mocked. In response, Rupert grinned and stuck two fingers up at him.

They drove to the address on some industrial estate thirty minutes from the hotel. It was typical of the genre: wide roads, a range of different sized buildings housing small production units and distribution warehouses. The Dallas Polo warehouse was easy to find and this time, unlike in Dallas, it had a large sign proudly identifying the unit.

Entering the unit, they were met by a receptionist who asked them to take a seat. Don Cheam, the manager of the store, was a true middle management employee full of 'hale, hearty and well met' cheer.

Well-built with gym muscle and beach blond hair, he came

forward, all smiles, "Hey, good morning guys, good to see you. Gus called and said your wife would be over but I understand that she had accident, my secretary told me. She OK?" he asked, all concern. Rupert tried to decide if it was an act; if he was genuinely programmed to care for someone he had never met or that he knew exactly how she was hurt and why. He could not decide, so continued with the bonhomie.

"Oh thank you, that's really kind of you to ask," was his refrain whilst shaking hands with the earnest Mr Cheam. "She is fine, but as she is pregnant, we wanted to play it safe and give her some more rest before we fly back later this week."

"Yea, sure thing. Now Gus tells me that your wife is doing an article for *Polo Express Magazine*? Sounds great." He had that annoying Stateside manner of finishing every sentence with an up-lift in his voice, making everything sound like a question whether it was intended to be or not. Rupert decided that he had better move things on before Chris punched him in the nose; he could sense his resentment rising with every spoken word. To his credit, Chris fixed a smile in a death like rictus and held the mask in place. Rupert explained the background to Claire's article and how she came to be involved.

"Oh, so good that you're here to see the polo. I love it. Do you like to play?"

"No, well a little bit of stick and balling; my wife is the real enthusiast. Loved it ever since childhood," Rupert enthused. "Now, could we see the warehouse and how the distribution works, it would sort of round up the story that my wife says the magazine wants? The main focus, you see, was on the manufacture of your splendid polo balls and how they get transported all over the world. Great story."

"Oh sure, we are the world's biggest manufacturer and distributor, but come on up to the office and you can see from there and then I'll take you on a tour." He led them up to the first floor office, which had a large glass window overlooking the inside of the warehouse, providing a bird's eye view of the whole area. It was stuffed to the brim with all manner of things to do with polo. But one area was given over to cardboard boxes, identical to those they a had seen being delivered to Bill Lester's doorstep.

"Now, can I get you a drink? The coffee here is real good, I make sure of it." To Chris's surprise, Rupert accepted and so as not to be left out, he too asked for a cup. Don Cheam got up and moved over to the adjacent room. They heard him filling the machine with fresh water, loading the filter and getting three mugs. He shouted through, "Cream? Sugar?"

They both asked for black, no sugar.

"Best way, get the pure taste that way." He returned in minutes, carrying three mugs of steaming coffee which smelled delicious. Rupert just had time to avert his eyes from the desk where Cheam's diary had been open. They proceeded with the coffee, chatting about the Game, the distribution and local markets.

Rupert took some photos through the open window and then Cheam took them down to the warehouse itself. It was, Rupert noticed with approval, a 'cross docker', in that the goods came in from the left with docks and sliding doors, then through a well ordered system with goods out to the right. Another run of docks and doors were apparent, with a warehouse man in charge of a ledger at each side overseeing the process.

"Seems pretty efficient, good system, in and out," Rupert pointed out, then took some more photos and while Don Cheam and Chris focused on the stores, he discreetly took a photo of the open ledger then wandered over to the boxes of balls. "So all these get moved out of here and on to shops and suppliers around the world? Oh and I nearly forgot, you sell them in bulk to Argy grooms and players too, to take to the UK and Europe, don't you?"

For the first time since they had chatted to him, the 'good

ol boy' attitude disappeared and the mask slipped, there was a harder tone to his voice, "Well, we sell them to whoever wants to buy them. Simple as that. If the Argy's want to buy them here and take some with them, why should we care? Its saves shipping them ourselves and what the heck, its good business; they buy a lot. Why would you be interested anyway?" he asked rather defensively.

"Oh nothing, we just saw a load delivered to Bill Lester's place and also at Meredith's ranch," he replied, amicably interested in Cheam's response. "It seemed like a lot of balls."

He shrugged. "Well, as I said, good business. Now guy's, are you done?" They nodded and made to move off, but as they were leaving, Cheam said, "You won't put about the fact the Argy's distribute the balls, will you?" he asked. *So that was it,* thought Rupert, *he was worried about his firm's reputation.*

"Oh of course, we won't mention a thing and I am sure Claire will let you see the draft article before it goes to print." They shook hands and parted company with Cheam waving them off. Once they were back in the car, Chris asked, "Did you get it?"

"Yah, one of the very important skills an agent needs is to be able to read upside down. So many times someone's left their day book unguarded; you wouldn't believe the deals I've picked up by reading upside down. Well that took care of the date for the deliveries and the photos of the delivery book I've got here," with which he waved the instamatic camera, "will give us the addresses. All we have to do is go through the addresses; one will stand out, I'm sure of it. Two are going out this afternoon and we'll get these processed in an hour, then we'll have the addresses."

CHAPTER 29

After Rupert and Chris left the hotel, Claire showered and dressed, deciding what to do for the day whilst they were away. It was then that the phone rang.

"Claire Brett," she answered.

"Claire hi, its Vikki Meredith. I heard what happened, it sounds terrible, are you OK?"

"Hi Vikki, yes I'm fine, really, just badly shaken up, a bit bruised and concussed, you know the usual holiday things," she replied with light irony.

"You Brits crack me up, do you ever take anything seriously?"

"Oh we work on the basis that everything can be fixed with a cup of tea," she said. "But how are you? We had a visit from the sheriff and I understand that things have been pretty grim there as well?"

Her voice lost the forced jollity as she replied, "Yea, kind of. Listen, could we meet up, maybe go out watch a game, anything to get away from here?"

Claire sensed the desperation in her voice. "Certainly, a game sounds fine, but can we get in? It is the quarter finals, tickets only, I understand?"

"We have tickets for all the main games; Daddy's on the board. Come on, I'll pick you up and we can go for lunch there and watch the game. Will Rupert and Chris be coming or are they working?"

"No, working I'm afraid. But I'll call him to let him know where I'm off to."

"Great, I'll be around in about half an hour." She cut the call and was gone. Claire then called Rupert on his mobile. It went straight to voicemail so she left him a message.

Despite feeling a little out of sorts, Claire was, she realised, delighted to get away and see some more polo; the quarter finals in any tournament were always exciting. So it was with some enthusiasm that she met Vikki outside the hotel reception, having left a note for Rupert just in case he did not pick up the unreliable message service on his mobile answering machine. The two women embraced after Claire slid into the seat of her BMW.

"Oh Claire, it's so good to see you and to get away from the house; I feel its jinxed or something."

"Oh don't be silly, anyway, the pleasure is all mine; the quarter finals no less!" she enthused. The car sped away as Vikki felt she was breaking free of some intangible hold over her. The roof of the convertible was down and the two women enjoyed the feeling of the wind blowing in their hair, and much to Claire's delight, Cheryl Crow blaring out 'All I wanna do is have some fun…' on the radio.

"Oh I love this song," she called out above the noise of the wind. "It will forever remind me of our holiday here."

Upon arriving at the club they found the panoply of The *Quarters* in full flow with all the razzmatazz that America can muster. The car park was jammed full and everyone seemed to have turned out for the big day's sport.

"Wow, what an atmosphere," Claire said. "I just love it." Vikki, too, was caught up in the feeling as they headed for the clubhouse.

"Yea but just wait for the after party tonight in the club up-stairs, they are so wild. Some of the stories I've heard about what goes on and it's not just the drugs and booze."

"Oh do tell, don't stop now," she ordered as Vikki pushed open the doors to the clubhouse and a wall of sound emanating from a chorus of people.

"Well, last year they had a chocolate fountain. Then one of the 'boys', I can't remember who, Steve Lamb I think, doesn't matter, dared one of the women that she wouldn't take her bra off and dip her tits into the chocolate so he could lick it off. Well, he had three takers, one was a titled English lady, would you believe it? Anyway-"

"Vikki, how are you? So sorry to hear your news, it is just too terrible." As both girls looked round, there was Samantha Lester, dressed immaculately as always, suddenly embracing Vikki in a hug. "And Claire, I hear you've been in the wars, too. Are you OK? Baby and everything?" she asked pointing down with her eyes to Claire's stomach. There appeared to be genuine concern in the voice, so Claire decided to treat the concern appropriately despite her reservations.

"Oh, you know, went for a swim and forgot to get out of the car," she laughed it off. Vikki and Sam caught the joke and joined in. "But everything is fine and I appreciate your concern." She hugged Samantha in response .

"Now come and join us for lunch, we have some people here. But where are Chris and Rupert?" She looked around and Claire noticed that it was Chris's name she mentioned first, not Rupert's.

"Oh, off working, I'm afraid. Probably tying up some deal or other on this Sub-Prime market that everyone is so excited about," Claire said lightly. Samantha gave her a look which could have been taken in any number of ways.

"Ah, yes, of course, I am sure that Bill will be involved

somewhere. Now, come through and meet some people." In reality, Claire and Vikki would rather have been left to their own devices but the social force that was Samantha Lester swept them forward. "I hear it was just awful about that waitress being killed as well. To think that she worked here too, terrible, just terrible."

"Did she?" Claire asked. "I didn't know that, how do you know? And what was she doing at the Meredith place, serving?" she asked disingenuously. Vikki frowned at Claire, fought back a question that rose on her lips, realising that Claire was dissembling, but not sure why.

"Oh I don't know, polo gossip, you know how it is. Nothing is sacred here for long, everyone knows everything. But no, I hear she was dating one of the grooms and went into the stallion's stable by mistake. Couldn't get out and well, that was that really," Samantha finished flippantly, not seeing the hurt look on Vikki's face as she sashayed forward through the crowd, smiling as she went.

God she can be such a thoughtless bitch sometimes, Claire thought as she grasped and squeezed Vikki's hand in support, smiling sympathetically at her. In a moment of inspiration, Claire said, "I'll be there in a minute, always need the loo at the moment."

Before Samantha could object, they both turned and fled for the Ladies. Unperturbed, Samantha shouted back, "Sure, see you at our usual table on the terrace." She pointed and then disappeared in a flurry of social kisses.

If Claire was making light of things, Tir Brennan was not. He had tried Siobhan's mobile number twice late yesterday evening and it had gone straight to answer machine. This morning he had tried again and a man answered saying he was a deputy sheriff, so he had cut the call straight away. He swore harshly, worried and blaming himself for letting her go alone to deal with the Argy's.

Like Chris, he knew how brutal the drug cartels could be. He was pacing around the floor, considering all possibilities, none of which he liked. The back door went and he spun around, hand reaching behind to his waist band for his Glock. It was Doyle returning from a trip out to gather what information he could.

"Well?" Brennan demanded without any precursor.

Doyle's face said it all before he spoke. "Not good. Apparently she went to the Meredith place to see her Argy contact there, as you said she would. But she didn't leave, she was killed by a horse apparent-"

"A horse?" Brennan exploded. "Remember, I told you she knew horses, was part brought up on her uncle's farm."

"I know, but we got one of the lads to go up there on a fake delivery. When he got there he asked around, as he saw all the police cars about. Anyway, they say she went into the stallion's stable by mistake, couldn't get out and tried to shoot it as it attacked her. It kicked her to death," he said quietly. "Terrible, just terrible, I'm really sorry. But, and this is really interestin', they also say that another guy died and three more in hospital. Apparently there was a hell of a fight; an intruder put them all in hospital and that the guy who did it had a hood on like a mask. Do you think they are tryin' to finger you?"

"What? A guy with a balaclava?" Brennan's mind raced, spinning through the possibilities. "Look, it wasn't me, you know that and it couldn't be the Argy's or cartel men or whatever. So who was it? A third party? Not the DEA, they would have operated officially and not as a masked man. This feels like security forces to me. Who the fock was it? I need to speak with your informant, it all doesn't fit right."

"OK," Doyle replied. "I'll get him here for you." He picked up his mobile and dialled a number. "Kev, it's me, can you come round for a beer tonight and a game of poker with the boys? Me missus is out and I'm on me' own. Good. What say, 7.00? Grand, see you later.

"Right, he'll be here at seven. You can talk to him then. In the meantime, I'll see what else I can find out." Doyle left the house and Brennan continued to filter the information, swearing he would kill whoever had murdered Siobhan.

CHAPTER 30

Rupert and Chris took the film to be developed at a local photo shop on an hour's service. Whilst waiting, they grabbed a sandwich at a Starbucks and sat in the shade.

"Nice chain operation," Rupert commentated. "I wonder if they'll ever spread to the UK? Be great to do acquisition work for a chain like this."

"Do you ever stop being an agent?" Chris chided him.

"Er, let me think about that, no. But I could say the same about you. You've checked the street three time since we sat here, had me do numerous counter surveillance manoeuvres on the way here and from the polo factory."

"I know, it's a habit," Chris replied, knowing that the second unofficial mantra of The Regiment was, *How can we do it better?* "But it's one that will hopefully keep us alive and well. Now when will those photos be ready?"

Rupert checked his watch. "About ten minutes. Let's pay up here and walk across, they may be ready early." At that moment his mobile buzzed and a voice message sign came up. He played the message back, hearing Claire's voice in his ear.

"Everything alright?" Chris asked.

"Yea, just Claire saying she is going to the quarter finals with Vikki."

"Don't look so worried, she is in company and if anything happens someone will rush her to hospital. It'll take her mind off things."

"No, you're right and I did suggest that she go, after all," Rupert conceded.

Upon arriving at the photo shop, the film was indeed ready ahead of time and they returned to the car with the still slightly sticky photos. Sorting through the pictures Rupert had taken, two showed the detailed pages of the 'Out Goods' ledger that he had photographed. They had bought a cheap magnifying glass at a hardware store and this blew the names and addresses up to full legibility. Rupert pounced on one name and the size of the order.

"There look, yesterday, 50 boxes of balls to Lopez Sports Equipment, Unit 6 Hunnerton Estate, East Street, Wellington. That has to be it, no one orders fifty boxes in one go. I know it's a long shot but it's the only one that comes anywhere near."

Chris shrugged. "Let's give it a try, times running out and we have no other leads."

They headed back to Wellington and bought a map of the local area. The industrial zones were marked and they found East street and the Hunnerton Estate. When they arrived, Rupert was disappointed. It was well run, with smart units and a good array of tenants, some of whom were household names. The units were a mix of sizes but of similar construction, with a flat roofed office pod to the front and the main building of pitched construction to the rear.

"What were you expecting? A shabby unit with baddies armed to the teeth, guard dogs and a big sign saying 'Drugs Dealers R Us.'" Chris laughed. "No, this is a good front. Who would suspect a drug operation here? But what do we do now? We can't just march in and ask to see the premises."

But in response, Rupert just smiled. "I am going to do what

I am trained to do; be a surveyor. To Chris's puzzled expression he explained. "I will canvass the estate see if anyone wants to sell into Sub-Prime, just like I would in the UK. You know, out here looking for real estate, loans. You name it, we do it. Have you still got Philip Rosti and Matt Woods' business cards?" Puzzled, Chris dug into his wallet and produced one of each, handing them to Rupert.

"Perfect just as we do in the UK; if you want to remain anonymous and get around a building incognito, use someone else's card. It always checks out and you are completely in the clear."

"But why more than one card?" he saw Rupert pocket them with those he had in his wallet.

"Because I can ask information on the way, remember your Mosaic thing? By the time I get to their unit, I will know who their grandmother is and what they had for breakfast, this is what I do for living remember? Also if they see me roaming round, which they will, it'll look less suspicious when I knock on their door."

"Alright, but stay out of trouble. Claire would never forgive me if anything happened to you," he warned.

Rupert, note pad in hand, went off grinning, singing an old Jamo Thomas song: *"I spy, for the FBI, I spy for the FBI..."* with Chris just shaking his head.

Rupert walked to the first of the units marked as a distribution company and began his spiel, getting it right for the American market and by the time he came to the final unit in the row, he was getting into the swing of it. He pushed through the outer door which led into a small office, a Latino secretary was behind a desk, bashing away on a keyboard in front of a computer screen. She looked up as he entered and a smile was etched on her face together with a perfunctory 'Good afternoon'.

Rupert's in-built assessor of every firm he had ever visited, from his first day at CR back in the early 80's came into play.

He reckoned almost without fail that he could assess the firm, its' attitude and mentality, just by the smile or greeting of the receptionist. To him it spoke volumes. He instinctively knew that this was the place: there was, to his sensitive antennae, a feeling of nervousness, a wariness of strangers who turned up unannounced and a slight hostility despite the smile and casual courtesy.

"Ah, good afternoon," he began in his best Hugh Grant foppish manner.

"Ah sorry to disturb, Matt Wood, down from New York office of HBJ Realtors," he continued not put off by the slightly puzzled expression on the receptionist's face. He turned the smile up to maximum wattage and continued. "Yes, looking at properties down here for Sub-Prime investors; been around the other units and now here. Wondered if I might have a word with the manager or owner if they are about."

Despite herself, the receptionist's smile deepened at the innocuous drivel Rupert was spouting.

"Do you have a card?" she said in heavily accented English as Rupert passed her Matt Wood's business card. "Wait here." He muttered a thank you as she got up, pressed the code on the keypad and slipped through the door to the factory area behind. Rupert had a brief glimpse of men in masks, one stood around with an automatic rifle, the noise of what sounded like electric drills making a screeching sound and the unmistakeable smell of hot or burning plastic.

Bingo! He thought, *whatever happens we are in the right place.* Rupert looked around the office, lost in thought and then noticed the security camera up on the wall above the door through which he had entered. A minute or so later, the receptionist returned, followed by a swarthy individual of Spanish origin, and a face scarred by pock marks of small pox or some similar disease. The eyes were dead, with a thinly masked brutality behind them.

Once again as the door swung shut, the obnoxious smell of hot plastic emanated from the factory.

"*Señor* Wood, this is *Señor* Lopez the owner," the receptionist introduced them.

"Ah good afternoon, Matt Wood, how d'do?" he asked in the same manner. Lopez shook hands and clearly not in the mood for niceties, asked straight away," So how can I help you?"

"Well, as you see from my card, I work for HBJ out of the New York office and we're looking at new areas to invest in with the Sub-Prime market taking off, you know." He received nothing in response, just a blank stare. Unperturbed, he continued with his spiel, "Anyway, we're looking at acquiring properties, keeping the businesses going but buying in and letting them back to the owners. We call it sale and leaseback. I wondered, therefore, if you would be amenable to having a chat about the possibility of structuring some sort of deal.

"I have spoken to others on the estate and one or two are potentially interested. Obviously, the more we can bring together, the better from our point of view." Rupert waited patiently, letting the silence build; he was a past master of the silent treatment himself and he knew what a weapon it could be. Lopez just looked at him as though trying to make sense of his words.

"Why here? I mean, why this area."

"Well, as we expand, we wanted to get in down here before others do, in the good areas. Very wealthy here, of course, Palm Beach, the polo, in fact that is why we're here at the moment down to see the tournament for the finals. Thought I'd mix a bit of business with pleasure, you see?"

"Who's we?" he asked in a flat response with no reaction at all to the mention of polo.

"Why, me and my colleague. He is out on other parts of the estate talking to other owners as well. Look if it is not a good time, maybe we can make an appointment and come back later?" he asked.

"No, I don't think so, we are not interested. We like the unit and won't sell. Goodbye." With that, he shook hands and opened the outer, door making it very clear that Rupert should leave.

"Ah well, that is a pity. Never mind and thank you for your time. If you change your mind you have my card. Goodbye, Mr Lopez," Rupert responded cheerily. Lopez watched him walk away to the car and drive to the next terrace of units as Rupert continued with the pretence of his excuse for the visit.

Once he was out of earshot, Lopez said in Spanish, "Pris, as soon as he is gone, go to the others you know on the estate, see if he asked the same thing of them, OK?"

"Yes, of course. Are you worried about him? He just seemed a stupid *cringo* out to make money and his accent was funny, he was English, I think, not *Americano.*"

"I am always suspicious when something out of the ordinary happens. Now go and find out once they have left," he barked in response. "But do it casually and only to those we know." Lopez looked down at the business card again. *Once Pris was back with the news, he would call the boss,* he thought. *Better safe than sorry.*

Outside, Rupert and Chris carried on the pretence with a visit to other units and the adjacent estates.

"You know the irony here," Rupert laughed. "I reckon I've got about ten or so owners who want to do what I have suggested. I could get huge fees from this canvassing. Dear old Matt Wood is going to get a lot of calls which he won't know anything about. Now what do we do?"

"We go away back to the hotel and wait until this evening. Then *I* go back and take a closer look," Chris replied.

Rupert protested. "Oh no, I will be the driver and you take a look. For a start, I can cover you and let you know if anyone is coming."

"Rups, there will be people there anyway. They're not going to let a load of cocaine lie around unguarded, are they? No, it will be tricky, but I bet they'll be another shift on and I should be able to spy something."

"OK but I still say you need a driver."

It was now getting towards late afternoon when they set off, each lost in his own thoughts. They arrived at the hotel to find Claire back and lying down. She was as eager for their news as they were for hers.

"So you're going back again tonight? But if they've permanent guards in position and they're armed, how are you going to see anything ? You'll just alert them to the fact that they are being watched and close it down or try and trace it back to you and Rupert. That   will be dangerous. Why not just tell the DEA chap or Sheriff Reed and they can raid the place."

"Claire, just leave it to me; I know what I am doing, I have a sort of plan. Now I need to go and report what we've found, but I'm not proposing to tell either Sheriff Reed or Meacham until we are certain and I don't want their size 12 boots plodding around messing things up. Each time we've found that they are ahead of us somehow. I mean, who's to say that someone on the inside isn't bent or they have bugged the Sheriff's office? I don't know, I just want to play it my way for now."

They all went for supper together at a restaurant in Palm Beach that was reputed to serve the best ribs anywhere in the US. They were not disappointed: three huge racks of ribs arrived, dripping with sweet, hot, barbecue sauce.

"Look at these, we'll never finish them," Claire commented.

"You just watch me; it's been a long day and it'll be an even longer night," Chris exclaimed tucking into his rack with gusto. They gave up further discussion of the day's events and tried to take the evening as a holiday with limited success. Both Chris and Rupert had their minds on the evening ahead and how it was going to pan out.

"Right Claire, when we get back to the hotel, order room service for about 11.30 and when the tray arrives make sure that you talk to 'someone' in the room. Make a sarcastic comment and give the waiter a large tip so that he remembers the event. He will also remember more than one person being there, even if he doesn't see them. OK?"

Claire nodded in agreement.

"By which time we will be back to the industrial unit early and see what is really happening inside."

The meal finished, they drove back to the hotel. Claire had both sets of keys to the rooms, so they appeared occupied on the hotel computer and made ready to order an evening snack.

CHAPTER 31

BOGOTA

Ballesteros was still in his country *rancheria* so Rojas put a call in on an unlisted number to inform his boss of the progress.

"*Jefe,*" Rojas spoke in fast Spanish, "it went well. The agent *Shivren* is dead and the latest consignment is ready. The distribution points will be clear, with shipments in the next two days." He waited for the next question, noting that there was not the usual pleasure in hearing a main enemy had been taken down.

"*Si* but I hear that all is not well, eh? Four men down and by who eh, by who?" he demanded. *Shit,* Rojas thought, *how does he know?*

"Yes, *Jefe,* I know; one dead and three injured. Whoever it was, he was good. He took out four, including Rizzo who is badly hurt. Also is Ramon back safely yet?" he asked, referring to the driver of the Trans Am who had run Rupert and Claire off the road.

"Yes, he crossed the border last night in the tunnel. Good work there, shame they are not dead, but I hear that things have

285

gone quiet and the woman, the wife of the *cringo*, was badly hurt. They should now back off and return to the UK, if not, kill them. Now Rizzo and the others, they are still in hospital?" Rojas confirmed they were. "Right, well make sure they don't talk. Anyone goes near them on a regular basis, silence them, OK? No leaks. Who did this to my men?"

"We think it must be Brennan. We know he made contact with *Shivren* and met with her. She must have planned it with him. We are lucky that she was killed and he was unable to help her. Only someone as dangerous as him could do such damage, one of the others may yet die."

"I don't care. Get someone who is better. Find Brennan, and kill him or I will send you, *comprende?*" A shiver went down Rojas spine as he muttered that he would sort it.

* * *

WELLINGTON

There was no moon, little wind to blow the clouds away and a promise of storm. For Chris, it was perfect. He was dressed in black again and had his Yukon night vision binoculars. There was still activity on the industrial estate; some of the tenants clearly ran night shifts. Rupert pulled into the service area and made straight for one of the units to the back of the estate. Chris dropped and rolled out of the slow moving car without it stopping. Rupert parked up with the interior light off and hardly any profile showing within the vehicle.

It was the flat-roofed office pod at the front of the building that had attracted Chris's attention and allowed him to form a plan on how to get a better idea of what went on inside. The pod stood proud from the main unit, but was only half the width. In each corner cast in shadow was a down pipe, running down from the gutter surrounding the flat roof. Being industrial units, they were not plastic but galvanised tin, with wide gutter apertures and square box-like down pipes.

Upon leaving the car, Chris sprinted for the sanctuary of the shadows as there were, of course, no windows at ground floor level. The units were constructed of brick and corrugated tin on the upper elevations, with roof lights set into the gently sloping apex of the main roof. This again was a regular characteristic of all the units on the estate.

In shadow, Chris made his way around to the corner of the pod and tugged hard on the downpipe. It didn't budge. Carefully using the edges of the bricks for footholds, to minimise the strain on the pipe fittings, he began to climb. It was only twenty feet and he reached the top with little effort. He pulled himself up over the gutter and onto the flat roof, expecting at any moment to be bathed in a security spotlight, highlighted against the shiny surface of the flat roof. He hurried on the balls of his feet to the relative shelter of the eaves, cast in greyer shadows. Chris stilled his breathing, focusing, absorbing all the ambient sounds and listened intently to sense if anything was out of kilter.

Satisfied, he carefully moved to the lowest point of the gable end and hoisted himself up as quietly as possible onto the pitched roof. Then crab-like, keeping as low as possible, he moved laterally across the shiny corrugated tin, balancing speed and silence with the fear of sliding downwards to the edge as he gripped the corrugations tightly with strong fingers.

He managed to successfully travel along to the first roof light; a three foot by four foot panel of safety glass set into the roof and offering natural light to the unit in the day time. Lying flat against the tin roof, he carefully edged his head over the glass, prepared at any moment to pull back and if necessary slide down the roof and off the edge. He peered into the well-lit factory space twenty feet below.

Armed guards patrolled up and down with what looked like Colt AR 15 assault rifles on slings. Stretching before him the whole thing was like a production line. Boxes of polo balls were at one end, in a sectioned off area, this fed the rest of the factory via a conveyor belt, with workers emptying out the balls. Then at the next stage, they found the dimple like impression where the injection had taken place originally, which Claire had described from her visit to the Dallas factory. Each ball was then placed in a hollowed plastic cup and an electric drill was pulled down on a drill clamp, it was halted half way through drilling. The operator then flicked a recessed clip on the bit and restarted. The process was reversed with the withdrawal of the bit. *So that is how they are doing it.* Chris thought. Then another person in the line sucked out the dust and debris with a small vacuum like pump, as used by dentists.

The balls were then passed to the next person in the 'production line'. He or she wearing a white mask, then filled the hollow ball with the white powder from a thin tube fed by a hopper above. The balls were then placed on a slow conveyor belt, holding them with the opening upright. The next process was fascinating as another set of drills were loaded with a small piece of coned plastic, just like those that Josh had photographed in Rizzo's room. The hole was plugged with a cone and then spun around by the drill, making an horrible screeching noise, before finally sealing due to 'friction welding'.

The final process was just out of sight and Chris had to carefully edge along to the next set of roof lights. Here he saw the plugged balls taken up and a hot blade cutter, shear off the proud end of the dowel, literally like a hot knife through butter. At this point he smelled the noxious fumes of melting plastic coming through the roof vents at the apex of the roof. He creased his nose in disgust. He saw that the finished balls, now containing cocaine, were thrown into plastic crates and went nowhere near the original cardboard boxes. Then Chris's world was bathed in headlights.

Two lorries entered the industrial estate and headed for the unit. He held his breath and tried to embed himself into the rigid corrugated steel of the roof. The two lorries' headlights on high beam flew down the side of the unit to the loading bay at the gable end.

Rupert in the waiting car saw all this and prayed for Chris on the roof top. As soon as the lorries started to stop and reverse nosily up to the loading docks with the beeping of reversing horns, Rupert had the wherewithal to start the car. He then turned on the headlights as though he had every right to be there and drove away from the adjacent unit, using it as cover. By the time the electric roller shutters were up, he was pulling out along the front of the adjacent unit and out of sight, where he stopped with the engine running. His mobile phone buzzed and an SMS message showed from Chris: 'Slowly round front now'.

In the noise of the roller shutter doors opening, Chris allowed himself to slide slowly down the pitch of the roof, using the lip of the gutter to stop his graceful progress. Here he rolled onto his stomach and using the gutter as leverage, slipped over the side and dropped the fifteen feet or so to the floor, immediately rolling to break the fall. He came up on the balls of his feet and ran to the Ford as it crept slowly by the front of the unit, slipping into the passenger seat.

"Get out of the estate, pull over about a hundred yards away and we wait for the lorries to leave," he ordered. Rupert, knowing him well, made no move to engage him until they were safely away. They pulled in amongst other parked cars in a side street which gave a view either way out of the industrial estate.

"Good, from here we can see but not be seen," Chris commented approvingly.

"Now tell me, what did you see?" Rupert asked impatiently.

"Very interesting and now nearly all our questions are answered," he responded and began to tell Rupert of all that he had seen.

"But you said a drill bit. I still don't see how it can be done, What did they look like, how do they get in and ream out the inside with only a small hole?"

"Yea, well I looked through binos and there were spare bits lying on the table, but I couldn't see properly in detail, only that somehow they managed to hollow out the balls.

"Wow so that's how they're doing it. No wonder Rizzo didn't want poor Harding to get that information back to MI6. Those must have been samples he had in his room. So simple and clever once you know the answer. What now?"

"We wait. Those lorries will load up with the filled balls which I am assuming will get transported to another place not contaminated with any of the cocaine. They will then be washed in a form of bleach or something similar: the drug sniffer dogs can't detect through the smell of bleach. And providing the balls are hermetically sealed, which they obviously are, they could pass any inspection."

"But why bother, why not just from one area to another in the same building?"

"Because the sniffer dogs are really sensitive and even a slight trace of cocaine, no matter how microscopic, and they would pick it up. This way, no one with contact to the exposed cocaine gets anywhere near the sealed units. The cardboard boxes will probably go by a separate van or something, maybe even new boxes marked accordingly, then they will be repacked afterwards, just smelling of plastic, bleach or whatever they use. Bang." Chris snapped his fingers, "all done and safe. We learned a lot in Colombia on the anti-drug raids," he finished in answer to Rupert's raised eyebrow. "Mind you, I've learned a lot from being a 'surveyor' too, like how to analyse industrial units and see how they are put together: you taught me well Rupert, you taught me well!" He clapped Rupert on the shoulder and smiled.

They waited for about half an hour and then saw the head-lights of the lorries leaving the factory.

"Right, start the car up, but no lights yet. Just get ready to move and keep low, I will look to see where they are going," Chris ordered. The lorries turned left out of the industrial estate and passed the entrance to the side they were parked in.

"Shall we go yet?" Rupert asked, eager to give chase.

"No wait one; there I knew it, an escort car, probably armed and to make sure the lorries are not tailed," he pointed as a Chevy passed by, just after the lorries. "OK take it easy, now we go just close enough to see, no more."

Rupert turned on the lights and pulled out just after another car went along the road, which would give them perfect cover. They proceeded to 'cat and mouse' the trailing car, ignoring the lorries as they were certain that the 'guard car' would follow the route.

"Now if the car turns off, stay with the lorries, it may do so and then come back on again just to check."

As Chris had thought after ten minutes and heading out of town, the 'guard car' pulled into the side and stopped. "Keep going, Rups. I'll keep an eye on the car, you follow the lorries." With that he pulled out the night scope and turned to face backwards. They had now left the street lights of the town and the night binoculars came into their own as they went deeper into the countryside.

"There they go. Just as I thought, pulling out without lights and tucked in behind someone else. OK, at the next legitimate driveway, pull in as though you own the place."

Within a few hundred yards, Rupert saw a driveway and pulled in with late signalling. He carried right up to the house and cut the lights. The following 'guard car' went slowly past and they both sensed eyes on them, then it was gone. Rupert quietly flipped the car through a sharp two point turn and was back down the drive and onto the road. They saw the distinctive shape of the Chevy in front and waited back about three hundred yards, matching its pace. Now they were entering suburbs again and small industrial estates appeared on both sides of the road. Then the Chevy just disappeared from view.

"Right, when we get level, slow down a bit but do not stop, all we need is to mark the spot. Then we go past and park somewhere whilst I go back on foot," Chris instructed. They passed the entrance to what looked like a small estate and pulled into a fast food burger drive thru.

"We must nearly be back in Wellington. If this is where they distribute from, it is perfect for the polo set. I'll get a burger for show and will park up at the back over there," he pointed.

"I'm good to go. See you later." Chris slipped from the car and melted into the darkness away from street lights, assuming cover of the vegetation behind the carpark. Five minutes later he was inside the estate, having climbed the chain link fence and dropped inside.

It was smaller than the Hunnerton estate with no more than 20 units. *What Rupert would call 'nursery units' of about 2,500 to 5,000 square feet,* Chris thought to himself wryly, *I've been around him for too long.*

He slipped from unit to unit, heading for the end of the first parade where the two lorries were being unloaded adjacent to the Chevy 'guard car'. He stayed in the shadows, not wanting to venture near. There appeared to be no easy way to access or view the units: no office pod; no convenient flat roof to shin up to; but they did have windows at ground floor level which to his mind was good and bad news. He could see in: they could see out. Much more risky. They finished loading, the shutters rolled down, but the lorries stayed in place and so did the Chevy, parked at the front of the unit.

The ensuing silence seemed much more ominous. Chris knew he had a decision to make: he had confirmation that this was where the drugs were distributed from; so should he go further and risk exposure or get the hell out and phone Sheriff Reed or Seth Meacham? He needed to know for sure, he decided.

Keeping to the shadows of the buildings and avoiding the arc lights dotted around the estate, he made his way successfully to the unit, there he saw a sign. Sports Distribution Inc. *Original,* he thought. He eased himself up to full height and looked at an oblique angle through one of the windows. He saw nothing, they had been painted in sun reflective paint which rendered them opaque. *Sod it,* he thought. He moved further around and finally ended up at the rear of the unit by the roller shutter doors.

They stood proud of the rear wall by a good two feet, in a sort of brick housing and formed part of the shallow loading dock. Chris sniffed the air and moved in close to the roller shutter doors: too close. They creaked in their slides, harsh against the still night. He caught his balance and moved backwards. Swearing silently, he held his breath, hearing a quiet conversation inside.

The pedestrian door on the side creaked open, very fast and a figure appeared carrying an automatic pistol, silhouetted against the factory light. Chris had ducked back into the shadow of the rear loading wall. It was a poor hiding place and easily exposed. But he knew what he would do if he were inside: send an obvious man out of the back and maybe one or two quietly from the front to nab any intruder in a pincer. He knew that he had maybe seconds to deal with this and be away.

A man coming out into darkness carrying a gun will turn to the right first if he is right handed, it is a natural thing to do. Chris knew this and waited. They had been taught that the human body was designed to take punishment from the front. All the muscles are there, big strong muscles and a rib cage to protect the organs. The head itself has a jaw and a neck and tendons ready to absorb frontal assault and protect the head from damage, absorbing energy. What the body is not good at, is absorbing assault from behind or the side. There is a point they had been shown, just behind the hinge of the jaw, where if struck with force will cause an instant knock out on pretty well anyone. It is where every boxer dreams of connecting: the guaranteed knock out.

The guard moved just past the wall pier and Chris launched a smashing straight left in the wing chun style, landing just on the hinge of the jaw and slightly on the pressure point behind the jaw. It was a perfect blow, his fist almost breaking the guard's neck. He just had time to catch him as he started to drop. He grasped the pistol, left the guard in a heap and ducked behind one of the lorries, pulling himself onto the bumper at the front of the cab. As he expected, two men appeared suddenly, one from either side and nearly ended up shooting each other. Seeing their colleague lying in the doorway, they swore in Spanish and looked around. One immediately dropped down, looking under the two lorries for signs of legs but saw nothing. They fanned out; one rushing into the unit and one back around the front.

Chris seized the moment, dropped off the bumper and ran to the next unit along and continued using them as cover until he gained the fence. But he knew it would make a noise if he attempted to climb it. Then he heard voices of the other guards who were now combing the estate, working systematically. He pulled out the Nokia and sent an SMS message to Rupert. *Pull up near the front then wheel spin and pull away fast.* Within a few seconds he heard the car arrive, brake hard, revving engine screaming as all eyes turned to the front of the estate and they ran towards it. Rupert revved the engine, and squealed away. They fired after him into the darkness and in the chaos Chris was over the fence and away. He called Rupert: "Yea?"

"Drive three blocks, round in a circle and pull up in the street opposite the drive thru. I'll be there."

"Roger that."

A minute later Rupert pulled to a halt and Chris emerged from the darkness, ducking into the car. They pulled out onto the road in the opposite direction to the industrial estate and drove off sedately. They immediately saw signs for Palm Beach. "Well, you certainly know how to have a party. Are you alright?"

"Fine, they missed!"

CHAPTER 32

Claire was pacing the room, worried. *Come on,* she thought, *come on, where are you? It doesn't take this long to look at a shitty shed!* She checked her watch again, two hours. Then she heard her mobile go, trilling a metallic ring. She saw the number and recognised it.

"Chris, where are you? Is everything alright? Where's Rupert?"

"Don't worry. We're 3 miles away. Rupert's fine and by my side, he's driving. See you in five, got to go."

"Ohh!" she ranted at the silent mobile, "bloody irritating man." And threw it on the bed in frustration.

* * *

Claire was not the only angry and frustrated person that night. The guards of the unit at the industrial estate were furious and slightly frightened. It did not do to fail within the cartel organisation. If you did, it often meant the ultimate penalty.

The leader of the guards, now called a number in America; the boss who orchestrated the whole US operation. There was no answer from the mobile. There was a landline, but only to be used in the direst emergency and if anyone else answered, not the boss, they had been instructed to hang up immediately. He swore in Spanish. Rizzo was still in hospital, who else was there to call?

The line was not secure to dial internationally back to Columbia and he really did not want to face Rojas, yet. Besides, he reasoned, what harm had been done? A snooper knocked out a guard and ran off. Nothing stolen; no security breached; could just be an opportunistic burglar, he tried to persuade himself of the fact, but knew in his heart that it was more than that. Santos, the guard who had been knocked out, had seen nothing, one minute upright, searching, the next unconscious and concussed. No, he would keep quiet and try the boss again later.

Chris and Rupert having made good their escape were nearly back at the hotel.

"So you smelled bleach from inside?" Rupert asked.

"Yes, but mixed with something else, unsurprisingly a sort of plastic, sweat smell. I can only assume that they wash the balls in bleach and then wash them again in something else to disguise the smell."

"It would certainly work and as you say, the dogs would be unable to pick it up. With the amount of balls going over, they could take tons of the stuff unnoticed and if it's pure, by the time it was cut and on the market it would be worth a hell of a lot more."

"Yea, providing they don't mix it with plastic and talcum powder!"

Arriving at the hotel, Chris quickly changed back into his casual clothes, not wanting to draw attention to himself. He put the clothes and trainers into a small bag and carried them through the hotel lobby upstairs, with both he and Rupert looking every inch the tourists back from a night out.

They split up and agreed to meet again in Rupert's room once Chris had tidied himself up. Chris entered his room, dropped the bag by the door and moved quietly across to draw the curtains. Guided by ambient light, he hated to find himself silhouetted against the window. He became aware of an outline above the armchair that should not be there. He reasoned that he would already be dead if that was the intention, so he froze, maintaining his composure. A desk lamp flicked on, illuminating the occupant of the chair.

There before him was the beautiful face of Samantha Lester.

"Hi," she said coolly. "You're a hard man to track down." She placed her drink on the side table and stood up in an elegant fluid move, aware of both her body and her sexual allure. She was wearing pastel pink eye shadow, highlighting her eyes and the golden tan of her skin and a lightly pleated flowing turquoise dress, which clung to her breasts. It was obvious that she wore very little underneath; Chris had to admit that she looked sensational. Once again he was consumed by the heavy scent of white musk and jasmine and found it intoxicating.

He asked the obvious question. "How did you get in here? The room was locked."

"In this town, money and influence go a long way, so don't be so naïve. Anyway, aren't you pleased to see me? I missed you at polo today and I haven't seen you since you slinked off ill at lunch; not that I believed a word of it." She moved closer, her eyes drawing him in like a hypnotic snake mesmerizing its prey. Her lips parted and the tip of her tongue slid sensually from one side to the other of her glistening lips.

Slowly, oh so slowly, it seemed to Chris, she moved her hand up and slid the strap from her dress. Shrugging her shoulders forward, the dress slithered down her body in a whisper of silk to pool around her high heels. Chris gazed down from her beautiful face, taking in the tanned, high, firm breasts, flat stomach and flaring hips, a tiny triangle of black lace, the only thing covering her nakedness. "Well?" She murmured her voice a rasping whisper and made to step forward.

Chris woke as if from a trance and held up the palm of his hand. "No, I'm sorry Sam, but no. I don't sleep with the wives of friends or people I know."

Her eyes betrayed a burning anger of disbelief. "Hah friends? You mean Bill? My God are you mad? He's not your friend, he is an avaricious business man who's out for all he can get. You, along with Rupert, just happen to be a solution. My God, I don't believe it!"

"Alright then, business associate and I don't want to kill the deal. Look, I freely admit I have very few morals, but that happens to be one of my rules. If I met you under other circumstances, well then it would be different."

Sam, cocked one hip, unfazed by her nakedness and assured of her allure.

"What is it about you? What are you afraid of, him, me or both? It was the same at lunch the other day. I know that awful tart Anita was there, but there is an intensity that I can't fathom: yes, you let people in, but as soon as they start to go deeper, an almost imperceptible wall comes down. Or maybe I should say breached?

I don't know, look at you, even now you frown, then grow distant. You're clearly not affected. I am obviously not the first person to say this. Well?"

As with all good cover stories, Chris fell back on partial truth. "I was an orphan, grew up on the streets, learned early never to let anything get to me." It helped to keep the truth from her and was a perfect reason to hide his true persona.

"It is not just that. You seem perpetually prepared, ready. Why, I bet if I turned into a genie now, you would spring forward with a jar and a stopper at the ready. There is something intangible about you." She sighed and bent forward exposing a perfect cleavage, and gently slipped the dress back in to place. "But I tell you this, watch out for Bill, things are not what they seem there. He is in desperate need of cash and will do anything to get what he wants. Even I get frightened of him sometimes," she admitted.

Chris pushed his luck and wanted to see if he could get more from her. "Is that why you play around?"

The resounding slap on his face was like the crack of a whip. He saw it coming but forced himself not to block the blow. It would have required exceptional reflexes. "I don't play around with just anyone. And you try being married to someone old enough to be your father!" she retorted.

"You chose to marry him." Sam didn't respond but picked up her handbag and walked to the door.

Then, as a seeming after thought, turned to Chris with a parting shot, "You may live to regret this." She turned and left with a surprisingly gentle close of the door. Chris shook his head in disbelief and immediately went to check on the briefcase in the wardrobe. It was in a slightly different position to that which he had left it, but the locks still appeared intact. He frowned in concern and went to tell Rupert of what had just occurred. Claire beckoned him to come in after he had knocked and he found Rupert on the mobile phone to Meacham, telling him of the evenings events. It appeared from the one sided conversation that he was not best pleased.

"Have you told anyone else?" Meacham demanded.

"Yes, we have let Sheriff Reed know. We tried you earlier but you didn't answer your mobile."

Meacham swore down the phone, ignoring the jibe. "What is Reed going to do?"

"I don't know, Agent Meacham."

"OK, leave it to me, I will liaise with Sheriff Reed and we will work together. Oh… and thank you, it was good work."

"Not at all, glad to be of service. We can just back out completely now and enjoy the last two days of our holiday." He put the phone down

"You're never going to believe what just happened to me." They both looked enquiringly at him. "Sam Lester was in my room and just tried to seduce me."

"What?" they both exclaimed.

"I warned you, Chris, the woman's a nightmare. What happened?" said Claire , so he explained in detail the events of the last few minutes. Claire was not surprised but Rupert was much more suspicious.

"And she said she was frightened of Bill Lester?" he asked after Chris finished his narrative.

"At times yes, but she didn't say why."

"You know, all along we have been looking only so far and we are sure that there is someone here orchestrating everything. We already have our doubts about Lester with his finances and cashflow problems. I think that this could be the final clue we need to proving that he is the boss of the operation north of the border. I mean, he has always known of our movements, seeing clients, it wouldn't take him much more effort to work out where we're going; and he has the contacts and financial clout to make things happen."

"He also has a lot to lose," Claire speculated. "So much of his wealth or potential wealth is tied up in property. It would all fit if it was him."

"Let me just say this," Chris interjected, "we don't need to know. It is not our job or the reason that we came here. We, or rather you, Rups, were asked to get to the bottom of the drugs route and how they were being smuggled out. We have done enough and my job was to protect you. Well, I'm doing that now.

Let it lie, I want you both, and particularly you Claire, safely back in the UK, so from now on let's just enjoy the last two days of the holiday, see some polo maybe, lie by the pool, but leave everything to Reed and Meacham, they are quite capable of tying this up without our help."

Looking at his watch he continued, "I should think that even now Sheriff Reed is mounting a posse, (if they still do that) to raid the two warehouses and Meacham won't be far behind him. All we have to do is let Johnston know in the UK and our work here is done. I'm knackered and off to bed."

"You're right, of course," Rupert conceded. "It is just so easy to get caught up in everything. I need to get some sleep too."

Chris left their room bidding them goodnight. He felt tired and emotionally drained, the way he always did post action. Entering his room he opened the briefcase containing the sat phone, entered the security code and sent a report of all that had happened to London, in the event that any polo teams left early for the UK, as they so often did once knocked out of the tournament. The border forces would then be alerted and could investigate any large quantities of balls being brought in by the Argentine teams. Following the report, Chris then downed a stiff whiskey, undressed and was asleep almost immediately when his head hit the pillow.

* * *

If Rupert was content, Tir Brennan was not. Earlier that evening he received more information concerning Siobhan's death from the truck driver who had visited the Meredith ranch. He became more convinced than ever that a special operative was at work.

But to his mind it posed more questions than answers, as he propounded to Doyle.

"So it was definitely the Argy groom Miguel who saw her last and she somehow got shut in a stable with no way out and a nutty stallion. But if that was the case, then who the fuck was roamin' around smashing up the other Argies and why the hell didn't they help each other? It was on home ground for them. All this guy Miguel had to do was shout. So maybe the grooms were taken out before Siobhan, if so, by whom? It just doesn't make sense. But I'll tell you what, there is another player in this game and the answers all lie at the Meredith ranch. I need to go there," he said emphatically.

"No, Tir, you need to keep a low profile. Let me get someone else to take a look."

"No! I'm going, no one else. If I find that fucker Miguel, he and I are going to have words."

CHAPTER 33

The following morning, Rupert was awoken by the trilling of the bedside telephone.

"Yes, Rupert Brett speaking."

"Mr Brett, Sheriff Reed. Good morning, how you doing?"

"Fine, Sheriff, fine. I think a little early maybe. What can I do for you?"

"Well, I'd like to meet up with you and Mr Adams, can I come around in about half an hour, get a cup of coffee with you both?"

"Certainly, Sheriff. We'll see you in the dining room, we'll be having breakfast."

"Good. I'll see you in thirty minutes. Bye."

Rupert looked at the humming receiver in puzzlement.

"Now what the hell was that all about?" he mused quietly. It was half an hour later that Sheriff Reed entered the dining room of the hotel and made his way to their table, attracting more than a few interested glances from the other guests. Upon seeing them all shake hands and receive a kiss from Claire in greeting, they soon lost interest with no apparent drama to intrigue them. Once coffee was ordered, Sheriff Reed began to explain the night's happenings.

"Well, we got there and of course I knew of the estate. We found the unit, but it was clean. Just a receptionist in the front and some guys in the back, cleaning off benches, some machinery, a conveyor belt, that was it. No boxes of polo balls; no drugs, nothing. But here's the thing: the whole place was being pressure washed and there was a strong smell of chemicals probably bleach or ammonia. Someone got wind of our proposed visit and did a fine clean-up job."

Rupert and Chris exchanged glances.

"Well it begs the question, either they got a tip off or Chris nearly being caught at the second warehouse alerted them to the possibility that they needed to close it all down. I suppose in reality if they left all the equipment in place it wouldn't take long to clean it all away. The second storage warehouse, was that also cleared out?" Rupert asked.

"Yup, 'fraid so. However," here he smiled, "they're not quite as clever as they think. You see they covered all the machines, drills etc., in plastic. I assume they'd wiped them all first and didn't want the spray to get into the works. Well," he continued, seeing the interested looks on their faces, "they left something behind." He reached into his brief case and produced an item inside a clear polythene evidence bag.

Inside was a metal drill bit, unlike any other that Rupert or Claire had seen before. This is what Chris had seen below from the skylight and on the bench. The stem of the drill was about six inches long and nearly half an inch across. The sharp end was tapered like a countersink. Reed took the drill out of the plastic. "Don't worry it's been dusted for prints," he assured them, offering it to Rupert.

Upon closer inspection, Rupert saw that recessed into the barrel was a small, sprung lever. Using a finger nail, he pulled it outwards and the parts of the tapered head sprang open to produce razor sharp barbs that shone evilly in the light.

"Incredible, look at those," he exclaimed, gently touching one and immediately regretted it. It had sliced his skin like a paper cut. "Ow, shit!" he exclaimed. "But I've never seen anything like it. Oh it's so simple and clever. Just as you described, Chris."

Chris responded with a nod. "See, they drill so far into the polo ball, release these lethal looking spines, which spin out, effectively hollowing out all the plastic bubbles inside. Then, once it is hollowed out as much as they can go, they retract the spines, pull it out of the ball and hey presto, a hollow ball. Very clever. I couldn't quite see how it was done from the roof. But this is what poor Josh will have died for. He obviously stumbled on to it without realising the full importance of what he had found," Chris surmised.

"So what now?" Claire asked "Do you have enough to put Rizzo and his cronies away or is that the province of the DEA."

"Well, I spoke with Seth Meacham last night and again this morning. He seems pretty pissed at the whole thing. Sort of blaming you guys in a way for spoiling his pitch. But I don't agree, we couldn't have found them without you and to be fair, I didn't really give all the credibility to your story that it deserved. But as to Rizzo and his men, they're under guard at the hospital and we'll see what the state prosecutor has to say in due course. All in all, pretty slim pickin's, but at least we've stopped their game and we can watch out for it in due course. Now, I suggest you folks enjoy the rest of your holiday and the sunshine before you head back to the UK and rain," he joked.

"Sheriff," Chris asked, "have you ever been to England?"

"Once, a long time ago with the army. Stayed for a week on training and then shipped out again. It rained every day!" They all laughed and Sheriff Reed stood to leave, shaking hands with the men, kissing Claire on the cheek and wishing her well with the future and her child.

"Well, if it's a boy, we might even call him 'Slim'."

"Well now, I hope not, 'cause I'll let you into a little secret: my real name's George." He patted his stomach in emphasis of how he got his nickname, chuckled and left them to finish their breakfast.

"I like him," Rupert commented. "And I think I might not answer any of Agent Meacham's calls, sounds like he is not a happy bunny!"

* * *

LONDON

Johnston picked up Sergeant Adams' message as soon as he arrived at his desk. It was the first information he assimilated that morning. Initially he was pleased but felt a little cheated, like a man who takes a bite of a chocolate biscuit, leaves it somewhere and can't find it again. *Yes deeply unsatisfying,* he thought. With that in mind, he picked up the telephone to call Webster, whose response was mixed, empathising with Johnston's frustration.

"Right, well I'll notify customs and border security to be on the lookout for anyone in the polo fraternity who comes in from Miami or Florida in general. We may check them carefully, but I don't want them alerted yet to the fact we are on to them."

"I agree. My instincts tell me we haven't quite got to the bottom of this yet and there is more to play out. Our friend Brennan is not going to very pleased. He might know more than we do and act as a catalyst. He has a pretty mercurial temper and might just light a fuse from which we may all benefit, but at least Mr and Mrs Brett are now safe, Sergeant Adams has done a good job and, to be fair, Brett was justified in asking for his protection."

"Indeed. We'll trace the Argentines coming through, lump up their vehicles and keep tabs on them. Won't make a move until they either move the drugs or try to sell them. Also, be useful to see where and how they break open the balls here and extract the cocaine. Then we can break their little operation from this side as well. Our friends at OCTRIS will be pleased as well. Not that they'll show much appreciation, but it all helps the entente cordial, I suppose."

"Fine, I'll keep you informed if I hear any more."

CHAPTER 34

FLORIDA

Claire had opted for a day by the pool, declaring that for once 'she was all polo'd out.' Chris and Rupert went for a run. Then he persuaded Rupert to go through some Wing Chun with him and extensive chi sao practice, the unique training within the art called 'sticky hands'. After, they both retired to join Claire pool side. It was, all in all, a very relaxed day with the only blot on the horizon being two avoided calls from Seth Meacham.

"I'll give him this, he's a tenacious little bugger, but I'm blowed if I will answer just to get a mouthful of his irascible temper. Serves him right anyway, he should of listened to us earlier."

The day passed without event and in the afternoon Chris checked the sat phone for messages and saw a brief comment from Johnston that they should lie low and enjoy the rest of the time there, but stay alert in case any reprisals may be forthcoming from Brennan or those connected with the drug smuggling.

It was at supper that their day changed. A discreet waiter approached their table and informed Chris there was a telephone call for him and that it was urgent. He walked to one of the booths offering some privacy and picked up the receiver.

"Chris Adams?"

"Chris, oh thank God I've got hold of you. I need your help."

"Sam? What's the matter, calm down, tell me slowly."

"Chris, can you come over, its Bill, I'm frightened and I didn't know who to turn to. The Argy's are on his side and I can't call the sheriff for no reason, it all seems such a mess. Please will you come over?" she pleaded.

"Sam, if this is some kind of ploy to get me into bed-"

"No, I'm serious," at this here voice took on a whisper as though she might be overheard. "It's not that, most of my girl-friends are at the polo after party and I want someone I can trust. You said you don't mix business with pleasure. Please, look, if you don't trust me bring Rupert as well, then you know I won't try and seduce you. Just come as quick as you can, it's all such a mess. I've got to go, he's coming, please think of a reason to come over." With that the line was cut. Chris looked at the dead phone and replaced the receiver. He walked back to the dining room, lost in thought, his mind turning over the conversation in his head.

"Everything alright?" Claire asked, concerned at the per-plexed expression on Chris's face.

"No, not really, I've just had a call from a very distraught Samantha Lester asking me to come over. Says its urgent and she needs someone to help her. She sounded really upset and frightened."

Claire was not impressed. "The damsel in distress act? Come on, Chris, don't fall for it. If she's that worried she can call the police, can't she? Please, Chris, she is a man eater, don't be fooled," she urged.

"Humm, I know what you mean but she sounded really wor-ried and I was as cynical as you, called her bluff and she said that if I didn't believe her I could bring Rupert as a chaperone. Well she didn't use that word but you get my drift. She wanted me over there now and that all her friends were at the after party at the polo club. Asked if we could call over casually on some pretext of work. Anyway, it's not like it's the Meredith place where everything seems to happen. We'll be fine and with Rupert to act as chaperone to protect my virtue, I will still remain a virgin," he joked.

"Well, just see that you both come back safely," Claire retorted.

"Yes mummy," was Rupert's flippant reply as he left the table after kissing her goodbye. Claire frowned at their departure, she wasn't happy and something was nagging at her; *call it woman's intuition,* she told herself. She thought for a while, staring into space and chewing her lip absentmindedly. Claire then made a decision; she left the dining room, returned to her room and picked up the telephone.

Outside in the reception foyer, Chris had more preparations to make.

"Wait one, I know maybe I'm being over cautious but I am going prepared for anything." They both returned to Chris's room and he proceeded to remove the bath panel again, retrieving the hidden Sig and conceal holster, strapping it in place; putting on his linen jacket and weighting it as before with coins in his wallet. Rupert looked on interestedly, curious as to the preparation and knowing that Chris never did anything just for fun.

"Interesting, why the thing with the wallet?" he asked and in answer to Rupert's question, Chris appeared to sway slightly and turn as though to face him with a view to answering the question. His right arm following the movement of his body, blurred and in his hand, as if by magic, appeared the Sig.

"Wow! Unbelievably fast."

"I've been practising and it was the best way I found. OK, we're good to go." They left Chris's room and went down to the car park.

* * *

Whilst Rupert and Chris drove out to the Lester's house, Tir Brennan was making his own way to the Meredith's ranch some 5 miles away. Just as Chris Adams had, Brennan entered the estate via the wooded cover from the road. And just like Adams, he was dressed in black including a makeshift balaclava; he knew the value of hiding a white face. The whiteness stood out making you a target. He moved stealthily through the shrubs, keeping close to the shadows. *How many times,* he wondered, *had he done this in his own country before making a kill and then getting away before the URC or army arrived?*

The van driver had drawn the layout of the buildings for him and they appeared familiar as they came into view. He worked his way around, moving carefully from barn to barn, avoiding the sensor splays of the security lights. There appeared to be no one about as, unbeknownst to him, all were attending the after party. All bar one. Miguel was on stable duty, fast asleep in his bunk above the barns. He didn't hear any noise from Brennan who moved quietly and fluidly around the complex of buildings, finding nothing. He cursed to himself with disappointment then he froze, hearing the yapping of a terrier in the distance.

The only other person who had not gone to the party was Vikki Meredith; she was not in the mood and knew that a barrage of well-meaning questions would be asked of her if she attended. Eschewing the company of others, she had curled up with a film and her terrier for company. It was Bob the terrier who had heard or smelled some alien presence on the ranch. He bounded up and started barking at the back door leading to the stables and yard.

Vikki frowned slightly, worried by the recent events, but this was her home, *no one was going to frighten her here,* she thought.

She grabbed a jacket and a hefty Maglight torch, as much for a weapon of comfort than a means of lighting her way. It was hefty and solid in her hand, giving her confidence.

"Bob, heel!" she called and the feisty terrier came back, strutting stiff legged, hackles raised, still offering a guttural growl. Something was wrong, she knew; her dog didn't react to ghosts or shadows. She continued down to the barn, pulling out her Nokia mobile phone, preparing to dial 191. She stopped and listened.

"Quiet Bob, shut up!" she snapped and in the ensuing silence she strained to hear any incongruent sounds other than that of horses snorting or wood creaking. Nothing. But looking at Bob, he was still aggressively alert, ears pointed forward. She bravely moved forward and Bob barked making her jump, but she was not to be deterred. Upon reaching the barns, she pulled on the big switch, flooding the bays with electric light and entered the first barn. Bob proceeded her and stood barking, sniffing the air in defiance.

"Who's there? Come out, I know someone is. I'll set my dog on you."

"A wee thing like that won't hurt me," a harsh voice from behind rasped in the hard accents of Belfast. Vikki jumped and started to form a scream, when a hand came over her mouth. "I'd hate to hurt a dog, I like them, but I don't care about humans. Now call him off or I'll shoot you, then him." Bob had launched himself at Brennan, grabbing his ankle through his boots. "Do it now!" he urged, forcing the cold barrel of the pistol into her neck.

"Bob leave!" she commanded and the plucky terrier released Brennan and backed off, growling and barking at him.

"Shut him up. Is anyone else around?" he demanded.

"A groom upstairs, more will be coming back soon, they've gone to get food." She grasped at straws, terrified of the masked figure holding her. He snorted in disbelief.

"No, I don't think so. Now who are you?"

"Vikki Meredith, we own the ranch. What do you want, to come back and finish what you started the other night, killing that poor woman?"

Brennan tensed at the mention of Siobhan's death. "That wasn't me, I came here to find out who it was, how she died and for what reason. Are there any drugs here with the Argy scum? Tell me and you won't be hurt; I've not come for you and won't kill you if I don't have to."

Vikki's mind span and like most people, her reasoning took the path of least resistance, believing the masked intruder and relieved that he was not after her, just information.

"Look, I don't know who it was who came the other night, everyone seems to be looking for something here. There's nothing here, we searched everywhere-" Brennan cut her off.

"We. Who's 'we'? Did you and Siobhan look together, is that why she was killed? Tell me."

"If that was the woman who was killed, I never met her, except at the barbeque earlier in the evening; she was there with Miguel, his girlfriend. She seemed very nice, I don't know why anyone would want to hurt her. No, I meant with Claire; we looked for anything unusual, to find out why Josh Harding was killed but there was nothing." Then she wished she had bitten her tongue, realising her mistake.

"Who the fuck was Josh Harding and who is this Claire woman?"

"She is just a friend of mine from the UK, visiting with her husband while he is doing some property work or other."

"A Brit, is it? So why is she interested in anything unusual here?"

"Because her husband knows the family of my boyfriend, Josh, who was killed. He was British and the shitty Argy's killed him," she cried, tears tracing lines down her cheeks. Brennan removed the gun, but continued to hold her by the shoulder; he sensed the truth here and wanted to learn more.

He interrogated her further and soon learned the whole story of Josh's death and how Rupert, Claire and Chris had become involved. His grip relaxed as he became momentarily lost in thought and seizing her moment Vikki broke free and ducked away through the barn door, Bob scurrying after her. Brennan reacted fast but stayed his hand, not pulling the trigger on his raised Glock. *What was the point*, he reasoned, *she was not a part of it*. He was more interested as to why the Brits were involved. From outside he heard a human collision, a fall and a scream followed by a muffled voice of recognition.

"Oh, Miguel, it's you."

"*Que pasa?*" he heard a Spanish voice call.

"Quick, get away. He has a gun, get away." It was the name that spurred Brennan on; *Miguel! The one responsible for Siobhan's death*. Brennan sped through the door and ten feet away were the retreating figures of a man and a woman. He took a quick shot, aiming low and on the second attempt was rewarded with a scream and the fall of the groom. Vikki kept running for the house with Bob by her side.

Brennan knew he would have only about 15 minutes before the police arrived. He ran up to the stricken figure and saw dark arterial blood pumping from the leg wound. The bullet, he realised, must have nicked the main femoral artery in the inside of the leg, a place where every knife fighter aims for. If he didn't do something Brennan knew Miguel would bleed out quickly. He pulled off the grooms belt and using it as a tourniquet stemmed the bleeding. Miguel in his pain looked relived and puzzled.

"Now you're going to tell me what I want to know, or I let go and you bleed to death. You're choice," he told him in Spanish. He, along with others from the IRA, had helped train members of FARC in the past and two of his fellow IRA members were still in prison as a result, his Spanish, therefore, was pretty good.

"What do you want to know?" asked the hapless groom.

"The drugs, where are they?"

"Drugs there are no drugs. I don't know what you mean I-" Brennan knelt on the wound and he screamed in agony.

"OK, OK, in the truck, over there." He pointed at the shabby looking lorry Claire and Vikki had looked inside.

"Where inside?" Brennan demanded.

"In the polo balls at the back, in boxes."

"In the polo balls, what the feck do you mean?"

"Inside, we smuggle the cocaine inside the balls. Break one, you'll see, *por favore señor*, leave me alone." Brennan looked down at him suspiciously.

"Right, you stay put, I'm going to check. If you're lying, I'll be back to hurt you," he warned and went to the lorry. Pulling down the loading ramp, he found the boxes of balls at the back. He broke open a box and looked at the plastic spheres all neatly packed. Covering his eyes, he fired two rounds into the balls. Looking inside he saw one of them had disintegrated, revealing a white powder that was falling everywhere. Brennan put a finger into the mess and touched it to his tongue. "Well, I be damned. Cunning little fuckers."

Realising that about 5 minutes had probably elapsed since Vikki escaped, he went and grabbed two armfuls of straw from the stables and a box of matches from the tack room. He struck a match and lit the straw, which caught quickly, catching the cardboard of the boxes almost immediately to the accompaniment of acrid burning plastic. He returned to the prostrate form of Miguel.

"OK, you were right, so I won't shoot you."

"*Gracias señor.*" The groom exclaimed, holding tightly to the belt around his leg.

"But I will take this and it's better than you deserve." With that he kicked Miguel's hands away and ripped up the belt from his leg, immediately blood started to pour from the wound.

"Noooo!" he screamed.

"That's for Siobhan." With that he started sprinting for the shrubs again to be suddenly lost in the darkness. He made it back to the car with Doyle waiting patiently behind the wheel.

"Did it go alright, I heard a shot or two?" he asked as they pulled quietly away.

"Yea, sort of, I caught the shite who killed Siobhan and destroyed their drugs. But I have some more questions I need answering."

CHAPTER 35

Rupert and Chris went along the now familiar journey to Bill Lester's sumptuous house and as they travelled down the drive, passing through the electric gates, all seemed quiet with the usual Marie Celeste approach to lighting, the main house glowed in the night with seemingly hundreds of twinkling bulbs. There were no unusual cars parked in the drive, everything appeared as it should be to Rupert and Chris's eyes.

"This all looks worryingly normal, are we on a wild goose chase?" Rupert asked rhetorically.

"Yea, that's what worries me. Right, rules before we go in. You stay slightly behind me. I always enter any room first with you giving me room to move. We never leave each other alone at any time and always expect the unexpected. As soon as we enter a room, we look around not just forward, before we say or do anything and be prepared to back out on my command. Got it?"

"Roger that." As always the relationship between Rupert and Chris see-sawed depending upon what situation they were in. When first they worked together it had proved more difficult, now one relinquished control to the other as of right, without conscious thought.

As they approached the end of the horseshoe shaped drive, Chris gave one final order.

"Carry on around the drive and point the car away from the house, just in case. Take the keys with you and lock the car. I don't want any surprises inside if we have to make a quick exit." Rupert nodded in acknowledgement and parked accordingly. They left the car, walked up to the front door, rang the bell and the door was answered by a Latino maid. As instructed by Samantha Lester, they initially asked for Bill Lester not his wife. The maid disappeared and returned a minute later from the direction of the den they had been entertained in days ago.

"*Si Señor* Lester is in the den finishing a call, please go through." She indicated a door at the far end of the entrance hall with the sweep of her hand. "Can I get you gentlemen a drink at all?"

The two declined and she then departed in the direction of the kitchen. They passed through one door to another short, wide corridor and ahead was the door to the den. It was closed. Chris stood to one side listening and hearing nothing. He knocked quickly and the door was flung open. Samantha Lester appeared, looking a little distressed. Upon seeing Chris, she jumped forward and flung her arms around his neck. He smelled her intoxicating perfume and had a glimpse of her figure in jeans, cowboy boots and a blouse before he was engulfed. His senses screamed at him, it didn't feel right, but what had his subconscious told him that he couldn't assimilate?

"Oh Chris, you came, thank you and you too, Rupert," she cooed over Chris's shoulder. Disengaging herself from the embrace, she moved to his left and walked him into the room which looked unoccupied with various seats and chesterfields empty and Lester's large leather swivel chair to the right, which was turned to face a TV screen showing stocks and shares, looking as though it had just been vacated. Rupert followed Chris and mindful of his warnings looked around him, keeping his distance. The curtains were drawn and there was a recessed window seat to his left into which he could not see into, but all appeared normal. The door remained wide open.

"OK, Sam, now what is this all about, you'd better not be wasting our time?"

"Oh, Chris far from it, I'm sure you will appreciate what I have to show you." Her voice and manner had changed; no more the little lost girl, and with the brittle tone of voice, she disengaged from him completely, moving to her left out of the line of fire. For the swivel chair had spun around and in it pointing his service issue Glock straight at Chris was Seth Meacham. At the same time, the door through which they had entered closed with a crisp thud and behind it was an unknown Argentine groom holding a long knife, looking like he knew how to use it. Samantha backed well away to the large desk, and the window seat revealed two more grooms each armed with knives. Chris snorted, half closed his eyes in disgust and gently shook his head. "Special Agent Meacham, well a good evening to you."

"You just couldn't leave well alone, could you boys? I kept telling you to back off. But oh no, you had to keep pushing your noses in, stirring up trouble. Couldn't leave well alone."

"Well it all makes sense now," Rupert offered. "How you knew where we were; the identity of Siobhan and where to find her; running us off the road; the fact that the warehouses were empty when they were raided. Shit you nearly killed my wife and our unborn child, you bastard! Did you order that?"

"No I did," Samantha answered

"You? Then Meacham isn't the boss?"

Samantha Lester shook her head in disgust. "For someone who is obviously intelligent and deals in unscrupulous markets, you can be awfully naïve, Rupert. Your chivalry will get you into trouble, although it looks as though it already has."

"But why? You've got a great home, wealthy husband, all the trappings, why get wrapped up in this?"

"Great marriage? I'm married to man twice my age, with no independence. I have to ask for money. I married a dynasty, not a man. That man by the way is about to lose all his wealth and me with it. I first used cocaine casually then realised that I wanted more and became very valuable to the new cartel, working my way into the organisation. This way, I have power, wealth and can do what I want.

"I am the boss north of the border, commanding all the Ballesteros' cartel operations. That makes me untouchable. We have judges, politicians and police in our pay; and the DEA." She waved a hand towards Meacham. "Once Bill is gone, I will have it all and be young enough to enjoy it." Her tirade was cut off as a mobile lying on her desk started to ring.

"Yes?" She listened for a few moments and answered in Spanish. "What! How the hell did that happen?" She listened intently then cut the call saying she would call back. In all this time, Meacham had kept the pistol focused on Chris and Rupert, it took concentration and the call distracted him slightly, but to Chris's disappointment he still remained focused.

"What, not all going to plan?" Rupert taunted.

"Rupert, you want to tread carefully, it's not just you but your lovely wife who are exposed here, think on that before you start to wind me up. Yea, that's taken the smile off your face, hasn't it? She was meddling down in Dallas where she shouldn't, I suppose she put together the polo ball aspect. But too late, the first batch is in the UK; home and dry. With you two out of the way the whole consignment will be delivered as planned."

Rupert could not resist. "Minus, of course, the lot it sounds as though you've just lost following that phone call. Well, you can't blame us for that. Where was it, the Meredith ranch?"

"Very clever, Rupert, but it won't help you. Besides, some losses are all part of the game."

As their lives were apparently going to be forfeit, Chris

wanted to know something: "So tell me, you mentioned police on your payroll, does that include Sheriff Reed?"

"No, the dependable Reed is clean," answered Meacham, "but if you think he's going to come rushing through that door like the 7th Cavalry, think again. He's off elsewhere as I told him I was going to see you two." He nodded at them.

"And why you, Meacham?"

"Oldest reason in the world: money."

"So you sold your soul to the devil." Chris sneered. "It always comes down to the same thing: greed and money. You dress it up with fine words justifying your corruption. But do you know what, really it's just greed. Living in this pseudo bubble of false values and wealth. I'm sure that you used to be a good man once, now you're just a puppet for the cartels and this witch!" he finished, pointing at Samantha Lester

"Don't get all pious on me. I started as an eager DEA agent; off to save the world, fight the good fight; keep America safe. Instead, I found a government who actually liked the fact that drugs got through, a huge black economy sloshing money around. As an industry it's worth billions; the government don't want to stop that, they can't afford to.

"Oh, they make showy efforts from time to time, making great news of high profile drug busts, but so much more gets through. The damn borders are so porous; the poor sods on the border are as disillusioned as me. They don't have the funding or the back up from their superiors. Even then, until they build a solid wall, which'll never happen, they'll never stem the tide of drugs.

"So I was approached by the cartels. I allow some loads to be caught and look good, but make sure so much more gets through." As he spoke, he smiled, his concentration and the gun just slightly relaxing in its aim. In small arms training, the Regiment soldiers are taught about concentration and reaction times, it still takes a period of time to react rather than to take the initiative. This reaction time is what anyone gambles on. Chris turned slightly to his right, looking over his shoulder at the groom behind with the knife, his hand at waist height pointing with his thumb.

"So, what's it going to be? Matey boy behind me going to stick me as I try 'breaking and entering' or–" He continued his return movement back to face Meacham; the jacket swayed outwards, his hand a blur, appeared holding the Sig, spouting flame, once then twice, a double tap straight to the central cerebellum of Meacham's head, all motor function destroyed. As Chris knew, a Glock takes approximately 5.5 lbs of pressure, to pull the trigger, all on an index finger, to his mind that was nearly three bags of sugar. He gambled on no last minute instinctive reaction to pull on a dying whim. Chris gave no warning, no heroics, or speeches like in the movies just instant death, with the smell of cordite wafting in the air. He immediately focused on the two grooms to his front.

As Chris had turned, so Rupert had followed him to partially face the evil looking groom behind. He had no liking for a man standing behind him holding a knife at his back. He realised what Chris was about to do and as he had resumed the turn, so Rupert stayed partially facing the groom.

After Chris had introduced him to Wing Chun, Rupert continued to study once a week and enjoying them, had kept up the classes over the last five years. After about two years and with everyone improving, the instructor had asked all the students to bring an old white t-shirt to the next session. Bemused, the students complied and found that they were going to learn about knife defence. They were each given a 'knife', amounting to a thick gem pen taped to a small handle and then to told to attack each other. They mostly finished the exercise proudly displaying hardly any cuts to their torsos. Their arms were, however, covered in 'slashes' of black. *'Very good' the instructor had said sarcastically, 'you've now got no tendons left in your arms and all your arteries are slashed open, in other words you're all dead!'* It had been a salutary lesson and he then proceeded to show them how to block properly.

The groom thrust the knife forward at Rupert's midsection, the free left hand distracting, as all knife fighters do. Rupert ignored this, with his weight evenly distributed, he pivoted on his right foot turning into the oncoming knife; thrusting both arms across his body, left above right, forming an X shape, scooping the knife arm and trapping it. The kwan sau block looked simple but had immense power and by virtue of the wide splay of the arms was almost guaranteed to connect. Rupert then rotated his left arm, whipping it down in a lap sau, using the forward motion of the groom to assist him, and struck cleanly over the groom's left ear with a palm strike with his right hand. He received a satisfying 'pop' as the eardrum burst, causing the groom to lose balance. But Rupert was not done. As the groom flailed downwards, he smashed an elbow strike into his face and he dropped like a stone, unconscious. The whole series of moves had taken a couple of seconds from start to finish and the hapless groom lay in a heap on the floor, blood pouring from his face and ear.

The other two watching the fighting remained powerless to intervene as they were covered by Chris's weapon. Samantha's face was a mask of contorted rage and it seemed to take all her willpower not to leap forward as her hands went rigid, fingers like clawed talons.

Chris was aware of everything and knew they were not yet free.

"You two, down on the floor, arms behind your back. Rupert, open the door there and keep an eye, and keep out of my line of fire." The two grooms were on the floor, with only Samantha standing. "Right, come behind me and call Sheriff Reed. We need to get this straight before madam here twists things. Then get on the phone to Johnston, straightaway. From your mobile but remember be careful, it's still an open line but be as candid as you can, tell him Meacham was a double working for the cartels. He'll put wheels in motion."

Samantha Lester's face grew more amazed with each word. "Who the hell *are* you?"

"Just a simple realtor, just like your husband is a simple property man. Now, you too, lie down, on your front." She hesitated. "I don't like shooting women but it doesn't mean I won't. Do it now." She reluctantly complied, lying down on the carpet of the study, her head to one side shooting daggers at Chris. Rupert left the room to make the call to Johnston, but kept within Chris' line of sight. He spoke quietly and quickly to Johnston, telling as much as he could directly without being too indiscreet.

Cutting the call, he turned back and headed for the den, calling Sheriff Reed. But it was the next command and person through the door that was the biggest surprise.

"Put the gun down and hands where I can see them-now!" And there, framed in the doorway, arms extended in a classic pistol stance, pointing a Glock at them, was the re-doubtable Sheriff Reed. As calmly as he could, Chris complied, gently and slowly bending forward to place the Sig on the floor, whilst keeping his other hand raised and in sight. Rupert had turned to face the sheriff his hands raised.

Samantha Lester recovered her composure quickly: "Sheriff, thank God you've come. He went berserk and shot this poor man who said he was an agent for the DEA. They were trying to rob us, I think, wanted to know about drugs and real estate deals. They were waiting for my husband to return, I was so frightened."

And to complete the picture perfect, she gently raised herself off the floor and proceeded to break down into tears, every inch the frightened housewife. If he could, Rupert would have applauded the performance; but he was equally aware that the two Argentine grooms had also got up on to their knees and were about to rise. Sheriff Reed now flanked by two deputies interceded.

"Boys you just sit, *comprende*? Mrs Lester, ma'am, I'm sorry for your distress, we'll look after you now, don't you worry." He then turned to look at the slumped body of Seth Meacham, a spray of red and grey matter all over the back of the high backed chair which masked the horror of what had been the back of his head.

"You shoot him?" he asked of Chris.

"Yes, Sheriff, but it was self-defence, they were about to shoot Rupert and me; blame it on a home invasion, and Seth Meacham was complicit in it all, he was crooked, Sheriff. It was him all along, working for the cartels."

"At this moment, I see a dead DEA agent, whom you admitted you killed; you in a house, where you don't belong and where the owner is clearly upset and calling you a killer. I am arresting you both on suspicion of murder and complicity to the act. Deputy, cuff them both." He then read Chris and Rupert their rights and proceeded to order two more deputies in who had been waiting with the cars outside. They had arrived silently without 'blues and twos' wanting the element of surprise on their side. The two remaining grooms were cuffed and he asked Samantha Lester to accompany them to the station to make a formal statement. She made to protest.

"Sheriff, can't I just make a statement here and await my husband? I'm so upset I just want my husband with me," she mewed.

"I'm very sorry, ma'am, but we really do need you to come to the station, there may be more questions and we'll have a female officer look after you, don't you worry." He was gentle but firm and the tone in his voice indicated that there would be no argument. At that point, sirens could be heard heralding the arrival of at least one ambulance.

Rupert and Chris sensed that at this point there would be no mileage in arguing and complied meekly to the deputies orders, offering no reason for brutality or prejudice to their position. Chris especially knew that given the strong relationship between the US and UK governments, strings would be pulled and doors opened. The next team through the door some five minutes later were CSI and the coroner's department. There seemed, to Chris's mind, a rather premeditated efficiency to all this and he wondered what powers had been at work to bring the sheriff and his team here so quickly.

However, Rupert had one more comment to add, "Sheriff, I just want you to listen to one more thing and no it's not a protestation of our innocence." He cut short the sheriff's protest, continuing. "The polo balls we mentioned? Well somewhere on this ranch; in the groom's area; down by the barns; in the tack room or even in the lorries, sorry trucks, as you would call them, you will find a large quantity of boxed balls. They were delivered only a few days ago and Bill Lester will verify this, ask him. When you find them, break one open and inside you will find the cocaine." The sheriff studied Rupert, then made a decision.

"Web, come with me. Stu get on the phone to the DEA, tell them what has happened and that we need a drug squad down here pronto." At this point Rupert looked across at Samantha Lester and saw the look on her face, it was twisted malevolently, in a mask of pure hatred. *How did he ever think she was beautiful?* he thought.

Outside, other eyes were watching the proceedings with interest. Tir Brennan and Doyle, armed with the information from the injured groom at the Meredith ranch, had proceeded to make their way to the Lester estate. They were securely hidden in scrub and rhododendron bushes, watching the procession of official vehicles arrive through binoculars.

"Looks like a fun party," Doyle commented laconically. "Now

where are they off to?" He had spotted the sheriff and the deputy called 'Web' head down to the barns and trucks parked near the stables and commence a search. They disappeared inside the various barns, intent on their search. No one had moved from the house, all appeared to be awaiting the result of the search and the arrival of the DEA. After what seemed an age to all concerned, the air was filled with the wup, wup, chatter of rotor blades and the howl of a turbine engine. The DEA had arrived.

CHAPTER 36

LONDON

Rupert's call on the open line to Johnston at MI6 had caused all sorts of signals to be sent to various departments from the Foreign Office downwards. Webster had been gratified at the justification for starting an investigation and was happily monitoring, through his own men, the whereabouts of the cocaine filled balls that had already been brought into the UK.

Johnston had more to worry about regarding the position of both Rupert Brett and Chris Adams. *It would not do,* he thought, *to have them brought into the court and face charges of murder and conspiracy to murder, along with whatever else may be thrown at them.* With this in mind, he called his contact at the DEA. However, having one of their supposedly top agents killed by an undercover British serviceman may not go down too well, he reflected ruefully as the secure line rang with the usual long distance ring tone.

"Special Agent Calder," answered the head of intelligence division at the DEA.

"Stephen, its Simon Johnston calling, how are you?"

"Simon, well, thank you. Good to hear from you. What news? I haven't heard from Seth Meacham for a couple of days, I was going to call him for an updated report." He was all business no pleasantries, just straight down to the details. Johnston coughed rather delicately in that particular way that British civil servants have before presenting bad news.

"Ah yes, well, I have some news in that department."

"Do tell," was the heavy response. With careful refrain, Johnston began to tell the DEA agent all he knew that had occurred. He was interrupted on a number of occasions as Calder swore harshly down the telephone line. Johnston finally finished when all the details were laid bare.

"So your boy, decided, based on circumstantial evidence, to act as judge, jury and executioner on special agent Meacham, who is even now cooling his heels in some county morgue. In his absence, he is accused of complicity with drug cartels; aiding and abetting a supposed drug lord up here, who also happens to be the wife of one of the most prominent citizens. Have I covered everything?"

"Er, yes, I believe that is a fairly concise, if rather oblique, view."

"There will be hell to pay over this. I'll get back to you." Stephen Calder slammed the receiver down. *I hope you are right, Rupert, you had better be for all our sakes.* Johnston prayed.

* * *

FLORIDA

Brennan and Doyle watched the incoming helicopter circle, hover, then float downwards on a cushion of air, forcing all the localised vegetation to be blown in every direction at once. Emblazoned on the side of the aircraft in large black letters was the legend 'DEA'.

"Time we're out of here. Nothing more for us to do now those boys have arrived, place will be swarming with feds for the next few hours and one thing's for certain, those drugs will be locked down with no chance of stealing them," Doyle opined. With that both men shuffled back out of the shrubs and made for the road and their car which had been left innocuously some distance away in a small layby.

Upon his return to the main house, having left his deputy to guard the drugs, Sheriff Reed found a febrile atmosphere prevailed with the arrival of the DEA agents. The two agents from the helicopter identified themselves as special agents Cole and Hughes and had initially been furious at the scene before them. Then with further explanation from Sheriff Reed and the confirmation from Bill Lester that the polo balls had indeed been delivered to the grooms some days earlier, Chris and Rupert's story started to have more credibility. There were unanswered questions which only seemed to be resolved by the pair's explanation.

With Rupert and Chris on their way to the police station, along with the grooms and Samantha Lester, it was left for the various departments present to supply answers. The DEA was of the opinion that as a federal matter it should be their jurisdiction and the prisoners handed over to them. Sheriff Reed dug his heels in and opposed the motion saying it was a murder enquiry and until proved otherwise, he held sway.

Special Agent Cole, the most senior of the two agents, then took a call from his boss, Calder, on his mobile and left the room to talk in private. He was gone for at least fifteen minutes, locked in a detailed discussion with his boss. He returned red-faced after the call ended.

"OK, my boss says to give you custody for now. But I would like you to give me a full rundown of what we know and what has happened to date."

"Sounds fair." He proceeded to give them a full run down, from the death of Josh Harding; the meeting with Rupert and Chris; their admission of involvement; progress through the idea of connection to polo and the idea for the balls as smuggling items for the cocaine. He then completed the picture with the abortive raid upon the two warehouses and included that only three people had known about it: his office; the Brits who informed him; and finally Seth Meacham. The final conclusion helped sway the view, rather reluctantly, that there was more to this than met the eye.

"OK, I have questions: one what was Meacham doing here? Two, why did these two Brits Brett and Adams turn up at the house. Three, and why did Meacham end up dead? Was he crooked? Because if so, we need to have proof. My boss Calder, against his better judgement, has put in place searches on Meacham's accounts, we'll see what those reveal. I don't like it, but I'm starting to go along with you."

"As soon as I get ballistics, CSI and post mortem reports, I'll pass them along. But I'll say this, I reckon Mrs Lester is in this up to her pretty ass. I had to arrest Brett and Adams anyway as a matter of form. You can come down to the office and speak with them later."

The den was filled with the gentle hubbub of procedure, with cameras flashing, measurements being taken, notes being made and calculations of trajectory. The quiet but frenetic activity of the legal process in action.

The station house of the sheriff's office was built along familiar lines; reception, offices and interview rooms on the ground floor and a secure basement housing the cells and other secure holding areas, making breakouts very difficult. To the rear was a secure fenced compound for police vehicles. It was to these that Rupert and Chris were taken in separate cars and then through logging procedures of fingerprints, and identification to the waiting cells below. The sheriff arrived half an hour later and proceeded to interview each man separately; going through their story and with the verification of the telephone call made by Samantha Lester to the hotel and the paging of Chris Adams to take a call from her earlier that evening. The story now rang true and provided the reason for their presence in the house backing against the rather scant story that Samantha Lester had offered. Chris, familiar with procedures, had asked the sheriff about the alacrity with which they had arrived at the scene.

"Well, you can thank Mrs Brett for that. She was unhappy with the way things were panning out. So she called the polo club first to see whether Bill Lester was indeed home or at the after party. Well, as you know, he is a well-known figure and it didn't take her two minutes before she spoke to someone who confirmed his presence at the party. After that she smelled a rat and called me directly, putting forward her suspicions and that you boys were heading into a trap. Either, she said, for a Badger Game or something worse."

"A *Badger Game*?"

"Yea, well I guess you boys don't know it as that but back in the days of the Old West, a crooked couple running a scam would lure an unsuspecting man back to her room and once in a state undress, her 'husband' would rush in and demand satisfaction or just shoot the guy and take his money. Well, you see how it works, it was she thought a variation on that theme.

"To be fair, without her call and warning I would have been far less sympathetic to your position when I first arrived, but the death of Seth Meacham really threw me. Didn't see it coming at all."

"Good old Claire, I owe her a big hug when we get back."

"Indeed. But it was the drugs stash which Mr Brett told us about that bears out your position more than anything and I've since had a call from a very nervous State Department official clarifying your position with information received from the head of your secret service in the UK. The biggest problem is the killing of a Federal Officer, but I dare say that will be dealt with higher up the food chain. So, for now, I'm going to let you and Mr Brett go but stay around for questioning, if you would. When do you fly back?"

"Day after tomorrow."

"OK then, well we'll see how this all goes. Between you and me, I think that if your story runs true and they find evidence of a bad agent, it will be swept under the carpet and some cock and bull story will go out about Agent Meacham dying in the line of duty, in the best traditions of the service or some other bullshit."

For his part, Chris had known one or two situations in his operations where a similar line had been taken and an eminent citizen's reputation had been preserved for the best of all concerned. "Indeed, Sheriff, I've come across it before."

"Right, you and Mr Brett are free to go. Your car is outside, I had it brought round from the Lester's house. Your weapon, I'm afraid, is part of States evidence and cannot be returned in the foreseeable future. And please, try and stay out of trouble for your remaining 48 hours here."

Chris grinned rather sheepishly at the sheriff. "Will do, Sheriff."

"You special forces boys are always getting into trouble. Seen it a hundred times, can never leave well alone."

"Sheriff, I'm a retired RGJ and a surveyor, not SF."

"Of course you are." The sheriff agreed, shaking his hand in a crushing grip and receiving one in return. "And say hello to that lovely wife of Brett's, she is a special lady."

"Will do, Sheriff, will do."

The pair were reunited in the reception area, cars keys were retuned and they were free to go under caution.

"Well, I'm just glad you were around on this trip," Rupert sighed as they got back into the car and compared notes on the interview with the sheriff.

"Yea, it has been interesting but I have to say Rupert, whenever you get involved in one of your 'expeditions', it never turns out to be boring. And this time it is Claire you have to thank for saving our bacon."

"Amen to that."

The lady in question had been worried sick until a kind call from the sheriff informed her that all was well and that her husband would be retuning in the next two hours. Upon returning to the hotel, they found her awake and relived to see them return from jail.

"I leave you both alone for five minutes and you get into a gun fight, arrested and thrown into jail. You're not safe to be let out unsupervised!" Then threw herself into Rupert's arms and after turned to Chris, "Thank you for keeping him safe."

"Well, I think in this instance it is you we should be thanking. We would've at least spent the night in jail and it could have gone a lot worse if the sheriff wasn't already on side."

"What made you call the sheriff?" asked Rupert.

"Call it woman's intuition. You two might happily go off 'Famous Fiving', happy to tackle regular danger, but the female can be more dangerous than the male, as the song goes. When Sam Lester clearly wasn't trying to entrap Chris in a romantic entanglement with offering to have you along, I became even more suspicious. It just seemed out of character for the predatory bitch. I also couldn't see Bill Lester missing out on a party, it went against the grain. Then, when I found out that my concerns were justified and he wasn't at home terrorising 'poor' Sam, I wanted to pre-empt any issue and phoned Sheriff Reed. I'm glad

I did, although I should think Sam Lester is pretty pissed off at this moment and has a lot of explaining to do."

"I think she'll wriggle a lot and come up with some fabulous story avoiding all knowledge of the drugs. After all, there is no direct evidence to attach her to them unless they can get hold of what will undoubtedly be some off shore bank accounts tucked away somewhere."

The phone lines between the States and the UK had been hot over the last few hours with midnight disturbances for those in the top echelons of the American government and early mornings for their UK counterparts. In the end, a compromise was reached on the official outcome of their enquiries, which as Sheriff Reed had predicted, differed greatly from the real events that had taken place; no department wanted its dirty washing aired in public.

More statements were made by Rupert and Chris along the lines suggested by the DEA and sheriff's department and after everything was settled, Sam Lester was charged on various offences. As expected, a heavy hitting lawyer was employed and she was allowed out on bail, supported by her foolish but loyal husband.

Vikki Meredith had come around to the hotel to say her goodbyes.

"Claire, I'm so sad that you're going. Who will I have to turn to? Can I visit in the UK, I know it's very rude of me but I'd love to come visit."

"Vikki, I'd love to see you in England. Come over in the polo season and I'll take you to Cowdray and we can watch the Gold Cup." They came together in a tight hug.

"I promise I will. If Rupert doesn't mind too much," she winked in Rupert's direction. Rupert smiled in response and assured her that she would be very welcome.

"Now, darling, we must be off," Rupert urged. There were more hugs and then they left in the car.

Unperturbed and desperately needing the money, Bill Lester had begrudgingly carried on with the deal that he and Rupert had put together. He was a pragmatic if arrogant man and knew that he would need all the financial muscle he could get when the scandal of his wife's alleged impropriety hit the press. Rupert, Claire and Chris caught their scheduled return flight home much to the relief of Claire and Sheriff Reed, who had stated that life was a little too exciting while Chris was around.

Epilogue

LONDON

Three days after landing in the UK, Rupert and Chris were called into MI6 headquarters to be debriefed by Simon Johnston. It was no 'tea and biscuits' affair despite the success of the mission; both Webster and Johnston were annoyed that Brennan had slipped through their fingers.

"So, no news of Brennan then?" Rupert queried.

"No unfortunately and Detective Chief Inspector Webster is not best pleased either. His sprat has disappeared from the face of the earth or so it would seem. Still, he should be pleased that the flow of drugs from the US has been halted, albeit almost certainly on a temporary basis until they find another way."

"It almost seems a waste of time when you put it like that," Rupert commented in a desultory manner.

Johnston stared at him fiercely and quoted, "*The only thing necessary for the triumph of evil is that good men stand by and do nothing.* You would do well to remember that. And Burke also said: *To speak of treason in mild language is treason to virtue.* Which I think in this case is very pertinent, don't you?"

Rupert acknowledged the barb with a nod of his head and let Johnston continue.

"Having said that, we are once again grateful to you for all your efforts. Without you, we would almost certainly not have found the answer and from what I understand from Sergeant Adams, a lot of that credit goes to your wife. Please pass on to her our grateful thanks. Your country owes you a debt once again, Mr Brett. And, dare I say it, until the next time?"

"You just don't give up, do you? The answer is firmly no, even with Chris at my back, enough is enough," he declared. In response, Johnston smiled tightly, agreeing to disagree.

"As you wish. Now gentlemen, I must get on. Sergeant Adams, thank you for looking after Mr Brett in exceptional circumstances and I am sure we will meet in due course." They shook hands and left the building. Outside, the two friends shook hands.

"What now, Chris? Back to Columbia?"

"No, orders are to return to Hereford; the Headshed want a debrief and then who knows, wherever I'm posted. Sophie is back soon, so that'll be good."

"Well bring her down if you get time. Claire especially would love to see her. Chris, thanks for everything, you kept us safe yet again," he lauded.

"Oh bugger off and get back to your deals. You'll be making me blub next!"

"Ha, well as they say, the cheque's in the post and no arguments." And with that he laughed and turned away with a wave.

* * *

FLORIDA

Tir Brennan and Tom Doyle had slowly driven away from the Lester place the evening of the arrests. For his part, Brennan was very disappointed that he could not steal the cocaine filled polo balls and sell the profits. He was also aware that a debt of honour existed between him and the cartel and someone he had cared for now lay dead as a direct result of the orders. He was a vengeful man and he also wanted to send a message to Ballesteros.

Over the next few days, he carefully thought out a strategy for revenge and went through his plans in detail with Doyle.

"Where can you get detonators from?"

"Oh that's easy. The quarries have them lying around, it's nowhere nearly as difficult as I understand it is in the UK. What else do you need?" he asked, making notes

"I'll need some explosives, Semtex preferably, but not Anfo; I'll need too much and it'll be bulky," he commented, referring to the ammonium nitrate and fuel oil explosive that was readily available over the counter in the States. "Or PETN as it has nearly the same TNT rating as Semtex."

"Sorry, TNT rating, what the hell's that?"

"All explosives are rated in terms of units of TNT, it is a sort of common denominator," he explained. "PENT and Semtex are pretty high up on that scale. Although, to be strictly accurate, PENT is one of the main ingredients for Semtex."

"Well, you learn something new every day, but I'll take your word for it, I'm just the fixer. Again it's not as restricted as you may think. How much?"

"Good. If it's Semtex then 4lbs should do it and I'll need a small transistor circuit board. Get me a new radio and an electric garage door remote and I can make it workable. No make that two of each." He then reeled off other incidental sundries that he would need, all of which Doyle confirmed he could obtain without any problem. *Amazing*, thought Brennan, *America must be so secure with its lack of terrorist threats. If a group ever plotted a strike, it would be a terrorist's dream come true.*

Two days later, he had all the materials that he had requested and set to work making alterations to the transistor boards. Doyle saw him take the garage remote controls apart and start to change the internal circuitry.

"Are they OK?"

"Yea, most garage remotes work on a frequency of 40 MHz, but the manufacturers set them with a series of codes in each batch and then jumble them up so hopefully your neighbour won't open your garage and vice versa. They're all done on a binary code so I am altering the encoding and restricting it still further; I don't want some dick to open his garage and blow me to kingdom come now, do I?"

"Pretty intensive stuff."

"Yea well, we had some good people train us, brought over from the US, Middle East and elsewhere. I learned a lot, although some poor fuckers lost fingers and a lot more before we got it right. But Semtex is pretty stable, even if you drop it, it wouldn't go off."

Brennan had two of everything in case one unit failed to function. Since the night of the fire at the Meredith's ranch, he had kept a very low profile, not leaving the house except at night in the boot of a car and only then to go to the countryside to run and keep fit. The house had a small gym with weight machines and he proceeded to build up strength and stamina for the job ahead.

When Brennan was ready, he had a final meeting with Doyle.

"All the arrangements have been made, it'll be fine. It is much easier to leave the US than enter; no one really cares and border security on the other side is lax. You'll be met by our contact from FARC and the details are all on the note. Once you've committed it to memory destroy it. And good luck!"

"Thank you for all the help, Tom. I may not see you again so stay well, yea?" Brennan acknowledged the debt. He was dressed prettily shabbily in innocuous clothes, had let his hair grow and in a secluded part of the garden, had carefully sunned himself in the Florida sun, adding to his natural Celtic dark skin, he now looked almost Hispanic. He had a false passport in the name of Martinez Figuero, that showed he was a native of Bogota.

They shook hands in a final gesture of farewell, then Brennan slipped out of the door to the garage and into the waiting car. The driver was unknown to him and he did not wish to chat or know his name. He travelled by car to one of the many small marinas dotted around the south Florida Keys. Then on to a fishing smack doing day trips for tourists. Finally, a transfer at sea to a 'Cigarette boat' with a sleek, fibre glass hull and capable of out-running almost anything on the water. They island hopped on the drug routes familiar to smugglers going in the opposite direction. Then skirting Cuba, they slipped through the gap between Haiti, and straight down to the northern port of Barranquilla on the Colombian coast.

The huge carnival city was a relief to Brennan after the hours of endless ocean. It was a very modern environment with tall sky scrapers, parks of green vegetation dotted all over and a bustling busy port in which it was easy to become lost with so much other sea traffic going to and fro. He was met by the contact from FARC who was to transport him the 600 miles to the Colombian capital in a simple innocuous truck.

He was taken to a small house on the outskirts of the city, just outside the slum areas of the metropolis. Here for the next few days he acted as a delivery driver's mate. Refining his accent, fitting in and learning the layout of the streets and where everything was. He planned escape routes; lines of fire; where the police stations were and the one way streets. The plan he had was refined by knowledge. After two weeks, he was ready.

Twice he had been driven up into the hills by the delivery driver and scouted the layout of Ballesteros' house. It was, he discovered, well-guarded with men inside the perimeter, but no one patrolled the roadside and a high wall flanked the property. The two guards at the hut by the gate checked everyone thoroughly, but as with many secure operations, once you were in it was assumed that you were harmless, with an emphasis on manpower with guns not sophisticated alarm systems. The wall, he decided, was easy to scale and once inside, he could deal with dogs and men. But it was still an operation fraught with difficulties. He did not know the layout internally and no one was allowed past the gates who was not known and friendly to the cartel. Brennan was patient, like many successful assassins, and he took his time assessing all movements and habits.

History showed that the original cartel bosses and their followers, including Pablo Escobar, had been assassinated by ruthless gunfire or kidnap, torture and death. Usually by researching planned routes and exploiting clever ambush points. Once or twice a frontal assault had been made on houses by groups in a brave, but obvious, display of machismo. The subtle approach was not the norm in Latin America.

Four weeks after his arrival, Brennan watched with approval as Ballesteros moved his operation to his ranch in the countryside at his *Finca* on the shores of *Emblase de Muna;* this is what he had been waiting for. Open ground, and a complete reliance on men and weapons, with vehicles left out in the open. The security was great. With an open expanse of flat ground the area provided a perfect killing ground and an army could be seen coming. Ballesteros felt safe.

Brennan found a good place for a hide within four hundred yards of the house and waited. The lights were on in the Casa, singing sounded from within, everyone was relaxed. Some dogs patrolled but he had always been good with dogs.

In the depth of night, he covered the ground, moving from cover to cover. Once a Doberman caught his scent pulling at his leash. The guard sensing the change, released him and the lithe animal bounded across the rough dirt courtyard. Brennan waited until the last minute and pulling a spray from his pack, sprayed a mixture of mace and skunk fluid directly in his face. Yelping, the animal retreated, temporarily blinded and wreaking of skunk, back to his disgusted owner. He shouted at the errant animal that he was stupid to chase a skunk and took him back to the stables to wash his eyes. He shouted to two other guards, pinpointing them for Brennan, who smiled quietly to himself in the cover of darkness. As things quietened down again, he progressed not to the house, but the armoured Range Rover parked under a sun canopy. In the city it was kept in a secure garage; here with all the other vehicles, it was left in the open.

Upon reaching the vehicle, Brennan shuffled under the Range Rover and attached the 4lbs of boxed Semtex beneath the centre of the car. Securing it in place with 'Rare-earth' magnets that clung to the steel armoured panels beneath. He preferred these magnets as they were pound for pound up to three times stronger and more durable than their traditional cousins. Looking closely Brennan saw, as he suspected, that Ballesteros had the armouring done locally as a post factory fit. He knew from past experiences, that in order to armour properly, the plates had to be overlapped, then welded. Welding them when abutting the plates or to the existing chassis rails was not enough to fully protect the occupants. The rails themselves had to be strengthened, along with the A and B pillars of the car or the vehicle just collapsed and disintegrated. This had clearly not been done.

Pleased with his work and findings, Brennan then reversed his movements, disappearing into the night like a ghost. He had boosted the range of the garage remote controls to 400 yards and so he moved this time, within range of the main entrance to the estate. Every vehicle entering or leaving had to pass this point manned by two armed guards. The next day, as often happened, Ballesteros planned a trip to the local village with two of his guards and a driver. The driver went out and started the engine, pulling up to the front of the house to collect Ballesteros.

Brennan watched as the vehicle approached and the guards opened the gates, nodding and waving to their boss. As the Range Rover was parallel to the gates, he pressed the garage remote control. The Semtex tore into the steel plates curling the metal upwards at the point of the welds and un-strengthened chassis rails, shooting gases, shredding metal and air through the car at around 2,000 feet per second in a deadly maelstrom of destruction. The car ignited in the blast, incinerating everything in its wake and killing the two men guarding the gate. Brennan permitted himself a wicked smile. "That's for you Siobhan, RIP."

He then slipped down from the rock plateau behind which he had been hiding and jumped onto to his waiting Suzuki RD trials bike, pressed the starter, kicked the gear lever and was off before anyone knew what had happened; skidding and slewing across the grass land in the shortest route to the waiting pick up some two miles away.

* * *

LONDON, three days later

Rupert, in his Richmond home, was sat relaxing in an armchair reading the Sunday papers which, he reflected, yet again seemed to consume half a rainforest to produce. He was expecting the arrival of Chris and Sophie for lunch and looking forward to the prospect of seeing his two friends again. He read further and reaching the International News section of the Sunday Times, he glanced at the headlines: '*Suspected drug cartel boss dies in explosion at country ranch.*'

He read further, shaking his head in amazement, as the story told of a car being blown up and supposedly containing the now infamous drug boss Juan Ballesteros, who was killed instantly. No one was reported as being held responsible for the atrocity.

"Claire," he shouted through to the kitchen, "You will never guess what…"

To start reading Book4 visit:
https://books2read.com/u/bovAoR

A MESSAGE FROM SIMON

Once again my grateful thanks to Natasha Orme for her splendid editorial work. My family for their continued love and support.

This was another trip abroad and a lot of detail needed to be researched on police procedures at sea, polo clubs and how they used to be; through to explosives, fight scenes and weapons.

With this in mind a special thanks to the Marine Police Unit at Hamble especially to Tim, Billy & Ben. Also thanks for all their time to: Will Lucas, Dr. Geraldine O'Sullivan, Steve Rawse of Injection Mouldings Ltd, Cheltenham, Simon Robinson, Henry Stevens, Stuart and Sifu Dave Taylor.

A DEAL ON ICE:
DEAL SERIES BOOK 4

Rupert faces his greatest challenge yet-get out of Russia live!

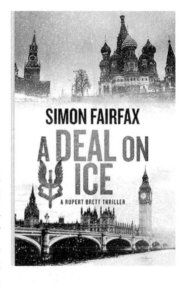

1999 and Rupert Brett is at the top of his game. He is head of Capital Markets worldwide and is given the challenge: open the Moscow office!

He finds corruption, powerful Oligarchs and a new Russian: Leader Vladimir Putin. The UK Government is opening new boundaries with immigration relaxed. The two worlds begin to collide with Rupert in the middle: desperate secrets need to be kept by both sides.

Framed for murder, Rupert will have to call upon all his street wise cunning as a game of cat and mouse begins among the streets of Moscow and the corridors of power in London. He calls upon his old friend, ex-SAS sergeant Chris Adams to help him escape and an international manhunt begins as he runs for his life!

To start reading book 4 visit:
https://books2read.com/u/bovAoR

ACKNOWLEDGEMENTS

Once again my grateful thanks to Natasha Orme for her splendid editorial work. My family for their continued love and support.

This was another trip abroad and a lot of detail needed to be researched on police procedures at sea, polo clubs and how they used to be; through to explosives, fight scenes and weapons.

With this in mind a special thanks to the Marine Police Unit at Hamble especially to Tim, Billy & Ben. Also thanks for all their time to: Will Lucas, Dr. Geraldine O'Sullivan, Steve Rawse of Injection Mouldings Ltd, Cheltenham, Simon Robinson, Henry Stevens, Stuart and Sifu Dave Taylor.

HISTORICAL NOTES

(NOTE: there are spoilers in this account if you are reading this before you read the book)

When starting to write this third book, I was only vaguely aware of the Sub-Prime market as with almost everyone else, we all knew the final cataclysmic effect with the collapse of Lehman Brothers bank in September 2008, sparking the worst recession in living memory. I doubt whether anyone in those early days of the mid 90's would have foreseen the mighty forces that the relaxing of the mortgage lending rules as I have described, would have on the financial world. But it really happened the way I described and history tells us the rest.

The Deauville polo club was in the mid 90's just as I described and much higher in importance in the international circuit than it is now. The same applies to Palm Beach Polo Club where I set the fictitious events of the parties and play. It has changed since then and is much more international with tarmac roads and a super smooth environment. Although the essence of small polo ranches surrounding the area is still very much alive.

Pablo Escobar was assassinated and all his cohorts decimated by a real group called Los Pepes in conjunction with FARC at exactly the time my book is set. There really was a tunnel under the border from Mexico to San Diego and it was found years later by the border patrols and closed down.

The helicopter prison escape about which I write really did occur as I describe and three IRA members were sprung free from Mountjoy Prison; but it actually happened in October 1973 so I took poetic licence with the date to suit my timeline.

The first text messages were available to send in 1995 and they were called SMS messages, with mobile phones becoming internationally compatible across many continents.

The polo balls are indeed imported into the UK in large numbers as the main manufacturers lie abroad and as I walked through customs one year with new equipment (including a bag of new balls, which are about ten times the price here) unchallenged just because it was sports equipment, a germ of an idea came to me. What if...?

Printed in Great Britain
by Amazon